Advance Praise for
The Ghost Manuscript

"Absolutely addictive—Indiana Jones with a female lead. And I would follow heroine Carys anywhere: she's funny, warm, smart, and vulnerable. The fact that she's leading us on a treasure hunt—accompanied by a ghostly monk, no less—makes this a buddy story, a detective story, a thriller, a terrific read you will never forget."

—JENNA BLUM, bestselling author of *Those Who Save Us, The Stormchasers, The Lost Family*

THE
GHOST
MANUSCRIPT

THE
GHOST
MANUSCRIPT

KRIS FRIESWICK

Post Hill
PRESS

A POST HILL PRESS BOOK

The Ghost Manuscript
© 2019 by Kris Frieswick
All Rights Reserved

ISBN: 978-1-64293-024-5
ISBN (eBook): 978-1-64293-025-2

Cover art by Whitney Scharer
Interior design and composition by Greg Johnson, Textbook Perfect

Post Hill Press
New York • Nashville
posthillpress.com

Published in the United States of America

To Peter and Sylvia—
who taught me to love Wales.

To Sidney and Priscilla—
who taught me to love words.

To my handsome Welshman—
who taught me to love.

PROLOGUE

Thursday, June 21

The pain pierced Carys Jones's abdomen, and every other sensation she'd been feeling was consumed. Gone was the hard coldness that had seeped into her core, the unexpectedly deafening sound of her own breath, the confusion of the black water that surrounded her, the throbbing in her ears. Her body drew into a fetal position and she held her breath. She pinched her eyes shut and held perfectly still. *If I don't move, the pain might stop*, she thought. *Please stop.*

Carys began to drop through the darkness. Then something grabbed one of her shoulders and spun her around. A red light filled her closed lids. She raised her hands to push it away, but hands grabbed hers and the light faded quickly. She slowly opened her eyes. Dafydd stared back through a wall of silvery bubbles, his forehead furrowed behind his mask. He jutted his thumb up. *Surface now.*

She could not move. Dafydd held her hand and began to kick slowly, towing her back the way they'd come. Out of the cave. Back to the surface. For an instant, it was all she wanted. To lie down and unfold and die on land. She almost looked forward to it.

Then a thought broke through the pain.

In.

She tentatively inhaled. Then exhaled. The pain eased slightly. The word came again into her mind, louder, more insistent. *IN.*

She took another shallow breath and squeezed Dafydd's hand. He turned back to look at her. She shook her head and pointed behind. *In. I want to go in. It's there. I know it is.*

He sharply jutted his thumb up twice. *The dive is over.*

Uncurling, Carys threw off his hand, turned around, and swam. Each kick of her legs shot the pain higher up, into her arms and shoulders, but she would not stop, even if it killed her. They were so close.

Dafydd grabbed her fin to stop her. She slipped out of his grasp and kicked harder. She pointed her flashlight out in front of her, where its long, thin beam hit nothing but the tiny fish fleeing the light, and sea matter suspended like dust in the water. There were no cave walls anymore, just blackness and water. There was no up or down, left or right, or upside down. It did not matter as long as she was going in, away from the cave mouth, away from Dafydd. She wasn't going to stop. It had to be here. She beat her legs up and down and searched the darkness with useless eyes.

Suddenly, Carys's head emerged out of the water into cool air. She ripped the regulator out of her mouth and gasped. The air was stale and tangy on her tongue, but it was oxygen. She inflated her diving vest. Her legs dangled in the water beneath her as she pulled off her mask. She strained to see something, anything. There was only blank space. She tried to relax, but her entire body felt like stone.

Then, all at once and completely, the pain subsided as quickly as it had come.

Dafydd surfaced next to her and pulled the regulator out of his mouth. He pointed his flashlight at her.

"What's wrong?" he said, his voice high and scared.

"I'm okay," she said, steadying herself with her hands on his shoulders. "I'll be okay."

"We have to get you back out," he said. "What's happening?"

"I don't know," she said. "Whatever it was, it's done."

Dafydd's face clouded over. Carys was breaking every diving rule ever written, and he was angry. Rightfully so. She was endangering them both. Again. But tonight, none of the rules applied, and they both knew it.

His face softened. He turned away and raised his flashlight to examine the space they were in.

It was a vast cavern, a cathedral of stone with walls thirty feet high. Yellow and red stalactites, like long, thin statues of the saints, hung down from the ceiling, some extending through the surface of the water. Dafydd turned and swept the beam of the light behind him.

Carved into the wall of the cavern, clearly made by human hands, was an enormous niche, like the ones built into the walls of churches to display statues of the Virgin Mary and the apostles. This one was much bigger, ten feet high at least, and another ten deep. In it, dirty white and ruggedly chiseled, lay a stone sarcophagus. An ancient Christian cross had been etched into the side facing them.

"Oh my god," said Dafydd, his voice barely a whisper. "It's here."

PART 1

Boston

Friday, June 8

The sight of the envelope on Carys's desk set her left eyelid twitching. Her name and work address were hand-printed on the center of it in small, compact letters, set in unnaturally straight lines. It could have been her own writing.

When Carys was thirteen, she'd tried to change how she wrote so it didn't look like this. She had tried flowery and sloppy, loopy with slashes, exaggerated crosses and dots, and sloping angles. None of it took for very long. Her handwriting still looked just like her father's.

She stared at the letter for a couple of minutes. She sipped her coffee and wondered why he was still trying. The eyelid twitching got worse. She turned the envelope over on its face and slid it away. She'd toss it out later.

"Carys," said Janice from the adjoining desk. Carys looked over, and Janice notched her chin toward their boss's glass-walled office.

The room usually resembled a shaken snow globe. Today, George Plourde's papers were organized and there was only one mug on his desk. He'd cleared the floor of the crumpled paper, the stack of extra ties and shoes, his collection of obsolete charging cables, and his ratty briefcase. Plourde sat at his desk, his back rigid and his face frozen in a smile—or what she assumed was a smile beneath the tangled mass of his salt-and-pepper beard. A bald man sat across from him.

"Who's that?" asked Carys.

"Martin Gyles," said Janice.

"What?"

"I know," said Janice.

"What's he doing in Plourde's office?"

Janice shrugged.

"How do you know it's him? I thought he was never photographed."

"*Art and Auction* got one," said Janice. "He was in the background in a photo of a crowd at a British Library exhibition. I recognized him when he came in this morning."

Carys stared at the back of the man's shiny head.

"How long has he been in there?" she asked.

"About half an hour," said Janice.

Martin Gyles rose, slid open Plourde's door, and strode toward the elevator. He was five foot seven or eight but looked taller in his tailored navy suit, made of a fabric that moved like water over his muscular shoulders. Beneath his left French cuff, a gold watch glinted.

Gyles pushed the elevator button and turned to survey the office. His eyes connected with Carys's. She almost looked away but found herself holding his gaze. She nodded a hello. He was not good-looking. Not even close. Slightly bulging eyes, thick eyebrows, and not much of a chin. Yet, he was confident, holding himself as if he owned the company. He probably could if he wanted to. He was likely worth a fortune.

He did not blink or look away. She broke the gaze first. The elevator door opened, and Gyles, the leading cultural antiquities repatriation expert in the world—the man who had returned more stolen treasures to their owners and countries of origin than anyone else in history—turned and stepped into it. When the elevator door closed, Carys shot Janice a puzzled glance.

"White whale," said Janice.

Carys's email notification pinged. She slid aside a stack of private-collection catalogs and nineteenth-century English gilt-edge psalm books that blocked the computer screen.

"Come see me," the email said. She closed her eyes, inhaled, and exhaled.

"Time for my morning ogling," she said.

"Find out what Gyles was doing here," said Janice.

Carys pulled her shoulder-length black hair behind her ears, buttoned her cardigan all the way up to her neck, and draped a scarf around her angular shoulders and full chest.

"Good morning, Ms. Jones, good morning," Plourde said as he waved her in, glancing at her breasts.

"Good morning," she said. She sat down and crossed her arms. "What was Martin Gyles doing here?"

Plourde's dull eyes sparked. He opened his mouth to speak, then closed it, shuffled some papers from one side of his desk to the other and looked back at Carys.

"We had some business matters to discuss," said Plourde.

"What busin—" she said.

"We got an interesting call a couple of days ago," said Plourde. "There's a collection I want you to look at. The owner is indisposed indefinitely, and his son is selling the family home and wants the books sold as soon as possible. I need you to head out to the house and confirm the catalog, evaluate condition, appraisal estimates, the usual. You can start today. You'll probably be there a week or two. We're doing a private sale on this one, not an auction."

Carys's eye twitch got worse. She normally reviewed manuscript collections at Sothington's Auction House, where she'd worked for nearly a decade, or in private warehouses. She did not like to do appraisals or authentications in the owner's home. People were messy—especially rich, obsessive book people. The last time she'd been in the home of a collector—an inbred Boston Brahmin with no chin, a Pinckney Street address, family portraits by Jennys on the wall, and a pair of khakis that looked and smelled like he'd been wearing them for two years straight—the man had spent three hours bent over her while she worked, trying to convince her that his Shakespeare first folio of *Romeo and Juliet* was authentic. It was not. She did not like people interfering with her process. That was just between her and the books.

"Send Jim," said Carys. "I'm busy."

"No. You're most familiar with the collection," said Plourde.

"Whose is it?"

"John Harper's."

She blinked.

A smile formed within Plourde's beard. "Well, he's not selling it. As I said, the son is."

He leaned across the desk slightly, and the cloying scent of his musky, cinnamon-tinged aftershave invaded her nostrils and started her eyes watering.

"Harper's been committed to Waggoner Psychiatric Hospital in Belmont. He's gone quite insane," he said.

Carys's hands went cold.

"His son, John Jr. or JJ, or whatever he goes by, has power of attorney," said Plourde. "The doctors don't know when or if Harper will be coming home, and JJ wants the books gone. Here's the catalog."

He handed Carys a black hardcover Moleskine notebook.

She opened it, but she already knew what was in it—page after page of handwritten notes, details on the books in the Harper Collection, the finest collection of British Dark Age manuscripts on earth. She had located and authenticated many of these books for

Harper and they were like beloved ancient relatives, wizened and wise and keeping their secrets.

They had been resurrected at great cost, and often great peril, from vaults and monasteries, caves and cathedral walls, war loot stashes and other forbidden places, and pulled into the present, one by one, from the most illiterate era since the birth of Christ. And they all lived now in Harper's home in Wellesley.

As she paged through the catalog, the smell of Plourde's aftershave drifted away and her eyelid stopped twitching.

♦ ♦ ♦ ♦ ♦

"Jesus, you're ugly," mumbled Carys.

The huge gargoyle door knocker on the front door of Adeona, John Harper's sprawling Greek Revival mansion, stared back at her. Its black wrought-iron beard, wild eyes, and fanged, sneering mouth dared her to reach out and knock. It was out of place on the house, an architectural anachronism, inappropriate aesthetically and historically. Not a mistake, though. She was sure of that.

If she knew Harper, this was a replica of a gargoyle on a church or cathedral built during the Dark Ages somewhere in the British Isles. Or maybe it was an original. Her breath caught briefly at the idea, and she leaned in to inspect the gargoyle more carefully.

The door swung open. She jumped back.

"You must be Carys," said the man who opened it. He was a good six inches taller than her, which was unusual. She rarely had to look up at men. His tousled bird's nest of blond hair belonged to a much younger person, not the mid-fortyish one standing there with the dark, gray-black circles under his brown eyes. He had the angular, slightly hollowed-out cheeks of someone who spent his days clenching his teeth from worry or anger.

"Yes. Carys Jones," she said. She extended her hand. He shook it once and dismissed it.

"I'm Mr. Harper's son, John Jr. Call me JJ."

She followed him into the home's foyer, its pale blue walls soaring above them into a domed ceiling like an early-spring sky. On the walls hung Audubon prints, a Picasso sketch, a blue Rothko, and a Cézanne. A pendulous chandelier hung from the peak of the dome down nearly to the top of the floral arrangement on the circular mahogany table that dominated the center of the foyer. She did not want to be impressed, but the poor kid in her was.

John Harper had become a tech billionaire in the early 1990s when he invented a new type of computer storage. He and Harper Technologies had been surfing the smooth face of the tech wave ever since. Adeona, named for the Roman goddess who guides children home, was one of six or seven homes Harper owned. He kept his library here, so Carys assumed this was his favorite, to the extent that she could suppose anything about a man she'd never met in person. They'd done all their work together via email, letters, and FedEx. She'd kept every bit of their correspondence, even the emails, which she printed out, in a folder in her desk drawer.

"It's lovely," she said.

"Thank you. My mother designed this house," said JJ. "She died a few years ago."

"I'm sorry."

"Thank you," he said. "Breast cancer. She was very brave. More than I can say for myself or my father. Let me show you the library."

JJ walked to the wide wooden door on the far side of the foyer, underneath the overhanging second-floor balcony, and produced a skeleton key. He slid it into the brass keyhole, entered the library, and ducked behind the opened door. She heard him typing a code on some kind of electronic device, and then he reappeared.

"This was the only room my mother didn't decorate," said JJ.

Carys stepped into the library. It took a moment for her eyes to adjust to the low light. As they did, she smiled. She was completely surrounded by books, manuscripts, pages of parchment. Thousands and thousands of them. They filled her vision and formed a pattern like a geometric quilt of brown leather spines and golden edges and creamy white pages, repeated over and over until it became a rhythm that thrummed in her head, like she'd stepped into her favorite dream. For a moment, she felt drunk.

It was the most beautiful private library she'd ever seen, built entirely of warm, glowing wood, with a wraparound balcony about eight feet off the floor. The bookcases—every inch of every one packed with manuscripts and parchments—filled the walls of both levels, extending all the way up to the high, coffered ceiling. Directly opposite the door on the far wall were three tall windows, side by side, offering a view of the expansive backyard and providing the only natural light in the room, though it wasn't much. They were covered with tinted filters—common in home libraries—to keep out UV light.

Harper had furnished sparsely. A simple wooden desk and Harvard chair faced the windows. There was only a lamp and a leather blotter on the desk. To the left was a long wooden table with a Tiffany lamp at each end. A velvet settee and standing lamp occupied the space between the desk and the library door. It was a reading seat.

Carys would never leave if this room were hers.

"My father spent most of his waking moments in here," said JJ. He looked up at the balcony with a wistful expression that folded into sadness. "He has no use for it now."

"Mr. Harper," she said. "I know this is none of my business, but this collection is one of the best Dark Age collections in existence. It would be a tragedy to—"

"I know," he said. "Selling these books is the last thing he wants. I…I don't…." He stopped midsentence, then cleared his throat.

He handed the skeleton key, on a ring with a dozen smaller keys, and his business card to Carys. "These keys open the cases. I've written the security code for the library door on the back of my card. The security directions are on the plaque under the keypad. It's on the wall behind the door after you enter. When you come into the library, you have two minutes to shut off the alarm. When you are leaving, reset the alarm, and then you have thirty seconds to lock the door with the skeleton key before the alarm goes off. Please let Nicola know when you're leaving."

"Nicola?"

"The...the housekeeper," he said. "I've kept her on to clean the place for the showings while it's for sale. How long do you think this will take?"

"It's hard to tell. Three weeks at the minimum. It depends on how complete the catalog is."

"Yes, of course," said JJ, picking some lint off his sleeve and looking up at her, again, with a brief half smile. "I'm sure you'll do an excellent job. My father would be glad to know you're here."

Without saying goodbye, JJ walked out of the library and left the house, closing the front door quietly behind him. His silent departure sent a pang through Carys—his sadness felt familiar.

The crunching of car tires on the stone driveway slowly faded. She stood in the center of the library and took a deep breath through her mouth to reset herself. Exhaled. Then she inhaled deeply through her nose. The scent of old manuscripts was perfume to Carys, old and animal and dusty and always triggering the same physical reaction. Her shoulders relaxed, her fingers spread apart and stretched, her brain became quieter and more focused. In this library, and libraries she had seen like it around the world—though none this grand—she felt most at peace. Especially when she was alone.

Arrayed around her was Harper's life's work, the physical manifestation of his decades-long, single-minded devotion to early Romano-British Dark Age manuscripts. Harper never lost an auction at Sothington's, or elsewhere. When Harper's bidder was in the room or on the phone, there wasn't much point in trying to win. He always went as high as necessary, and eventually even the museums stopped bidding against him.

There were very few collectors as obsessed with the time period as John Harper. He couldn't have cared less for ornate illuminated manuscripts—he even passed on a previously unknown fifth volume of the Book of Kells. He didn't want first editions or Shakespeare folios. But he would spend a million dollars on a single-page letter if it was dated to or dealt with the time period of AD 400 to 700 in the British Isles.

Carys pulled her white cotton work gloves from her briefcase and put them on. She slid the key marked "I" into the lock of the first bookcase and opened the door, climbed the rolling ladder, and pulled the first manuscript on the top shelf. She gazed at the book's worn animal-hide cover and ran her hand across it. The hair follicles of the animal's skin rose like Braille under her fingertips through the thin gloves. She climbed down, closed the bookcase, and walked to the settee.

"Hello, gorgeous," she murmured at the manuscript as she sat down. She opened it, held it up to her nose and inhaled deeply, savoring the rich, ancient smell.

Usually, after she was done smelling a book's odor, a mix of skin and decay and earth, she'd see how much of it she could read. The manuscripts she'd procured for the Harper Collection were all in Latin, and she'd contrived a way for many of them to make a pit stop at Sothington's—for verification purposes, of course—before they took up residence in this room. She estimated she'd read about a quarter of the manuscripts he owned.

She'd read the elegantly composed Roman parchments that told of everything from love affairs to legal transactions. She'd read Latin transcriptions of some of the earliest Greek Christian scriptures, though they were of less interest to her. What she loved were the letters, written in Roman cursive, a chance to see inside the minds of men dead for fifteen hundred years. Roman verbosity and literacy made the sudden silence of the Dark Ages in Britain all the more stunning—there was barely anything written in the British Isles except by monks after the illiterate Anglo-Saxon hordes had finished ravaging great swaths of the country and its people in the mid-sixth century.

Carys flipped to the manuscript's first page and began to read. It was an accounting of land holdings in what the catalog surmised was far western England, perhaps Cornwall. The information wasn't particularly historic, but the manuscript itself was a rare artifact written by some regional administrator's hand, likely in the years between AD 420 and 460. The writing was small, but sure and steady and clear on the page. It was one of the manuscripts discovered in an impoverished Irish church's ancient vault. She had acquired the entire collection eight years earlier for auction at Sothington's.

As she read, the walls of the library seemed to fade away, replaced by the stone walls of an imperial administrator's office in a small British settlement, nestled safely in a valley between rolling green hills, ignorant of the devastation flowing like cold blood down from the north.

At first, Carys barely noticed the singing. When she finally became aware of the sweet female voice, she assumed JJ had left a radio on somewhere, tuned to a Celtic music hour.

"*Gwenu'n dirion yn dy hun,*" came the voice, unaccompanied by instruments. It didn't need any. It was lilting and clear.

Then Carys's brow tightened. She knew this song. It was a Welsh lullaby. "Suo Gan." Her father used to sing it to her. Her stomach clenched.

"*Ai angylion fry sy'n gwenu,*" the voice continued in that impenetrable language. She never had been able to master it. The song unlocked a memory she hadn't had in years—she and her father singing this song, he in Welsh, she in English. The English version flooded her mind, like it had been waiting just below the surface to be remembered.

"What visions make your face bright? Are the angels above smiling at you, in your peaceful rest?" Carys sang.

◂

The woman's voice stopped.

"Good lord!" it chirped. Carys jumped up.

On the other side of the library, up on the gallery level, was an older woman wearing a baggy T-shirt and yellow rubber gloves, wielding a spray bottle and a crumpled-up newspaper, about to clean the glass face of one of the bookcases.

"You scared me half to death!" said the woman, patting her chest with her hand. "I didn't see you."

"That makes two of us," said Carys. The woman studied her for a moment.

"Are you the woman from Sothington's?" she said with a thick Welsh accent. She dropped her cleaning supplies and started down the gallery stairs.

"Yes, I am," Carys said.

"JJ said you'd be coming by today," said the woman as she walked toward Carys at the settee. She had very white skin, and her hair was long and gray, tied back in a ponytail. She was about Carys's height and was soft around the middle, maybe in her late-fifties. The sparkle in her green eyes, her elegant, narrow nose, sharp jawline, flawless complexion, and the high arch of her eyebrows were all remnants of a face that had been very beautiful once—and still was, in its way. "And you know the song. You're Welsh?"

"My father was," said Carys. "My mother was American."

"So that makes you half Welsh. Better than no Welsh! Where was he from?" asked the woman.

"Mumbles."

"You're joking! I used to live in Swansea. What's your father's name?"

"Anthony. Anthony Jones," said Carys. She hadn't said that name out loud in years.

"Well, there's only about a million Anthony Joneses in Mumbles. I knew about twenty of them in my time there. How old is he?"

"I'm not sure. Early sixties. I haven't seen much of him since I was seven," said Carys.

The woman's friendly smile faded. "I didn't mean to pry."

"It's okay. My name is Carys."

"I'm Nicola," the woman said. "Nicola Powell. Housekeeper. JJ's been kind enough to let me stick around until the house is sold."

"JJ doesn't live here?" asked Carys.

"No, no. He's got a brownstone on Beacon Hill," said Nicola. "He's a partner at a hedge fund downtown. Got a PhD in computers and mathematics or some such. Very, very bright. Dates supermodels. He's quite the catch. Are you single?"

"Sort of," said Carys.

"Hard to do better than the handsome son of a rich man," said Nicola. "Although JJ is entirely self-made. Never took a dime from his father. Even paid his own way through university and post-grad. He's a good boy. Loves his dah to death but always wanted to be his own man."

"I'm probably not his type."

"You're saying you're not a supermodel?" asked Nicola with a grin.

"And I'm much too old for him," said Carys. "Thirty-seven."

Nicola laughed. "Oh yes. You may be right. Well, I'm sure that you have many other fine qualities. It's very nice to meet you, Carys. Did your dad ever tell you what your name means?"

Nicola was lovely, but her accent was grating on Carys's nerves.

"Yes. He did," Carys said.

It means love, she thought. *Not that it mattered.*

2

<small>◇◇◇◇◇◇◇</small>

Saturday, June 9

Carys was at the center of everything. The world spun by, blurry and colored and full of fast lines. The cars sounded like they were circling around and around her. Past her spun Mum and Dah, waving. The flat, gray ocean. The street full of stone buildings. The cars. The swing set. Rocking horse. Mum and Dah again, still waving.

She tilted back her head and above her was sky, the color of the dust that gathered under her bed. Why was it always gray here? A white bird flew above her in bigger and bigger circles, until it flew right out of her view. Goodbye, bird.

Dah hopped on the merry-go-round next to her. His hair was blowing all over the place into funny shapes, and his eyes were wet from laughing. Carys smiled. They were both at the center of everything then, the world spinning around them slower and slower. Mum was next to them when they stopped. She was drinking her beer. She scooped Carys up. She smelled like warm clothes out of the dryer. She hugged Carys and said what she always said.

"My brave big girl."

Carys smiled in her sleep, then remembered and woke up.

Steven lay snoring softly next to her in the king canopy bed, and her heart sank. She rolled over and tried to relax herself back into sleep, or something close to it. It was no use. It never was after that dream.

The sky brightened a couple of hours later. She watched through the open window as the mountains surrounding the Vermont village where they were spending the weekend turned from black to darkest green. When the sunshine finally lit up their peaks, Steven rolled over. His body was boxy and muscular, his semi-successful college football career close enough in his rearview mirror that he still worked out daily to maintain it. He'd be up and off to the gym every morning at six, except on vacation. On the two mornings a week when Carys stayed over, he'd get back from the gym sweaty and horny. She normally found delight in his body. Not this morning. That dream.

Steven smiled at her and rolled over onto her, reaching his big hands around her waist. He kissed her, probing her mouth with his tongue. She pushed him off, got out of bed, and headed to the bathroom.

"Hurry back," he said. As she turned back to look at him, a lock of his straight, brown hair dropped across his broad forehead and thick eyebrows, so artfully arranged that it annoyed her. *Crap*, she thought, *here it comes.*

She forced a smile and closed the bathroom door. Naked, she stared at her reflection in the mirror. New crow's feet trod lightly around her eyes, although her forehead, like Steven's, was uncreased. There were random grays sprouting along the part in her black hair. There were a few grays in her eyebrows. Her cheeks were beginning to drop a bit, and her tall, wiry body, which she could always count on to mask her true age, hadn't been keeping up its muscle tone quite the same way it used to. A fatty pooch was forming at her belly. Daylight truly was burning.

"Carys," Steven said from the bedroom.

"Out in a minute," she said. "Can you call for some coffee?"

"Yup," he said. The bed squeaked as he rolled over to pick up the phone. Two buttons pushed. Coffee ordered. Phone back in its cradle. Bed squeak as he rolled back over.

"What do you want to do today?" Steven asked.

Her throat clenched. She inhaled and exhaled as quietly as she could. Her body always knew it was over long before her brain did.

That night, halfway through dinner and a bottle of burgundy in front of a roaring fire at a French bistro just outside of Bennington, Steven said he wanted to talk. Carys hadn't done much talking for most of the day. She hoped her changed heart wasn't too obvious. But he wasn't dumb.

"Thirty-seven years old," he said, his sleepy, heavily lidded green eyes staring into his wine glass. "You've never had a relationship longer than this one?"

"I'm incredibly picky." She smiled, but his face stayed dark.

"I'm tired, Carys," he said. "I am not sure what I'm doing wrong here."

"You're not doing anything wrong," she said.

"I feel like there's a wall."

She kept her mouth closed. There was a wall, of course, but it had nothing to do with him. He was a good man. So were the ones who had come before. Each time, after a few months, she couldn't see the point of continuing.

"I'm sorry," she said. This was true.

"You're completely closed off," he said. "You won't talk about anything. You don't like talking about your work, or your friends." He lowered his voice. "You refuse to talk about your family or your mother's suicide. For chrissakes, Carys, I could swap you out for a sex doll and I'd barely notice."

She took a slow sip of her wine. They were done here.

"Let's get the check," she said, smiling to try to bleed off some of the anger that was rising up in him. It didn't work. He put his knife down a little too hard.

Getting to this conversation with Steven had taken longer than usual. Six months he'd made it. She was impressed at his persistence. It appeared she had finally exhausted it. She tried to never let her relationships get to a point where her lover was angry when it ended. Still, it always ended the same way—with him closed out, perplexed by a woman who wasn't actively seeking what he believed all women want, and Carys just this side of indifferent. She never pushed or implied that it was ever going to be more than it was, which, with Steven, was dinner twice a week followed by sex. This weekend was the first time they'd gone away together overnight. It was obviously the last.

They didn't speak until the check arrived. He reached for it.

"I've got it," she said, and pulled it out from under his hand. He looked up angrily, staring at her, challenging her to fight for it. She looked down at the bill, reached placidly for her purse, and extracted a credit card. Steven's face turned blank.

They walked out to his car. Steven opened her door and his eyes searched hers for a response, a conversation, some sort of dialogue. She just slid into the passenger seat and sat silently as they drove back to the inn.

"Aren't you going to say anything?" he finally asked as she reached over to turn out the light next to the bed.

"There's really not much to say," she answered.

The next morning, after brushing her teeth, she bared them to the mirror. Her gums were red and healthy, her teeth straight, strong and white. *Not yet*, she thought. *I'd still rather be alone. As long as I have all my teeth.*

They came back to Boston that morning. There was no talk of next time when he dropped her off at her apartment. He hugged her briefly, sadly, and drove off, the wheels of his black BMW spinning in the road dirt at the end of her driveway.

3

Monday, June 11

It always felt this way—a weight gone. The departure of a man, or anybody who was cluttering up her life, brought Carys profound relief, like looking at a clean, flat sheet of paper. Untouched, uncomplicated, simple. There was probably some sort of psychological diagnosis that claimed this feeling as a primary symptom. She didn't care. She loved it. It was never loneliness, just simplicity. It gave her mental space to do her work. She drove up the driveway at Adeona with a blank mind and a smile on her face.

The front door swung open as she approached the doorstep. Nicola smiled back at her.

"JJ's not here," she said. "Let's have a cup before you start. I made some muffins."

Carys followed Nicola into the enormous kitchen, a riot of gleaming copper pots, wrought-iron racks, wood-faced appliances, and vases full of pink and white peonies. Nicola already had teacups set out, and, without asking if Carys wanted any, poured out dark tea from a pot surrounded by a puffy light blue cozy.

"Milk?" Nicola asked.

"Please, and sugar."

As Nicola spooned the sugar from a blue clay pot, her hand started to shake and the sugar spilled across the countertop. She grimaced.

"I'm sorry about that," Nicola said. She grabbed a sponge and wiped up the sugar. "It's the MS. One of the symptoms is the shakes. Sometimes I lose the feeling in my hands. And sometimes I can't get out of bed for three or four days."

"Have you had it a long time?"

"About ten years," Nicola said. "I'm on good meds, but it likes to assert itself every once in a while. Would you mind pouring the milk? Unless you'd prefer to wear it." She laughed. Carys smiled.

"I'm glad you're here," said Nicola.

"I'm glad, too," said Carys.

"You know the collection better than anyone but Mr. Harper, don't you?" Nicola asked, looking at Carys over the edge of her teacup, which shook slightly.

"Part of it," she said, "but the total collection surpasses my involvement. He has books here that I've seen only in museum catalogs. It's remarkable. Who else was he working with on this?"

"Oh," said Nicola, dropping her eyes, "I don't really know. I never really paid attention to the other people. You were the one Mr. Harper mentioned specifically. He was very impressed with your work. He said you were a very good hunter after you located that copy of the *Annales Cambriae*."

Nicola pronounced the words—the Latin name for the Book of Wales, written in AD 550—perfectly. Strange.

"So, how did a smart woman like you decide to spend her life surrounded by musty books, then?" asked Nicola.

"As a kid I read voraciously, especially the classics," Carys said. The truth was that her mother had refused to spend money on cable, and her frequent, months-long bouts of depression made books

Carys's most dependable companions. Nicola didn't need to know that part.

"Classics?" said Nicola. "Very advanced."

"I got addicted," she said. "When I learned they were all based on older stories, I became obsessed with tracking down the original tale and its author. Like following a stream in the woods back up to its source. I mean, Shakespeare was the biggest plagiarist of all time, wasn't he?"

Nicola laughed. "He was that."

"Once I had an ancient handwritten manuscript in my hands, I was a goner. I guess I am a hunter in that way."

"Where did you study?" asked Nicola.

"Smith undergrad. BU for my master's. PhD at the University of London."

"What did you do your dissertation in?" asked Nicola.

"Paleography of Romano-British manuscripts."

Nicola lifted her tea in a little salute. "Well done, you."

"I'm a little surprised I made an impression on Mr. Harper," said Carys.

"You did," said Nicola.

"You seem to know a lot about the collection."

"Mr. Harper was kind enough to indulge my curiosity about the books," Nicola said. "At first, I think he just wanted to impress upon me the importance of keeping the security system on at all times. Eventually, he started teaching me about the manuscripts. He seemed pleased to have someone in the house who appreciated his work. His wife couldn't have been less interested, bless her soul, and JJ never got the bug—although he always supported his father's passion. JJ even bought him a very rare manuscript a few years ago. Mr. Harper was very touched by that."

"What brought you to the U.S.?"

Nicola paused, raised her teacup and sipped, then smiled lightly.

"Just a lark," she said. "I'd finished college and decided to see the world for a few years."

"What did you study?" asked Carys.

"Celtic languages at University College in Aberystwyth. You ever been up to that part of Wales? Truly gorgeous country," said Nicola.

Carys paused mid sip. Her appetite dissipated.

"No, I haven't," she said. She stood up. "I should get to work."

"Of course," said Nicola. "Let me know if you need anything."

Carys went back to the library and took a deep breath. Aberystwyth—a town she'd never been to, and never would. The return address on the envelope on her desk last week. The town where her father now lived.

She'd heard enough about Wales for one week. For one lifetime, really. She turned her attention to the books arrayed before her. They would ease her mind. They always had and always would.

Verify and authenticate. That was her job. Steven had jokingly called her a "highly educated, glorified fact-checker" when introducing her at an office party. It stung a bit, but he wasn't the malicious type and she didn't take offense. He didn't understand what she did all day—not his fault; she'd never discussed it with him.

He wasn't wrong. This part of her job was fact-checking. She had to make sure every item listed in the Harper Collection catalog was physically here in the library. Then she had to make sure the description in the catalog was right. That a thing described as Vulgar Latin wasn't actually Medieval. That the ink used was carbon black and not metallic. That the handwriting style had been in use when the manuscript was written. That the binding technique and material were available when the book was created. That there wasn't something else hidden behind the words in the manuscript...like a barely visible earlier text, the remnants of writing that had been erased by an ancient hand so the precious papyrus or parchment could be reused. Those types of books, palimpsests, caused so much excitement in the world of ancient book collecting because there was always a much, much older document hidden behind the visible writing—the ghost of a previous author. It was like finding a da Vinci hidden behind a Kandinsky.

Once that part of the authentication was done came the fun part: verifying the book's provenance, determining the route it had traveled and the owners who had held it, naming every person or institution that had bought or sold it, from the moment of its creation to the moment it landed in Carys's hands. It was like doing the biggest puzzle in the world. She would spend months reverifying the documented provenance of a rare manuscript if even one single bit of it smelled funny. Buyers relied on this provenance information to make sure they were weren't buying war loot, or stolen items, or forgeries, or a manuscript formerly owned by a Jewish family in Berlin during World War Two—a family exterminated except for one survivor, who decades later legitimately could claim ownership of the priceless text, leaving the buyer empty-handed, out a large sum of cash, and possibly under indictment, if it could be proved that he or she participated in any way in the deception.

It happened more often than Carys could have ever imagined when she entered the profession. The sheer volume of manuscripts and other ancient artifacts pilfered and winding their way through their rarified little world, with fake provenance, with buyers and sellers turning a blind eye to the obvious truth of it as a way to keep the item from being confiscated—it was a booming industry. Doing the most diligent provenance work possible was her small way of getting the real owners justice and giving back to the manuscripts their true history.

In the end, she was speculating on all of it—making her most educated guess. Her guesses were, it was widely acknowledged in her field, among the best. It was the only thing in her life of which she was deeply, jealously proud.

Her final job was to estimate the value of each book. She didn't care much for that task. In her mind, these manuscripts, every single one, were priceless. Utterly irreplaceable. An auction's purpose was to determine what the market thought the price should be, so her estimates were merely a starting point. Of course, there would be no auction of the Harper Collection. It was a private sale. Whoever was buying would inevitably be well known to Carys—the collecting community was tiny. It would be either a university, a huge private library like the Morgan (the publics would never be able to afford the items here), or one of the strange, mercurial billionaires who collected these books as obsessively as Harper did. And they had better bring a hundred million bucks if they wanted the whole thing.

She unlocked the first bookcase again and opened the glass door. So far, every book, manuscript, and parchment was exactly where the catalog said it would be. Except for the one that was now directly in front of her face.

It was a modern notebook wedged between two ancient manuscripts. She pulled out the unexpected volume and opened it to its first page, which read simply, "Cross-referenced Index of Contents." It was grouped by subject headings and subheadings, each entry pointing to a specific paragraph and page within one of the manuscripts in the library, then listing the manuscript's location in the collection. For Carys, it was something else entirely: a glimpse into Harper's mind, an inkling of what he was obsessed with within these books, what drove him, what steered his book selections during his entire collecting career. She leaned her back against the wooden bookshelf dividers and began to read.

Her eyes danced over the handwritten words for a few moments. Then she began to page back and forth, checking and rechecking. A minute later, the nature of Harper's obsession stared back at her.

Mons Badonicus, Gwynyfr, Camlann, Merlin, Glastonbury, Arcturus Rex. It was all Arthuriana—topics relating to the hunt for the mythical King Arthur.

"You are shitting me," she muttered. "Please, please, Harper, tell me you weren't obsessed with King Arthur."

She flipped rapidly through the pages, trying to find some reference to another subject. There were lists of names and places, none that looked familiar. But there were no major subject-matter headings other than Arthur and things she vaguely recognized as topics peripheral to him. She closed the notebook sharply, slid the index back on the shelf, and made a note of its existence in her own notebook.

Carys felt numb. She'd never, in all the time she'd been dealing with Harper, picked up on this. None of the manuscripts that she'd found for him fit into the traditional requests that book dealers were all too accustomed to receiving from Arthur chasers, a particularly earnest and scholarly group of crackpots—sometimes highly educated and university-funded crackpots, but crackpots nonetheless. They chased the legend, convinced that some gold lay at the end of their quest. Unlike the chasers who could be counted on to demand the oldest written versions of the source material for such works as the *Mabinogion* and *Gothic History* by Jordanes, or *De Excidio et Conquestu Britanniae* by Gildas, it looked like Harper focused his efforts on Roman land records, census data, and personal letters, none of which had ever been considered primary source material for the pursuit of Arthur. Her arms were heavy with disappointment.

Her phone buzzed. Plourde.

"Carys. How is it going at the Harper asylum?" Plourde asked. She could hear him grinning.

"Fine."

"How long do you think it'll take?"

"At least a month, maybe two," said Carys.

"We can't take that long."

"It's one of the most comprehensive Dark Age libraries on the planet," she said. "I think our buyers would expect the most detailed attention possible to this task, don't you?"

"Of course, but JJ is eager to get rid of it as fast as possible," Plourde said.

"JJ should donate the whole thing to a museum or college, get a gigantic tax break for the estate, and be done with it."

There was a brief, all too rare, silence from Plourde.

"You know what would be a sin, Ms. Jones?" he said. "If any representative of Sothington's suggested to a client that he endeavor to dispose of a collection in any way that deprives Sothington's of a substantial commission. Are we clear?"

"Of course."

"Brilliant. I want the final appraisal report in my hands in two weeks."

"That's not possible."

"Make it possible. If you have to cut a few corners, that's fine. I'm sure the catalog is already in excellent shape. Time is of the essence, Ms. Jones."

"Fine." She hung up, took a deep breath, held it, then exhaled hard, a technique she used frequently at work to keep from throwing something across the room.

There had to be another index focused on another topic, like ancient medicine or the evolution of law or something worthy. She tossed the catalog on the desk, and it landed with a bang that echoed through the library.

"Everything okay?" Nicola asked from the library's door.

"Yeah," she said, startled. "My boss. He's sort of...difficult."

"I heard what you said about the collection," said Nicola. "I'm sorry. I didn't mean to eavesdrop."

"I wasn't exactly keeping my voice down."

Carys sat at the desk, put her elbows on it, and rubbed her temples with her fingers.

"It really is a shame that JJ doesn't want to donate this collection," said Carys. "I hate the thought of its being broken up or being sold to someone who doesn't appreciate the importance of what Mr. Harper has collected."

"Yes," Nicola said. "It is a tragedy."

Carys turned around.

"Has anyone tried to talk JJ out of it?" she asked.

Nicola studied her face.

"I'm sorry. It's none of my business. I should just get back to work here," Carys said.

"He'd like to donate it," said Nicola. "But he's more concerned with keeping his father's name out of the papers. He's very protective of him. Especially now that he's so sick."

"Nicola, the sale of this collection…. It'll be like someone set off a publicity bomb. A donation could be arranged to be completely private and undisclosed until JJ wanted it disclosed."

"That's not what Mr. Plourde told him," said Nicola. "He said that a private sale with Sothington's was the only way to preserve the family's privacy at this difficult time. He said those words exactly, according to JJ. He said that Sothington's was the only house that could handle such a sale with discretion. He said a donation would be far too public."

"Mr. Plourde does not know what he is talking about." She turned back to the Harper Collection catalog on the desk and flipped to the page where she'd left off.

She didn't hear Nicola leave the library.

◆ ◆ ◆ ◆ ◆

"Can I buy you a drink?"

A man's high-pitched voice cut through the din of the after-work crowd at O'Hara's. Carys turned around and examined him. Tall, high cheekbones and very white teeth, polyester jacket, slicked-back hair. Salesman. Totally out of place in this particular drinking establishment, where Southie's long-predicted gentrification was still a laughable rumor, the only acceptable suit was Carhartt overalls, and ordering wine by the glass was still a very bad idea. He smiled at her with his very white teeth.

"No, thank you," she said. She turned back to the bar as her cocktail arrived.

"Bitch," he mumbled, and faded into the overwhelmingly male crowd. The bartender shrugged an apology. Carys sipped her scotch and soda.

"Still a hit with the boys I see."

Carys smiled and turned around. Her best friend, Annie Brennan, stood there, her long blonde hair flowing over her broad shoulders and framing the neckline of her mostly unbuttoned white button-down oxford. Behind her, a couple of men admired her ass. Annie hugged Carys and wedged herself into an open space next to her.

"One day, you might try bein' nice," said Annie.

"What's the point?"

"Well, sex, for one," said Annie. "Speaking of which, how's the sex machine?"

"Gone. Dumped me Saturday night."

Annie studied her face.

"Are we sad?" asked Annie.

Carys shrugged.

"Reason?" asked Annie.

"The usual. He wanted to talk. I didn't."

"That sucks," said Annie. "Aside from the dumping, how ya been?"

"I hate my boss. I got another letter from Anthony on Friday. But I like my cat."

"What did the letter say?" asked Annie.

Carys sipped her drink.

"Seriously," said Annie. "Thirty years. Don't you think it's time to open the door a crack on this one?"

"No. How's Detective Hottiecakes?"

"Still very, very hot," said Annie with a devious grin.

"Still very, very married."

"Yes, sadly," said Annie. "I'm meeting him at the Green Dragon in Haymarket after his shift."

Carys winced.

"Which part of that didn't you like?" said Annie. "The meeting part or the Green Dragon part?"

"That's where my parents met," she said. "Saint Patrick's Day. I think she thought he was Irish. I boycott the place."

"They're not responsible for hookups on their property," said Annie.

"You're playing with fire with that detective," said Carys.

"Indeed I am," said Annie. "I like fire. You should call your dad."

"No, I shouldn't."

"Well, I'm glad we cleared that up." Annie gestured to the bartender. "I'll have what she's having. Carys, why not just let him know you're well, update him on what you're doing?"

"I don't want to."

"Yeah, you do. You're just being stubborn."

"No, I am not. If I wanted to talk to him, I'd call him."

"Why don't you?" asked Annie.

"You know perfectly well why not."

Annie opened her mouth to speak, thought better of it, and leaned over, wrapping her arm around Carys's shoulder. They'd been having this same conversation for almost twenty-two years.

"So, how's The Dick?" asked Annie.

"You want the whole story? Or just the highlights?"

"Highlights."

"He's rushing me through a project on what is probably the most important Dark Age collection on earth. I helped build it. Wants it in two weeks. It's like his hair's on fire…which I'd actually pay money to see."

"What's the rush?"

"Commissions. We close this sale out by the end of June, or else it's like it didn't even happen. If we make the deadline, the entire sale amount will go straight against his bonus. And trust me, it'll be huge."

"A sale?" asked Annie. "I thought Sothington's was an auction house."

"We are, but we also do private sales. It saves the client the risk of not earning the minimum bid. The clients pay double what we charge for auction commissions."

"But it sounds like they'd earn more at auction for this collection, right? It must be famous."

"The client's father actually owns the collection. He's sick. My client is terrified people will find out what's wrong with him if they have a public auction—he's at Waggoner Psychiatric Hospital."

"Ooh. Not good," said Annie.

"Apparently, The Dick convinced the son that a sale will be more discreet than an auction or a donation. The problem is that the minute we approach potential buyers about this sale, every single one of them will know exactly where the manuscripts came from."

"So why are they doing it this way?"

"His housekeeper…"

"His what?"

"His housekeeper," said Carys. "She says that the son wants to donate to a museum and keep the collection intact. But Plourde told me today that the client wants to sell it as fast as he can."

"How did the client seem to you?" asked Annie. "Did he seem in a rush?"

Carys thought for a moment.

"He seemed sad," she said. "And tired. He asked how long it would take, but he didn't seem like he was in a big rush about it."

"Why would a housekeeper know so much about his feelings? Isn't that odd?" asked Annie.

Annie saw conspiracies everywhere. Hazard of her job as a criminal defense attorney.

"I guess," said Carys. "But she's been working for the Harpers for years, and she's still living there until they sell the place. She seems more like part of the family."

"How do you know what's wrong with the father?" asked Annie.

Carys opened her mouth, then stopped. Nicola's exact words played back in her head: Plourde had said that a private sale with Sothington's was the only way to preserve the family's privacy. She hadn't really heard what Nicola was saying at the time, but now it made perfect sense.

"Fucking Plourde," Carys said.

"What?" asked Annie.

"Plourde is blackmailing him. The Magic Rolodex."

"The what?"

"The Magic.... Why do you think The Dick has been so successful at Sothington's? Why do you think he's my boss, when I know for a fact that he wouldn't know a first-folio Shakespeare from a Superman comic book?"

"He slept his way to the top?"

"He wishes. He makes money. Lots of it. He brings clients in that no one else can snag."

"And he does that how?" asked Annie.

"If shit hits the fan with anyone who owns anything valuable in the northeast corridor—D.C. to Portland—he knows before it even splatters. He has a network of people he pays to get information—nurses, police detectives, psychiatrists, tax collectors, garbagemen who go through trash for him. He's like the TMZ of the auction world."

"I don't understand," said Annie.

"He gets the dirt, reaches out to the unfortunate rich person, offers his condolences on their troubles. They're horrified, of course. How could he know? He suggests that if they need to raise some ready cash, he would be more than happy to expedite the auction of, say, the Chippendale bureau or the Matisse. He assures them of complete privacy, but he leaves no doubt that their little situation just might find itself all over Page Six if they don't come through in a timely fashion."

"That's horrifically amazing," said Annie.

"None of these clients complain, because they know if they do, he'll spill. So they sell the Chippendale."

"How has he not gotten caught if the Magic Rolodex is such an open secret?" asked Annie.

Carys wiggled her thumb and middle finger together in the universal sign for money.

"Most lucrative branch in the entire company—even more than the one in London," she said. "They'll just write a check to anyone who complains. It'll never cost Sothington's more than what he brings in."

"You think he is blackmailing JJ into selling the Harper Collection?"

"I'd bet my life on it."

"It's a big leap," said Annie.

"He's never done anything on this scale before. I mean, this is a huge collection, Annie. One of the most important in the world. For real. The world. Minimum seventy-five to a hundred million."

She could hear her heart beating in her ears, and her skin was growing hot. She caught herself. She did not like the way anger made her feel, like she would jump out of her skin. She sat facing forward on her stool, examining the bottles behind the bar.

"It's not right," she said softly.

"Whaddaya gonna do about it?" asked Annie.

"What can I do? He's still my boss, and the client has agreed to a private sale. My hands are tied."

"Maybe not," said Annie. "Maybe not. Are you pissed off enough to do something?"

This was an excellent question, and Annie already knew the answer. Since they'd known each other, Carys had made it a point not to allow herself to get too pissed off about anything. Being angry required action, unless one relished being angry all day every day, and she did not. She wanted to go through her life doing her best to ignore the things that sent others through the roof, things like Plourde. Anger was for people who believed they could manage outcomes.

"I could lose my job if I get involved," said Carys.

Annie shook her head.

"So then, you don't really care about the collection?" asked Annie.

"See, I know what you're trying to do," she said, waggling a finger at her friend. "First you'll try to make me feel guilty. When that doesn't work, you'll change the subject and tell me all about some big miscarriage of justice you corrected this week and how great it made you feel even though it was really hard."

"I don't even know why I bother showing up for drinks," said Annie. "You could just play out the whole night in your mind without me here, and I could save a few hundred calories on whiskey."

The two sat in silence for a moment.

"Eventually you have to take part, Carys," said Annie.

"Ah, the direct approach. I haven't seen this move in a while," she said, staring down at her empty glass.

"I mean it. You helped to build this collection. Why don't you take all that energy that you're using trying to not feel mad and use it to stir some shit up?" asked Annie.

One of the things that Carys loved about Annie was her willingness to fight. That's how she got the four-inch scar on her right shoulder. When Annie was fifteen, a Southie punk had started giving her crap about her father, who had just landed in Walpole State Prison after a botched robbery of the downtown Bank of Boston branch. She gave the punk a concussion and a broken jaw, and relieved him of four teeth. She didn't realize he'd cut her until a friend mentioned the blood soaking through the back of her shirt.

"A guy like that has to have some skeletons in his closet," said Annie. "Something that you could use to convince him to keep his mouth shut about your client."

"I wouldn't even know where to start," said Carys.

"A criminal record search," said Annie. "I've got access to databases you wouldn't believe. I have friends in the Attorney General's office who will do a search for me, and whatever I can't get to through them, Detective Hottiecakes can find. Get me a fingerprint. If he's ever been booked for a crime of any kind in North America, we can find it. We've got two weeks, right?"

"That's illegal, isn't it?"

"No!" said Annie. "Well, sorta. But procuring a fingerprint is not illegal. Surely you can do that. Just get me his mug. Or a used plastic water bottle."

Carys knew that if she agreed to get a fingerprint, they'd be jumping off a cliff. It wouldn't faze Annie. She jumped off cliffs like this before breakfast. But Carys would free-fall. She'd be risking her job, but more terrifying, she would have to use whatever Annie dug up. She'd have to do something.

Carys was rooted to the bar stool like a tree growing around a rock. Then she thought of the manuscripts—the hundreds and hundreds of beautiful books, Harper's manuscripts, but they were her manuscripts, too—flying in a million different directions never to be in the same place together for the rest of eternity.

"Let's do it," said Carys, lowering her head. "But if anything even smells like it might go wrong, I'm going to abort. And I advise you to do the same."

Annie beamed next to her.

"Excellent."

They clinked their glasses and drank whiskey and remembered the bad old days.

◆ ◆ ◆ ◆ ◆

CARYS WAS DRUNKER THAN SHE'D BEEN in a long time. With great effort, she opened the front door of the Sothington's building and committed herself to the task of acting sober. *Speak clearly to the security guard. Smile. Yup, forgot a reference book I need. Good to see you, too. Have a good night. Smile again.*

Carys's purse slipped off her shoulder as she walked to the elevator, and she overreacted while trying to catch it. A lipstick, a sunglasses case, and house keys spilled onto the floor. "Fuck," she murmured.

She turned back and saw the guard glance at her. She waved, collected the items, and put them back in the purse. Key fob swiped. Elevator button pushed. Door opened. She stepped in; door closed. *No, don't hold on to the guardrail to steady yourself. The guard is probably watching the elevator camera. Still, better than falling over in here.* She grabbed the railing. *Who cares if I'm drunk? The guard probably is, too.*

The elevator door opened on her floor. The computer monitors and exit signs over the stairwell doors bathed the vast, darkened space in a pink light. Carys took a deep breath and navigated her way to her desk. She picked up a small, hardbound guide to Latin idioms and stuffed it into her bag. Plausible deniability.

Plourde's office was lit by the glow of his computer screen. *Probably doesn't know how to turn it off*, she thought. She walked unsteadily toward his office door, willing it to be locked. It wasn't. The glass door slid silently to one side with a push.

She stepped in and scanned the top of his desk. There was a smudged water glass on his blotter. Probably residual grease from his morning doughnut. *Krispy Kreme. Who eats Krispy Kremes in Boston?* She pulled a tissue out of her purse, picked the glass up by the rim, and put it in a plastic bag provided by Annie. *'Cause my badass best friend drives around with evidence bags in her glove box*, she thought, grinning.

Waved to the guard on the way out. "Thanks much. Have a good night." She stepped through the glass doors back out into the cool spring air and let her shoulders drop.

Annie beamed as Carys hopped into her car. Then the two women fell silent. It wasn't the comfortable silence they had developed over the years. It was more like a stopper in a sink. If they didn't talk, then Carys couldn't talk herself out of what was going to happen. Annie drove her home—she'd always held her liquor better than Carys. She would take a cab into the city to retrieve her car before heading back out to Adeona in the morning.

"I'll call ya tomorrow as soon as I hear something," said Annie.

"Thank you," said Carys as she clumsily extricated herself from the car.

"You know it, babe."

Once back in the brightly colored triple-decker Victorian in West Newton she called home, Carys felt like some boundary had been crossed. She was now on Annie's side of the invisible line that had always divided them. Annie always did what needed to be done. Carys thought if something required too much work, it wasn't worth having.

She walked up the two flights to her top-floor apartment. There were floor-to-ceiling bookshelves throughout, books in stacks on the floor, books on just about every flat surface. There was very little furniture except for the antiques from the tiny apartment she had shared with her mother, Patricia.

Carys was fifteen when Patricia finally made good on her threats to kill herself. The next day, Carys had moved in with Annie and her mother, Priscilla, who had been Patricia's best friend. There, she waited for her father to come back from Wales to collect her. He never did.

When it became clear that Carys would be staying for a while, Priscilla emptied Patricia's apartment into a storage unit to save for Carys until she had a place of her own. Carys didn't know she'd done that until the day the movers unloaded the deep red leather lounge chair from the truck in front of her first apartment in Somerville. The sight of it wrenched free the first tears Carys had cried in many years.

It had been her father's chair, and there was a round worn spot on the left armrest where he had always placed his glass of beer between swigs. She'd sit in his lap in that chair and watch the news with him, his warm heart beating against her back, his free arm wrapped around her. It was one of her few memories of him, and like the rest, it started happy and then turned dark.

Carys tossed her coat onto her green muslin couch and bent over to pick up her tabby, Harleian—Harley for short. She nuzzled him and put him down, filled his food and water bowls, and threw herself into the red chair. It smelled like her mother's house, even after all these years. She drifted off with her shoes still on and woke with a start at four in the morning. She dragged herself to bed and slept more deeply than she had in months.

4

Tuesday, June 12

The next morning, Carys's cell phone rang at nine and jolted her out of a dreamless sleep. It was Annie, laughing so hard she could hardly speak.

Three hours later, palms sweating, heart beating, Carys rapped lightly on Plourde's door.

"What a nice surprise!" Plourde bellowed as he waved Carys in. His eyes landed on her breasts. "How goes it at the Harper asy—"

"It goes fine," she said. She closed the slider behind her. "I think you should reconsider the private sale." She sat in the chair in front of his desk.

"We've already discussed this, Carys."

"A donation is the right thing for JJ to do," she said, leaning back in her chair. She was sure she was pitting out her sweater dress.

"JJ Harper has signed a contract. We will respect the client's wishes," said Plourde.

"These are not the client's wishes, and we both know it. He's only doing it because you threatened to expose his father's illness."

"Ms. Jones," said Plourde, glaring. "I resent the accusation."

Something shrank inside of her. *I can't do this*, she thought. *I'm throwing everything away.*

Plourde sat there, his arms crossed, a defiant half-smile on his face. He was poised for a fight. He wanted one. She couldn't do this. She couldn't.

But Annie could. Annie would take no prisoners. What would Annie say?

Carys's shoulders relaxed a bit.

"George, you're making a mistake," she said. "A big one."

Plourde lowered his chin, leaned toward Carys, and glared.

"I told you. We are doing the...." Then he stopped. His eyes notched slightly wider, and the corners of his mouth inched up into the beginning of a smirk. "Fine. Why don't you tell me why I am making a big mistake?"

Carys cocked her head to the side and lowered her chin, as if she were examining an insect, considering whether to crush it. Just as Annie did during closing arguments. She swallowed.

"It's wrong to use people's secrets to make them do what you want. It's blackmail," she said softly.

"I have not blackmailed anyone," said Plourde with half-hearted indignation. "We have a contract that JJ signed of his own free will."

Plourde paused. His face cracked into the full grin he'd been stifling. "And frankly, even if I had used some information that has come into my possession to persuade young Mr. Harper to sell the collection, that's just good business, is it not?"

She was struck dumb. She had prepared for every type of denial that Plourde could possibly concoct, but she hadn't expected that he'd just admit it. Why on earth would he do that? Didn't he realize he was confessing to a crime? The answer became obvious as his eyes danced over her breasts again, then brazenly lingered. He was bragging. He was trying to impress her.

The male ego, she thought. *So dangerous and fragile*. A mix of delight and rage shivered through her as she reached into her purse and pulled out a folded piece of paper.

"No one deserves to be blackmailed," she said. She slowly slid the paper across the desk to Plourde.

He furrowed his brow and took the paper. He unfolded it quickly, impatiently. Then he froze.

It was a thirty-year-old Los Angeles County Record of Arrests and Prosecutions—a rap sheet. Plourde's rap sheet. The mug shots had surprised Carys, too, but not for the same reason they were surprising Plourde, who was now ashen. She was amazed by how very skinny and very young he'd been. In the photos, he was nineteen, and he'd been named Mark Littleton, a Pittsburgh street kid charged with two counts of indecent exposure, two counts of resisting arrest, one count of solicitation, and one count of possession of narcotics.

Carys watched his face as he examined his young self. The seconds ticked by as she waited for the explosion, but it didn't come. She reached back into her purse and drew out JJ's business card and slid that across the table. Plourde's eyes flickered over to it, but he didn't pick it up.

"JJ will be happy to hear that you now believe a donation to a museum is the most discreet way to handle the collection," she said.

Plourde opened his mouth again, but only air escaped. She stood up, reached across his desk for the phone, spun it around, and dialed the numbers on JJ's card. She heard the other end ring twice, and JJ picked up. She handed the phone to Plourde. His body seemed to come to attention, but his eyes were still glazed.

"Hello, this is…uh…George Plourde from Sothington's," he said, looking up at Carys. "I'd like to talk to you about the…uh… the collection."

By the time the message was delivered and JJ released from his private-sale contract with Sothington's, blood was beginning to return to Plourde's cheeks.

"You can't do this," he said through clenched teeth. "My record was expunged. I went through a program. This isn't even supposed to be publicly available. Where did you get this?" His voice rose ominously, and he stood up, his fist wrapped around the paper. "Where did you get this?"

"I have a Magic Rolodex, too," she said.

"Ms. Jones, you don't know who you're fucking with," he seethed. The veins on his forehead pulsed.

"If you tell a soul about Harper's condition, or try to get me fired, everyone in this company, and your wife, is going to get a copy of that," she said. "I'm assuming you've never told her. She's Harvard Club, right?"

Plourde's cheeks went bright crimson, and he began to pant.

"Yeah, I thought so," she said. She stood up and turned to go, then looked back at him. "I'll finish the Harper appraisal. They'll still need it for the donation. Don't assign anything else to me until I'm done. I don't know how long it will be. I'll check back into the office a couple of times a week."

Carys turned and walked out of his office. As she approached the elevator, she heard Plourde's phone ringing the distinctive "Rule, Britannia," which meant his boss in London was calling. He did not pick it up.

◆ ◆ ◆ ◆ ◆

RADIO BLARING, CARYS BASHED OUT the drum solo to "Flirtin' With Disaster" on her steering wheel as she sped down Route 9. Plymouth State College, 1999. Her first rock concert. Molly Hatchet was on a nostalgia tour, but it was all new to Carys. The Williams College rower she was sleeping with had taken her to the show in New Hampshire, and they did shots of tequila in the car in the parking lot. The band went onstage while she was in the bathroom discovering why she'd never drink tequila again. She was on her knees, staring into a toilet full of vomit, when the bass line of this song started pounding through the bathroom walls into her gut. Some sort of fiery energy slid up through her body, and she was instantly sober. She ran out of the bathroom, straight into the beat and the lights and the crowd and the consuming wash of sound. For a moment, everything else melted away. It was one of three times in her life she'd been so vacantly happy. Today was the fourth.

She drove up the driveway to Adeona too fast, and sent stones spinning as she braked by the front door. When she'd called Annie and told her about her meeting with Plourde—with dramatic flourishes, which she felt she'd earned—Annie laughed so hard, she didn't make any sound. Just occasionally gasping for air.

At the front door, Carys gripped the hideous, Plourde-like gargoyle door-knocker by its beard and banged it against its metallic face three times.

Nicola opened the door.

"Good morning," said Carys. She smiled and brushed past her into the foyer.

"You're in a fine mood," said Nicola.

"Have you spoken to JJ today?" asked Carys.

"No. Is something wrong?"

"Quite the contrary. Sothington's has released him from his private-sale contract. I'd like to talk to him about some candidates for a donation."

Nicola grasped her throat with one hand.

"How…" said Nicola.

"Not important. It's done, and we can start making arrangements."

Nicola grabbed her and hugged her.

"Oh, sweet child! You can't imagine what this means to us… to Mr. Harper," she said. She held on tight. Carys wasn't sure what to do with her hands. She finally raised one and patted Nicola on the back.

Nicola released her grasp.

"I'm so glad," she said.

"I'm glad, too," said Carys, pulling back from the embrace. "This is the right thing to do for the collection. I'll still need to appraise it for a donation and for tax purposes. I hope JJ will allow me to work on that."

"I'm sure he will," said Nicola. She turned and moved quickly toward the kitchen.

Carys unlocked the library door and set to her methodical reckoning of the room's contents. She'd been back at her work for about half an hour when Nicola came into the library.

"Sorry to interrupt," Nicola said.

"No problem," said Carys, not turning from the desk and her notes. "Come on in."

There was a moment of silence behind her. Then Nicola said quietly, "I need to tell you something."

Carys turned around to face her. Nicola looked different, more present. She was standing differently; her shoulders were back, and her gaze was straight and strong. She looked taller. It was unnerving.

"There's a manuscript here," said Nicola. "A palimpsest, actually, that isn't in the catalog."

"That's not a problem. That's why I'm here. To make sure we catch anything that's been omitted."

"It's been omitted from the catalog on purpose," said Nicola. "Mr. Harper left it out. You won't find it in his catalog, or any catalog."

"It's got to be in a catalog somewhere. How old is it?"

There was silence. Carys pushed the chair out and turned fully around to face Nicola.

"Around AD 550," Nicola said. "It's been carbon-dated to within thirty years."

"That's not possible," said Carys. "If there is a palimpsest from AD 550, it's in a catalog somewhere."

"Mr. Harper has made sure that it's completely off the grid," said Nicola.

"Why are you telling me about it, then? How do you even know about it? You're the house—"

"The housekeeper?" said Nicola. "You really aren't very observant are you, my dear? Head stuck in those books too long."

Nicola moved toward her and sat on the settee. Carys just stared at her.

"I work for Mr. Harper. On the library. I'm not his housekeeper. Well, I pretend to be to keep JJ at bay. There are some things he doesn't need to know."

Carys furrowed her brow. Her head started to ache slightly.

"Your focus, your dedication to these manuscripts, is why we are telling you about this," said Nicola.

"We?" she asked.

"Mr. Harper and I. We needed to be sure we could trust you before we showed the manuscript to you," said Nicola. "When Mr. Harper was hospitalized, the doctors were convinced it was a permanent condition. No one knew what was wrong with him. After six months, JJ decided to sell Adeona and the books with it. I don't blame him. This house is too much for him right now. He's dealing with his father's illness. John is his last parent, and he's scared. We both are. And he has no conception of how priceless this collection is. Eventually, John realized there was nothing he could do to stop it, so he told JJ to call Sothington's to do the appraisal. John knew you would be the one they'd send. We thought we could make a donation, establish a Harper Library at a college somewhere, endow a fund to maintain it, so we'd still have access to the books. We thought we'd have more time to deal with this. And we would have a chance to see whether you were worthy."

Carys felt cold. "Deal with what? Worthy of what?" she asked. Nicola didn't appear to hear her.

"We never anticipated Plourde would blackmail JJ into doing a private sale, but as it turned out, that was a fortunate little piece of business, wasn't it?" said Nicola.

Carys's slackened jaw drew a smile from Nicola.

"Yes, JJ told me about the blackmail," said Nicola. "I don't know how you got your boss to back off. But now we know this collection is as precious to you as it is to us."

"Nicola, what are you talking about?"

"It might be best if you heard about the palimpsest directly from Mr. Harper," said Nicola.

Carys's throat closed up. She coughed to regain her voice.

"I don't understand," she said. "Surely he's too ill for visitors if JJ was planning on selling the house and everything in it."

"He's not ill, Carys," said Nicola. "He's had some sort of psychotic break. But I suspect you already knew that. Didn't you?"

Carys didn't speak.

"Of course you did," said Nicola. "He's at Waggoner, under the name of James Weldon, in the Webster House. I'll call them and tell them to put you on the visitor list."

"I...can't," mumbled Carys.

"This manuscript has been off the grid since the sixth century," said Nicola. "Isn't it worth just a few minutes of your time to find out why?"

Hospitals were Carys's vision of hell. She'd spent too much time in them as a teenager. Three weeks. Solid. She ate, did her homework, and slept in the chair next to her comatose mother watching her suicide attempt succeed in slow motion. The smell of antiseptic, the beeping, the dripping liquids, the needles, the bandaged wrists seeping dots of blood, the yelps from down the hall, the way her mother's hands felt cold all the time, the aftertaste of chemicals when Carys kissed her cheek.

"I really can't," she whispered.

"But you can. Haven't you always wanted to meet the man who amassed this?" asked Nicola, gazing up at the bookshelves above them.

◆ ◆ ◆ ◆ ◆

THE PERFECTLY MANICURED, rolling green lawns of Waggoner Psychiatric Hospital looked like a college campus, complete with a soundtrack of murmuring leaves. Groups of buttercups huddled here and there across the lawn like wandering patients. It was beautiful—but still a loony bin.

Carys parked in front of the Webster House, a square, brick, two-story Federalist-style building with a white wooden porch and white trim. This was where the very wealthy and the very private came to have their very embarrassing psychiatric problems addressed discreetly. She turned off her car and sat for a moment tapping her finger on the steering wheel, willing her legs to move.

After five minutes, she grew disgusted with herself. She punched her thigh, heaved the car door open, grabbed her purse, and walked briskly up the steps and through the front door before she had time to reconsider. The nurse at the reception desk looked up as she entered.

"I'm here to see John Har…James Weldon. I'm here to see James Weldon," she said. "My name is Carys Jones. He's expecting me."

The nurse looked her up and down. Without a word, she picked up the phone, dialed a single digit, and spoke in inaudible tones to the person on the other end.

"Take a seat over there," the nurse ordered. Carys obeyed.

The reception area looked like an expensive hotel lobby. Antique chairs and end tables, which she figured to be mid-nineteenth-century, filled it. Portraits of the hospital's founders, one by John Singer Sargent, lined the walls. A large oak buffet table with two candlestick lamps was placed against the wall across from the reception desk. She sat in one of the wingback chairs that flanked it. A few moments later, a man in a suit walked briskly into the reception area and approached the nurse. The nurse nodded at Carys. She rose.

"May I please see some identification?" said the man. His face was hard.

"Oh, of course," Carys said. She reached into her purse, extracted her license, and handed it over. The man read it and seemed to relax a little.

"I'm Doctor Frankel."

"I was told he was expecting my visit."

"Yes, I know. Carys Jones. I just need to make sure that you know what you are going to be dealing with," said Frankel.

"I don't. Not at all. I have no idea what is wrong with him. If you feel that he's not ready for visitors, I'm more than happy to come back at another time." She pulled her purse onto her shoulder.

"I think a visit may be very helpful, actually," Frankel said. "If you want to follow me, I'll take you to his room."

She stood where she was, looking at him.

"Are you okay, Ms. Jones?"

"What is wrong with him?" she asked.

"He's having hallucinations, and he's exhibiting some sporadic manic episodes," said Frankel. "Nothing dangerous, but it can be disconcerting. Can you handle that?"

"I have no idea," she said.

"There's no danger. But we'll have someone with you just in case."

Frankel motioned for Carys to follow him. They went through a door at the back of the reception area into a long, softly lit corridor. It was carpeted with a discreet gold and beige block-patterned wool rug. A chair rail ran the length of the hall at hip height. The wall above the rail was covered in a gold-print wallpaper, and there were gold candle wall sconces between each of the doors that led—Carys assumed, because of the locks on the outside—to the patients' rooms.

He stopped at a door at the end of the hall. The corner unit, of course. He unlocked the door and led her into an apartment that was far nicer than her own. There were floor-to-ceiling windows with light-green silk curtains on two walls of the living room, which had a velvet couch, a coffee table, and two reading chairs.

"Wait here a moment," he said. He stepped out of the foyer into the main living room, passed a dining table against a far wall, and knocked on a slightly opened door on the other side, which she assumed was a bedroom.

"Mr. Harper," he said quietly. "Your visitor is here."

Carys strained to hear the response.

"She came," a frail voice said. "I didn't think she would. She's shy."

"I can see that," Frankel said quietly. "So be nice to her." He came out of the room and motioned for Carys. She moved her leaden feet slowly toward the opened door.

"We'll need to notify Mr. Harper's son that you came by," Frankel said. "He's next of kin."

"That's fine," she said.

John Harper was sitting uncomfortably in a chair in front of an enormous desk between the bedroom's two large windows. His white hair was unwashed, and he was wearing a gray sweatsuit. Behind him was a king-size, mahogany four-poster bed—a bed she had dreamed of having when she was a little girl—its duvet smooth and clean, its pillows covered with matching shams.

"I'll have Elizabeth wait in the foyer, Ms. Jones," said Frankel. "If you need anything, just call."

She turned to see a small blonde woman in a light-blue uniform by the door. The woman wouldn't meet her eyes.

"They're afraid I'll attack you," said Harper quietly. He stood slowly, gripping the desk on his way up. He was taller and more muscular than she thought he'd be. An older version of his son.

"It's a pleasure to meet you in person," said Harper. A trace of his Brooklyn childhood remained in his accent. He moved toward her unsteadily. She smelled his dirty hair as he approached. "Forgive my appearance. The medications they have me on are kicking my... uh...butt."

He extended a slightly tremoring hand. She swallowed the spit that was accumulating uncomfortably in her mouth. She shook his hand. It was cold.

"Sir, your collection is...I can't even find the words," said Carys. "I'm honored to have been a small part of it."

"Have a seat," he said, motioning out of the bedroom to the living area.

"Elizabeth," he said as they approached the couch. "Wait outside."

"Mr. Harper, Doctor Frankel asked me to stay in the room," said the woman.

Harper seemed to shrink.

"Had twenty-five thousand people working for me once," he muttered. With great effort, Harper sat on the couch and motioned for Carys to sit next to him. She obeyed. She could smell his stale breath.

"The walls have ears," said Harper quietly.

He may be nuts, but he got that right, she thought. *Who here ratted him out to Plourde?* She eyed the nurse warily.

Harper smoothed his sweatpants. Then he sharply turned his head toward the bedroom door, saw something, pursed his lips in exasperation, shook his head "no," and looked back to Carys.

"Are you alright, sir?" she asked, tensed to run if necessary.

"Fine. Just...distractions," he said, his voice barely above a whisper.

"I'm here about the manuscript, Mr. Harper," she said. "How is it possible that it's not in any catalog? I don't understand."

"It's been on quite a journey," he said, then turned to face her fully and leaned in. His voice dropped to a barely audible whisper. "You must not tell. Anyone."

"Of course," she said.

"Thank you for stopping the sale of the collection," said Harper.

"I'm pleased I could help," she said. "At least now it'll be kept intact. And you'll be able to access it at whatever museum or library gets it."

Harper shook his head again. "I asked JJ not to sell Adeona. I begged him. I keep on telling him that I'll be well soon."

Harper looked up to the bedroom door again, but this time fought off the urge to react to whatever it was he saw there.

"How is it possible that the manuscript hasn't been cataloged?" she asked.

"The book has been on a long trip," said Harper. "Its provenance is, unfortunately, all word of mouth, but it is quite a tale."

She hated verbal provenance. It wasn't verifiable. She liked catalogs.

Harper leaned closer. She started breathing through her mouth.

"It is the personal journal of a monk," he said. "A very important monk from what is now Wales. Written in Latin, of course. But at the end of the journal, it changes to very early Welsh. The only written example ever found. It's a Rosetta Stone. That alone makes it nearly priceless."

Her eyes widened.

"That's not why this book is important," Harper whispered. "The author was named Lestinus. He took the journal when he traveled to Saint Catherine's Monastery at Mount Sinai sometime in the mid-sixth century."

He stopped and rubbed his eyes. Carys could feel him reaching for his thoughts.

"He joined the monastery," he said. "When he died, the monks erased his journal so they could reuse it for a psalm book. It ended up in one of the monastery's libraries. It was there for thirteen hundred years. The conditions at Saint Catherine's are freakishly good at preserving parchment. Tischendorf bought—some would say stole—the journal on his 1859 expedition to Saint Catherine's. It ended up in Tsar Alexander's library at Alexander Palace."

Carys was now oblivious to anything but the story.

"It was there until the Russian Revolution," whispered Harper. "Tsar Nicholas's ministers cleaned out the libraries and fled to all points of Russia. The book ended up in a minister's home in a town near Leningrad. When the Nazis were looting the area during World War Two, a German soldier broke into the home and started ransacking the library. The minister begged the soldier not to take this one specific manuscript. He explained the book's history, how he ended up with it, and why it was so precious to him."

Harper sipped some water.

"The Nazi was apparently unmoved by the tale. He shot the guy in the heart and stole the manuscript, and half the contents of the house. After the war, the soldier fled to Buenos Aires and the only thing of value small enough for him to carry was the manuscript."

Harper drank again and a drop of water escaped down the side of his chin. He didn't notice.

"In 2003, just before he died, the soldier told his children about the book's history. He also confessed to killing the minister in cold blood—clearing his conscience just in time to meet his maker. For whatever good it did. Friggin' Nazi. His children sold the manuscript to a local antiquities dealer—friend of the family—and passed the tale on to him. He called me," said Harper.

Carys marveled, as she always did, at the incestuous nature of the rare-manuscript community.

"I flew down and bought it," he continued. "I got it home and I started translating it. The topmost writing was Latin. Just Old Testament passages. I started examining the traces of the original handwriting that had been erased. It was barely visible. I had to use"—he struggled to find the words—"uh…multispectral, UV, and X-ray fluorescence techniques on it. There was this passage at the end that was written in a language I'd never seen. It had traces of Celtic origins, so five years ago I hired the best Celtic linguist I could find to help me translate it."

"Nicola," she said.

Harper smiled with a fondness that surprised her.

"No one besides my wife, Nicola, and the bookseller knew I had this book, and it was vital we kept it that way," said Harper. "Nicola is now the only one living of those three. We concocted a cover story that she was our housekeeper and my wife's caretaker. She didn't like that idea much until she saw the manuscript. JJ never figured out what she was really doing there—he didn't spend much time at Adeona. He still thinks she's only a housekeeper."

Harper's face broke into a grin at the memory.

"It took Nicola and I a year to figure out what the language was that the writer used toward the end. It was primitive Brythonic and the beginnings of archaic Welsh. Then it took us four more years to translate that section."

"Amazing," said Carys. She'd forgotten where she was. "What did the text say?"

At this Harper stopped, looked toward the foyer, and took her by the hand. He put a finger to his lips, stood, and began walking toward the bedroom door. Every survival instinct in Carys went haywire, but still she followed.

As Harper shuffled her along, he stepped around something that wasn't there. They quietly entered the bedroom, and Harper closed the door almost all the way. He motioned for her to sit at the desk. She did as she was asked. Harper moved next to her, leaned against the desk, and bent over next to her to whisper into her ear.

"Lestinus was the personal priest of King Arthur," said Harper.

Carys's heart sank.

"His name wasn't Arthur at the time," said Harper. "It was Riothamus Arcturus. His people called him Dux Bellorum—the Duke of War. The monk's manuscript is the only original document ever found that chronicles King Arthur's existence contemporaneously."

She leaned back. Harper's eyes were burning brightly, his face the picture of mania. He saw her body language change.

"You must listen," he said. Then he turned to the door and hissed at the thin air, "Be quiet. Let me explain it to her."

She was trapped. Harper's body was blocking her path to the door. He didn't appear threatening. Still, she began to fidget fearfully. "You have to listen to me. Please. I just need one more minute," he said. "I want you to have this manuscript."

"Why would you want that?" she asked.

"I want to offer you a deal," he whispered, his eyes growing wilder. "This journal leads to the final burial place of King Arthur. One of the most significant historical finds in centuries. Pick up where I left off and find the tomb. Follow the information in the journal wherever it leads."

Harper shook his head hard. Then stared at the desk. Then back at her. His eyes were glazed over and far away.

"When you find the tomb, you can have the book," he continued. "The book. You can have my entire library. I know JJ intends to get rid of it. It would be so much easier to tell him about all this. But he doesn't appreciate the work I'm doing. He wouldn't understand why those books are so vital. He would never understand this search. He'd try to stop it."

She could feel how much pain this state of affairs with JJ caused Harper, despite his obvious insanity. She wondered if Harper knew just how far JJ was willing to go to keep his health a secret.

"But if we can find that tomb before a sale goes through, then it'll all be worth it. JJ will have no choice but to keep the library intact and at Adeona once we prove it leads to Arthur. And you can have it. All of it. All I want is the right to claim that I was the one responsible for finding the King's burial site and anything in it. That's all. That's all. That's all I want." Harper started shaking his head again, back and forth, back and forth.

"Mr. Harper," she said as gently as she could. She wanted out so badly. She put her hands on the desk and began to push herself up from the chair. "I'm going to—"

"I know it's him," said Harper, his mania beginning to build. "I know because Riothamus Arcturus is mentioned in the documents that were written during the time that he was alive. His name is in the land records, personal letters, census data. There are all sorts of clues. But there's only one version of these documents. No one thought them worth copying. I bought every single one I could find. You found them for me!

"The journal specifically mentions the battle of Mons Badonicus, of Dubglas, Urbe Legionis, Tryfrwyd. It tells of a great leader who delivers his people from the invading hordes and dies at the hand of the Usurper," said Harper. "The author was there. He witnessed the battles. He rode with the man."

She pulled further back. This was a psychotic rant. Why would a woman as smart as Nicola believe any of it?

"When Arcturus died," Harper whispered, "his people buried him with one of the richest treasures of the time. The journal lists just a few of the objects. It makes King Tut's tomb look like a goddamn Kay Jewelers." His dirty hair flopped into his eyes.

Carys sat still, waiting for an opening to get around him to the door.

"It's filled with precious gems, gold, lots of gold…and Excalibur," he said.

Carys's eyes widened, and Harper grinned to himself.

"In the manuscript, it's called Caledfwlch." He pronounced it with a perfect Welsh accent—*KAH-led-voolk*. As he spoke the word, there was the familiar wrench in her stomach.

"It will be a cultural treasure in the country where it's found, which is probably Wales. But that's beside the point. Arthur's burial site must be protected. There are people who would do whatever is necessary to get what's in that tomb. If they succeeded, if they somehow found it, we would never see it again. Every speck of it would end up on the black market. It would be lost to us forever. I simply cannot allow it to happen."

Carys, despite her fear, found herself unexpectedly sucked in.

"Does anyone else know you have the manuscript or what it leads to?" she said.

"No," said Harper.

"Then what's the rush?"

Harper's eyes cleared for a moment, and she saw a glimpse of the man she imagined Harper had been before.

"Because we have to find it before JJ gets rid of the library. Those manuscripts collectively form airtight backup and confirmation of what's in the journal," he said. Then he lowered his head. "And I'd like to live to find the tomb."

Carys swallowed. "I'm sorry."

"Don't say that," he said. "Just say yes."

"I can't," she said. "I have a job."

"Quit. I'll give you my library and half the money the local antiquities authorities will pay us when they seize the treasure as cultural patrimony," said Harper.

Carys could only stare at him.

"I'll pay you a stipend and all your expenses," he said, and paused to let the offer sink in. "But we have to keep it secret. We don't want to set off a race."

Harper was clearly exhausted from his efforts. Dark circles, just like JJ's, began to etch themselves deeply underneath his eyes. Whether he was right or wrong about the origin of the book, or the identity of the man the monk had written about, or the treasure it supposedly revealed, Harper believed every word he'd just said.

She was almost afraid to ask the obvious question.

"Mr. Harper, there were many warriors and leaders all over the British Isles who fought off the invaders during this period. How can you be so sure that Riothamus Arcturus was King Arthur?" she asked softly.

A light sweat broke out on Harper's forehead. He breathed deeply.

"It's all been researched, cross-referenced. It's all in the library. It's Arthur. I know it is." Then Harper's face seemed to drop, and his eyes glazed over.

"And *he* told me it was Arthur," he continued. He started shaking his head back and forth again.

"Who told you?" she asked.

Harper stopped shaking his head and looked at her. His eyes were crazed and wet. He leaned in closer.

"Lestinus told me," he whispered. "The monk who wrote the manuscript. The monk who traveled with him. He told me it was Arthur."

The blood drained from Carys's face, and every muscle in her body tensed.

Then Harper whipped his head around to his left.

"Of course, she doesn't believe me," he said sharply to the thin air. "It'll take her time. I didn't believe you either, at first."

She stood up, pushed Harper gently to one side, and flung the bedroom door open. The young nurse was standing behind the bedroom door, and it almost smacked her. Carys walked past her into the living room.

"Ms. Jones?" said the woman, flustered.

As Carys walked out the door into the hall, Harper called out to her.

"You'll be back once you've read it," yelled Harper. "And once it has read you."

This, she thought, *is why I prefer books to people.*

◆ ◆ ◆ ◆ ◆

CARYS DROVE IN CIRCLES for two hours through the suburbs near Belmont.

Harper was completely, certifiably, institutionally insane. She'd seen mental illness before, up close and far too personal, but nothing like that. She wanted to just drive back to her old life.

But as the miles rolled by, she couldn't keep the questions at bay. What if…?

What if he had something as ancient as he claimed? It would be like finding another Codex Sinaiticus. Whether or not it pointed to King Arthur's tomb, packed with riches and Excalibur—which was probably just the crazy talking—the journal was a historian's gold mine, not to mention its value as a collector's prize.

What if she took him up on his offer? What if she followed the manuscript's directions wherever they led—even if, as was virtually certain, they led to a tomb that had been looted within a hundred years of its occupant's death? She still would have kept up her end of the promise. Harper would have to give her his entire library. Was he even legally able to make such a bargain if he was crazy? Probably not.

"Stop," she said to herself. "You're being as crazy as him."

Carys steered her car abruptly into a gravel turnout on a country road in Wellesley and put it in park. It was late afternoon, and a lazy sunlight filtered through the forest around her and warmed her car. She shut her eyes and tried to relax. But soon, Harper's face and exhausted eyes appeared. Her head swirled with their conversation, and behind it all, one sentence bubbled up and repeated over and over.

"It would be lost to us forever."

Like people's voices when they die. Or run away.

The next thing she knew, she found herself pulling up in front of Adeona. Not to accept the assignment, but to get some answers.

Nicola searched her face the moment she opened the front door. Seeing no resolution there, her expression softened.

"You saw him?" Nicola asked. "How did he seem?"

"He seemed insane," said Carys sharply. "I'm sorry. I'm just completely out of my element here. He made me a crazy offer. I need to understand what is going on."

She went into the library and sat on the settee while Nicola made tea. The peace that usually enveloped her in this space was gone, replaced by disquiet. Nicola returned and put two mugs on the desk, where they steamed merrily, oblivious.

"What are your questions?" said Nicola.

"Does the book exist?"

"Yes. It's been carbon-dated. It is from the mid-sixth century. As I said."

"There were dozens of books written by monks in the sixth century. Why is Harper willing to give me this entire library to go searching after the ghosts in this one?" Carys asked.

"He's convinced it's Arthur, and please realize that that is not a decision he came to lightly," said Nicola. "The information in the journal is cross-referenced, confirmed, and dated using the primary research material that you see here in this library. Together, this room forms airtight historical verification that the man referenced in the journal is the one who came to be revered as Arthur. You could redo his research, which took him nearly five years of full-time work, or you could just take our word for it."

"But King Arthur. Seriously. It's practically a cliché," said Carys.

Nicola's eyes flashed angrily.

"Maybe," she said. "It also happens to be true."

Carys shook her head. "Of all the things he could have cared about, devoted his money to…"

"We don't get to pick our passions, Carys," said Nicola. "They pick us."

"No one has been able to prove that a single King Arthur existed. At best, he's a mash-up of a few Romano-British warriors who lived during the Anglo-Saxon invasions."

"No one has ever had the journal, or the primary source material that Mr. Harper has collected," said Nicola. "No one. He is the only person who has been able to put the evidence together. Now he wants you to do what he no longer can—prove it to the rest of the world."

Nicola's eyes grew sharp.

"And you should be honored you've been asked," she said.

"Nicola, why me? Why not you? Why not JJ?"

"JJ couldn't care less about this library. All the library is to JJ is another sad reminder of everything he's lost in the past five years. He loves his father, but JJ never understood his obsession," said Nicola.

"I'm having the same problem," said Carys.

Nicola ignored her.

"I would do it," she continued. "I would. Happily. Joyfully. But my body has other plans at the moment. The task falls to you. Harper is convinced that you're the right person for the job. I have learned throughout our years together that Mr. Harper's reasons are always sound, even though they may not be apparent."

"But he's lost his mind," said Carys. "How can you believe anything he says? In his state, the offer isn't remotely legally binding."

"It'll be binding," said Nicola. "Don't worry about that. And John did most of the work on this project before he got sick. His mental health deteriorated so badly in the past year that when he could no longer function, we had to take action. But inside he's still John. He's still the same man. The same mind. I believe that."

Nicola looked at Carys, her eyes damp.

"We will not ask again," she said. "If you decline, we must make other arrangements as soon as possible. But I need you to understand the chance we're giving you. You could write your own ticket once this is done."

Nicola stood up. "I'll let you think for a while. Shout if you want more tea." She left and softly closed the library door.

Carys sat for half an hour, breathing in the smell of the room, trying to clear her mind enough to think. It was fruitless. Finally, she got up and started walking along the perimeter of the library, running her hand across the glass fronts of the bookcases. She opened the first one, grabbed the cross-referenced catalog, flipped it open, and looked with fresh eyes at the entries within.

Listed were places, battles, and names that she had seen in the Dark Age manuscripts that she'd procured for Harper and had the chance to read. But she'd never seen a mention of a man named Riothamus Arcturus. Or maybe she had and just hadn't noticed it. She'd never sought the name Arthur or its Latin or Celtic variations when she gave herself the pleasure of reading these manuscripts. She was more interested in how the people lived at that time, how their daily rituals were like her own and how they were different. How love was the same. How fear, jealousy, passion, and grief were the same. Their motivations and fears were the same. It was all there, exactly like today. The only thing different was the language they used.

Carys reached back into the bookcase, placed her hands on the manuscripts on the shelf directly in front of her, and smoothed the parchment with her bare hands—a sacrilegious act. The oils from human skin could deteriorate the material. She ran her fingertips over the remnants of the hair follicles on the parchment, the ancient goat skin as soft as silk and still pliable fifteen hundred years later. She inhaled deeply, relishing the dusty, ancient smell. She smiled at this one familiar thing. When she turned back around, Nicola was standing in the doorway holding up a key like an unspoken question.

What do I have to lose? she thought. *What do I have?*

"I need to verify some things for myself before I start," said Carys.

Nicola smiled, closed the library door, and walked to the desk. Carys walked to her side.

"Put on your gloves," said Nicola. She did as she was told. Nicola handed her the key.

"The desk drawer," she said.

Carys slid the skeleton key into the drawer lock, turned it, and slowly pulled the drawer out. A solitary pencil rolled to the front of the drawer. She looked up at Nicola, confused.

"Reach into the very back," said Nicola. She reached in and felt something taped to the rear of the drawer. She pulled on it and retracted her hand. She held another key, this one more modern with a small black chip on it. Nicola backed away and motioned to a huge ficus plant in a pot on the floor by the window. "Slide that aside, please," she said.

Carys bent over and with a grunt slid the pot to one side. There was a circular brass plate on the floor with a small key slot in the center. She inserted the key in the slot and turned it.

There was a thunk, then a mechanical sound came from the other side of the library. Carys looked up to see an entire bookcase sliding slowly forward about three feet into the room. It stopped after about ten seconds, leaving a space barely big enough for a human to slide behind She looked up from her crouched position at Nicola, who reached down to help her up. Carys moved the plant back into place.

The two women walked to the bookcase and slid into the space behind it. There was another door with a keyhole and numbered keypad. Nicola motioned for Carys to use the same key. She did, and Nicola tapped in a code on the keypad. The door slid to the side. Nicola stepped in and flipped a switch to the right.

Dim lights flickered on, illuminating a staircase. Carys descended and found herself in a large windowless laboratory filled with machines that made it look like a hospital MRI facility. In the center, away from the equipment, was a table with a rectangular glass case on it. It was much cooler in this room than in the main library. There was a thermometer and a hygrometer on the top of the glass box. Inside was a small book, about seven inches tall and five inches wide and three inches deep. A codex, with a cover made of animal hide. It took Carys's breath away. These ancient works of art always did.

Nicola came forward, now wearing her own gloves, and lifted the cover of the glass case. She reached in, took the book in both hands, lifted it from the case, and turned to Carys.

Carys stood, her eyes glued to the codex. She was overcome by a desire to touch it, to open it, to learn its secrets. To crawl inside the life, the head, and the heart of the man who had written it. Even if she had to go to the one place she vowed she'd never go.

"I'll do it," Carys whispered as she reached for the manuscript.

5

◇◇◇◇◇◇◇◇

Wednesday, June 13

From the moment she'd been shown the manuscript the previous day, Carys's world had shrunk to the size of the book vault. She'd spent the remainder of the previous afternoon, and into the evening and wee hours of the morning sitting in the chair next to the glass table that contained the manuscript, her white gloves cradling the precious book. She flipped slowly through its heavy skin leaves. Every few pages, she stuck her nose between the sheets and inhaled the warm, musky smell deeply into her lungs. She was in a place as close to heaven as she'd ever been.

Her first order of business should have been to take a tiny section of the parchment out of the manuscript and send it to a lab for another radio carbon dating to ensure the previous readings were accurate. The technology had gotten so much better, even just in the past couple of years. She should also have busied herself collecting the tiny traces of dust and dirt that had accumulated between the parchment pages to send for analysis. Analyzing the handwriting and the ink, the form of the Latin used, and so many other details, were the purpose of her profession. But holding the book in her own hands blocked out all thoughts of what should be done. She would get to all that eventually. When she was done reading.

I am Lestinus. I am a Christian monk. My village, my home, and my family were murdered by invading armies seeking to destroy all that is good. Only I survived. I wish they had taken my life with them. Instead, I am saved by a great leader, Riothamus Arcturus, and am in the service of he who fights the tyranny of ignorance and hate. I set down the exploits of my most exalted master, so that the children who live and their children will know that brave men fought for them. I write here in the language of the learned, safe in the knowledge that my words can be read only by them and never by those who destroy.

The Latin handwriting rolled across Carys's eyes like a wave climbing a smooth, sandy beach. First, she read the X-ray photo image of the palimpsest's page—it showed Lestinus's tiny Latin handwriting emerging from the overlaid, newer writing on top of it like a faint whisper. Then she read a few pages of the English translation—done, she assumed, by Nicola. Lastly, she held up the manuscript itself, peering behind the newer writing to find any traces of Lestinus's actual hand. Parchment was almost as precious as gold back when it was used for manuscripts, and older manuscripts were frequently erased entirely and reused, as this one had been. It was why so many of the oldest examples of written language had disappeared. Some monk, in the grips of religious myopia, fixated only on writing another psalm book, had judged the ancient writing not valuable enough to preserve.

After sleeping a few fitful hours back in her own bed, Carys drove back to Adeona. She knocked on the door, and JJ opened it.

"Hi," said Carys. "JJ. This is a surprise. Is Nicola here?"

"She's not awake yet," said JJ, moving into the foyer. "I think she's having a bad morning."

"That's too bad," said Carys.

"Yeah," said JJ. "She was my mother's caretaker for years, and the whole time, she was sick herself. She's such a trooper. Listen, I've got to leave for a meeting in ten minutes, so I'm going to cut to the chase here. The sale is off. Mr. Plourde released me from the contract."

"Yes," said Carys. "He told me."

"It's, ah, it was a bit of a surprise," said JJ.

"I'm sure it was," she said.

"Were you aware that your boss was blackmailing me?" asked JJ. He stood next to the big round table in the center of the foyer. He didn't look angry or accusatory, but there was a tension in his shoulders that unnerved her.

"Did you know that he threatened to reveal my father's illness if I didn't sell the collection privately through Sothington's?"

Admitting anything would give him grounds to sue the auction house, and as much as she hated Plourde, she wasn't interested in being responsible for that. Her mouth hung partially open as she tried to figure out what to say.

"Your silence answers my question," said JJ. "Did you know from the beginning? Were you in on it?"

"No," said Carys, before she could check herself. "As soon as I realized what was happening, I insisted he cancel the contract."

"Why would he listen to you? Don't you work for him?" said JJ. "And what's to prevent him from spreading rumors to get back at me and my family?"

"It's complicated," said Carys. "You won't have any more trouble with Mr. Plourde. I promise. I'm so sorry, Mr. Harper. If you feel you need to work through someone else to get the collection ready for a donation, I completely understand. Just know that Mr. Plourde does not represent me or the people who work at Soth—"

"No, no," said JJ. "I'm not blaming you. Plourde, however… well, I'll deal with him. I'm not used to being threatened. If it had been anyone but my father, I would have made sure that Mr. Plourde never worked in this industry again—and he would have had trouble eating for a few months. Him and his buyer."

"He had a buyer already?"

"Yes," said JJ. "I thought you knew."

"No. And I'd be very surprised if he actually had one. It would take months for him to arrange a sale of this magnitude."

"Well," said JJ, "Plourde had one. One person who he said was going to buy the whole thing. He brought him over here to view the library last week. Very early Friday morning. British guy. Martin Gyles."

"Martin Gyles? How the—"

"Plourde brought him over," said JJ. "He wanted me to open the bookcases, show him the manuscripts. Made me sick to my stomach."

"I can't believe Plourde contacted Gyles so quickly. I mean, a man of Gyles's reputation—he's a renowned antiquities specialist. And Plourde is…"

"Yeah," said JJ. "A dirtbag. They're quite the odd couple."

"A collection of this size and value would usually go to a few different buyers, and they'd all want to see the catalog first. No one commits to a sale of this size without airtight provenance," she said. This certainly explained Gyles's visit to Sothington's.

"I swear, Carys, if I hear a single word about my father's illness in the press, I will sue Mr. Plourde, Sothington's, and this Gyles person," said JJ. "And I'll expect you to testify to everything you told me today."

"Of course," said Carys. She sincerely hoped it wouldn't come to that. "Have you told your father about any of this?"

"No," said JJ. "That's the last thing he needs to hear in his condition. The hospital called and said you'd visited him yesterday. What did you talk about?"

"He asked to see me," she said.

"It's fine," said JJ. "How did he seem? What did you talk about?"

"The collection," she said, swallowing swiftly as the lie came out. "I feel like he wanted to have a hand in the appraisal. He said he didn't want to sell the collection or the house. He insists that he'll be home soon."

"I know," said JJ. "It's so sad. He's been saying that for six months. But he isn't getting any better. I wish I could do something. This is one of the few times when throwing lots of money at a problem doesn't make it go away."

JJ looked up at the sweeping foyer staircase above their heads and took a deep breath. He smiled wistfully.

"I used to ride down that railing when I was little," said JJ. "Used to freak my mom out something awful. She couldn't even be in the room when I did it. But Dad thought it was the best game ever. He'd stand down here, and I'd get on up there, and he'd make sure he was underneath me the whole way down so if I fell off the railing he could catch me. I never fell, though." JJ kept looking up at the railing above them for a moment longer, and when he looked back at Carys, his eyes were watery.

"I've got to get going," he said. "I'll be in touch later for some recommendations for the donation. Please tell Nicola I was here and said hello. Thank you, Ms. Jones. I really appreciate your honesty about all of this."

"Please let me know if there's anything at all that you need, or that I can do."

"You've already done plenty," he said.

As JJ left, Carys's heart ached. JJ was about to lose his last remaining parent. He knew it, too. She knew all too well how it felt—like looking down a long tunnel and seeing a headlight slowly coming toward you, and you can't get out of the way or make it stop. All you can do is watch. She wouldn't wish it on her worst enemy. Even Plourde.

It didn't take long for her conversation with JJ to dissipate once she was back in the book vault. She dove back into the manuscript, and before long, she was sure that the translation by Nicola and Harper was impeccable. Latin had been one of the few languages she had immersed herself in throughout high school and college, and she read it as confidently as she read English. Her sophomore-year teachers at Boston Latin Academy used to tell her it was so typical of her—the solitary, scholarly Carys Jones, bent on spending all her time and energy learning to read and write a language that no one spoke—another way of shutting out the living. The living were too messy. Latin was the perfect language for her.

Ironically, her mastery of Latin was the reason she had a career. But the best reward for all her study was in her hands at that moment. It was the direct connection with the actual thoughts and words of a man dead for fifteen hundred years.

It became obvious quickly that the monk had been young and afraid but determined to avenge the deaths of his people.

I am forbidden to fight. My master has instructed me to tend to the needs of those who have fallen under the sword or who have been forced from their villages. He bids me save minds and souls and leave the killing to him. I ache only to swing an axe at a savage's head.

He described the villages they passed through, or what was left of them. Carys could feel the pain and his sadness in his stark language. *Next to the well, the infant and its mother were felled together with a single sword stroke. In death, the mother clutched the babe with the arm she still possessed.*

Violence and depravity had not changed a bit in the ensuing fifteen hundred years. Neither had war.

I smell of earth and blood and my own shit. We march from dawn until dusk in pursuit of the enemy. All discomfort falls away when we engage. Then there is nothing else.

Lestinus described his master, Riothamus Arcturus, as confident and immensely compassionate, but filled with rage at the aggression of the invaders and their brutality. Arcturus was willing to listen to his men, but he had usually already chosen his course of action. He fought with the ferocity of a bear.

His cross/shield held high he drew down fourteen men.

Lestinus mourned the need for them, but knew that these battles were being waged in the defense of a life, of a culture, that was on the verge of destruction. As he described his terrible black grief over the murder of the parents, sister, and three nieces he never got a chance to save, tears formed in Carys's eyes.

The first time through the manuscript, she read for love. She didn't question a single fact or bit of potentially erroneous translation. She read only to know this monk and hear his words from a millennium and a half in the past. She saw the names, Legionum, Badonicus, battles that had oozed their way up through the sediment of history to become attached to the Arthurian legend. But there were other battles and towns of which she had never read or heard. As the journal progressed, as Arcturus's victories increased and it looked like he and his forces might have succeeded in stopping the advance of the hordes, Lestinus began to describe the leader more thoroughly, as if he'd realized that the task of memorializing the great man's exploits had fallen exclusively to him.

He was born near Aquae Sulis to Roman parents who wore the purple. He was educated by priests and joined the army as a young boy, as he hoped to carry on the brave work of his great King Ambrosius Aurelianus. He chose not to hide behind his status, and he came among the people to be with them. His wife bore him two sons. He led men into battle from his sixteenth year and earned his great renown at our finest battle, Mons Badonicus, at his age of thirty. We flung the savages into a funeral pyre and they did not rise up again. In the peace that follows, our people begin to return to what is left of their homes. Ambrosius considers Arcturus among his most important war generals and has gifted him with a ring to honor his bravery and selflessness, which Arcturus wears proudly each day. It is a band of solid gold, the width of a man's thumb. Set into it is an emerald, the size of a thumbnail. On either side are two blue sapphires. The emperor's seal is on the inside of the ring. My master now approaches his forty-fifth summer, his greatness past all imagining.

Carys came up for air only when Nicola placed a blanket on her shoulders, which she hadn't realized were shaking. Nicola said nothing and left the vault as quietly as she'd entered.

Arcturus has returned from Aquae Sulis, where he went to visit his wife and children. There he heard that a new clan king had risen in the north and threatens to extend his lands south to the peaceful people, whom Arcturus has spent a lifetime defending. My master orders that we bring our legion together and set out. We will wait until the great wave of the Sabrina Flumen can carry us north.

The passage ended there. On the next page, in a different, sloppier handwriting—a style that looked almost tired—came the final passages of the manuscript.

My grief is never ending. The Great Bear, my leader and master, is dead, murdered by the Usurper. After Arcturus drove our legion north on the river, we marched over land for two days to seek out the clan leader and create a truce that would save the peace. But a young king of Venedotia, great-grandson of Cunedda, Maelgwn, craved only power. He saw my great master as a threat to his dominion. It was at his hands that Riothamus Arcturus met his end.

At this point, the tiny, barely legible handwriting in the palimpsest, hidden behind the monks' prayers, changed from Latin to the strange words—Brythonic, the earliest form of written Welsh known to exist.

How, by what miracle, had Nicola and Harper figured out what it said? Carys read each line of the translation, then reread the impenetrable Welsh words shown in the X-ray image of the manuscript.

*Head toward the setting sun from Aquae Sulis up the great
   Sabrina Flumen
The bear unto whom is all the glory save our Lord
Protector, whose bravery is known to all,*

Is struck down in battle with the Usurper
They both fed the ravens along the mountain stream, running
red with their blood
The sword pierced his heart
The great Duke of War is dead
We and the river carried him down the four falls to a field of
flowers
Adorned with drops of his blood
They bloom at our arrival then die and fall as we pass
All nature and man mourn in unison
Then across the ebullition of the sea
We land on the island of the apples
There is a castle of defense under the ocean waves
Between the mother tree and the last light of the fat sun lies the
watery nest where we laid him
With the sword of Ambrosius—King Saint Protector
Caledfwlch
And his belt and ring bestowed
And the wealth of his people, awaiting his return
What castles that can never be
The sea guards better
And now he is the tree of our faith
From here his fruit will fall and the land will be fertile.

Carys sat for a long time with the poem ringing in her head. Why would he write such tortured, opaque clues cloaked in a language that almost no one could read—then or now? Did he want people to find the tomb or not?

The riddle posed a particular problem. The translation could not be verified, because this was the earliest version of Welsh and there was nothing to compare it with. It didn't surprise Carys that it'd taken years to translate it—and even then, she knew there was no guarantee that the translated version matched the original Welsh version or intent. She might end up chasing her tail, but she'd come into this expecting that to be the case. Carys's only hope was that the monk would prove not tremendously clever when it came to crafting word games, and that Nicola and Harper *were* tremendously clever when it came to linguistics.

Whatever his ultimate intent, one thing was sure; Lestinus was devoted to protecting the final burial place but felt an obligation to leave the world some proof that this man had lived, even as all record of their previous way of life was again being extinguished by the Anglo-Saxons, who had resumed their assaults at just about the time that the monk would have fled Britain. Lestinus's journey to Saint Catherine's Monastery in Egypt would have come years after Arcturus's death, which itself came decades after the final, decisive routing of the Saxons at Mons Badonicus—Mount Badon.

Lestinus had felt compelled to leave a trail to the lasting, physical proof that a civilized world once existed, in case his worst fears were realized and the invaders and their ignorance eventually succeeded in plunging humanity into darkness forever. It was a noble task. It was based on a hope that somewhere, one day, the light of learning and knowledge would shine brightly enough that someone would be able to read his words and find his great Dux Bellorum, the Duke of War, the honorific Lestinus used to describe his master over and over throughout the manuscript. She shuddered when she realized how close his fears had come to being realized—if not for Harper's obsession.

She felt bonded to Lestinus in that moment. The monk's mission had now passed from Harper to her.

Carys was beginning to believe, against her better judgment, that the Arcturus in the journal was the man who inspired the legend of King Arthur. Tomorrow, she decided, she would snip the parchment, collect dust particles for testing, and start the cross-referencing to the primary source material that Harper had collected. Harper and Nicola would be frustrated by her need to verify all the details that they had so clearly and painstakingly unearthed and verified before her, but she needed to be sure. She also relished the chance to feel just a hint of the sense of discovery and revelation that they surely had felt as the carbon-dating tests came back and as the names in the monk's journal began appearing in equally old documents scattered throughout the library.

There was no rush, despite what Harper had said. A house of Adeona's value would not be sold quickly. The library could not be donated to any notable institution or museum without a complete catalog, and she was in charge of creating that. Arcturus had either been in his tomb for fifteen hundred years or had not. That she had agreed to pursue this quest would have absolutely no impact on whether or not he was still there. Whatever the outcome, it could wait a few more weeks. The only urgency came from Harper's health, and he was receiving the best medical care money could buy.

She put her nose in the folds of the parchment and inhaled its scent—an intimate goodbye for now. She closed the manuscript, running her hands gently across the nubbly surface. She cradled it in her hands and lowered it into its glass case, closed the lid and locked it. She turned out the lights and for the first time felt the cold of the vault deep in her bones.

Carys emerged into the library. The sun was just setting over the trees at the front of the mansion, and the light streamed through the library door, which Nicola had left open as she put-tered around on the first floor. Golden sunlight fell against the wall with the vertical windows. The room had the bright, peaceful solemnity of a church, and Carys smiled. She closed the sliding vault door and typed in the security code to lock it, removed the key, and replaced everything where Nicola had shown her. She moved into the sunlight and looked out the long vertical windows to catch the view of the forest in front of her as it was bathed by the deepening golden sunset. It was a symphony of colors—a thousand shades of springtime green, punctuated with daffodils and roses. The sun on her back and the view combined to warm and relax her. She stood still, staring out, letting the colors seep into her brain and calm her swirling thoughts.

6

◇◇◇◇◇◇◇

Thursday, June 14

You know the exact moment when you break a man's nose. It's the sound. Like a dry branch wrapped in a towel being snapped in two. And this guy's nose was very broken.

The man's mouth dropped open, and the first hint of a scream began to come out as his eyes rolled back in his head. Frank Marshfield clamped his hand over the man's mouth. He'd be ready to talk now. Frank looked over at the man's giant desk, so neatly arranged.

"I'm going to take my hand away," he hissed. "If you make a sound, I'll kill you."

The man nodded, and Frank slowly removed his bloodied hand.

On the desk was a photo of the kids, a boy and a girl, both in that awkward, gangly stage. School insignias on both of their blazers. Solihull School. Big money. Huge money. Could buy a house with the tuition this twat was paying every year.

There was no paper on the desk. Frank yanked open the top drawer and saw a notepad and a pencil. He pulled them out and slapped them on the desk, then grabbed the broken man by his collar and shoved his face down toward them.

"Write down where we can find it, or I start breaking your fingers," he growled.

The man picked up the pencil, his hand shaking uncontrollably. He looked up at Frank, terrified, and began to mumble.

"I've got a business card," the man said through bloody drool as he put down the pencil.

Frank grabbed the guy's collar again and spun him around to face him, then took his free hand and started pressing on what was left of the bridge of his nose. The man's scream began, then caught in his throat. His legs gave way underneath him, and Frank found himself holding nearly all the man's weight in one hand. Fortunately, he wasn't a big guy and Frank was. He shoved the broken man into the chair in front of his big desk.

"The card for the person who has the icon?" he asked.

The man nodded, his face crumpled in agony.

"With his address?"

The man nodded gently again.

"Let's have it then."

The man opened another drawer on the desk, pulled out a neat stack of business cards and began rummaging through them. He pulled one out and handed it up to Frank.

"You know what'll happen if it's not there?"

The man nodded, his hands moving up to his nose, shaking, afraid to touch it.

"The kids still up at Solihull School?" asked Frank. "They must be due home any day now for the summer break, huh?"

The man looked at him from the corner of his eye, and Frank could feel a new kind of fear emanating from him. The man reached back down to the pile of business cards. He pushed through them again, pulled one out, and handed it to Frank. He took it and tossed the other card back onto the desk.

THE GHOST MANUSCRIPT ◆ 81

"Thank you," said Frank as he pulled back and landed his fist into the man's jaw.

The blow pushed in the side of the man's face. He and the chair tipped over sideways in slow motion. The man spilled onto his Oriental rug, where he lay motionless. A pool of blood began soaking into the rug under his head.

Frank adjusted his jacket and put the card in its side pocket. His finger toyed briefly with a hole in the bottom where the stitching was coming apart. Cheap-ass jacket. But it was the one he wore when he knew there would be blood. It had been dry-cleaned to near disintegration.

His burner phone vibrated, giving him a brief start. He flipped it open and answered it.

"Morning, boss," he said.

"Morning," came a Manchester accent, oozing through the earpiece. "How goes it?"

"Bloody, but I got it. I'm about to head over now. Should have the icon later this morning."

"Brilliant. As soon as you're done with that, I have something else for you."

"What you got?"

"I need you to go to the U.S."

Frank's shoulders stiffened.

"I told you, I won't go back there," he said.

"This is big, Frank. And I don't trust anyone else to do it."

"How big?"

"Quarter million pounds. That's your take. That enough to overcome your fear of the American constabulary? That case is officially considered cold by the way. Two dead junkies in L.A. Those are a dime a dozen. They barely even bother investigating overdoses."

"They do when one of the junkies is the sprog of an Academy Award winner," said Frank.

"Don't worry about it. You didn't know they had quit using—the dose you gave them should have been just right. All that matters is they told you where the statues were and we found the damn things before they ended up who knows where. They were way out of their league. It's their own fault they're dead. You shouldn't feel bad. Your soul is still intact, I'm sure."

"Bugger off," said Frank.

A high, tinny laugh came through his phone.

"More importantly, our clients were very pleased with your work," said his boss.

"Bloody murderous camel jockeys."

"Don't be racist. They're called Islamic fundamentalists, and they're our best customers. Show them some respect."

"They're bad news," said Frank. "Those two junkies were lucky they died before the towel-heads got to them."

"There you go then. A public service all around. I need you on a plane to the East Coast."

"What's the object?"

"Dark Age manuscript. Written by a monk."

The man on the floor was wheezing but was not quite conscious. Frank landed a solid kick in the man's rib cage, turned, and let himself out of the ornate office with its view of the twinkling lights along the canals of Birmingham. He locked the door from the inside as he closed it.

"Guess whose book it is," said his boss.

"Whose?"

"John Harper's."

"Figures," Frank said.

The billionaire had been a thorn in their side for twenty years—not that Harper had ever known that. Harper always got his hands on the rarest manuscripts, books that would have done very well in his boss's "antiquities location and redistribution investment trust," as he liked to call it. It was annoying.

God knows, moving books would be easier money than they were making right now. Ancient books are simpler to find, hide, transport, and sell than the clunky artifacts and sculptures they had been dealing lately. And book clients tended to be less…jihadist. His boss had recently climbed into bed with some terrorist cells that were funding their activities with antiquities pillaged from museums and archeological digs in war zones, and they'd both been making a bundle selling the goods into a network of illicit antiquity collectors: men and women who loved a thing more—and would pay way, way more for it—if they weren't supposed to have it. The icon Frank was about to go collect, from the unsuspecting man whose name was on the now bloodied card in his pocket, had been "misallocated" by one of the many handlers who had helped bring it over from Iraq. The bloke had no idea the hell that was about to be visited on him today.

But the whole operation made Frank nervous. He'd seen depravity during his time in the British Navy, but nothing like these jihadists could dish out. But the mean mother on the other end of his phone respected depravity—truth was, his boss could give any jihadist a run for his money in that department.

"Harper's in a loony bin. Lost his marbles. I need you to go retrieve the manuscript. And the translation of it as well. It'll be useless without the translation."

"Useless?" said Frank. "It's a manuscript. What's it do? Make you tea?"

"No. It bloody spells out the location of a tomb. Supposedly full of Dark Age artifacts and jewelry. If we're going to find that tomb, we need to know what the manuscript says, don't we?"

"Right," he said. "Where is it, then?"

"Well, that's where it gets sticky." His boss's voice turned. It was slightly lower, and his delivery, normally rapid fire, became more deliberate.

A loud squeak came through the phone. The boss was reclining in his big, black leather desk chair in his mahogany-paneled office in Piccadilly. This was bad. Frank knew from bitter experience that his boss spoke in this tone and leaned back in his chair when he was getting ready to do something truly awful. Like the time he had an antique dealer's private plane blown up for cheating on a deal. Or when he ordered Frank to arrange for the right hand of a young woman, an antiquities courier who had sticky fingers, to be "separated from its host" and FedExed to her boss in Paris. "Eye for an eye, hand for a hand, all that," he'd said.

"The manuscript is probably at the Harper mansion. It's in a posh town near Boston."

"I hear Boston is nice," said Frank. "Red Sox, lobsters, all that."

"Harper has a woman working with him. Carys Jones is her name. I want you to find her and do whatever you need to do to get that manuscript off her. Just don't leave any trace. At all. Fly out as soon as you can. I'll call you later with the pick-up arrangements. I'll get you details on Jones, and a weapon."

Frank started to sweat. He hated guns, although they certainly had their uses. But this job was maybe the one he had been waiting for. He'd promised his mum just before she died a few months earlier that he'd get out of the business. He hadn't meant it at the time, but over the following weeks, and the following crimes, and all the following blood, it had started to sound like a good idea. A big cash infusion right now would provide an excellent jump-start on his new life on St. Bart's.

"Right," he said. "I'll drop the icon at the usual location later this morning."

"Good work, Frank, my friend," said Martin Gyles. "Good day's work."

◆ ◆ ◆ ◆ ◆

CARYS HAD ARRIVED AT THE MANSION EARLY, eager to make a full day of it. She let herself in with the front-door key that Nicola had given her when she agreed to the hunt and walked into the kitchen to make some tea. Nicola was standing at the kitchen counter in a thin bathrobe, her hair up in a messy bun.

"Good lord, child," Nicola said as she turned toward Carys, clutching her hand to her heart. "You scared the stuffing out of me!"

"I'm so sorry," Carys said, stifling a laugh. "I didn't think you'd be awake yet. I wanted to get an early start. I was even going to make you some tea for a change."

"Well, next time give me a little knock and a hello so you don't catch me running around in my bra and panties," Nicola said.

"You do that? Cat's away, mice will play, huh?"

"Oh yes," said Nicola. "And the orgies. You wouldn't want to catch me in the middle of one of those." Carys shook her head, smiling, and sat at the granite-topped kitchen island. She accepted the ubiquitous cup of tea.

"What did you think of the journal?" said Nicola.

"I feel very bad for Lestinus."

"I know. Such tragedy. But that defined the era, sadly," said Nicola.

"The poem with the clues. Those will be a problem. How do we know the translations are even close?"

Nicola sat quietly for a moment. "They're accurate. You can rely on them."

"How can you be sure? There are no references for the written Brythonic."

"Yes, there were," said Nicola, looking down into her cup of tea. "But they were very difficult to find. We were able to do the very best translation of those passages that it is possible to do. I can't promise that some of the meaning of the phrases hasn't been lost over the centuries, but the words are solid."

"I'm not a linguist, but I sure would love to know how you pulled that off," she said. "Like deciphering Egyptian hieroglyphics without a Rosetta Stone. Quite a trick."

Nicola sat without speaking. Carys waited. When it was clear the conversation was over, she picked up her tea and headed for the library, then stopped at the doorway and turned back.

"I'll be taking a small cutting for carbon dating," she said.

Nicola inhaled.

"Is that necessary? We've already done the dating."

"Did Mr. Harper use gas or liquid scintillation technology?"

"No, of course not," said Nicola.

"Then you don't have the most accurate tests possible," Carys said. "I have a lab in La Jolla that can get us a date within sixteen years of the day they killed the goats. I also intend to send some of the sand and dust particles away to see if we can confirm anything about the provenance that Mr. Harper recited. It's all supposition, as you know."

"The manuscript is so fragile as it is," Nicola said, placing a hand on her hip.

Carys laughed.

"That book was built to last forever," she said. "It'll outlive us both and look the better for it."

"Do what you must," said Nicola. She left the kitchen and walked up the grand staircase out of sight.

Carys spent the next hour selecting a piece of parchment to use for the dating. She eventually chose a section from the last page of the manuscript that had very little of Lestinus's writing on it—just Lestinus's final words. "*Et nunc reclinat, patriamque navigamus. Dei gratia Riothamus Arcturus. Suscitate viveque.*" "And now he rests. We sail home. God save Riothamus Arcturus. Wake and live."

She took the tiniest piece of parchment she could, using a custom blade designed to slice this material. She placed the piece carefully in a tiny glass jar. Then, using a sterilized brush, she swept particles of dust, sand, and whatever else was hiding in the manuscript, from between the pages into another glass jar. She labeled them both with a code and put them in her briefcase. She let herself out of the house.

She posted the parchment via overnight FedEx to a lab in California she'd used before, labeled her request urgent, and included the billing information of the Harper estate. They were expecting the package tomorrow. The testing team at the lab, renowned for its accuracy, would extract a testable section of the sample and she'd have the results immediately. She'd paid for speed—or the Harper estate had.

She drove the dust sample over to an acquaintance at the chemistry department at Harvard. She knew him through her work at Sothington's, and he occasionally did her favors like this as a way to train his doctoral students on spectral imaging, and chemical and mineral analysis.

That afternoon, she returned to the mansion and began the work of confirming the names and places found in the manuscript. She quickly developed a routine. First, she'd read a section of the monk's Latin writing using the photocopied x-ray of the journal, Lestinus's words materializing up through the newer writing like an apparition. Next, she'd confirm that Nicola's translation of the Latin was to her liking. Then, using the index, she'd identify the corroborating material in the library. When she completed that, she returned to the vault to read the next section.

Every four or five rounds, she'd stick her nose into the spine of the ancient manuscript itself for a good deep sniff.

At first, the inhaling was just for the pleasure of experiencing the ancient odor of the parchment, a warm, earthy smell that was part barnyard, part perfume—her definition of perfume anyway. But after a few times, she began to get a little high. There was a light-headedness, a pleasant little whoosh that made her feel slightly giddy and, oddly, clearer and more able to quickly process the Latin. It was addictive. She'd never experienced anything like it when she inhaled the scent of other ancient manuscripts.

Using the index that she'd been so disheartened by on her first day in the Harper library, Carys quickly cross-referenced the various place names in the manuscript to the original material that Harper had accumulated. Many original administrative documents, to her surprise, did in fact list the names of both Lestinus and Riothamus Arcturus. They included census documents, bills of lading—innocuous slips of parchment recording the number of sheep sold to someone, from whom they had been purchased, and how much gold had changed hands. There were letters; there were activity reports from scouts. It was all the business of the last, fading days of the Romano-British empire, with its magistrates and local leaders rearranging the proverbial deck chairs on the *Titanic*.

Instilling order, thought Carys. *It is how we humans survive. Create a routine in the face of chaos, terror, madness. It won't save you, but you'll live a little longer with the illusion of normalcy. Sometimes that's all you need to make it through the day. Sometimes, that next day is when the chaos begins to end.*

And sometimes not.

Carys spent the rest of the day reconstructing Harper's work, which was proving flawless. She knew she would be expected to visit him soon and report on her work, even though he would likely just smile, roll his crazy eyes, and say, "I told you so."

◆ ◆ ◆ ◆ ◆

THE WEST NEWTON SKY was a thick blanket of indigo fringed by an orange glow coming from the lights of Boston five miles away. Carys got out of her car and went into her apartment, put on her sweatpants and a T-shirt, fed Harley, made and ate a tuna sandwich, got a glass of wine, and plonked down on her red leather chair with a modern translation of Gildas's bitchy little indictment of the British kings, *De Excidio et Conquestu Britanniae,* originally composed, it was believed, in the mid-500s. Her work on Lestinus's manuscript was just retracing steps that someone else had already taken, but it still gave her forward momentum. And she hadn't laid eyes on George Plourde for days, which was a lovely thing.

Around nine-thirty, her lids grew heavy, her head dropped, then jerked up, only to drop down again and stay down for about an hour. When she woke up, she realized that she was drooling slightly. She stroked Harley, who had ensconced himself on her lap on top of the book. She picked up the cat and gently placed him on the floor.

"Time for bed, furry boy," she said, rubbing sleep from her eyes with the other hand. Out of the corner of her eye, she thought she saw movement back in the hallway behind her. She turned sharply to her left.

There, in the middle of the hall, stood a man.

She gasped and froze.

The man was perfectly still, looking straight at her. He wasn't tall, but he looked big because of the robe he wore, made of a dark woolen fabric, belted at the waist with a rope. His head was shaved. He was smiling ever so slightly.

She wanted to scream, but it got stuck in her throat. After what felt like an hour of staring straight at the man, she forced herself to move.

She leapt from the chair, ran into the kitchen through the dining room, and grabbed a butcher knife from the holder on the counter. Adrenaline pulsed so hard through her veins that she thought her heart would explode. She swung around the other exit to the kitchen and into the hallway to face the intruder, ready to do whatever she had to do to protect herself.

He was gone.

"Get out of my house!" she screamed. She ran into the living room as Harley flew out of it and back down the hall. "Get out of my house or I will kill you!"

She moved in a circle, scanning the room.

There was nothing there that wasn't supposed to be there.

She ran to the door that led to the outside stair landing. It was still dead-bolted from the inside. All the windows in the living room were closed and locked.

The adrenaline sent electric shocks up her arms and legs, keeping her body prepared to fight.

Knife held out in front of her like a flashlight, she crept back down the hallway to investigate the bedroom. Both it and its clothes closet were empty, and there were no broken windows or signs of disturbance.

She backed out of the bedroom and returned to the hall. The bathroom door was ajar.

Standing in front of it, heart pounding wildly, she lifted one foot and kicked it in, and it slammed open against the bathroom wall.

Nothing.

She moved slowly, her hand slightly shaking, to the shower. She listened with every ounce of concentration for the sound of someone breathing or moving. There was no sound. She reached out, grabbed the curtain and yanked it back, her knife held high.

No one.

Her mind began to spin. Where the hell did he go? Should she call the cops?

A moment later, unfazed by the outburst or the door slamming, Harley brushed against her leg, purring. Harley hated strangers and would have been hiding underneath her bed if there had been someone else in the apartment.

She turned slowly around one last time, looking for anything out of place. She examined the floor for dirt, or large footprint impressions on the deep Persian carpet, any sign at all that someone else had been in the apartment.

She found none.

It was just a dream. It had to be. Please let it be a dream.

7

Friday, June 15

Frank sat in his rented Ford Focus in the parking lot of the Home Depot in South Cove. There were no quaint brownstones, there was no ocean, no Red Sox. Just a freeway, industrial parks, and what looked like acres of run-down council flats. It looked like his hometown of Tottenham, a neighborhood north of central London where you did not want to find yourself alone at night, or during the day.

It was a mystery why George Plourde had chosen this busy place to meet when there were so many other remote locations not under twenty-four-hour surveillance, like a beach or park. Plourde was probably scared to be alone with him. Rightly.

At 9:00 a.m., a black Jaguar XJ pulled up next to the Ford. The driver wore a tweed jacket and a light-green silk pocket square, all resting atop a mountain of stomach that barely fit behind the Jag's steering wheel. He had never met Plourde before. So far, he wasn't impressed.

The man looked over at him and nodded dourly.

Here we go, Frank thought.

He'd been hearing about this guy for years. Plourde started out as just another auction house executive, sourcing legal antiquities and art for the personal collection of Martin Gyles, world-renowned antiquities repatriation expert. It had all been aboveboard and legal. But at some point, Gyles learned that he and Plourde had something in common: they both had a second, less savory but far more profitable business. Plourde trafficked illegal items to unsuspecting customers, and along the way, he'd become an expert at creating fake but extremely authentic-looking provenance documents—customs forms and bills of lading, old sales agreements and invoices, or any type of document commonly used to prove a legal ownership trail. Gyles said they were the best he'd ever seen.

At first, Gyles dealt with Plourde anonymously. Gyles ran his illicit businesses under the pseudonym JB—the initials of James Brian, his deceased older brother. None of his customers or suppliers had ever met JB—well, they sometimes did, but they didn't realize it. JB maintained a network of secure and completely anonymous, hack-proof and encrypted electronic channels, bank accounts, and phones. When Gyles needed a human involved, he deployed Frank, and if he wasn't available, Tommy. They were the only two people who knew Gyles's true identity. Gyles had been very good, perfect in fact, at keeping his two lives completely separate. Even Frank and Tommy had never spoken to or met each other, although they were well aware of each other's existence.

But Plourde offered access to a new, lucrative line of business. To be exploited, Gyles had to reveal his other identity to the man. Gyles had taken the risk that it would be worth it, and so far, he'd been right.

Thanks to Plourde's exceptional ability to make illegal items look perfectly legit, and sell them into extremely reputable collections via Sothington's, many of those same trafficked items were finding their way into museum collections. Their deal was this: Plourde would tip off Gyles when one of these illegal items showed up in a museum collection, and Gyles would report the presence of the trafficked objects—discovered by "complete chance"—to officials in the object's country of origin. Then he'd extract a heavy repatriation consulting fee from said government. He'd give a cut to Plourde. The two men profited from both ends, and their deal helped Gyles burnish his professional reputation. They always waited until the item was several sales removed from Sothington's, so no reputational damage befell Plourde or the auction house. The few times the illegal items were traced back to Sothington's, Plourde's fake documentation proved as convincing to the authorities as it had to his buyers.

Even Frank had to admit it was a bloody brilliant setup. Only he, Plourde, and Gyles knew the extent of one another's involvement in this international scam, but they had so much dirt on one another that their silence was sealed by the threat of mutually assured destruction. Of course, the destruction of he and Plourde was far more assured than that of Gyles if something went amiss.

Frank got into the passenger side of the Jag.

"Nice wheels," he said. Plourde's cologne, or the car freshener, or whatever it bloody was, nearly choked him. He pressed the electric window button to let in some fresh air.

"Nice to meet you finally, after all these years." Plourde extended his hand.

"Likewise," he said, roughly shaking Plourde's hand. "Let's make this brief. I'd like to get to my hotel for some kip before I get started."

Plourde looked confused.

"Sleep," Frank said. "I need a nap."

"Right," said Plourde.

"Do you have the picture, address, all that?"

"I've got everything you need," said Plourde. "I should probably give you a little background on Carys Jones."

Gyles had warned him about Plourde and his stories. "Pretend you respect him," Gyles had said. "He'll do anything you want." Frank settled in and turned toward Plourde.

"My source at the asylum is a nurse's assistant who—"

"I don't need to know who your sources are," he said. "They'd probably prefer it that way, huh?"

"Of course. Right. Anyway, Carys Jones. She's a rare-book authenticator. Very good at what she does, but a total bitch. She's cute, late thirties, doesn't have a pot to piss in, essentially an orphan as far as I know," Plourde said. "Keeps to herself. She has a cat. She was authenticating the Harper collection for the private sale to Mr. Gyles, as you may know, but then things went, well, they got confused."

"That happens in this business," said Frank. "Nothing that can't be handled."

"May I ask what Mr. Gyles wants with her?" asked Plourde.

"He'll loop you in later," he said. That would not happen.

"Great. Whatever it is, if you decided to use a little more force than strictly necessary on Ms. Jones," said Plourde, "I would consider it a personal favor to me. As a thank-you for my assistance in this matter."

Frank leaned ever so slightly toward Plourde. Plourde backed away.

"Aren't you already being well thanked?" he asked.

Plourde's ruddy cheeks drained of their color.

"Yes, yes, of course," said Plourde. He fiddled with his pocket square. "I've got a briefcase in the trunk. It's got a photo of Jones, brief bio, home address, the address of the Harper mansion, and a handgun. It's unregistered, serial number scrubbed. Box of bullets as well."

"Brilliant. I'll grab it and be on my way."

"Is there anything else I can help you with?" asked Plourde.

"No," said Frank. "We'll take it from here. You received your payment for service and the weapon already, yeah?"

"Yes," said Plourde.

"Then we're through for now. Thank you for your help," he said. "Pop the boot, and when I close it, drive away. Cheers."

"Happy hunting," said Plourde.

He hopped out of the car, and the trunk swung open. He grabbed the brown leather briefcase out of the back, closed the trunk, and knocked on it twice. Plourde drove slowly away.

Frank got back in his car and dialed Gyles.

"I've got what I need here," he said. "I'm going to scope out the locations. Make contact later today. Should have something in hand by end of day. Anything new on your end that I should know about?"

"No," said Gyles.

The chair squeaked on the other end of the line. The sound always made Frank's hair stand on end. Gyles's low, slow voice came through the phone.

"This will be the easiest money you ever made."

"It will be the easiest money *you* ever made," said Frank, half joking. "What with you being safely tucked away on the other side of the Atlantic."

There was a long silence. The voice came again.

"Is there a problem?" asked Gyles.

"No problem at all, my man," he said, wiping his cold, sweaty hand on his trousers. "None at all."

♦ ♦ ♦ ♦ ♦

THE PREVIOUS NIGHT had been endless. Carys had lain awake, staring at the ceiling, listening with every ounce of energy she had for footsteps on the stairs, or an unfamiliar rustle, or the rush of a nervous breakdown she'd been half-awaiting her entire life. None of them came. Friday morning arrived like a bright blessing. It was only at dawn that she finally drifted off to sleep for two hours.

She left for the mansion very early and spent the entire day in the sealed vault with the manuscript, doing the slow, methodical work of cross-referencing the text and familiarizing herself with the book's narrative and points of verifiable historical basis.

That afternoon, the La Jolla lab called with the results of the carbon dating they'd done as soon as they received the parcel. As before, the parchment dated to the early 500s, likely between 490 and 510. Lestinus could have been recording all the exploits of Arcturus in real time. He'd carried this book with him for decades. No wonder the writing was so tiny—it was unlikely he would have been able to get his hands on another one of these parchments in the midst of war. She was thrilled anew at the knowledge that she was one of the few people who knew of its existence.

In the late afternoon, her cell phone rang. The ID said "Harvard."

"Hey, Bill," she said. "Didn't expect to hear from you until Monday."

"I know, but I knew you were excited to see the results. They're very interesting," said Bill. "The dirt contains high concentrates of alkaline granites, syenogranite, alkali feldspar granite. Some volcanics. I'm surprised to see it in these concentrations. Also, there's flakes of vegetable matter. Looks like it's papyrus."

"Egyptian," she said to herself. More confirmation that it had been in Saint Catherine's.

"Also, there's something else," said Bill. "There's a mold spore in there. Mixed in with the dirt. It's organic, so I can't really figure out what it's from without further tests. But it's definitely mold. Probably rode in on the papyrus. Do you want me to dig down on that?"

"There are always all sorts of things growing in these old books," she said. "That's what gives them their lovely smell."

"I think they smell like dead animal," said Bill.

She laughed. "Can you identify the spore for me?"

"Sure. It'll be longer for that, though. We'd need to send it off to another lab, and the prof who runs it is in Aruba for two weeks."

"No problem. Finding the granites and volcanics told me what I most needed to know."

"Where'd you get this manuscript?"

"Working on it for a client. Just trying to verify provenance right now. Looks like we just did," she said.

"That's cool," said Bill.

"Isn't it?" she said, smiling to herself.

Carys stopped her work and left the vault just as the sun was getting low. She sat at Harper's desk and kicked off her shoes. Nicola hadn't been at the mansion all day, and for a moment, Carys let herself imagine that this entire library was hers. It was the only place in the sprawling home where she didn't feel completely out of place.

She was suddenly overcome by an urge to explore. She normally wouldn't have given herself permission to wander around in someone else's private space, but she had broken so many of her personal rules in the past week that she figured she might as well take advantage of her newfound adventurousness in case the old Carys came back. She padded in her bare feet out of the library, leaving the door open behind her, then tiptoed up the stairs like a naughty child, glancing back occasionally to make sure she wasn't being observed.

She cracked the first door on the balcony and peered in. It was a sleek, marble-filled half bath. The next door, in the center of the hallway, opened into an enormous sitting area with a couch, a painting that looked like an original Picasso, several side tables with lamps, and a large fresh flower arrangement. On the far end of the sitting area was a hallway that ran the length of the mansion, from left to right. It had four doors along it. She walked to the far end of the hall and opened the first door. It opened into the most palatial bedroom she'd ever seen. Clearly the master suite.

An enormous canopy bed filled the right-hand wall. A wide stone fireplace, five feet tall, filled the space between two sliding glass doors that led out to the balcony overlooking the backyard. To the left was an entrance to a grand bathroom, decorated from top to bottom with marble. There was massive soaking tub and a shower large enough for eight people. The bathroom was bigger than her first apartment.

She walked back to the edge of the canopy bed. It was made up, a mountain of pillows stacked artistically. On the bureau to the right of the bed was a collection of family pictures, including a wedding photo of a very young Mr. Harper and a beautiful, willowy blonde who she assumed was the departed Mrs. Harper. Next to it was a scattering of smaller photos of Mrs. Harper at various ages, including one in which she was emaciated and clearly wearing a wig. She had what looked like a forced smile on her face, and her eyes were tinged, Carys thought, by anger.

On the left-hand bedside table was a half-drunk glass of water, with traces of pink lip balm on the rim. A set of women's black-rimmed reading glasses were next to it. They looked like Nicola's.

Then it all made sense: this was also Nicola's room. She and Harper were a couple.

The sharp grief she'd seen in Nicola's eyes the first time they met, her intimate knowledge of Harper, his life and passions—it all snapped into focus. She felt a pang of sadness when she thought of how big that bed must feel to Nicola without Harper in it. She sighed. She really did have her head stuck too far into the books.

She left the master suite and went back to the hall and opened the next door.

It was a sterile but artfully decorated room, done in gray and cream. JJ's room, she figured. She wondered if he knew the truth about his father and Nicola. There was a small photo of a young Mrs. Harper on the bedside table. On the dresser, below a picture window that offered an expansive view of the backyard, was an eight-by-ten photo. Mrs. Harper had sandy, beach-blonde hair and was slightly freckled. She hugged a child, Carys assumed JJ, then maybe five, who had a full head of the same color hair. They couldn't have been any happier. At that moment, Mrs. Harper probably thought she had a long, happy life ahead of her.

Carys felt her throat start to close up, and she instinctively looked up into the bright sky, knowing from experience that, for reasons she didn't really understand, it would stop the tears from welling. It worked and she looked down again to the forest.

Just behind the row of trees where the lawn met the forest, she saw something flash. Not like a camera flash. It was more like two small round reflections. She squinted and tried to see what was causing it.

Back in the forest, she saw a man lower a pair of binoculars and move behind a tree.

◆ ◆ ◆ ◆ ◆

CARYS ARRIVED HOME just as the sky was darkening. She sat in her car for a moment, trying not to panic. She had been followed. After she'd missed her exit on Route 16, she'd taken a series of right turns to get back on track. A blue Ford made all the same turns as she did. Now, that same car was conspicuously parked on the street two houses down from hers with a man in the driver's seat.

She should have driven directly to the police department, but the driver would likely peel off and try again later. It was too dark to read the license plate number. As she considered her options, she began to feel trapped, a feeling she thought she'd left in her childhood.

Slowly, her fear gave way to anger. Who the fuck did this man think he was? Maybe it was the same man who had appeared in her living room. Her breath came in short spurts. She gripped the wheel and forced her lungs to take a deep breath. The rage grew. For once in her life, she let it.

Carys opened the car door, stepped out, walked around to the trunk, popped it, and pulled out the tire iron. She slammed the trunk and turned to face the car. She saw the occupant shift slightly in his seat. With the iron held in her fist, dangling by her side, she crossed the street and walked as nonchalantly as she could manage down the sidewalk toward the car. Twenty feet from it, the occupant, a very large man in an ill-fitting suit and almost no neck, got out and faced her. His mouth smiled.

"Are you Ms. Jones?" he asked. He had a Cockney accent.

"What do you want?" she asked. It came out squeakier than she'd intended. She gripped the iron tighter and lifted the working end up to the palm of her other hand so it crossed her body, a small barrier between her and the stranger.

"I'm sorry to disturb you at home," he said.

"Who are you?" she said, less squeaky. *He knows I live here.*

"Ms. Jones, I'm here to offer you a business proposition."

"I have an office. You could have called me there instead of tailing me across half the county," she said. "I'm going to call the police, and if I ever see you on my street again—"

"I did not mean to frighten you."

"I'm not afraid," she growled from the back of her throat. "I'm angry. What gives you the right to—"

"I understand," said the man, who took a step toward her. She lifted the tire iron. He used his left hand to gently nudge back the edge of his coat, where, even in the fading light, she could see the handle of a gun. The blood drained out of her limbs.

"Just listen to my offer," said the man. His aggression was palpable through the cooling night air.

Brandishing the tire iron like a sword, she stood her ground.

"I would be happy to discuss this in my office tomorrow," she said. "As long as you leave that gun home."

"We prefer discretion," said the man. "You have something that we want. We can make you very wealthy."

The hand holding the tire iron began to shake slightly. He knew. "I don't own anything valuable."

"Well, technically you don't own it, but you can get it. In exchange, we'll give you three hundred thousand dollars. We transfer the money into any account you wish when you hand the item to me."

"What do you think I have that is worth that much?" she asked.

"Don't get smart," the man snarled, low and deep. "You know I'm talking about the monk's manuscript."

She swallowed hard. "I deal with dozens of rare manuscripts every week. I'm not in a position to sell any of them personally. You should contact my boss at Sothington's if you wish to make an off—"

"We want the book. You'd have lots of money and we would have what we want and no one would get hurt. Simple."

She stopped breathing.

"I'm afraid I can't help you," she said.

The man scowled.

"You shoulda said yes," he said. He turned and walked back to the car.

Carys stood frozen in place as the car pulled away.

♦ ♦ ♦ ♦ ♦

As soon as the man's car was out of sight, Carys rushed inside, hastily stuffed a suitcase with a few clothes, her laptop, some makeup, and a toothbrush. She ran downstairs and asked her neighbor to take care of Harley—made some excuse about a sick relative. She kissed the cat on the scruff of his neck and handed him over to her sweet, slightly confused neighbor, Milly.

"We'll take good care of him," said Milly. "Don't you worry."

"Thank you," she said. "I don't know how long I'll be gone." She opened the front door and looked both ways before walking briskly to her car.

Her first instinct was to drive to the mansion, but she thought better of it. Best to stay away from all the places that the man knew about. And how the hell had this goon found out about the manuscript? He even knew it was written by a monk. And who was "we"? After all these years, and all the secrecy, how did anyone know about it now?

She decided to head to the city—easier to hide in a crowd. On the way in, she called Annie and made arrangements to meet her at a bar in the Copley Place Mall. She could park in the underground garage, and the bar was near the garage elevator.

Then she called the hospital to speak to Harper. She got the runaround from the receptionist, because in her panicked state, she forgot the fake name under which Harper was admitted. Somehow, she remembered his doctor's name. The receptionist reluctantly agreed to bring him to the phone.

"Ms. Jones, it's Doctor Frankel. How can I help you?"

"I must speak with Mr. Harper. It's an emergency."

"We're trying not to create stressful situations for Mr. Harper right now," said Frankel.

"Please put me through. It is vitally important that I speak with him."

"I must put my patient first, Ms. Jones," Frankel said. "Perhaps if you can tell me about the problem, I can help you."

"It's private...it's—"

"You could come by tomorrow to discuss it with him in person, in a controlled situation, when you're not as...emotional," he said. "He's been making good progress this week, and we don't want to interrupt that."

"Fine, I'll come by tomorrow morning. What time will you allow me in?"

"Anytime after ten."

"I'll be there at ten sharp." She hung up just as she drove into the parking garage off Huntington Avenue.

She sat in her car and dialed Nicola. When she answered, Carys spilled out a flurry of words that made no sense.

"Slow down, slow down," said Nicola calmly. "What is happening?"

"Where are you right now?"

"At Adeona," said Nicola. "Tell me what's wrong."

"This big goon with a gun followed me to my house tonight, and when I got out and confronted him, he tried to talk me into selling him the manuscript," she whispered into the receiver. "The monk's manuscript. He specifically said that. He knew all about it. Nicola, I swear I haven't told a living soul about that book. How did he know about it? How did he know about me? He was trying to scare me. He had a gun. I'm afraid they're going to try to get into the mansion to get the book. I saw someone in the backyard tonight."

Nicola was silent.

"What should I do?" Carys asked.

"We need to get the manuscript, the translations, and you out of harm's way as soon as possible," Nicola said. "Did you call John?"

"They wouldn't let me speak to him. I'm going by at ten tomorrow morning. I don't think it would be smart to stay at the mansion tonight. Go somewhere. A hotel, friends, whatever. I'll meet you at the hospital in the morning, and we can figure out what to do next. You've got to get the manuscript out of there."

"I'll bring it with me tomorrow," said Nicola. "God. I…it's my fault, Carys. This is my fault."

"Did you tell someone about the manuscript?"

"No, but I sent copies of some of the Welsh sections out for translation, many years ago. It's the only time that the language in the manuscript has been seen outside of the vault. I sent some to my old colleagues at the University in Aberystwyth. I never told John that I did it. It was so long ago, I thought that my translators had been discreet. None of them were told where the manuscript was from, and they each got such a tiny portion of the text that I thought they'd never be able to put it all together. That's the only thing I can think of."

"I'm sure that's not it. There has to be something else. We can talk about it tomorrow."

"I'm going to call John right now," said Nicola. "We need to warn him."

"I don't think that's a good idea. He'll get so agitated, they won't let us see him in the morning. We don't want to set off another one of his hallucinating spells. He's safe there. We don't have to worry about him."

"You're right, you're right. Where are you staying tonight?" asked Nicola.

Carys was on the verge of tears.

"I'll be safe. Don't worry. Take care and I'll see you tomorrow, Nicola. Please, please be careful."

"I will, sweet girl. I will."

Carys got out of her car and ran to the hotel's elevator, took it up to the first floor of the Mall, and walked quickly to the bar entrance. Annie had already gotten a booth in the back when she arrived.

"What the hell is going on?" asked Annie, her face rigid with concern.

"I think I'm…" she said, throwing herself into the booth, tears of frustration welling up in her eyes. "I'll tell you everything, but you have to swear that you will not repeat a word of this to anyone. I'm afraid that I'll put you in danger if they see me talking to you."

"If who sees you talking to me?"

"The people who are after the manuscript."

For the next half an hour, Carys whispered the story of the monk, the manuscript, the hunt for the tomb and its likely occupant, and meeting crazy Harper, who maybe wasn't so crazy after all. Annie sat silently until Carys told her about the man with the gun. Annie's jaw dropped open.

She grabbed Carys's hand. "This is real."

"I know. And they won't let me in to see Harper until tomorrow morning. I don't know what to do."

"We'll stay at a hotel here tonight. I don't want you to be alone until you're safe."

"You can't stay with me forever."

"Hopefully, you'll be safe long before that," said Annie. "But I'm gonna stay with you as long as it takes."

"It'll just be for tonight. I'll have a plan tomorrow once I talk to Harper."

"I told you, I'm not leaving your side," said Annie.

"What about your job?"

"I'm so far over my billable quota this month, they should give me a medal," said Annie, smiling.

"You need to get a life," said Carys with a wan smile.

Annie's eyes flashed up at her, and she opened her mouth to speak, then closed it again and looked down at her drink.

All Annie did was work. It was a form of atonement. Annie had quit the U.S. AG's office several years earlier. She couldn't stand putting dumb, small-time criminals—guys like her father—behind bars and destroying their lives and families. Annie told her that being a defense attorney felt nobler somehow. But once you've won an acquittal for a man who bilked retirees and pension funds out of billions, you've crossed a moral line that you can't uncross.

Sometimes, their friendship felt like one more way that Annie was seeking absolution from the universe for working on, and profiting from, the wrong side of that line.

Carys was convinced that Annie's affair with the cop was another form of penance. It kept Annie from embarking on a real life—love, marriage, kids, things Annie had long claimed she wanted but which Carys suspected Annie didn't think she deserved as long as she was defending the scum of the earth.

Carys smiled at her best friend, the woman closer to her than anyone else, a woman who would put herself in harm's way to keep Carys safe. It was the very last thing she wanted.

◆ ◆ ◆ ◆ ◆

FRANK HACKED THROUGH THE UNDERBRUSH in the forest surrounding the Harper mansion, tree branches clawing at his hair. It was drizzling—like London but without the grime. His shoes were damp. They were nice shoes, too. He didn't have another pair. Crawling around in the woods wasn't something he normally packed for.

Trying to bribe the woman had been a bad idea, but he had to give it a try. He was sick of blood. The woman was terrified of him, but she'd still lied to protect that manuscript. She didn't understand that he was doing her a favor. Must be some book.

Reporting the incident to Gyles went exactly as he'd expected.

"I made contact with the Jones woman. Tried to bribe her. She denied knowing anything about the book."

"Why the fuck did you do that?" yelled Gyles. "You've got a gun. Why didn't you fucking use it?!"

"I was hoping not to have to kill any more Americans this year," he said through gritted teeth.

"Look, we know the manuscript is in the mansion somewhere. Just go get it. You're an excellent B and E man, if I recall."

"Yeah, sure," he said. "The place has alarms everywhere. I trip one, I'll have coppers up my chuff in two minutes."

"Then don't trip any alarms," said Gyles. "Just get me the manuscript and the translation, and do it tonight. Then get the hell out of there and back here. Easy."

Frank knew better than to try to break in. That was a fool's errand. And he was no fool, despite what Gyles seemed to think. He could see from his position in the trees that an older woman was still in the house. He'd been watching her for a while. She'd been reading until a phone call came in a little earlier, and then she began moving quickly, back and forth. She was packing, then she was putting on a coat, picking up some keys, in a hurry. This was his chance. The minute she opened the front door, he'd convince her to let him in. He could be very convincing.

But he did hate this part. He was good at it, but he hated it. He pulled on a ski mask and leather gloves, crouched down, and began to move silently across the lawn.

As Frank reached the edge of the stone driveway, the front door swung open. He ran across the driveway and arrived at the door just as the woman was coming out. She looked up at him with a start and began to scream, quickly backing up into the house.

She tried to close the door, but he got to it before she could close it all the way. He jammed his foot into the doorway and pushed the door into the woman as hard as he could. The woman fell backward, smacking her head on the marble floor.

Her large purse flew off her shoulder and skittered to rest underneath the large wooden table in the middle of the foyer. Frank entered the house, slammed the door behind him, bent over her, pulled her to her feet roughly, and marched her to the alarm panel next to the front door.

"Disarm it," he said. "Type in the code now. And do it right or I promise you you'll be dead before the police get here."

Her face was drawn and pale, and he could feel her thin body shaking hard in his grip.

"What do you want?" she said, barely a whisper.

"The code!" he yelled. She jolted. Her hand slowly lifted to the panel and typed in six digits, which Frank quickly committed to memory. The panel flashed and then a synthetic voice said, "Alarm off." He frog-marched her to the door of the library.

"Open it," he said.

"I don't have the key with me," she said. "It's in the bedroom."

"Well, let's go get it," he said. She was shaking so hard, it felt like she was having a seizure. He saw a tiny trickle of blood on the back of her neck. The last thing he needed now was for her to pass out.

They climbed the stairs to the second-floor balcony and went through a door, down a long hallway, and into a huge master bedroom.

"It's in there," she said. She raised a hand to the back of her head, and it came away bloody. She let out a whimper. He shook her arm.

"You'll be fine. Keep moving."

She retrieved the key from the top drawer of the bedside table, and they walked back to the library. With a shaking hand, she slipped the skeleton key into the door, unlocked it, and entered the library, flinging the door all the way open. Frank marched her to the desk in the middle of the room.

He looked up at the second level and marveled for a moment at the walls of books.

"Where's the manuscript?" he said. "Get it for me now."

"Which one?" she said.

He shoved her down onto the desk chair. She seemed to fold in on herself. He bent over her and put his face inches from hers.

"You know which book," he hissed. "The monk's manuscript. Get it for me or I will kill you."

She started to cry.

"I don't know what book you're talking about," she said, tears streaming from her eyes, the blood soaking the neck of her blouse. Frank almost felt bad.

Normally, he'd smack her around a little bit, but the head wound made that a bad idea. He needed her conscious. He picked up a reading lamp from a long table, yanked it out of the electrical socket on the floor, and walked over to one of the glass-fronted bookshelves. He covered his eyes with his arm and swung the lamp hard into the glass. It exploded into a million shards.

He dropped the lamp and reached in, grabbed a few of the ancient manuscripts, and threw them onto the floor. He picked another, pulled it out, and let it flop open. He pulled on the pages. It wasn't paper. It was something thicker and harder. It wouldn't rip.

"Stop! You'll destroy it!!" the woman screamed as she jumped up from her chair and began to move toward him. He dropped the book and pulled out his gun in one fluid motion.

"Sit the fuck down," he said, barely raising his voice.

She stopped short. Then she seemed to stagger slightly to her right. She backed up unsteadily and sat back down.

He picked up one of the books on the floor. "These are tougher than they look, aren't they?"

She looked up at him, but this time, there was something going on behind her watery eyes. He could see her thinking.

"Don't do anything crazy, love," he said. "Just give me the manuscript and I'll be on my way."

Her face seemed to change. She was still shaking but now her green eyes were sharp, strafing him. He reached back into the bookshelf and grabbed another book, one that looked like it had paper pages.

"You're going to kill me," she said.

"That depends on whether or not you give me the *fucking book*," he yelled, and ripped out several pages before throwing the book on the ground. The woman's face hardened, and her eyes narrowed to slits.

Suddenly, a violent grating alarm began to rip through the silence of the library. It echoed off the walls and sent daggers of pain into Frank's ears. He spun around, scanning the walls for an alarm system keypad.

Then, out of the corner of his eye, he saw movement. When he turned toward it, he saw the woman running at him faster than he thought possible, a look of pure rage and determination on her face.

Instinctively, he raised the gun. She kept coming. His finger squeezed the trigger and the gun barked in his hand.

The bullet tore through the right side of the woman's chest, up near her armpit. It spun her completely around and she hit the floor.

"Fuck," he muttered. He stood paralyzed, shoulders climbing up toward his ears. "Fuck."

The woman lay perfectly still. Blood started pooling underneath her immediately, shiny black against the wooden floor. *Second time I've seen blood in two days*, he thought. She was still breathing, although it sounded like a child's rattle.

He holstered his gun and moved quickly but purposefully out of the library, through the front door, making a mental note that he had not touched anything with his bare hands. He sprinted across the lawn and back into the woods. He'd have to come back for the manuscript later. After the cops—and the ambulance—had left.

◆ ◆ ◆ ◆ ◆

CARYS AND ANNIE GOT A ROOM at the hotel at the mall complex and had a bottle of wine and a plate of popcorn shrimp, which Carys barely touched. She didn't bother getting her overnight bag out of the car. She was too afraid. Instead, she crawled into bed in her underwear, knowing full well that there would be no sleep. As Annie dozed peacefully in the next bed, she turned on the TV and muted the volume. Light flickered across the room.

She drifted off for a couple of hours and woke with a start. She rolled over to look at the alarm clock—2:30. The TV was still on, and she sat up to look for the remote control.

On the wall to her right, about three feet from her edge of the bed, a dark shadow formed, created by nothing. It started out as simply an area on the wall where the TV flicker seemed darker than the surrounding light, but it slowly grew more opaque. Carys watched, confused, unsure if she was awake or asleep.

Slowly, the shadow turned solid. The dark areas transformed into nubbly woolen robes, then a rope belt appeared around them, then arms, the white of a bald head, a chin, cheeks, mouth, nose, and lastly eyes, serene, gazing down at Carys. The man had a slight smile playing across his pale face. It was the man from her living room.

She wanted to shake Annie awake, but she couldn't move. Her throat was clamped shut.

I'm having a dream. It's a dream. I don't need to panic. Her heart bashed away inside her chest.

"*Non time, Carye,*" the man said. "*Tibi non nocebo. Amicus tuus sum.*"

He was speaking Latin. Her heart was now beating so fast that she could hear it pounding in her ears. She tried to focus her mind and translate the words. The concentration helped her regain some control over herself.

He was telling her not to be afraid. That he wouldn't hurt her, that he was her friend.

"*Te succurram. In periculum es. Debes nunc abire, eumque petere,*" he continued.

She closed her eyes, trying to process his message, though she could barely breathe. *I am here to help you. You are in danger. You must leave now. You must go seek him.*

"*Arcturus nunc te sperat. Eum debes invenire ante isti sic faciunt. Dux Bellorum tibi reperiendus est. Desere!*" *Arcturus. He is waiting for you. You must find him before they do. You must find the Duke of War. Leave now.*

Carys looked down at the covers of her bed. She glanced over at Annie sleeping peacefully. The sheets lay damp with sweat against her legs. She closed her eyes tightly, opened them again. The man stood there, still, gazing beatifically down at her.

This is a dream. This has to be a dream. Please let this be a dream.

"I am Lestinus," the man continued in Latin. "I rode with him for years. He saved my life. And now I will save yours. You must not wait until sunrise. You must go now. Get the journal and leave tonight."

Her throat released slightly, and she inhaled enough air to speak.

"Where?" she said.

"Across the sea."

"Why?" she asked.

"*Dux Bellorum tibi reperiendus est,*" he said evenly, without emotion. *You must find the Duke of War.*

Carys could see his lips moving, moist, full, his teeth crooked and dull, his facial stubble as real and defined as the stubble on her own legs, his mouth enunciating the Latin words perfectly.

"He was a leader and a man in a time of great fear. I hid my journal so that the evil ones would not find it and unearth his tomb.

Only the learned and worthy may find him," Lestinus said calmly. He began to slowly fade.

When the space on the wall returned to just a dark shimmer, she found her voice and her feet and jumped out of bed.

"Wait!" she said in a loud whisper in English.

"Wait for what?" asked Annie sleepily.

Carys froze. The last thing she needed was an involuntary hospitalization—although that would be one sure way of staying away from the no-neck British goon.

"I need to get out of here," she said.

"We can't do anything tonight," said Annie.

"I'm not going to sleep another wink."

"Then just lie down and try to relax. I won't let you go back to the mansion until it's light and we can see what we're getting ourselves into."

"There is no 'we' on this thing. It's me. My problem. I will not get you involved in this."

"Too late," said Annie. "Whatever it is, I'm involved. I will not let some tea-drinking bastard threaten my sister."

"I'm not even your real sister. I'm some stray cat your mom picked up."

"You're my sister. And you will now shut up and go to sleep."

Carys lay back down, cold to the bone and shaking. The image of Lestinus, as real as anything she'd ever seen, swam behind her closed eyelids.

Please, let it be a dream.

8

◇◇◇◇◇◇◇

Saturday, June 16

The knock on the door startled Carys awake.

"Relax, Sleeping Beauty," said Annie, already dressed and at the door. "It's room service."

Carys rolled over on her side and tried to slow her heartbeat as the valet brought a pot in on a tray and placed it on the coffee table next to the room's small couch. Annie signed the bill and sent him away, then poured a mug, put cream in, and brought it to Carys.

"You had nightmares last night," said Annie. "You kept me up all night mumbling."

"I've gotta call Nicola," she said as she reached for her phone. She dialed the numbers. The phone rang. And rang. The voicemail message played and the beep sounded. "Nicola, Carys here. Call me. Please. As soon as possible. Bye."

"I'm sure she's fine, hon," Annie said.

Carys looked at the clock. Quarter to nine. "Shit," she said. She hopped out of the bed and headed for the shower. She dressed and got back into her clothes from the night before. She and Annie checked out and walked back down to the garage. Her hand shook slightly as she put her key into the door lock.

"We have to assume that they're still following you," said Annie. "Keep your eyes peeled for any vehicles behind. Make a few trips around the block, check in your rear-view." She gave Carys a smile. Carys didn't reciprocate. "I'll follow behind you and I'll call you if I see anything strange. I'll call Jimmy at the precinct…"

"No," she said. "I don't want you to get your damn boyfriend involved in this. Let me talk to Harper and Nicola and find out what they want to do. I don't want to bring the police into this until we absolutely have to."

"A guy threatened you with a gun," said Annie. "I'd say we absolutely have to."

"He didn't threaten me with it. Just made sure I saw it. I promise I'll call the police as soon as I talk to Nicola and Harper."

The two women drove around the block twice. They turned down a side street, onto the Massachusetts Turnpike on-ramp, and headed west. No one followed.

◆ ◆ ◆ ◆ ◆

"MR. HARPER IS EXPECTING YOU," said the nurse at the reception desk. "Doctor Frankel has cleared this visit but asked me to remind you not to do anything that might upset Mr. Harper."

"Of course," said Carys, knowing this would be impossible. "Mr. Harper's friend Nicola will be arriving shortly as well."

The same nursing assistant followed her down the hall.

"I need some private time with Mr. Harper. Can you please stand outside? What we have to discuss is very confidential."

"I'm sorry. You know the rules," the tiny woman answered, not meeting Carys's eyes.

The assistant unlocked Harper's door and Carys knocked before opening it. Harper's hair was washed and combed, and he was slightly less disheveled than he'd been on her previous visit. He had a half smile of expectancy on his face. It vanished when he saw Carys's expression.

"What's wrong?" he asked.

"Can you please wait here in the foyer again?" she said to the assistant. "We'll keep the bedroom door open."

The woman shrugged as she entered the small foyer and leaned against the wall. Carys and Harper went into the bedroom and closed the door almost all the way. She sat at his desk, and he sat on the bed. She leaned in.

"A man just tried to buy the manuscript from me."

His jaw dropped.

"How did he know about it?" he whispered loudly.

"I don't know. He was a big guy. He had a gun and was pretty clear that he would take it by force if I didn't agree to sell it. I saw him in the forest behind the mansion, then he followed me to my house and offered me three hundred thousand dollars."

"Three hundred?" snorted Harper. He looked confused, and his eyes darted back and forth to the door.

"I told him I didn't know what manuscript he was talking about and that he should call Sothington's if he wanted to purchase such a thing," she said.

"How the hell did this happen?!" he said, his voice rising. She put her finger to her lips.

"I called Nicola and let her know. She said she would meet me here at ten."

"He knows where I live," he said. "Nicola could be—"

"She'll be fine." She wanted so much to believe it. "I called her last night to warn her. What do I do?"

Harper stood up and began pacing.

"I need to get out of here."

"That's not going to happen."

"I know, but I can't help if I'm in here."

"You're safer in here than you would be if you were out," she said. "You'd just be another person this guy could come after."

"You need to take the manuscript away," said Harper. "Nicola will have to go somewhere safe. JJ, too. I don't know how I'll explain this to him, but I'll figure it out. You need to take the manuscript to Wales and follow the clues right away. If you leave today, they won't even know you've gone."

Carys was stunned.

"Why don't we just take the manuscript out of town and lie low for a while?"

"If this guy knows the manuscript exists and he has already tried to bribe you for it, he probably knows what's in it," said Harper. "He'll know what it leads to. It's not the manuscript he's after—it's the tomb. The tomb and its contents."

"But he can't find the tomb without the manuscript," said Carys. "If we just hide it—"

"We can hide it, but as long as you, Nicola, and I are still alive and know where the manuscript is, none of us will be safe. Not us nor our families."

Carys thought of Annie outside in her car. Then a fleeting thought fell to her father, in Aberystwyth—but surely they knew nothing of him. She barely did.

"The only way to stop him is to find the tomb and make public whatever is inside. That is the only way to protect ourselves," said Harper.

"Doesn't it make more sense to report this to the police and—"

"The police can't help us," said Harper. "We can't make this public until we find the tomb, or we'll set off the biggest treasure hunt and antiquities lawsuit in history. That manuscript is war loot. An ancient British relic. Only we can help ourselves."

"But I haven't even finished authenticating—"

"Goddammit, Carys!" said Harper. "Don't you believe this yet? Don't you see what this is? Has a single thing in that book failed to check out? What more do you need? What?!"

He turned sharply to his right.

"Be quiet!" he yelled to nothing.

Carys sat rigid, her mouth slightly agape. Harper caught himself and sat down on the bed again and put his head in his hands.

"I'm sorry," said Harper. "It's just…I can't do anything here." He looked up at her, his eyes beginning to fill. "I'm sorry I brought you into this, Carys. This wasn't supposed to go this way. We were supposed to be able to work at our own pace, give this search its proper due. But that can't happen now. You need to leave right away."

"How am I supposed to get the manuscript without them seeing me? What's to prevent them from just jumping me once I have it? They already know what I look like and where I live," she said.

Harper leaned toward her and whispered, "There's a secondary entrance into the vault. You'll have to go in that way. There's a hatch in the forest directly across the street from the entrance to my driveway. There's a very large pine tree, about a hundred yards back from the edge of the road. It's the only tree like it in that area. There's a hatch in the ground directly behind it. It opens with a code. It leads right to the vault."

He scribbled numbers on a pad of paper on the desk, ripped off the sheet, and handed it to her.

"You can grab the manuscript and anything else you need out of the library without anyone seeing you go in."

He handed her the codes, and she shoved them into her pants pocket.

"Book a flight, round trip so it doesn't send up any flags. Fly into Heathrow, not Cardiff. Get a car and head to Wales. Get a hotel room and stay there until you can figure out the clues and get started. Do not leave messages here. Don't leave any voicemail messages for anyone, least of all Nicola. Get a new SIM card when you—"

Carys's phone rang. The caller ID said "JJ Harper."

"I should take this," she said.

She answered the phone.

"Carys. It's JJ Harper."

"Hello," she said. "What can I—"

"I know you're with my father right now. The hospital called and said you were visiting. I…I have some bad news, but I don't want you to say anything to my father."

"What is it?" she asked.

"There's been an accident," he said, his voice catching and wavering. "At the mansion. It's Nicola. I…I know it's Saturday, but I…if you were planning to come work at Adeona today…you shouldn't."

The blood drained from her face.

"Hang on one moment," she said to JJ. She turned to Harper.

"I've got to take this," she said. "I'll be back in a minute."

She left the room calmly, then ran back down the hallway and out the front door, where she stood on the front steps and got the second-worst news of her life.

◆ ◆ ◆ ◆ ◆

ANNIE PUSHED HER CAR to the limit down the Mass Pike toward St. Augustus Hospital, where Nicola was in intensive care. JJ was at the house. He said the investigators were finishing up and he was about to leave for Waggoner to speak with his father.

Carys didn't go back inside to see Harper. She just grabbed her bag out of her car and hopped into Annie's—she knew she wouldn't be able to drive.

"What are you going to do?" asked Annie.

"I have to get the manuscript and go to Wales," she said. Even she couldn't believe she was saying it.

"How will you get it without them knowing?"

"There's a passage into the vault."

"Maybe someone else should get it?"

"No," she said. "It has to be me. I won't endanger anyone else."

They drove in silence until the car pulled up in front of the emergency entrance at the hospital. Carys jumped out, then stopped and leaned in through the window.

"Can you get me a fake passport?"

Annie thought for a moment. "Yeah. I'll figure it out. When do you want it?"

"I'm going to try to get a flight out of here tonight."

"I'll call you later this afternoon," said Annie.

"Don't text or leave me a message. In case they can hack my phone," she said.

"Jesus," said Annie.

"I hate to put you in the middle of this, but I'm going to need you to talk to the cops. Go through back channels, whatever you need to do. They need to get whoever did this to Nicola, and they need to protect Mr. Harper," she said. "But they can't know anything about the manuscript. It's a British antiquity and war loot—Mr. Harper could lose everything if they find out about it."

"I understand. I'll take care of it."

"Love you."

"Love you back."

She ran through the front doors and to the information desk. She lied and said Nicola was her sister, and they directed her to sixth-floor intensive care. She checked in at the nurse's desk and was led to a glass-walled room. There was a police officer posted outside. He checked her ID. She held her breath as she pushed open the door, and the officer followed her into the room.

Nicola's face was paper white. There was an oxygen tube under her nose, tubes came out of her arms, and beeping machines surrounded her. Her upper body was wrapped in bandages, and a quarter-size patch of blood was seeping through them near Nicola's armpit. It made Carys's head swoon.

"She's heavily sedated right now," said the nurse who was tending to Nicola's IV. "She lost a lot of blood and shouldn't move. You can't stay long."

She nodded. She took hold of Nicola's hand. It was cold.

"Nicola, it's Carys. I'm here. Can you hear me?" she whispered into the woman's ear.

Nicola squeezed her hand.

"Did you see who did this to you?"

She squeezed again.

"Nic, this is important. Did they get the manuscript?"

Nicola shook her head very slightly *no*.

"Did you tell them where it was?"

Nicola squeezed her hand tighter than she had so far, and shook *no* again.

"That's good. That's good. I didn't think you'd tell them. I'm so sorry. I'm going to take the manuscript and go to Wales. Harper gave me the codes to the passage. I can get in and out without them seeing me."

Nicola's forehead creased, and she tried to speak.

"Shh. Just try to relax. You and John are safe now. Once they realize I'm gone, they'll come after me. You'll both be safe. You'll get better and this will all be over soon. And you and John can get back to all that fooling around."

Nicola continued to struggle to speak, her brow furrowed. She squeezed Carys's hand again, and tugged her closer. The sounds came out of her like a long gag.

"Baachhhh," said Nicola.

"I don't understand. Try again, Nic."

Nicola's heart rate monitor began to beep more quickly.

"Baaaaahch," she said.

The door swung open, and an anxious nurse stepped in and moved briskly to the monitors.

"You'll have to leave now," said the nurse.

"But I—"

"Now," said the nurse firmly. "I'm sorry."

Carys backed away from the bed as the nurse took charge of the area with her bulky presence.

"You get better. I'll check in as often as I can. I'll have my friend Annie look in on you," she said as she moved toward the door.

She could see Nicola struggling to open her eyes.

"Just rest. Save your strength. I'll make sure they find who did this to you. I promise."

The sound of the frantic monitor lingered in her ears as she stepped back into the hallway.

◆ ◆ ◆ ◆ ◆

WALKING THROUGH THE ENDLESS CORRIDORS of St. Augustus, Carys closed her eyes and inhaled deeply, then exhaled, then inhaled again, willing herself to process the situation in a linear fashion. She opened her eyes and looked up.

The monk, the one who'd said he was Lestinus, was standing across the hall, staring at her.

She gasped.

She was wide awake. This wasn't a dream. She was hallucinating. Or something.

She closed her eyes again.

"*Debes nunc abire,*" intoned the monk. *You have to leave.*

Carys opened her eyes and scanned the hallway. Maybe he'd go away if she ignored him. He had to go away. She couldn't be crazy. Not now. She had too many things to do. She looked up at the robed man again. He was as real as the pregnant woman in a wheelchair being pushed past her.

The man pushing the wheelchair gave Carys a wide berth and glanced at her suspiciously.

Her mother had never hallucinated, or at least she'd never told Carys she had. She probably would have been too embarrassed to admit it. She wouldn't have wanted to worry her. There had been enough to worry about in their home.

"Walk through this place, find a side door, take the carriage away from here," the vision said in Latin.

She put her hands on her ears and closed her eyes. She wanted his voice out of her head. *Not now. This can't be happening to me now. I'm not insane. I know I'm not. Go away.*

She opened her eyes. He was still there looking at her.

"Go," he said.

"You're not real," she said aloud. "I am not…"

Then a moment of clear thought cut through the panic.

The carriage. He was talking about the subway. It was just across the street.

It was a good idea. It was the fastest way out of Boston, and she wouldn't have to linger outside waiting for a cab. She could take it all the way to Cambridge and get a cab from there.

She looked at the vision's face. Then she glanced down the hallway to find a red exit sign. She looked back for the monk.

He was gone.

For a split second, Carys was disappointed, then a wave of relief covered it. Her hands were shaking badly.

She turned and walked down the hall to the small hospital convenience store. She stepped in and bought a dark-blue hoodie and a Red Sox cap. She bought a duffel bag, into which she put her purse. She also bought a disposable cell phone and a mini-flashlight and set of batteries in case the tunnel wasn't lit. She turned off the GPS and all locator programs on her phone, yanked out the SIM card and dialed Annie on the disposable.

"I'm going to go get the manuscript," she said. "Are you okay?"

"Hi, Roger," Annie said. "I can't really talk right now. I'm with the police. Some nasty business with a client. Can I call you back later?"

"Yup," said Carys. "Any luck on the passport?"

"Absolutely," she said. "I'll have it by two-thirty. I'll give you a call later and we can arrange a meeting."

"Annie, we need to assume they're following you also. Perhaps you could leave the passport somewhere and I'll come by and pick it up."

"Okay, I'll talk to you later."

Carys pulled on the sweatshirt and the hat, and followed the signs to the ambulatory care center on the western side of the hospital. Just as she stepped outside, her phone rang. Annie's phone number popped up. She stepped to the side of the hospital's courtyard, in a shadow beneath a tree.

"Where are you?" asked Carys without greeting.

"Outside the police station. I don't think I was followed. About this passport," said Annie. "I can drop it wherever you want after two-thirty."

"Okay. I'll also need a flight out of Boston to Heathrow," she said.

"I can book the flight and put it on my credit card as soon as I know the name on the passport. I'll get you some cash," said Annie.

"Can you drop the passport at the Boston Athenaeum on Beacon?" she said. "I'm practically family over there."

"You and your moldy-book friends," said Annie.

"It's better than having ex-con friends," she said, managing a smile.

"Not when you want a fake passport it isn't, and don't you forget it."

"Annie, I can't tell you how much—"

"Then don't."

She closed the phone and walked to the edge of the curb, waited for the walk signal, then jogged across the street and into the MBTA station. As the station's glass doors swung shut, she glanced back.

The British goon walked out of the hospital into the courtyard where she had just been standing.

She gasped and turtled into her hoodie. At that instant, the goon stopped and scanned the area. Their eyes met. He stopped walking, his eyes widened, and then he sprang into a sprint toward her.

Carys ran farther into the station, jumped the turnstile, and ran up the stairs leading to the platform. She could hear the rumble of a train but couldn't tell if it was going east or west. She hit the westbound platform just as the boxy silver train pulled up.

She ran down the platform to the lead car and jumped on just as the doors were closing. She sat with her back to the platform and put the duffel bag under the bench.

"Ladies and gentlemen," a voice intoned over the train's loudspeaker. "Due to traffic ahead, we are being temporarily held here by the conductor. We apologize for any inconvenience."

"No no no no no," she whispered to herself. She picked up a discarded *Metro* newspaper from the seat next to her to shield her face. She peeked over the top of it to watch the reflection of the platform in the windows on the opposite side of the train.

The goon ran up alongside the train right next to her car. He pressed his face to the windows, looking in at the passengers. In the reflection, she saw him see her. He began pounding on the windows, then he ran to the door. She held her breath.

"Open the bloody doors—it's an emergency!!!" he yelled in his deep British brogue.

Just then, the train jolted and began to ease slowly out of the station. The goon ran alongside it, banging. And banging. He reached the end of the platform, and the banging stopped.

Carys realized as the train rattled down into the tunnel on the Cambridge side of the Charles River that she was still holding her breath. She looked up at her fellow passengers, who seemed unfazed by the strange man's outburst. As the seconds ticked by, she felt the tension slowly draining out of her.

When the train made its final stop, she grabbed the duffel and bolted through the doors, up the stairs, and into the first in a line of cabs under a covered waiting area. She gave the cabbie directions to the stretch of dirt road near where the hatch was supposed to be hidden. She figured she'd bushwhack to the hatch rather than risk being spotted getting out of the taxi on the road in front of the mansion. She had no idea how many people were involved in this, out there looking for her.

When the cab pulled up at the spot near the woods in Wellesley, she paid the driver an extra thirty dollars to wait for her. "It's really important that you're here when I get back," she said as she hopped out of the cab.

"I'll be here," said the cabbie. "I don't wanna know anything else."

"If it looks like someone is watching you, call this number," she told him, and handed him a slip of paper. "Okay, my friend?"

"Okay, sweetheart," he said, and tossed the number onto his dashboard along with a dozen other scraps of paper, gum wrappers, and dust.

She walked into the woods, duffel slung over her shoulder. It was a sunny, cool day—the woods were starting to smell alive, and the tree pollen tickled her nose. Any other day, these woods would give her peace. Today, the hair on her arms stood up.

After ten minutes of walking, she began to doubt her direction. Then she heard cars passing—she was close to the street that ran by Adeona's driveway. She broke out in a nervous sweat, convinced she'd missed the vault. She crouched low and scanned the forest for a tall, solitary pine tree.

Finally, she spotted it, slightly off to her left—she could see its dark green peak above the canopy of newly green leaves. She walked to its thick trunk and began kicking at the undergrowth at its base.

After several moments, she uncovered an unnaturally flat area. Using her fingers, she identified the boundaries of it, then ran her hand across it looking for the device that ran the hatch. She found what felt like a bubble. She tried to pull it up with her fingers, but they kept slipping off, so she used her keys to pry one edge up. The bubble lifted up, like a coffin top. Below it was a keypad. She blew some leaves and grass away from the numbers on the keypad, retrieved the code from her pocket, took a deep breath, and typed in the code slowly and carefully—there was no telling what would happen if she typed it wrong. She heard a slight thunk, then one end of the hatch began to rise as if it were on a hydraulic lift.

Once the hatch was fully open, she peered down into the hole below. A metal staircase went straight into blackness. She pulled out the flashlight and took the first few steps, her heart thumping so loudly that she couldn't tell if there was any sound inside the tunnel. She started to hum the melody to "Happy Birthday"—it always calmed her down. This time, it didn't work.

At the bottom of the staircase, she shined the flashlight around. There was another keypad on the tunnel's cement wall. She re-entered the code, and the hatch closed down again. She turned around to survey the tunnel.

The passageway had clean, smooth cement walls, ceiling and floor, and it was more than head high. It smelled musty. She'd been expecting a dirt tunnel and was relieved to see vents, lights, and a light switch, which she flipped on. Fluorescent lights, one after the other, each farther away, flickered on to reveal a long, seemingly endless hallway. It dipped down slightly on its way toward the mansion. She turned off the flashlight to conserve the batteries, stuffed the code back in her pocket, and started to walk.

After just a minute in the dank space, her breath began to catch in her throat. Sweat beaded on her forehead and neck, and her head began to swim. She stopped walking and put her hand against the wall to steady herself. The feeling of cold cement didn't help. Her chest felt tight.

She couldn't do it—she didn't even know she was claustrophobic until that moment. She decided to go back outside, compose herself, and try again. She turned around and looked back where she'd come from.

Lestinus stood between her and the stairs. She startled at the sight, and her heart set off racing.

"*Timor solus est*," he said calmly, his voice like a warm blanket. "*Ambula te statim*." *It's just fear. Keep walking.*

Oddly, the sound of his voice made her heart slow down a little, and she began to feel steadier on her feet. *Alright*, she thought. *He comes out when I'm panicked. Or just waking up. Is that a good sign or a bad one?*

"When you get in, you must be very quiet," he said.

Carys continued to lean against the wall, breathing heavily, trying to keep the fear at bay.

"What are you?" she asked.

"I'm here to help you," he said. Then he smiled. A genuine, loving smile. Her breathing steadied, and she stood up straight. She turned down the long corridor and began to walk.

After what seemed like an hour, she saw the end of the tunnel up ahead. There was a steel door with a similar number pad next to it. She carefully typed the code again.

The door opened directly into the book vault. She'd never even noticed the door when she'd been in the vault before. But that wasn't all that surprising. Her mind had been totally immersed in the monk's tale.

Carys walked into the vault, leaving the door behind her open. She didn't intend to be in here long. She swept her flashlight around the dark room, and the light bounced off the smooth white walls, the machinery, the filing cabinets. Everything seemed to be in its place. No one had made it in. She felt her shoulders relax a little. Nicola had stopped them outside. God, she was so brave.

Lestinus moved across the vault and waited for her by the glass-topped display case. She walked to it and aimed the flashlight in.

It was empty.

Carys's mind went blank.

It had to be there.

She pointed the flashlight into all the corners of the case. Nothing.

She spun around and aimed the beam of light on the counter where Nicola always kept the hardcover black notebook containing the translation. It wasn't there either. She moved the light to the bookshelf above the counter. She scanned each row, growing closer to a full panic with every sweep of the light across the spines of the books, none of which were the transcription notebook. She started pulling the books down from the shelf to see if maybe the transcription or manuscript was behind them. Nothing.

"Oh my god," she said, turning to Lestinus. "It's not here." Tiny stars began to form at the periphery of her vision. "She said they didn't get it. Where is it?"

Lestinus stood calmly next to the staircase up to the library.

"*Saccus*," he said in Latin.

Carys just looked at him, perplexed.

"*Saccus*," he repeated.

She stared at the vision. What the hell was he talking about?

Saccus. She went through her translations in her mind. Sack cloth. Rough fabric. Sack. Then it hit her. *Saccus*. It could mean bag. That's what Nicola had been trying to say in the hospital. Bag. But that made no sense either.

"What bag?" she asked him.

Lestinus smiled.

"She was leaving," said Lestinus. "She was saving them."

She'd called Nicola last night and told her to get out of the mansion. She must have put the manuscript and the translation in her bag.

"It's in the house," said Lestinus.

"Maybe it's in the hospital room."

"It wasn't there," he said. "It's still here."

She grabbed her phone out of her purse and called the floor nurse at the ICU, who confirmed that no personal effects had been transported to the hospital with Nicola.

The reality of what she had to do next struck her like a punch to the chest. Nicola usually kept her bag hanging from the back of one of the tall chairs at the breakfast bar. She had to go out there.

What if someone was there? Maybe JJ or the cops had come back?

She climbed the stairs out of the vault and took a deep breath. The vault door slid open when she hit the button, revealing the thin wooden panels of the back of the movable bookshelf. Two thin strips of light shone through the narrow gaps on either side of it.

When she hit the final code number, the sound of the bookshelf moving forward would alert anyone who was in the room. She held her breath, staring through the tiny slit on the right, looking for any movement, and listening as hard as she could.

She could hear nothing. No one was in the library.

The room's door—always locked—would provide cover for her to get out of the vault without anyone seeing her. Getting to the kitchen would be another matter.

She exhaled and typed in the final digit. The bookshelf thunked quietly and began to slide forward. She pushed the button that stopped it. She stuck her head into the crack formed between the moving bookshelf and the fixed one to the right.

Just then, she heard a noise, a cracking sound. There was someone in the house.

She was about to touch the button again to slide the bookshelf back into place, but Lestinus moved up close to her.

"We have no choice—we have to get it," he said.

"You mean I have to get it," she said.

Somewhere in the house, a set of heavy, quick feet stomped back and forth. It definitely wasn't JJ. He wasn't that big. Maybe the cops?

She pushed the button again, easing the bookshelf only far enough forward so she could slip through the space. She stuck her head around the side and surveyed the library.

The scene stopped her breath. There was a huge dark stain on the floor by the desk. The desk chair had been knocked over. The glass faces of almost all the bookshelves were smashed, and books had been pulled down and were strewn across the floor.

The library door was wide open, nearly flush with the library wall.

Fuck, she thought.

She ducked back behind the bookshelf. JJ must have forgotten to lock it when he left. He was probably in shock. All that blood. Carys swallowed hard but her throat was too tight to let the spit go down.

She could wait until the person left the house. She *should* wait. But who knew how long he'd be there. And there wasn't time. She needed the book and translation. She needed to get to the Athenaeum. Then, she needed to get out of town.

Whoever was in the house wasn't expecting her to be there. She could avoid him or her. She had to.

Carys slipped out from behind the bookshelf and walked along the wall of books to her right. She moved silently behind the opened library door so she could hear what was happening in the rest of the house.

Someone was in the kitchen opening cabinets and drawers, pulling things out, throwing them to the ground, swearing in frustration—with a British accent.

The goon.

She began to tremble. She hadn't given Nicola enough warning. He'd come back here and somehow got into the house and shot Nicola. And now he was back, looking for what he came for last night.

The smashing and slamming meant he hadn't found it yet.

This was the only good news.

If he found the manuscript now, in the handbag probably hanging off the back of the chair in the kitchen, then Nicola's suffering, and all the years she and Harper spent on this search, would be for nothing.

Carys couldn't let that happen. She scanned the library for a weapon. She knew there were scissors in the desk. She would kill this man herself. Except he had a gun.

She slowly closed the library door, but only enough so she could see out into the hallway through the crack between the hinged edge of the door and the doorjamb.

Lestinus walked slowly into the center of the library near the desk. She almost told him to stop and hide, then remembered he wasn't really there. He raised his arm and pointed out the partially closed door.

"It's there," he said.

Carys looked back through the crack. Just then, the goon stormed into the foyer. Carys pressed her back against the wall. Within seconds the smashing continued in the living room on the other side of the entranceway—it sounded like he was ripping the pictures off the walls and turning over the furniture.

"There," said Lestinus, continuing to point out the door. She scanned the foyer through her narrow vantage point but could see nothing. She looked back at Lestinus.

"Where?" she whispered.

Lestinus stood there, pointing.

She looked into the foyer once more, and that's when she saw it.

A section of a thin black leather strap was peeking out from underneath the massive wooden table in the center of the room. Nicola's bag.

The commotion continued in the living room. Carys could not try to grab the bag until he had moved on to another room. It looked like he'd already scoured the library, so he probably wouldn't come back. Probably.

The wait was interminable. With each new crash, adrenaline jagged through her veins and sweat soaked through her shirt. After what seemed like a lifetime, the man reappeared and mounted the steps to the second-floor balcony. The moment she heard his footsteps above her, she edged around the door and stepped silently into the foyer.

It wasn't far—maybe fifteen feet—but it was a mile. She could hear the man slamming around above her. It sounded like he was dumping the contents of a bureau on the floor. Like they'd hide a priceless manuscript in a bureau. Idiot.

Carys took a deep breath, crouched low, and moved as swiftly and silently as she could toward the strap under the table. She grabbed it and yanked, and Nicola's purse came sliding out. She clutched it under her arm and quickly scanned the floor. Only a lipstick and an eyeglass case remained behind. She spun and crab-walked on all fours back to the library.

Once inside, she ran back to the extended bookshelf. As she turned her body to slide behind it, something on the floor caught her eye. A business card. She grabbed it and scanned it quickly. A man's name, a U.K. address, and a bloody fingerprint.

Above her, she could hear the brute thumping back down the stairs. She put the card into Nicola's purse, slid behind the bookshelf, and hit the button to close it. She shut the vault door behind her before the shelf was fully retracted. Only when she was at the foot of the stairs in the vault room did she allow herself to look in Nicola's bag.

There was the translation notebook. Inserted between each notebook page, right where Carys had put them, were the photocopied x-ray images of each page of the journal—Lestinus's tiny writing peaking through the newer psalms. At the bottom of the purse, underneath Nicola's wallet and a small package of tissues, was a Ziploc bag. She pulled it out and unzipped it. Inside was an object wrapped in a silk cloth. She slowly unwrapped it.

The manuscript smiled up at her from her hand. She looked at Lestinus, standing next to the tunnel door. She opened the book and gazed at its pages, so small and ancient. She felt as happy to see these pages as anything or anyone she'd ever seen in her life. She lifted the book to her nose and deeply inhaled the scent, as familiar now as that of a friend or a lover. Her head swerved but cleared again in an instant.

Carys wrapped the silk around the book, put it back in the bag, and placed it, the notebook, and the bloody business card into her duffel. She left Nicola's purse on the counter.

She had been gone for more than forty minutes, but the driver had waited. She gave him another twenty. "Did you see anyone?"

"Nope. Barely any cars passed the whole time you were gone," he said, glancing at her in the rear-view. "You okay, miss?"

Carys nodded.

"I need to go to the Boston Athenaeum. On Beacon Street and Park," she said, then dialed Annie.

"Are we all set?" she whispered.

"Yup, the package has been delivered. The flights have been booked out of Logan. Your name is Jane Roberts. You're from Waltham."

"I'm flying first class, of course," Carys said.

"As a matter of fact, you are," said Annie. "I left your luggage at the Athenaeum. I repacked it into a big legal briefcase."

"Listen, there's something else. The goon was at the house when I was there. If you tell the police to head back there right now, they might be able to catch him. Maybe they can get some prints. He's ransacking the place. Also, I found a business card on the floor in the library. It's for a guy with a British address. There's blood on it. I don't know whose blood, or if the guy in the house is the guy on the card, but can you check it out? I'll leave it at the desk at the Athenaeum."

"Sounds good," said Annie. "I'll call the Wellesley cops as soon as we hang up."

"I'll call you when I get to London," she said. "Please check in on Nicola while I'm gone. And tell Harper I've left."

"Will do," said Annie.

"I'm afraid."

"Be careful," said Annie.

There was a soft click as Annie hung up. It felt final.

♦ ♦ ♦ ♦ ♦

FRANK PRESSED THE DOORBELL for the first-floor unit of the apartment building in Newton where the Jones bird lived. After a few minutes, the front door opened a crack and an older gentleman peeked through. He turned his eyes up to Frank and recoiled. People sure were skittish in America.

"Hello, sir. I'm Matthew Williams and I'm looking for Carys Jones," said Frank, using his very best posh British accent. "I've come from London for a meeting with her about an auction at Sothington's, and we were supposed to meet this afternoon here, but she's not at home. Do you happen to know when she'll be back?"

The man eyed him coldly.

"She's away," he said. "She left last night to visit a sick relative. We're watching her cat. I don't know when she's due back. Excuse me. I've got food on the stove." He didn't wait for a reply before he closed the door. Frank was going to knock again and then thought better of it.

So, she'd made plans to leave town right after he'd tried to bribe her last night.

He walked back to his car, got in, and dialed Gyles.

Gyles answered and he could hear what sounded like a party in the background.

"Hang on a moment, please," said Gyles, his Manchester accent gone, replaced by a thick, landed-gentry articulation. He addressed someone nearby. "Your excellency, I'm afraid there's a bit of a situation at the Guggenheim. May I beg your indulgence for a few moments while I get it sorted?" He could hear Gyles walking away from the voices, then down an echoing hall, and finally into a small room without an echo.

"What's happening?" Gyles asked.

"There's a problem," he said. He could feel the bruises on his hands from wrecking the Harper mansion. He wouldn't have known the monk's manuscript if it bit him, so he'd focused on finding the translation, which at least he could have read. He hadn't found anything.

"A problem," said Gyles. "Of what nature?"

"I went to the mansion to try to get the maid to give me the manuscript, and there was an accident," he said, glancing in the rear-view mirror. His collar was soaked with sweat, and there was dirt on his lapels. That explained the neighbor's reaction. Should have looked in the mirror before he went to the door.

"An accident?" said Gyles.

"I shot her."

"Jesus, man," Gyles hissed.

"She lunged at me. The goddamn gun Plourde gave me had a hair trigger," he said. It was true. He had not intended to shoot anyone, not on this trip anyway.

"She dead?" said Gyles.

"I don't know. Ambulance took her away. I tossed the mansion after the cops left this morning. I scoured the place. Came up empty."

"So just follow the Jones woman," said Gyles.

"That's the other thing," he said, steeling himself for what would come next. "I lost her."

"What do you mean you've lost her?" said Gyles. His voice went up an octave. "How could you—"

"I found her at the hospital, but then she got on the subway, and it left before I could get on."

"Fuck! Did you go back to her house?"

"I'm here now. She told her neighbors last night she was leaving town. What do you want me to do?"

"She's probably got the manuscript and translation," said Gyles. "Goddammit!"

Gyles was silent for a few moments, then his voice returned, calm, low, and malevolent. "She's gotta come up for air at some point. When she does, we'll find her."

Frank often wondered if this silky, malignant voice was the last thing that Gyles's big brother, James Brian, heard before Gyles snapped his neck.

The twelve-year-old Gyles had sworn it was an accident, and the authorities agreed, but his parents knew better. They'd promptly shipped Gyles off to a notoriously horrific boarding school because they couldn't stand to look at him anymore. "They had no idea what that place did to me," Gyles had told Frank in a rare emotional moment between them, years back. But Frank knew. That place did nothing that some twist of nature hadn't already done. Gyles came out exactly as evil as he had gone in.

"We'll find her," said Gyles. "Don't worry."

For a moment, Frank couldn't help but feel bad for Carys Jones.

PART 2

Wales

1

Sunday, June 17

Each step Carys took was leaden. The ground was soft and wet and strewn with strangely shaped rocks. Her feet were black with mud. The smell of something like raw meat clung to the inside of her nose. She stumbled and landed on an object, soft yet oddly unyielding.

A human leg. Not attached to anything.

She screamed, but there was no sound. She tried to jump up but felt as though she were underwater. Slowly, she stood and backed away from the severed limb.

Ahead of her, on a small rise in the vast hillside before her, a man... Lestinus...was down on one knee looking at something on the ground. Farther on, beyond where he knelt, there were clusters of men moving down the hillside in groups of twos and threes. Some were limping; others supported them. All were covered with the same dark mud that covered her feet, knees, and hands.

Lestinus was sobbing. Before him lay a man dressed in a white tunic bearing the image of an ancient Christian cross. It was spattered with blood. Lestinus crossed himself and then clasped his hands together at his chest in prayer.

"Suscitate viveque," *he said.*

Wake and live.

Carys woke with a jolt. Her heart was pounding, and her eyes were blurry. A high-pitched whining filled her ears, and her brain creaked into motion trying to figure out where she was. She inhaled deeply to slow her heart. They were around her, the men in cloaks and the dead. She could feel them.

The bag on her lap started to slide off. She grabbed it just before it hit the floor. Standing next to her was a pretty, tall woman in a red suit and a crisp white shirt.

"Tea and scones, Ms. Roberts?" the woman asked.

Right. Airplane. I'm on an airplane, she thought.

"Yes, thank you," Carys said. She wiped some drool from her chin and tucked the bag containing the manuscript and translation into the space between her hip and the armrest.

An hour and a half later, she stood in the immigration line, her palms sweating furiously.

"Destination?" asked the immigration agent.

"Wales," said Carys.

"Purpose of visit?"

"Pleasure."

"How long are you staying?"

She didn't know. She'd forgotten to look at the return ticket Annie bought.

"Two weeks, but I may extend it by a week if the sun comes out," she said with a forced smile.

"Good luck with that," said the agent, smiling slightly back. He turned to his monitor and studied the passport picture that appeared on it.

"Where will you be staying?" he asked.

"With family near Cardiff," she lied. He stamped her passport and handed it back to her.

"Enjoy your visit."

Relief washing through her, she passed into the aimless, anxious mobs in the international terminal. Normally, she'd lose her mind in spaces like this, with the crush and noise and the smell of unwashed, jet-lagged humans all around her. Instead, all she could think of was that she was finally safe. No one could have followed her. She changed dollars for pounds at an exchange kiosk and paid cash for a prepaid phone card in an electronics shop before hopping the shuttle to the rental car office.

She realized, too late, that even though she could pay cash for the rental car, they'd need to put a hold on a credit card for the deposit, and the only one she had was her own. There was no alternative. As the customer-service rep swiped it through the machine, dread seeped through the jet lag.

She walked to her car, a red Vauxhall, and started to get in it on the wrong side. She'd forgotten that she was going to have to drive on the left. While jet-lagged. She walked around the front of the car and got in behind the right-hand steering wheel, pulled out of the lot, and concentrated as hard as she could on simply following the car in front of her, around an endless series of confusing roundabouts, nearly colliding twice with oncoming traffic.

Half an hour later, as Carys drove west on the M4 through the English mist, she finally relaxed a bit. The highway was easier. Her shoulders moved away from her ears, and she started to see the countryside through which she was passing.

She was seven years old the last time she saw the British Isles. Her parents were still together but would not be for long. She remembered that trip so vividly, which surprised her, because she remembered so little about the rest of her childhood.

The intense, uniform emerald of the British landscape had mesmerized her when she was a child—and it mesmerized her again now. All those decades ago, she'd thought the entire island was covered with the fluorescent green from her finger-painting set. She always wondered if that last trip was the reason her father had bolted. Maybe he'd remembered he loved this land more than he loved them.

They'd visited her father's hometown, a place named Mumbles, a tiny town on the Welsh coast that flowed like a gray mudslide down the seaside hills into Swansea Bay. There were endless beaches there, especially the one stretching for miles at Three Cliffs Bay. Wormshead, a rock formation off the coast of the Gower Peninsula, looked like a great sea monster rearing out of the ocean. Fog clung to the ruins of medieval castles perched on the cliffs high above the sea. It was a place out of myth and fairy tales, like a cloud city drifting above the rest of the world. When they got back to America, her father left them and returned to Wales, and nothing was good again. From that day forward, the sound of a Welsh accent nauseated her.

Now she was driving toward that country as fast as her underpowered Vauxhall would go. It had just become obvious where she should hide.

Two hours later, Carys was at a dead stop in a massive traffic jam. The M4 was closed in Bath due to a car crash. Sometime in midafternoon, she finally crossed the toll bridge over the Severn River, the water separating Wales and England. As she passed over it, Lestinus formed in the seat next to her.

This time, as the monk solidified into existence, Carys was neither half asleep nor completely panicked. As he took his full form, she was calm and, though jet-lagged and exhausted, completely awake. This time there was nothing on which she could blame the vision, except insanity. What else could it be? A ghost? Even entertaining that possibility was another kind of insanity.

Still, whatever it was, it had helped her save the manuscript. And it didn't seem like it was going to go away.

"We're here," said the monk in Latin.

"We're where?" she asked.

"We buried him here," he said. He gazed out the window down at the wide, flat Severn River below.

"How do you know?" she asked.

"This river. We traveled it in a boat. A wave pushed us that way," he said as he pointed upriver. "It drove us north. Toward the Usurper."

"It's called the tidal bore," Carys said. She reached for her phone and called Annie.

"I'm here. I'm safe."

"Where are you going?" Annie asked.

"It's probably best that I not tell you. The less you know, the better. How is Nicola?"

"She's stable. But the doctors aren't sure which way it's going to go," said Annie. "Has anyone been following you?"

"I don't think so. I can't imagine how they could have."

"Do you want me to contact Harper for you and tell him you're there?" asked Annie.

She thought on this a moment.

Lestinus turned to her. "He will be fine," he said. She looked at him for half a beat. His weight, his breath, his smell—old wool and a tinge of sweat—were palpable.

"Don't bother calling Harper. I'll call him when I have something to report."

"Be safe. Call me every day," Annie said.

"I will." She hung up.

Lestinus looked at her blankly.

"Find a safe place to read," he said.

Lestinus was visible for longer this time than any time before. She found his presence strangely calming. Then she'd snap back to the realization that she was most likely going nuts.

The car tires hummed soothingly as they sped down the M4 toward Swansea.

"What are you?" she asked him.

"A monk," he said. "In the service of my master, rest his soul."

Psychotic hallucinations don't tell you they're hallucinations, she thought.

"Where did you die?" she asked.

"Saint Catherine's," he said. "I longed for the green hills of home. The smell of rain. But there was no returning. It was too dangerous to come back."

"Western Wales wasn't that dangerous after you left. It was one of the only safe places in Britain," she said.

"I had heard these things, but it was too much risk," he said. "If they'd caught me, I fear what I would have told them. I saw many men betray all they held sacred rather than face their tortures. I did not trust myself to keep the secret."

"It must have been unbearable. During the invasions."

"It would have been if we had had no hope."

"And this warrior, Arcturus, he gave you hope."

"Hope and life," said Lestinus. He made the sign of the cross.

She took the exit into Swansea and drove along the road next to the bay for several miles until they hit the main street of Mumbles.

Jammed up against the hills, Mumbles was a former fishing village composed of three- and four-story white stucco and stone shops, restaurants, pubs, and homes pushed right down against the edge of the narrow main road. The street was so tight against the buildings that the people walking on the sidewalk looked as though they were in constant danger of being mowed down.

Carys had no idea where she could stay. Just as she was about to pull over into a parking spot and start walking the town, she saw a sign on the right for a B&B called the Farmer's Arms. She pulled into a parking lot next to it.

When she turned off the car, Lestinus was gone.

She walked into what she thought was the inn but found herself inside a partially filled pub instead. The men at the bar turned toward her, then back to their drinks. She stepped back out the door and inspected the front of the building while holding the door open.

"You looking for the inn?" asked the bartender, a gray-haired man with a craggy face and bright blue eyes.

"Yes, I am. How do I get into it?"

"You're here. Do you have a reservation?" he asked.

"No. No, I don't. Do you have a room?"

"Sure." The man reached behind the bar and grabbed a thick leather-bound book.

"How long do you want to stay?" he asked.

"Can we start out with a week and see how we go?"

"Sure thing. Name?"

She paused for a moment trying to remember her fake name.

"Jane Roberts," she finally said.

"Hi, Jane. I'm Peter." He reached across the bar and shook her hand. "May I see your passport?" he asked.

Carys handed it over. Peter scribbled her name and passport number in the leather book.

Her room was on the floor above the pub. It was small, with light-blue flowered wallpaper, dark wooden flooring, and a single casement window with cast-iron mullions and wavy ancient glass. Through it she could see down into the pub's courtyard, which served as a beer garden. The room had a small bed without a headboard, and a bureau, desk, and chair. The bathroom was indescribably small, and she couldn't imagine how she was going to be able to wash her hair inside the tiny glass cocoon of a shower.

"This is fine," she said. Peter handed her the keys and let himself out. Carys put her bags on the floor and sat on the edge of the bed.

Though she had slept soundly on the plane, a blanket of exhaustion fell over her. But it wasn't just jet lag. It was something else—a feeling like she was too weak to lift her arms. She rubbed her eyes, stumbled to the bathroom, and splashed water on her face.

When she stood up, Lestinus was behind her, staring back in the mirror. She jumped and almost yelled at him for startling her, then remembered there was no point.

"Read," he said.

She dried her face and retrieved the manuscript and translation from her bag. She sat at the small desk and opened the manuscript. She stuck her nose in it, inhaled, and swooned. Opening the translation, she went straight to the poem. She turned toward Lestinus and began to read out loud.

Head toward the setting sun from Aquae Sulis up the great
 Sabrina Flumen
The bear unto whom is all the glory save our Lord
Protector, whose bravery is known to all,
Is struck down in battle with the Usurper
They both fed the ravens along the mountain stream, running
 red with their blood
The sword pierced his heart
The great Duke of War is dead
We and the river carried him down the four falls to a field of
 flowers
Adorned with drops of his blood
They bloom at our arrival then die and fall as we pass
All nature and man mourn in unison
Then across the ebullition of the sea
We land on the island of the apples
There is a castle of defense under the ocean waves
Between the mother tree and the last light of the fat sun lies the
 watery nest where we laid him
With the sword of Ambrosius—King Saint Protector
Caledfwlch
And his belt and ring bestowed
And the wealth of his people, awaiting his return

What castles that can never be
The sea guards better
And now he is the tree of our faith
From here his fruit will fall and the land will be fertile.

"This is completely impenetrable," she said.

"I didn't write the poem," said Lestinus.

His eyes seemed to shine more brightly than before. He was so real. She could see his chest move in and out as he breathed.

"Who wrote it?" she asked.

"Taliesin," he said.

She balked. Then she laughed.

"Taliesin? Really. Taliesin wrote this. Not you?"

"He dictated it. He didn't know how to write," said the monk.

Her mind snapped back to a memory. Harper had been looking for Taliesin's works a few years earlier. She'd helped him locate several of the first transcriptions of the poet's epic works, which he had composed and delivered orally in the mid-sixth century. Taliesin never wrote a word. There was great controversy in the book world over whether any of the Taliesin transcriptions contained his actual poems, since they were written centuries after the poet lived. Harper still bought everything she'd found. But now, maybe, here was Taliesin, in this manuscript.

She scanned the words again. The rhythm, cadence, and phrasing were similar to those of the transcriptions she'd seen. If these words were his, it would be the only known contemporaneous transcription of his work—written down literally as he dictated it. The value of the manuscript would have just tripled.

"Why Taliesin?" she asked.

"I wanted this part to be created by a higher intellect, so the savages would not be able to find our master if they somehow found my journal," said Lestinus. "I never understood half of what Taliesin said, so he seemed a wise choice. I think he leaves some clear directions to my master's tomb."

"On what planet?" she said, dropping the translation notebook to the desk in frustration. "They wouldn't have been able to read this archaic Welsh anyway."

"What?"

"How did you expect anyone to be able to figure this out?"

Lestinus stood silently, gazing down upon her.

"Even if they had been able to read this language, this poem describes a place that has fruit trees near ebullient seas," she said. "That describes pretty much the entire coastline of Wales. And England. And Ireland. And France. And any number of other countries where you might have transported his body."

"He names *Aquae Sulis*," said Lestinus.

"Bath," she said to herself.

"There are baths there. Hot springs," said Lestinus. "We washed there. It was wonderful after being filthy for so long."

"Head from Bath toward the setting sun up the great *Sabrina Flumen*," she said.

"The river we crossed on the way here," said Lestinus.

"The Severn River?" she asked.

"*Sabrina Flumen*," he said. "We rode it north."

She grabbed her laptop, turned it on, and connected to the pub's Wi-Fi. Typed in "sabrina flumen." A Wikipedia entry for the Severn came up.

"The wave pushed us far upstream. Then we rowed a while. It was much narrower when we got out of our boats," said Lestinus.

She turned back to the transcription and pointed to a paragraph earlier in the text, where Lestinus described the battle with the Usurper and Arthur's death at his hand.

"In this part, where you describe where he supposedly died—"

"It is where he died," said Lestinus. "We left the boats and marched into the mountains to meet the Usurper. There was a terrible battle with the traitor. In the end, our master died not at the hand of a savage but one of our own."

Lestinus crossed himself.

"But where was it?" she asked.

"I don't know what it's called," he said. "We used another river to bring his body down to the sea. We passed through a field of flowers. Spotted red. And the flowers all died while we were marching through the field."

Sadness crossed his face like a cloud.

"I tried to tell the old man about the flowers," said Lestinus. "But he had been far past hearing for a long time. It all got jumbled up in his mind. He couldn't remember anything I said. So I stopped trying. I was waiting for you."

"The old man?"

"The man who found my journal," said Lestinus. "The man who realized what it was."

Harper.

"Did you…" she began, but the world seemed to shift around her. She grabbed the side of the table and was overcome by an intense exhaustion, like someone had opened a valve in her foot and all the energy in her body had drained out. As she moved to the bed, stars formed in her eyes and she realized she was going to pass out. She hit the bed just as her legs gave way beneath her.

◆ ◆ ◆ ◆ ◆

THREE HOURS LATER, Carys woke up. She was shaky and her head was swimming. She felt as if she'd been poisoned. It was half an hour before the shakiness subsided and she dared to sit up. Through the thin walls of the inn, she could hear the crowd below and in the beer garden outside her window.

Lestinus appeared, faintly at first, and then as clear as the desk next to which he stood.

"You must eat," he said.

She got up and walked back and forth in her room several times, testing her legs. When she felt strong enough to navigate the stairs, she put the manuscript and translation in her purse, left the room, and carefully descended the stairway into the pub.

The place was pleasantly active and had the tangy smell of beer and men. The lamps on the window ledges cast a yellow glow on the pub's dark wooden tables. Through the rippled glass of the pub's windows, she could see Swansea Bay, murky in the gray-brown light.

It was an enormous tidal flat, drained of water, like an expansive muddy parking lot. The boats, built to stay upright on the ocean floor when the water drained out from underneath them, sat like sentinels here and there on the mud. Walkers and joggers passed on the boardwalk that ran along the edge of Swansea Bay.

A decrepit playground stood, unloved. There was a merry-go-round in the middle of it, its paint chipped and faded; some of the wooden platform slats were missing. It reminded her of something deep inside herself that she couldn't quite name.

Then, like a gust of wind, a memory blew into her mind. The dream. She'd been there, on that merry-go-round. It was the last happy moment she'd ever had with her parents. It made her heart ache in that old, familiar way that she'd thought she'd finally outgrown. She looked away. Coming here maybe wasn't such a bright idea.

Peter was still behind the bar.

"We saved you a spot," he said to her, motioning to a space at the end of the bar. There were no stools.

She moved to the open spot, ordered a Coke, tried to put the sight of the playground and all the other thoughts that came with it out of her mind, and glanced at the bar menu. She ordered, paid Peter, took her drink, and settled at a small table in the corner of the room.

The bar was a low hum of pleasantries between friends and neighbors. It lulled her. A few minutes later, her steak-and-ale pie arrived. She bent over and stuck her nose into the steam rising from the brown crust. It had the rich, salty, slightly burnt smell of a family kitchen—not her mother's, though. It was more like the kitchen at Annie's house. With her first bite, she felt her energy instantly returning.

"Good?" said Peter from behind the bar.

"Amazing," she said. "Thank you."

The front door of the pub opened, and a man walked in alone. His thick black hair was damp and combed back. He was wearing a beige wool fisherman's sweater and jeans tucked into muddy Wellingtons. Several of the men at the end of the bar greeted the black-haired man with a holler and motioned him over.

When she glanced up a few minutes later, the man was standing at the bar with a glass of beer, looking at her. She smiled slightly and looked back down at her food. Her skin started tingling. She reached into her purse and pulled out the translation with the intention of looking busy enough that he'd stay away.

It worked. When she looked up again, the man was engaged in what appeared to be a heated conversation with another drinker. She finished her Coke and packed away the translation. She put her dirty dishes on the bar.

"Get you another?" asked Peter.

"No, thank you," she said. "But can you tell me where I can find the closest library? I need to do some research."

"What kind of research?"

"History of the region."

"There's a library just up the High Street," said Peter. "Celeste is the head librarian. I'm pretty sure they're open tomorrow. It's up Oystermouth Road, about a mile and a half on the left."

"Thanks," said Carys. "Have a good night." She turned and climbed the staircase to her room.

2

Monday, June 18

It took every ounce of energy Carys had to roll over and swipe her cell phone's alarm off the next morning. She fell back asleep instantly.

She woke again at nearly eleven. After a shower, she examined herself in the mirror. Her eyes were puffy, with dark circles under them that she'd never had before. There was a gray pallor to her skin. She looked awful. She felt awful, too. Her midsection ached. It was weird. She wasn't due for her period, and she hadn't had anything to drink the night before.

She pulled on jeans and a light sweater, grabbed her computer and the books, and headed downstairs. She needed coffee, but no one was behind the bar. She walked out the side door into the parking lot to get her car. It was misting and overcast, and she could smell the funk of another low tide. She slowly and very gingerly maneuvered her Vauxhall down the narrow street that ran next to the boardwalk, her knuckles white on the steering wheel. She kept her eyes glued to the bumper of whatever car was in front of her, mimicking its moves.

Stay to the left, stay to the left, she repeated over and over. Just when she thought she'd gotten the hang of it, she managed to navigate up and over the shallow center island in the middle of the Oystermouth roundabout, drawing a barrage of car honking and a slew of obscenities from several men on the sidewalk.

The stout "Oystermouth Library" sign hung on the front of a square, ancient, whitewashed building at the top of a hill with a panoramic view of the ocean. Carys pulled into a small opening in the tall stone fence next to the building.

The library's side entrance led her to a bright, fluorescent-lit room filled with metal book stacks. She approached the librarian's desk. Behind it sat an elderly woman with curly white hair and glasses pushed down to the end of her nose. She had a red cardigan draped over her shoulders.

"Good morning," said Carys, doing her best to be cheerful despite the gnawing ache in her gut. "I'm looking for Celeste."

"I'm Celeste," said the woman. "How can I help you?"

"My name is Jane Roberts. I'm looking for some information on…uh…I…" she paused, searching for the right words. Seconds ticked by. Her brain seemed jammed.

"Take your time, dear," said Celeste. "I'll probably live at least another week."

Celeste stared at her for a beat longer, then the woman's eyes twinkled.

"I'm kidding," she said.

Carys laughed self-consciously. The ache in her gut flared.

"I'm researching a flower species that is indigenous to Wales," she said. "And I'm also looking for the oldest map of Wales that you have."

"The oldest?" replied Celeste.

"Yes, please."

"Do you have research credentials?" asked Celeste. "We don't normally allow the public to view the ancient documents."

Her ears pricked up.

"Actually," she said, "I'm a…"

Then she remembered that she couldn't use her very excellent and appropriate credentials here. She was Jane. From Boston. And that was all.

"I'm looking for any information you have about the ancient path of the Severn," she said.

"I can do better than an old map," said Celeste. "I have an excellent modern geography text that shows the route of the river over the centuries. Would you like to see that?"

"Absolutely," she said.

"What era are you interested in?" asked Celeste

"Sixth century."

Celeste glanced back at her with an odd, almost amused expression on her face.

"Sure, love," said Celeste. "Follow me."

The old woman got up and shuffled down the long line of metal stacks. She paused, stepped into one of the aisles, pulled a set of rolling stairs toward her, and took three tentative steps up. She grabbed a large, thick hardcover book from the top shelf and handed it down to Carys.

Carys found an unoccupied table and opened the geography book. She flipped back and forth between the two pages that showed the Severn River's course—one from AD 1000 and one from the current era. According to the maps and accompanying descriptions, the river's course had not changed much since the beginning of the second millennium. It originated, then and now, from a spring high in the flat-topped Cambrian Mountains. It flowed down the mountains, which pushed it northeast, then it bent nearly due east into England. Its course then turned southwest until it met the sea right where she had crossed it the day before. There, it served as the border between England and Wales.

To Carys, it looked like an enormous question mark. And that's exactly what it was. How far up would Lestinus and Arcturus have ridden the famous Severn bore, a wave that flowed up the river, against the current, created by the second-highest tide in the world? Where did they march after that? Until she answered those questions, a key piece of the puzzle—the location of Arcturus's death—was missing.

She rested back in her chair and looked at the ceiling. *Be methodical*, she thought. *Tick off one thing at a time. Start with the easy things first. The flowers should be easy.* She rose and approached the librarian's desk.

"I'm trying to identify a flower, and I only have a very basic description of it," she said. "Can you help?"

"No pictures?" asked Celeste.

"No. I only have a description. It's a flower with red spots, and it blooms and dies quickly. And it grows in Wales. Probably in the northern portion, near the ocean."

"Is that all we have to go on?" asked Celeste.

"I'm afraid so," she said.

Celeste pinched the bridge of her nose. "I'll see what I can come up with. I may not be able to deal with this today though."

"That's fine. I'm grateful for any help you can offer. Also, I'm trying to figure out how far up the Severn the bore goes."

"I wouldn't know anything about that," said Celeste. "But I'm sure any local surfer could answer the question. When the tides are right, they can surf that wave up the river for miles. It never ceases to amaze me."

"Do you happen to know any surfers?"

"I'm afraid I don't," said Celeste. "But there are plenty of surf shops around here. Although a better bet is the lifesaving station at the end of the pier in Mumbles."

◆ ◆ ◆ ◆ ◆

As Carys drove back down the hill toward Mumbles, her stomach growled. She needed to eat. She couldn't risk another episode like the one the previous night. She pulled into a parking spot across the street from a small supermarket. The fruit and vegetable section was just inside the main entrance. Everything was labeled in Welsh and English. The Welsh words made her head ache. Eggplant was *wylys*. The cucumbers were *ciwcymbrau*. Oranges were *orennau*. Apples were *afalau*. She couldn't begin to imagine how they were pronounced. She picked up an apple. A tall, twentysomething stock boy with a severe part in his black hair stood looking at her.

"How do you pronounce 'apple' in Welsh?" she asked him. He smiled at her.

"A-val," he said. "F's are pronounced like v's."

"A-val," she repeated, and took a bite. "Thank you."

"*Croeso*," he said, and turned back to his work.

Carys grabbed a yogurt and another apple, paid, and went back to her car. She ate and mulled the facts. If she could find out where the Severn bore ended, she could at least narrow down the section of mountain range where Arcturus had been killed. The only other thing she knew for a fact was that once the guy was dead, his army had ridden a river or stream down from the mountains, down four falls—waterfalls, she assumed, unless the translation was off on that word—to the sea. Then they had sailed across turbulent waters to an island of apples. *Afalau*.

At the end of the boardwalk, a couple of miles around the bay from her inn, there was a long, narrow pier that jutted out a thousand feet into Swansea Bay. At the end of the pier was the Mumbles Lifesaving Station. It was an angular, modern building and looked completely out of place amidst the Victorian architecture of the buildings along the waterfront. She parked in the pay lot at the base of the pier and took the long walk out to the station. The front door of the building opened directly into a gift shop. She was greeted by a woman behind the cash register.

"Good afternoon," said Carys. "I'm looking for some information about the Severn bore."

"Let me get Fiona," said the woman. "She runs the place." The woman turned and made a quick call, and a few minutes later, a tall, solidly built woman with short brown hair, wearing an official-looking uniform, appeared in the shop.

"Hi," said Fiona. "How can I help you?"

"Yes. I'm doing some research for a book, and I've got a question about the Severn bore."

"Fire away," said Fiona.

"How far up the river does it go?"

"Normally, it stops at the weir in Gloucester," said Fiona. "But it's been known to go all the way up to the lock in Tewkesbury during exceptionally high tides."

"Do you know how far it would have gone before the weirs and locks were built?"

"I don't know," Fiona said. "But those locks have been there since the 1800s."

"And how far up is the Severn navigable for boats?"

"You're not thinking of going up it, are you?" asked Fiona, her eyes turning sharp. "It can be very dangerous for inexperienced boaters, especially below Gloucester."

"Oh, no," said Carys. "I'm just doing some research."

"I've been told you can get a boat all the way up to Welshpool," said Fiona. "Maybe even farther than that if you're in a rowing craft."

"Can you show me where that is on a map?"

"Happy to," said Fiona. "Follow me."

The woman led Carys up a flight of stairs and along a balcony that looked out over a bright, shiny orange lifeboat, suspended on straps in the middle of the building. Below it was a huge ramp that sloped down through a big door in the side of the building and into the bay.

"She's a beauty," said Carys, pointing at the boat. Fiona turned into an office. She followed.

"Yeah, she's just a couple of years old," said Fiona. "We're very proud of her."

"Do you go out?" asked Carys. Fiona reached up into a shelf behind the desk.

"Sure do," Fiona said.

"What's the roughest stretch of water along the northern Welsh coast?"

Fiona turned to her and smiled.

"It's all rough."

She pulled down a map book, placed it on the desk, and flipped it open. She pointed to a spot on the map.

"Welshpool," Fiona said. "And here's Shrewsbury."

Carys leaned in and examined the map in detail. By walking along any of the rivers near those two towns, someone could get from Welshpool or Shrewsbury up into the mountains within a couple of days. But this information was of no help. The map labeled the mountainous area Snowdonia, colored the dark green of a designated national park, with tightly stacked elevation marks running through it showing the steepness of the terrain.

"What's the roughest water along the coastline up here?" she asked, pointing to two peninsulas, each one with a large island at the end of it, along the coast west of Snowdonia. "If you wanted to sail from the coast south or north of these two peninsulas, would that be a very bad sail?"

"Not particularly," said Fiona. "But the ocean can get very nasty along the entire coast depending on the weather and the tides. Calm one minute, maelstrom the next. But if you're looking for rough"— Fiona pointed to a tiny island off the coast of the Llŷn Peninsula, which extended southwest away from the coastline—"that's rough.

Pretty much all the time. When the tide is coming in, the current around this island can get up to eight knots. I used to live up there and I'll tell you, there were days when that water looked like a giant whirlpool. I half expected sea monsters to appear."

Carys leaned over and looked at the map closely. Bardsey Island. A small island about two miles off the tip of the Llŷn Peninsula. "Which way would the current go when it's that fast, when the tide is coming in?" asked Carys.

"North," said Fiona. "Up through this channel here." She pointed to the water between the island and the peninsula. "When the tide is ebbing, south, it's not nearly as treacherous. Still pretty dicey though."

Carys thanked Fiona and left, even more confused than she'd been before.

Strolling back down the pier, she stared out into the ocean. She could see the water level slowly crawling up the pilings beneath the pier. The tide here was a force that dictated all, and had done so since people occupied these lands.

Jet lag was reasserting itself. She needed to move a little bit. Once off the pier, she decided to walk awhile along the boardwalk back toward town. About ten feet below was the mud of Swansea Bay, rapidly filling.

She had been walking for about ten minutes when she came to a marina and boat ramp. A beat-up pickup truck was on the ramp, hauling a trailer carrying a large inflatable that had just been pulled out of the channel. A man wearing a wetsuit was unloading scuba gear from the inflatable into the back of the truck. He had a broad back and black hair, and despite the cool damp, he had the top of his wetsuit unzipped and draped down around his waist. His honed muscles flexed as he lifted the heavy tanks. Carys let her eyes linger on his back.

The man turned toward the front of the truck and looked up at Carys. It was the man from the pub the night before.

Their eyes met briefly, then recognition crossed his face. He smiled and nodded a hello. Carys couldn't help it—she smiled back. Then she quickly turned around and headed to her car.

◆ ◆ ◆ ◆ ◆

CARYS GOT TO HER ROOM just in time for another wave of exhaustion to come over her. Before she would allow herself to sink back down onto the bed, she had to call Annie and check in.

"How is Nicola?" was the first thing she said when Annie picked up.

"Not good," said Annie. "Not good at all. I've been calling every two hours, and they downgraded her a little while ago."

Carys sat on the bed, staring at her shoes.

"You alright?" asked Annie.

"Yeah. I'm doing research, trying to figure out which island of the ten trillion islands on the coast is the one where they buried the King."

"Can I help?"

"No, honey. The locals know this area intimately. I'm in the best place I could possibly be."

"Which is where, exactly?" asked Annie.

She paused. She should tell her.

Just then, Lestinus formed by the desk.

"She does not need to know," he intoned. "Her ignorance is safety."

Carys had to agree. "The less you know, the better," she said.

"That's incredibly stupid," said Annie.

"I know," she said. "I need to lie down for a little while. I'll call you tomorrow."

◆ ◆ ◆ ◆ ◆

FRANK WAS LYING ON HIS COUCH, drinking a beer and watching a rerun of a Chelsea-Tottenham football match. It made him happy.

His father had been a big Spurs supporter, and he'd given the bug to Frank. His mother would make them sausage rolls and keep the two of them supplied with beer as they watched the matches when he was young, back when they'd had enough money to pay most of their bills. That ended when his father bolted. Never saw the fucker again. His mother wasn't qualified for any kind of work that might have earned enough to support the two of them. Poverty—and the Royal Navy for him—wasn't far behind. The woman hadn't deserved the life she got.

He shook off the memory. He'd been home for less than forty-eight hours, and his shoulders were just beginning to relax—a condition that was always temporary—and he didn't want to screw it up by thinking about his mother.

The disposable cell on his coffee table buzzed. It was Gyles.

"Frank, my man, two pieces of good news this morning," said Gyles. He sounded light, almost happy. "We got a hit on Jones's credit card. Rental car agency at Heathrow. Looks like the Jones woman is on the island."

"How did you—" he said.

"When you have someone's Social Security number, you can learn just about anything you need to," said Gyles. "And Mr. Plourde has it, of course."

"Why would she come here?" he asked. "Wouldn't it just be easier for her to hide back in the U.S.? It's a big bloody country."

"Well, that leads us to the second piece of good news," said Gyles with a smile in his voice. "Mr. Plourde informed me that he found a letter on Ms. Jones's desk last night. It's from her father. Plourde said he didn't even know her father was still alive. Letter had a return address on it. In Aberystwyth."

Frank was silent.

"That's in Wales, Frank," said Gyles.

"Sure," he said. He'd never heard of the town. He'd never been to Wales.

"The father's name is Anthony Jones," said Gyles. "I'll text you his address. I can't pronounce these Welsh words. Sounds like you're choking. Plourde googled the guy and said he's a professor. And, based on the letter, he and the woman are not exactly on speaking terms and haven't seen each other in a long time. But he's her only living relative, so if I know my damsels in distress, she's probably headed right there."

Frank's piece-of-shit father hadn't even called when his mum died. He'd never forgive him and he'd certainly never ask him for help—even if he knew where he was.

"I want you to find the father and keep an eye on him for a couple of days in case she turns up there," said Gyles. "I've got a man back in Boston keeping feelers out in case she pops up there. We're tracking her cell phone, although she hasn't used it since she disappeared."

Gyles let out a low, sinister snicker.

"Get up to Aberystwyth. Get eyeballs on the father. Call me when you find something. I've got a meeting in Lisbon tomorrow at the National Archeology Museum. A trafficked Roman bust from Iraq has landed there. God, this job is like shooting fish in a barrel sometimes. Anyway, if I don't answer, I'll call you back when I get somewhere I can talk."

"Sounds good," he said.

"Aberystwyth," said Gyles, and laughed again. "Of all the bloody places. Once you find her, grab that manuscript and the translation and get them to me. You won't even have to get your hands dirty."

Frank grunted. His hands always got dirty.

◆ ◆ ◆ ◆ ◆

CARYS NAPPED FOR A COUPLE OF HOURS and woke famished. She put the books in her purse and headed down to the pub to have another steak-and-ale pie. She greeted Peter, who was pulling beer after beer for the thirsty after-work crowd of mostly men who were lined up at the bar. She ordered the pie and a Coke and took a seat, the same one she'd had the night before. She pulled out the translation and began scouring it again for anything that might now stand out—something, anything she might have missed on the first dozen readings. The pie arrived just as the pub door swung open and the dark-haired man strolled in. Small town. Same rhythms, night after night. He wore a green cable-knit sweater and dark blue jeans that were just a little bit tighter than they needed to be, and he was carrying a red rubber raincoat. His hair was dry this time and combed back. He didn't notice Carys and instead greeted a friend at the other end of the bar. A male friend, Carys was happy to note. Not that she should care.

Carys turned her attention to the pie. It was just as good as the one the night before. She shoveled several more bites into her mouth and then realized someone was standing at her table. She looked up. The man was standing there, smiling down at her.

"Isn't that just about the best pie you've ever had?" he asked.

She tried to answer but her mouth was full. She raised her hand, signaled for the man to wait, and quickly swallowed.

"Yes," was all she could muster, faced with the bluest eyes she'd ever seen.

"I'm Dafydd Reynolds," he said. "You visiting?"

"Here for work," she said, trying her best to not stare at him.

He pulled out the chair at her table. She slid the translation closer.

"Is it interesting," he asked, "your work?"

"Yes. It is. Are you from around here?"

"Yeah," said Dafydd.

"Jane," yelled Peter. "If that bad man is bothering you, you just let me know."

Dafydd grinned and turned to the bar.

"Sod off, you old git," he said.

Peter laughed.

"Where you from, Jane?" Dafydd asked.

"The U.S.," she said, as she put the translation notebook back in her purse.

"I sorta guessed that with your accent. What part?"

"East Coast," she said.

"Boston, right?"

She smiled but didn't answer.

"We get a lot of Boston tourists here. What do you do there?"

She paused. He was entirely too inquisitive.

"Not a trick question," said Dafydd.

Carys rallied quickly to find a suitable lie.

"I'm a professor, geography, doing some research for a book," she said. "How about you?"

"I run a diving company. Take tourists out to wrecks, clean boat hulls, recover salvage. That sort of thing," he said.

"That must be fun," she said.

"It is. About half the people in this town do some sort of water-based activity, for work or fun. Diving, sailing, fishing, ferries, salvage," he said. "What do you do for fun?"

Again she paused, but this time it was because she wasn't sure of the answer.

"Am I making you uncomfortable?" he asked. "I can go if I am. You just looked like you could use some company. I didn't mean to intrude." He began to push his chair away from the table.

She took a deep breath.

"I'm fine," she said. "I'm just a little jet-lagged right now."

Dafydd pulled his seat back in.

"I…I don't do much of anything for fun," she said. "Seems I'm working all the time. I like to read."

"But don't you read a lot for work?" he asked.

She laughed. "Yeah, I suppose I do. I guess I'm not really very interesting."

"Oh, that can't be true. Geography is very interesting. And you obviously have an interesting job, because otherwise you wouldn't be here. So, what are you working on these days?"

"What do you do for fun?" she asked.

"I like to dive," said Dafydd.

"But don't you dive for work?" she replied.

"I guess I'm not really very interesting either," he said, and clinked his glass with hers. He took a long gulp. "Another?"

"Uh, sure. It's a Coke."

"That's a crime here, you know."

"I know. I like living on the edge," she said, warming up to the man despite her better instincts. He hopped up, got them two more drinks, and sat back down.

"What's your book about?" he asked

Her mind scrambled. She sipped her drink to stall for time.

"It compares ancient Roman place names with modern cities, geographic features—that sort of thing," she said.

"Have you been to the library yet? Celeste is pretty famous around here. She's got books in that library that are so old, she keeps them in special cases," said Dafydd.

"I've met her," she said. "I'm actually going back there in the morning to do some more research."

"What towns are you researching?" said Dafydd.

Carys stiffened and he noticed.

"Don't have to talk about it if you don't want," he said. "Just thought maybe I can help."

"That's very kind," she said. She couldn't help smiling. "But it's unlikely you could help unless you have an encyclopedic knowledge of the rivers and mountains of Wales." She sipped her drink.

"Well, Miss Jane, as a matter of fact, I do," Dafydd said, leaning back in his seat and crossing his arms. "I've been kayaking and hiking here since I was six."

"Fine," she said. "Let's give it a try. Have you ever heard of a river that starts in the mountains—"

"They all start in the mountains."

"Like all rivers, this one starts in the mountains, and it has four waterfalls. Then it passes through a field filled with flowers, and then empties into the ocean," she said.

"Well, that could be any number of rivers," said Dafydd. "But it sounds like it would be a Class Five river, with the waterfalls. Do you know roughly where it is?"

"Very roughly. I think it's within twenty or thirty miles of either Welshpool or Shrewsbury."

"That doesn't narrow it down much," said Dafydd. He pulled out his phone, typed briefly, and sat back.

"There are about ten rivers up there that are Class Fives," said Dafydd. "They all eventually flow down to the ocean. Some come out near Liverpool. Some come out near Barmouth, or Portmeirion, south of the Llŷn Peninsula. And some in between them." He handed her the phone.

Carys expanded the view on the screen. It was an alphabetical list of the most extreme kayaking rivers, posted on the North Wales Kayak Association website. She scrolled down slowly. Her head began to ache again just imagining how the words were pronounced. Afon Ceirw, River Clywedog, River Colwyn, River Conwy. Ugh. So many. She looked up at Dafydd.

"Can you show me where these are on a map?" she asked.

"Sure," he said. "If you're going to the library tomorrow, I can swing by and we can use one of the geographic survey maps. Those will be more accurate."

She looked back down at the list. Afon Croesor, River Einion, Afon Gamlan, Afon Goedel, Cwm Llan, River Lledr.

She looked back up at him and examined his face more closely. *Damn*, she thought, *those eyes.*

"I think that's a great idea," she said quietly, and took another sip of her Coke, which had become unsatisfying. "You know, I think I will have a whiskey."

Dafydd smiled. He got up and returned with two.

"Here's to kayaking," she said, and clinked glasses with him. "What time can you meet me tomorrow?"

"Early," he said. "I have a client tomorrow." Dafydd turned to the bar.

"Pete! What time does Celeste open up in the morning?" he hollered.

"She's usually there by ten," Pete hollered back.

"Client's at noon," he said. "I could meet you there at ten."

"I would really appreciate that."

"You didn't think I was going to be able to help you, did you?" Dafydd said, grinning.

"No. I did not. But I am thrilled that you may prove me wrong," she said.

3

Tuesday, June 19

"Afon Gamlan."

Carys's head hurt. She peeled one eye open.

Lestinus stood at the foot of her bed. He looked agitated.

"Afon Gamlan," he said again.

It sounded like he was saying "a-*von come*-lan."

She continued to stare at him.

"Afon Gamlan," he intoned again. "The river."

"What are you talking…," she said.

She stared at Lestinus for a moment longer, and he stared back. Then she heard what he was trying to tell her.

She jumped out of bed and grabbed her computer and searched for the kayaking website she'd been reading on Dafydd's phone the night before.

Afon Gamlan. Right there in the list of the most difficult kayaking rivers in North Wales. How had she missed that? Dafydd's eyes and the whiskey, most likely.

Gamlan. Holy actual crap.

It was a short etymological leap from Gamlan to Camlann, and even she knew that Camlann was the name of the legendary battle site at which King Arthur supposedly died. Camlann was, in fact, one of the most famous place names associated with the Arthurian legend—next to Camelot and Avalon.

What if the famous Battle of Camlann was named for a river, not a town, as had long been believed? The river they used to transport the King after he died. Down the many waterfalls. Through the field of flowers. And then to the island of the apples.

Carys scoured the web for a precise map of the river's course, but she couldn't nail it down. Google recognized the name, but it didn't show up on its map, no matter how much she zoomed in on the image and explored the terrain.

But Dafydd would know.

Once she figured out where the river was, she'd make sure its course today was the same as it was fifteen hundred years ago. Maybe Celeste would let her have access to one of the old maps to confirm it. Any map dating to within a few hundred years of Arcturus's death would be fairly accurate, at least in showing the location of the headwaters and valley the river occupied. That would be enough. Hopefully, with Dafydd there, a nice local boy, Celeste would give her access to those maps.

When Carys got out of the shower, she had a full-blown headache. Hangover. Probably. She smiled, but even that hurt. Dafydd had been nice. Cute. He had bought her a couple of whiskeys, and she drank them. He politely said goodnight after the second one and shook her hand. She'd been a little disappointed to see him go.

She dressed, grabbed the manuscript, translation, and computer, and put them in her bag.

The day was as bright as the previous one had been dark. She gazed out the pub windows at the sea, and her eyes ached as the sunlight drove into her head. But she couldn't bear to close them.

The view was breathtaking. When lit by the golden sunlight, the hills around Mumbles lost their tumble-down gray and muddy green and became a collage of a thousand shades of emerald and oddly sparkling stone against the deep blue of the sky above. Even early, the waterfront was teeming with far more people than it had been the day before. It was as if someone had turned on a giant light and everyone had woken up. Or maybe she just hadn't noticed the people before.

Dafydd was waiting in the parking lot when she got to the library. He hopped out of his truck as she pulled in, a wide smile on his face.

"Good morning," he said as she approached him.

"Hi," she said. "Are you always this energetic in the morning?"

"Oh yes," said Dafydd. "Annoying, really."

They walked into the library, and Celeste, who was standing behind her desk, turned toward them as they walked in.

"Look what the cat dragged in," Celeste said. "How are you, son?"

"I'm well, Celeste," said Dafydd. "And you?"

"Still kicking," said Celeste. "You know this woman, then?"

"Yes, I do," said Dafydd. "Helping her do some research for a book she's writing. Can you steer me toward a geographic survey of Wales? We'll need the lowest ratio you have. One to twenty-five thousand should do it."

"Right," said Celeste, as she looked over the top of her glasses at Carys. She detected a slight rise in her stock in the old woman's eyes.

A few minutes later, she and Dafydd were standing at a table with four enormous paper maps in front of them. Dafydd was leaning over one of the maps. His broad shoulders obscured her view. She didn't really mind. She let herself enjoy the nearness of a man, his earthy smell, his body heat, for a few moments.

She listened attentively as Dafydd went through each of the rivers on the Class Five list, pointed at their source, and traced them down to where they eventually reached the ocean. Afon Ceirw, River Cly-wedog, River Colwyn. River Conwy, Afon Croesor, River Einion.

And then, finally, Afon Gamlan. High in the mountains near the Llŷn Peninsula on the northwest coast of Wales, Afon Gamlan could be reached easily from either of the two towns along the Severn, Welshpool or Shrewsbury, that Fiona at the lifesaving station had told her about. You'd just have to walk up a river valley into Snowdonia. It looked like it would be a two- or three-day hike, more with an army, less with a highly motivated army. The headwaters of the Gamlan emerged from a spring on an expansive, barren mountain plateau dotted with small ponds—the perfect place for two warring armies to collide.

"This area, up here, just north of where the four waterfalls are," said Dafydd as he swept his hands across a small area, "it's called *Coed y Brenin.*"

"What's that mean?"

"The Forest of the Kings," said Dafydd.

"Why do they call it that?" she asked.

"Don't know," said Dafydd. "But it's some of the nastiest water I've ever run. The Black Falls, they're called. They drop sixty feet in no time flat. Unrunnable most of the time."

"What about higher up? Could you paddle down the Gamlan from close to its headwaters?" she asked.

"At high water, sure," said Dafydd. "Late spring, when all the snowmelt is coming down. Say, late May to late June. The Gamlan merges with another river, which merges with the Mawddach here"— he said, pointing to the spot—"and it flows down to the ocean here." He indicated a large flood plain near the city of Barmouth on the coast, just south of the Llŷn Peninsula.

"Does the river pass through a field on its way to the ocean?" she asked, sweeping her hand over the estuary.

"Yeah," he said. "Big, wide fields. Just beautiful. Not much fun, though. Slow. No real quick water. We usually get out after the Black Falls. But that section of the Mawddach is a popular canoeing spot in the high water."

Carys leaned over next to Dafydd and examined the map. If the Gamlan's course was the same fifteen hundred years ago, then she now had a very strong contender for the area where Arthur's body started its ocean journey to his "watery nest."

It was progress. Real progress. It gave her more energy than she'd had in days. She approached Celeste.

"You mentioned that you had a very old map of Wales somewhere in the library," she said. "Would it be possible to see it?"

Celeste examined her for a beat or two. Then she glanced over at Dafydd, who was still examining the maps intently.

"I suppose it would be alright for you to take a look as long as I'm with you," she said. "But it's a map of just Snowdonia. Not the southern portion of the country."

"That's fine," said Carys. "Perfect really."

"Follow me." Celeste came out from behind her desk and walked to the back of the library. Dafydd looked up at them from the reading table and followed. Celeste paused at an unmarked door on the far back wall, turned a key in the knob, and pushed it open.

On the other side of the door was one of the most modern rooms she had seen since she set foot in Wales. It was windowless, and there was a large rectangular table covered in white Formica set in the center of what looked like a laboratory. Around the perimeter of the room were display cases, clearly temperature-controlled and illuminated by low-emission lights. The temperature in the room was a good twenty degrees cooler than in the front room. Celeste waited for Carys and Dafydd to enter and closed the door behind them.

"This is a surprise," Carys said.

Celeste walked to a white metal storage chest along the far wall of the room, opened the drawer, and retracted three surgical masks. She handed one to Carys and one to Dafydd.

"What are these for?" asked Dafydd. "We doing surgery?"

"No, dear. I'm going to open the oldest map I have in the library. There are nasty things hiding in it," said Celeste.

The three of them put on the masks. Celeste opened one of the bookcases and pulled out a foot-long parchment scroll. She turned and placed the scroll on the table, gingerly unrolled it, and held the ends with her gloved hands.

The scroll was nothing like Carys had ever seen. It was in near perfect condition, and the colors that the mapmaker had used to indicate forest, mountains, and sea were, she imagined, as bright as the day it had been created. It was a map of what became known as Snowdonia and the northwest coastline of Wales. The coast was drawn in exaggerated scale in some places, and underdrawn in others, but the basic outline was clearly identifiable, as were both the Llŷn and Anglesey Peninsulas.

"Remarkable," Carys said.

"Yes," said Celeste. "It was found about forty years ago as part of a cache of old manuscripts hidden away inside a wall of a monastery in the Brecon Beacons. Quite priceless. The man who bought and renovated the monastery was an old family friend, and when he died, his estate donated his collection to the library."

"How big is the collection?" said Carys.

"About a dozen manuscripts and maps," said Celeste. "All dating to the sixth century and later. Some American man tried to buy them all from us a few years ago, but we told him no. They belong here."

Carys swallowed. She knew who that was.

"The region depicted in this map was considered among the holiest and most important by the monks who drew it. What are we looking for?" asked Celeste.

Dafydd leaned over the map, scanned it, and put his finger over a blue line that wound through what looked like drawings of mountains.

"There, that's probably the Gamlan," he said. "It has a pretty distinctive eastern track." His hand followed the blue line to a larger blue line—the Mawddach—down to a small bay on the coast. "That's where it comes out. That's where the field and estuary are today."

"Very good, Dafydd." Celeste's eyes beamed. "He knows his geography. You're exactly right."

The old woman looked coyly up at Dafydd, who rewarded her with a wink. The beginning of a blush came to the woman's cheeks.

"Oh, by the way, Ms. Roberts," Celeste said. "I think I found something for you on those flowers." Celeste stepped back outside the room briefly.

"Flowers?" said Dafydd. "I thought you were researching place names?"

She struggled for a quick explanation and was about to make up a lie when Celeste returned, holding another book, which she placed open on the table. It showed a picture of a yellow flower that resembled a small violet, but in its center were red spots the color of blood. Celeste read from the description.

"'Spotted rock rose, *Tuberaria guttata*, a flower of the west coast of Wales. Distinct crimson-spotted flowers. It blooms from June to August.' But here's what's interesting," Celeste said. "'It flowers only once during its lifetime and sheds its petals within hours of doing so.'"

Carys could feel the blood draining from her arms and legs.

They bloom at our arrival then die and fall as we pass.

"Hours?" she asked.

"Yes, hours," said Celeste. "The largest colonies are on Anglesey's Holy Island. This is Anglesey." She pointed to the large peninsula at the very northern edge of Wales, then at an island off its tip. "And this is Holy Island."

"Why do they call it Holy Island?" she asked.

"The remains of a sixth-century church are there," said Celeste. "And a Roman fort. Standing stones, probably Celtic in origin. It's been a religious site since long before the Romans invaded Britain."

Carys's heart began to pound.

"The flowers can also be found here," said Celeste, sweeping her hand over land through which the Mawddach flowed. Carys took a deep breath and stood up. She closed her eyes briefly and rubbed them.

"You alright?" asked Dafydd.

"Yeah," she said. It was a lie. She was exhausted again. But she had to think. The rock rose grew June to August. Snowmelt. High water. Both Afon Gamlan and the Mawddach would have been navigable by boat. The river passed right through the flower's current known habitat—and the monk's manuscript indicated it had been its habitat fifteen hundred years ago as well.

It all fit together. Arthur's army brought his body down the Gamlan, over four waterfalls, then down the Mawddach, where they passed through a field of spotted flowers that died as they passed. Then they met the ocean at the large estuary near Barmouth, just south of the Llŷn Peninsula. *My god*, she thought, *it's all real. Everything in the manuscript's poem is real.*

But she was no closer to knowing where they had sailed once they made it to the ocean. Which island, of all the islands large and small along the Welsh coast, was the *island of the apples*? Where the hell did they bury him?

"Celeste," she asked, "do any of the islands on this section of the coast have apple orchards?"

"Orchards?" Celeste replied. "You mean today?"

"No," said Carys. "Back then. When this map was drawn."

Celeste and Dafydd both looked at her.

"I'm researching a document that specifically mentions apples," she said.

"How old is the document?" said Celeste.

Carys began to balk. She couldn't get facts unless she shared some of her own.

"About the same age as this map," she said.

Celeste's eyes grew wide.

"How did you get this ancient document?" asked Celeste.

"It's part of my research," she said.

"What type of research do you do?" asked Celeste.

"I'm working with a private individual who owns this document who has asked for anonymity. I'm sure you understand."

Celeste's eyes examined Carys for a moment longer. Then she turned to the map again.

"The islands of Bardsey, at the tip of the Llŷn, and Holy Island both had apple orchards at the time this map was drawn," said Celeste, who then looked up at Carys pointedly. "Holy Island's religious history and its orchards have led quite a few King Arthur hunters to think Holy Island is Avalon. 'Apple' in Welsh is *afal*—it sounds like the first two syllables of Avalon…silly really."

Her heart jumped up into her throat. She could feel her cheeks reddening. Celeste noticed.

"It's the most worn-out myth in all of Wales," said Celeste, her eyes on Carys. "Of course, the first mention of Avalon at all was Geoffrey of Monmouth's *Historia Regum Britanniae*, and that wasn't until the mid-twelfth century."

"Of course," she said. Her voice wasn't entirely steady. "People are so gullible."

"How do you know all this stuff, Celeste?" asked Dafydd.

"You wouldn't believe how many people come here looking for information on Arthur," said Celeste.

Carys tried to sound nonchalant.

"Other than those two islands, do any of the smaller islands have apple orchards?" she asked.

"Not that I know of," said Celeste. "Most are just windswept hunks of rock sticking out of the ocean."

Dafydd pointed at Bardsey.

"I love it up there," he said. "Some of the best diving in the U.K. Its western shore is riddled with caves. Wrecks, too."

Just then Carys felt the world shift under her feet. She grabbed the end of the table.

Dafydd reached out to steady her by her elbow. She pushed it away lightly.

"Celeste, do you have any old detail maps of those islands—Bardsey Island and Holy Island?" she asked.

"I think so," said Celeste, and she turned toward the bookshelf again.

Carys took off her mask and sat down on a chair.

"Can I get you some water?" asked Dafydd, taking off his mask, too. "You look pale."

"I'll be fine," she said. "It's just that a very bad man made me drink whiskey last night, and it's not something I'm used to."

"Oh, that's awful," said Dafydd with a grin. "Now that you mention it, I do remember seeing someone pouring whiskey down your throat against your will last night."

She tried to smile back, but the world was spinning.

"I have to get going," said Dafydd. "I've gotta go get ready for my dive. Do you need me for anything else?"

"No, you have been incredibly helpful," she said, and extended her hand. He shook it firmly. "Thank you so much for your help on this."

"My pleasure. Maybe I'll see you round the pub. Bye, Celeste," he said as he turned to leave. "Give my best to Ian."

"Will do. Ta, son," said Celeste as she laid another manuscript covered in rich red leather on the table. She motioned to Carys, who stood up slowly and approached.

Just then the world began to go dark. She inhaled sharply.

"You know," she said. "I think it might be a good idea for me to go back to the inn for a few hours. I'm not feeling well at all. Probably jet lag or something." She tried to smile.

"You shouldn't drive," said Celeste. "I'll see if Dafydd can take you back."

She shuffled quickly out the door, calling Dafydd's name, before Carys had a chance to stop her. She sat down, worried she would completely lose consciousness. Her eyesight began to blacken around the edges. She felt the presence of Lestinus next to her, but she could not see him.

Carys heard Dafydd come back into the room.

"Let's get you back," he said, and she felt his strong hand on her arm, helping her stand.

"Celeste," said Carys. "May I come back and look at this tomorrow?"

"Of course, love," she heard Celeste say. "I'll see you tomorrow. I hope you feel better."

As she and Dafydd stepped outside, Carys's vision began to clear.

"I'm so sorry," she said. "I have no idea what came over me in there. The world just went black. I'm feeling much better now. You don't need to drive me back."

"Well, I'm going to anyway," he said. "Get in." He opened the passenger door of his beat-up pickup and guided her up to the seat before she found the strength to resist. The truck smelled like diesel, seaweed, and leather. Dafydd hopped in the other side.

They drove back to the Farmer's Arms, making stranger-type small talk about the weather. He pulled into the parking area.

"Do you need help up those stairs?" he said.

"No, oh god, no," she said. "And what would Peter think? I have a reputation to uphold."

Dafydd laughed. He reached into the cup holder between their seats and extracted a business card. "My cell number is on there. Call me if you need anything."

"I will," she said as she slid off the seat onto the gravel. "Thank you."

"You're welcome," he said and gave her a wave.

Carys somehow mustered the strength to lift her legs up each of the stairs to her room. She stripped off her clothes, climbed into bed, and fell into a dark, complete slumber. She did not dream.

♦ ♦ ♦ ♦

FRANK NEVER DROVE HIS OWN CAR for work. Too easy to trace. For
the drive up to Aberystwyth he rented a Mercedes S-Class using a
fake ID and credit card. He was done with crappy cars. Plus the Merc
was the only one with GPS. Frank had no idea where anything was
in the United Kingdom once he breached the loving embrace of the
M25 ring road around London.

Frank drove north into Wales. He loved the British Isles, but he
couldn't wait to leave. The relentless, overcast, misty, windy weather
was for plants and birds, not humans. He couldn't wait to move to
his place on St. Bart's. He'd get a tan or, more likely, a blistering
sunburn. Every day, he'd be out there on his lanai, just sucking in as
much warm sunshine as he could, skin cancer be damned.

The construction on the villa was just about done. Occupancy
permits were a few weeks away. Once this job was done, he'd just
stay in a hotel in Gustavia until the house was ready. Maybe do some
boating. He hadn't spent much time on boats since he left the navy
and fell into his current career as the enforcer-cum-business-partner
for a psychopath. Mum would have loved St. Bart's. But she still
would have found something to complain about, just so he didn't get
too big for his breeches.

In spite of the rain, Frank had to admit that this part of Wales
was one of the most beautiful places he'd ever seen, more beautiful
even than St. Bart's. He couldn't see very far—the clouds were so low,
they chopped off the top of the mountains, but there was something
about this land; the way the road dipped up and down, around and
through the villages, hidden in the same little valleys for a thousand
years. The rivers and trees were just where they'd always been, no
matter what happened around them. It gave him peace, which was
something in short supply in his world at the moment.

Six hours after leaving London, thanks to the female-voiced GPS, which he named Beryl, he found himself just outside the University of Aberystwyth, at 352 Gordon Court. It was a nice house, built of dark gray brick, the ubiquitous Welsh building material. The surrounding terrain was a low, windswept, treeless moorland. The houses on this little street were huddled up together to protect each other from the wind and rain. He parked a few houses down from Anthony Jones's house and waited.

Half an hour later, an SUV pulled up in front of the house. A pretty middle-aged woman and a dark-haired boy of around fifteen got out and went up the stairs into the house.

The kid looked just like Carys Jones.

The rain beat down on the roof of his car like an assault.

4

Wednesday, June 20

Carys awoke at eight o'clock that morning. She'd been in bed—off and on—for nearly twenty hours. She'd managed to drag herself downstairs for a late lunch at three the previous afternoon, then again at eight o'clock for some dinner and a very short walk along the waterfront. Her gut throbbed with a dull ache the entire time. This wasn't jet lag or hunger. Something was wrong with her. Each excursion was utterly exhausting. The last thing she saw before her head hit the pillow after dinner was Lestinus, standing like a sentinel at the foot of her bed.

"Do not abandon me," he said. "We must find him."

"I'm not going anywhere," she said. As her mind faded into darkness, she was oddly comforted knowing that he—whatever he was—was watching over her.

When she woke up that morning, she felt slightly better. Then she rolled over and the ache in her belly flared. Maybe the walk to retrieve her car would help. She rose, showered, dressed, collected her bag, and went downstairs to the pub.

No one was there, so she went straight out. She stopped at a small outdoor cafe along the way to the library and got a coffee and a scone, which she ate slowly, watching the people pass by. The tide was up. The water of the bay sparkled, and the sun beat down on her shoulders, warming her quickly. Even the wrong-way traffic seemed friendlier and more sedate. She was beginning to like it here.

Lestinus formed in the chair across from her.

"They live without fear," said Lestinus in Latin as he watched the people pass. "None of these people, not even you yourself, would exist if he had not."

"It's not true, Lestinus," said Carys quietly. There was a couple sitting two tables over. She shifted her body so they couldn't see her speak. If they did, she could legitimately claim she was practicing her Latin.

"If he hadn't held back the savages," said Lestinus, "everyone with Roman blood in their veins would have been exterminated, or bred and intermingled with them."

"The people you see here are the result of fifteen hundred years of intermingling with those savages," she said. "They took over the British Isles. The people who sit on the British throne right now have savage blood in their veins."

"It can't be true!" said Lestinus with disbelief. "How could it happen?"

"You presume that there are superior and inferior breeds?"

"Of course there are," said Lestinus. "If you had seen what these illiterate monsters were like, you would not question their inferiority."

"That's not very Christian of you. Didn't the Lord make all men in his image?"

"They weren't men. They were animals. The Lord had abandoned them and they him."

"I know the feeling," she said.

She arrived at the library just as Celeste was unlocking the doors. The old woman looked up and seemed surprised to see her.

"Good morning," Celeste said. "You look like you're feeling better."

"I do feel a bit better. I was hoping you'd show me those maps of the islands this morning."

Celeste looked her up and down, and then nodded in agreement and waved her in.

Moments later, they were back in the clean room in the back. Celeste pulled out two surgical masks from the tall cabinets. She handed one to Carys. Celeste put hers on, but Carys placed hers on the metal table. Celeste left briefly and returned carrying the red leather-bound manuscript. Celeste opened it very slowly, smoothing her hands over the parchment.

"Now, this one is my greatest treasure," said Celeste.

She flipped through the manuscript gingerly to an illuminated drawing, the thick, ornate gold lettering glowing on the parchment. Next to the text was a drawing of a small island, covered with ancient Christian crosses, which looked like plus signs with a circle drawn around the axis. There were mountains, streams and houses depicted as well.

"This is a map of Bardsey," said Celeste. "During the sixth century, this island was just as sacred as Holy Island. They called Bardsey the Land of Twenty Thousand Saints. There was a monastery, and it was said that three trips here was as sacred as a single trip to pray in Rome. There have been people there since the Iron Age."

"How did they get there?" she asked, leaning over the book. The thick black lines of the artist's pen were dark and clearly defined against the creamy parchment, the sign of impeccable preservation, and the colors of the illuminated drawing almost sang on the page. She found herself smiling.

"Boats, rafts, whatever they could put together, I imagine," said Celeste. "The Welsh have been mariners since prehistory. And Bardsey's not far from the end of the Llŷn. Nasty water though."

"So I hear," she said.

"The caves that Dafydd was talking about are along this section of the coast," said Celeste, pointing to the western shore. "Lose at least three people a year to cave diving there. Very, very dangerous."

Carys leaned over to more closely inspect the drawing, but before she even realized she was doing it, she stuck her nose into the bindings and inhaled deeply.

"You shouldn't do that," said Celeste.

"Do what?" she asked.

"Sniff the book. I had a friend who got sick doing that."

"Sick?"

"Yes. Very sick."

"How?"

"He was a researcher. A treasure hunter really," said Celeste. "He spent ten years of his life reading old musty ships' logs in the British Library looking for the location of privateer sinkings in the 1700s. There were hallucinogenic mold spores in the books. He spent so much time inhaling them that one day he swears one of those privateers—they were pirates really—made a house call."

Carys froze.

"That's when he quit treasure hunting," said Celeste. "He said the vision showed up for a couple of months after he quit his research, and eventually it faded away."

"What do you mean a pirate showed up?" she asked.

"He had a vision of one," said Celeste, "but it was more than a vision. My friend, Andy, said he was as real as you or me. Talked to him, too. The pirate told him things. Andy said he thought he was losing his mind."

Carys sat back down on the chair.

"From mold? It gave him visions?"

"Hallucinations, yes. But more vivid. And it also gave him a nasty lung infection," said Celeste. "It traveled to his kidneys. He's on a donor list. That's why I always wear one of these." She tapped the surgical mask.

Her hands began to shake. Celeste looked down at her.

"Ms. Roberts?"

"I'm sorry," she said. "I just realized that I…I need to get moving. Thank you so much for your help."

She turned and walked to the door and back out into the main library, then straight for the exit.

Outside, she leaned against the whitewashed wall of the library, warm from the sun, hoping the heat would penetrate her. She stayed icy cold.

Lestinus appeared next to her. He said nothing.

She turned away from him, walked to her car, got in, and drove back to town. But her hands started shaking so badly that she had to pull over on the side of the road in Oystermouth to compose herself.

He was a hallucination after all. One so real, she felt she could reach out and touch it. Have full, complex conversations with it. Be surprised by it, mesmerized by its tales. And learn from it.

She wanted Lestinus to be a ghost. She wanted him to be able to tell her things she could use in her search—new things. Things that she didn't know. That Harper didn't know.

And he had. He'd given her details that weren't in the book. Taliesin, for one. Where had that come from if he was just a hallucination? Hallucinations don't know things.

At least she wasn't going crazy. She was hallucinating, but it was because of a natural process, a toxic mold. She should have been more relieved.

Instead, she tilted her head back and looked up into the ceiling of the car, willing herself not to burst into tears. Her stomach growled mightily. *Please let that be hunger*, she thought, *and not a goddamn kidney about to explode.* Her friend at the lab at Harvard had told her about the mold. She hadn't processed or even deeply questioned it.

No one had ever said a thing, in all the years she'd been working in this industry, about mold in old books causing hallucinations. It was the craziest thing she'd ever heard. Not counting the monk's tale, of course.

Would it have mattered even if she had known? Did it matter now that she did? Would it have changed anything that was happening?

She was no closer to figuring out where the tomb was than she'd been two weeks ago. Nicola was in the hospital, clinging to life. The only thing she'd managed to do was narrow the search down to two huge islands off the coast of Wales. It would take her the rest of her natural life to figure out where the hell they'd stashed Arcturus's corpse. She was so, so tired.

◆ ◆ ◆ ◆ ◆

Frank dialed Gyles. He picked up in half a ring.

"What news?" Gyles mumbled.

"The father's on the move. He's got what looks like an overnight bag, and he's on the move."

"Any idea where he's going?"

"I'm following him south along the coast on the A487," he said.

"We can safely assume he's heading straight for the woman," said Gyles. "I need not remind you to stick to him like glue."

"Of course," he said.

"By the way, that woman you shot?"

"Yeah," he said.

"She died last night," Gyles said.

He felt a sharp twinge in his throat. He swallowed hard and it went away.

"Plourde called me a few minutes ago," Gyles continued. "As you can imagine, he was not pleased, since he gave you the gun that killed her. He is concerned about potential consequences."

"Do we know if she gave the cops a description? Any way to trace it back to me?" he asked.

"We don't know, but it's probably best that you've left the country," Gyles said.

"That Jones bird probably told the cops about me," he said. "She could give them a pretty good description."

There was a brief silence on the other end of the phone. Gyles's leather chair squeaked. A chill ran up Frank's spine.

"Is there any chance you left any forensic evidence at the location?" asked Gyles. "Anything that could tie you to the crime?"

"Absolutely not. I was wearing gloves and a ski mask, so there's no skin or hair. No video ID possible from the scene, even if they had surveillance. I turned off the alarm system and wore gloves and a mask when I went back to toss the mansion."

"Sounds pretty straightforward," said Gyles, his voice slightly lower and slower. "Keep on the father. As soon as you know where he's headed, call me."

He hung up. Tension settled into the space between Frank's shoulders as it dawned on him just how ugly things were about to get.

◆ ◆ ◆ ◆ ◆

CARYS GOT OUT OF THE CAR and crossed the street to the grocery store—the same one from the day before. The produce aisle was blocked by a large trolley loaded with boxes of apples. *What is it with goddamn apples today?* she thought. *Afal.* Avalon.

She was gullible. So very gullible. If Celeste had known what she was really up to, the woman would have laughed in her face. Maybe she had been laughing and Carys just didn't notice.

She approached the trolley, and the man unloading it looked up at her.

"I'm sorry," he said. "Let me move this out of your way."

"Thanks," she said.

"Try one of these," he said. He reached into one of the cardboard boxes on the trolley and grabbed an apple. "Best you'll ever taste."

It was smaller than the huge Red Delicious variety in the case. Less perfect. Less red. Roundish, with some small bumps along the sides. She took it, rubbed it against her pants, and bit into it.

As her teeth snapped into the crisp flesh, her mouth filled with the richest, sweetest essence of apple she had ever tasted. She chewed the firm meat, which dissolved into something that felt like sugar.

"These are amazing," she said to the man. "Thank you so much. I'll take two more."

The man reached into the cardboard box, pulled them out, and handed them to her.

"They're organic," he said. "No pesticides. None needed. They're from a stock of apple resistant to all diseases, and the bugs don't attack them."

"Are they bred to be resistant?" she asked. "Some kind of hybrid or something?"

"Nope," said the man. "Naturally resistant."

"No kidding," she said. "I've never heard of that before."

"Yeah, it's a variety discovered back in the nineties," said the man. "They're stock from the oldest apple tree ever discovered in Wales. Naturally disease-resistant and no one knows why. My family bought some cuttings from it and started an orchard up in the hills not far from here."

"Where's the old tree?" she asked.

"Island off the north coast," he said.

"Which one?" she asked. The hair on the back of her neck began to prickle.

"Bardsey," said the man. "They say that tree is over fifteen hundred years old."

She stopped chewing. The man moved the trolley aside.

"I hope you tell your friends," said the man, smiling wide. "We just started marketing these."

She smiled at the man and stepped around the trolley. She made her way to the refrigerator, grabbed a large bottle of water, and went through the checkout and back outside.

She went across the street toward her car, but then passed it. Slowly, almost without realizing it, she made her way down to the water and began to walk. She found herself standing back at the playground where she and her parents had spent that pleasant afternoon a lifetime ago.

There was the little merry-go-round, tired and worn-out and waiting for children. One red horse mounted on a giant rusting spring wobbled back and forth in the breeze, as if tilted by an unseen hand. She sat down at the picnic table, the one where her parents had sat all those years ago, and stared out at the sea.

She used her phone to do a quick search on the tree that the man had told her about. It was actually called the mother tree, and it grew on the west side of Bardsey Island. In the picture of it online, it looked like a gnarled old woman crawling up the side of a whitewashed farmhouse. She pulled the translation from her bag and looked at the words of the poem again. The field of flowers. Died as he past. His watery nest. The Afon Gamlan led to Barmouth. The spotted rock rose's natural habitat. The tides could have driven the King's funeral barge up the coast straight to Bardsey. And the tree. The oldest apple tree in the country. Tree Zero.

Was it the mother tree in the poem? Was it Bardsey? Or was there another old tree on Holy Island that also had orchards dating to the same time period?

Carys closed her eyes. What would Lestinus and his fellow warriors have done? She inhaled and exhaled. She let her mind drift.

Slowly, the playground faded away. The world became quiet. Her mind's eye filled with the view along a broad, flat, sandy beach, the sky gray with low clouds. She could barely tell where the sea ended and the sky began. The land was utterly barren. Nearby, a smattering of maybe ten to fifteen dirty, bloodied men were pushing a small boat. She moved closer, her vision gliding along the muddy flats until she was next to them.

She looked inside the wooden boat. A body—that of the man in the white, blood-covered tunic with the ancient cross on its front—lay in the bottom.

She turned and examined the warriors, their faces tight with fear and confusion. They yelled at each other, gesturing and pointing. Tears streamed down the dirty face of one man, creating narrow strips of clean skin from his eyes down to his matted brown beard. They were leaderless. Mourning. The deepest mourning any of them had maybe ever experienced. They were fleeing something. Panic coursed through them.

"We outran them," Lestinus's voice intoned in her head. "We sent the rest of the army back home. The Usurper's troops were on their way south to slaughter our people, who were unprotected. We needed to put the King somewhere where the hordes—and the Usurper's men—would never find him. Where there were monks sworn to protect the tombs. A place where his grave would be just one more of thousands and thousands of other tombs. And then we needed to get home."

Holy Island would have just been too far.

She opened her eyes, and Lestinus was next to her on the bench.

"We buried him on Bardsey," said Lestinus.

She stared at him.

"He's there," said Lestinus. "You must listen. Listen to me. Listen to yourself. You know it's true."

He was right. He stared back silently, his form never wavering. His eyes as clear and crisp as the light sparkling off the bay. Arthur was on Bardsey Island.

Then it dawned on her—Harper was so sick. He was hallucinating, too. It had to be from the manuscript. Even if he hadn't been inhaling the smell of it, like Carys did, he'd been around the mold for far longer than she had, years and years. She had to tell him. He probably didn't know that this was what was causing his illness. She had to warn him. She had to tell him so many things.

Carys searched and found the number for Waggoner Hospital and dialed. It was before dawn back in Boston, but she didn't care. She sweet-talked the receptionist into putting the call through to "James Weldon's" room.

"John Harper," he said. He didn't sound like he'd been sleeping.

"It's Carys," she said.

"Where are you?"

"I'm in Wales. I think I know where he is."

"My god," he whispered.

"Bardsey Island."

There was complete silence on the other end of the phone. She couldn't even hear him breathe.

"Oh, Carys. No," Harper finally said, his voice dripping with disappointment. "That can't be. That's the most obvious place in the world. That island's been picked over more than any other location on earth except for Holy Island. He can't be there."

"The flowers in the poem are spotted rock roses. The river that carried them—it was Afon Gamlan. Camlann wasn't a place, it was a river. It's high up in Snowdonia. And it has four waterfalls, and it flows right through one of two places in Britain where those spotted rock roses grow. The waters of the Afon Gamlan eventually flow out to the sea just south of Bardsey. The mother tree in the poem... it's the ancient apple tree on Bardsey. The ebullient seas. It's the rip currents around Bardsey. And Bardsey is riddled with caves. He's in a cave on Bardsey."

"It can't be..."

"There's something else. The hallucinations you're having—"

"They're almost gone. I'm doing much better. There's talk that they may be able to release me sometime soon," Harper said.

"You need to get a full medical checkup. Have them check your lungs and kidney function. The hallucinations are caused by a mold spore that was hiding in the manuscript. My friend at Harvard tried to warn me about it when he analyzed the dirt from the journal, but I didn't follow up with him. The mold gives you an infection in your lungs, and then it travels to the kidneys and causes hallucinations. If it's not treated, it can kill you."

There was a long silence on the end of the phone. Then Harper spoke very softly.

"Carys, have you been—"

"Yes," she said.

"Who was it for you?"

"Lestinus," she said. A great burden lifted.

"But how could that be? How could the same hallucination appear to both of us?" Harper asked. "How is that possible? It doesn't make any sense."

"It makes perfect sense," she said, surprised at her own logic in the face of something so insane. "The manuscript was written by him. We both immersed ourselves in that book. His voice was already rattling around in my head before he ever appeared to me. If we were going to hallucinate anything, it would be the thing we were most obsessed with, wouldn't we? And we are both obsessed with Lestinus."

"But he knew things," said Harper. "He knew things we couldn't have known ourselves. Hallucinations don't know things."

"I know. It's impossible. But Lestinus insists that they buried him on Bardsey. How could I know that?"

"If he's just a hallucination, then he'd say what you wanted him to say, wouldn't he?"

"Maybe, but he's told me other things, too," said Carys. "Like the poem."

"What about it?" asked Harper.

"He said it was written by Taliesin," she said. "How would I know that?"

"I have no idea," said Harper. "And we have no way to know that that's even right unless we analyze it. But that's the least of our worries right now. Have you told anyone about the manuscript?"

"No," she lied. Annie didn't count—she was essentially an extension of herself. "But I've been researching the area at the local library. I've told the librarian nothing. Dafydd recognized the Gamlan as the river with the four waterfalls. He kayaks it."

"Who's Dafydd?"

"He's a local guy," she said. "He's been extremely helpful."

"You've brought too many people into this."

She snapped.

"What the hell did you expect me to do? I needed to find this tomb, and I needed to do it as quickly as possible. No one here knows me. We have to hope that no one knows where I am—but we don't know for sure that I haven't been followed. I'm here all alone and I'm scared. Nicola was nearly murdered, and I don't want you or me to be next. I needed help."

There was a long silence on the other end of the phone.

"I'm sorry," she said. "I'm so sorry. I haven't even talked to you since she was shot. John, how is she?"

"It doesn't look good," he said. "JJ has been keeping me posted on her condition. He's been to the hospital every day. He's very fond of her. They grew close after my wife died. He's taking this hard."

"I'm so sad for both of you, but she's strong," she said. "I just know she'll pull through. But I have to ask. Why didn't Nicola get the hallucinations? She's been working with this book as long as you have."

"She had very little exposure to the original manuscript," he said. "She worked almost entirely off the x-rays of the writing behind the main text. I was the only one who really spent time with the manuscript." There was a pause. "I love the way it smells."

She smiled.

"Carys," he said, "if you're convinced the tomb is on Bardsey, then you need to go to Bardsey. Leave right away."

She looked over at Lestinus, still silently watching her.

"How do I figure out which cave it is?" she asked Lestinus.

"I have no idea," said Harper. "I mean the poem says—"

"I'm talking to Lestinus," she said. "I mean, my, uh, hallucination. Hang on a minute."

Lestinus looked up at her. "It is on a line between the last light of the fat sun and the mother tree," he intoned. "It points right to the mouth of the cave."

Carys stared out over the water and briefly mulled his words—the poem's words. She let them float around her head, and soon an interpretation began to take a vague shape deep in her mind.

"Are we sure the translation of the words in the poem 'fat sun' is accurate?" she asked.

"The original words were the earliest forms of the modern *rhef* and *houl*," he said. "*Rhef* meant large, fat, grand in ancient Welsh. *Houl*, sun, was pretty straightforward."

"Fat, grand, big sun," she said, thinking out loud. "The biggest sun. Could it maybe have been an eclipse? The sun looks larger during an eclipse."

"We could find out when there were solar eclipses in Wales," he said. "That would narrow it down."

"But what would it mean to be between the eclipse and the mother tree?"

"Maybe if you draw a line from the tree, aiming right at the sun during the fullest point of the eclipse when the sun is its fattest, along that line is where the cave is? I could do some research on my end. JJ brought me my laptop the other day when he came to visit. Meanwhile, get up to Bardsey as fast as you can. Call me in a few hours, and I'll tell you what I found out."

"I'll leave right away," she said. Then something occurred to her. She'd calmed down enough that it seemed obvious. "John, is it possible that we do know all of the things he tells us, somewhere deep in our minds?"

There was a long pause on the other end of the phone.

"Like in a fever dream?" asked Harper. "Or that moment right before you fall asleep when you can remember things you've struggled to remember all day long?"

"Exactly," she said.

Harper was quiet again. Then he exhaled.

"It's the only explanation," said Harper. "You and I know the Dark Ages better than almost anyone ever has. You say you read the books you found for me over the years, right?"

"Many of them," she said.

"Your brain never forgets anything," he said. "It just stores it somewhere that most people can't access. Maybe the hallucinations are letting us access it."

"But you know what I know," she said. "Why didn't he tell you all the things he's telling me?"

"I don't know, Carys," Harper said. "By the time Nicola was done with the full translation of the poem, my condition was already so bad that I couldn't think straight for more than a minute at a time. You've only been exposed to this mold, or whatever it is, for a couple of weeks. I've been inhaling it for years. Maybe there's an optimum amount of impairment that unleashes your knowledge, but past that point you go mad. It was like my brain wasn't my own anymore."

"You need to tell your doctor. There could be kidney failure. I heard about a man who—"

"I promise. I'll do it today. Leave for Bardsey immediately. I don't think I need to tell you to be careful."

"Tell Nicola I miss her and I'll see her soon," she said. "And please give my best to JJ."

"I will. I will."

Carys hung up and contemplated the bay for a few moments. She closed her eyes and let her mind drift back to the poem. The tomb was in a cave, a castle of defense under the ocean waves, a watery nest. It was a cave under or at the water. If she was going to get into the burial cave, she needed to be prepared to dive into it.

She opened her eyes and gazed out over the sea. Dafydd was out there, and she was sure, for the right price, he'd take her diving on Bardsey. Or at least he could hook her up with a dive kit. There was no reason to let Harper in on this portion of the plan. He'd have a fit and get stuck in that hospital for another six months.

When she stepped into the warmth of the Farmer's Arms, Pete, as ever, was manning the bar.

"I'm afraid I need to check out earlier than I'd planned," she said.

Peter raised his eyebrows. "Sorry you can't stay longer."

"Me too."

She sat at her usual spot next to the window and dialed Dafydd's number. It went to voice mail.

"Dafydd, this is Jane," she said, trying to sound light. "I have a business proposition for you. I'd like to hire you for a dive trip, up north, but we need to leave right away. Please call me back as soon as you get this number." She left the number to her prepaid and hung up.

◆ ◆ ◆ ◆ ◆

Two hours later, Carys drove north through the Welsh countryside heading for Aberdaron, a tiny seaside town where she could get a hotel and catch the ferry to Bardsey Island. She wanted to get the lay of the land. The sky had turned stormy, with great dark gray clouds looming low. They matched her mood.

Lestinus appeared next to her. She turned to speak to him, then remembered she was just speaking to herself.

"You need me," he said.

"You're a figment of my imagination," she said.

"Do not abandon me. You will die."

"Shut up," she said. The phone next to her rang. Dafydd's cell number appeared on the screen.

"Hello, Dafydd," she said, more cheerily than she'd intended.

"Hi," he said. "I got your voicemail."

The cry of seagulls and the clank of sailboat rigging sang merrily in the background.

"I want to go diving up on Bardsey," she said. "I need a guide and some gear, so of course I thought of you."

"Well, I'm glad you did. When are you thinking?"

"Tomorrow."

"Tomorrow? You realize it's quite a drive to get up there."

"Yes. I'm actually on my way up there right now. I'm heading to Aberdaron for the night. Can you meet me there? Also, is there somewhere up there we can rent a boat?"

"Hang on, hang on. I haven't even told you how much I charge."

"How much do you charge?"

"I hate talking about money on the phone."

"As I said, I need to dive tomorrow. Maybe the next day as well. Are there places to stay on Bardsey?"

"There are more things involved here, Jane. The tides. If the tides aren't right, we're not diving. Did you have somewhere specific in mind?"

"I'm not sure yet."

"I have some suggestions if you'd like to hear them. I know the island pretty well."

"Can we talk about it tonight? When can you leave?" she asked.

"What's your certification?"

Carys paused a little longer than she intended while she racked her brain for the name of her certification. It had been a long time since she'd been diving. She wasn't even sure her certification was still valid. She knew she knew it and she needed to remember fast. She glanced over at Lestinus.

"PADI," Lestinus said.

"PADI," she said to Dafydd.

"Do you have your card with you?" Dafydd asked.

"No, I don't. That's why I need you to bring some gear. I won't be able to rent up there without my card."

"You realize I could lose my dive master certification if we get caught, right?"

"We won't get caught," she said.

"It can be treacherous up there," he said.

"Dafydd, can you help me out or not?"

"How many days do you think?"

"I don't know," she said. "I'll pay cash."

"Get me a room. I've got some arrangements to make. I figure you for about a medium suit. Thick one. It's bloody cold in that water," he said.

"Thanks very much. I'll call you later to check in," she said.

Carys drove on for a few more minutes, then dialed Annie's number.

"Where the hell have you been?" Annie said.

The urgency in Annie's voice drained the blood from Carys's face, and she knew before Annie even said the words what had happened.

"What are you doing right now?" asked Annie.

"Driving."

"Pull over," said Annie.

Carys obeyed.

"I'm stopped," she said.

"Nicola died late last night," said Annie.

Her body went completely numb.

"I'm so sorry, Carys," said Annie.

"I just spoke to Harper. He didn't know."

Then, a sob exploded out of her, and she began to cry harder than she had in years—maybe decades. She pressed the phone against her thigh so Annie wouldn't have to listen.

Nicola did not deserve this ending. No one did, but especially not Nicola.

After a minute, she sharply inhaled so she could speak, and moved the phone to her ear.

"She and Harper were together," she said between jagged breaths. "He'll be heartbroken."

"Right now, I'm more concerned about you," said Annie.

She tried to breathe. She didn't have the time to cry right now. She inhaled and exhaled deeply, then wiped her nose on her sleeve.

"I'll call him later today."

"I have something else I have to tell you," said Annie. "It's not bad news. But I need you to know. I called your father."

"You did what?"

"Just shut up and listen," said Annie. "I was worried sick. You didn't expect me to sit here and wait around for you to call, did you? I had no choice. He is the only person on the whole goddamn continent who knows you and cares about you."

"He doesn't care about me," she said. "How do you even know where he is?"

"Just because you wouldn't communicate with him doesn't mean my mother didn't," Annie said. "Did you honestly think she wouldn't tell him how you were doing?"

"If he cared how I was doing," she said, "he maybe should have showed up at some point since my mother killed herself twenty-two years ago. You had no right to call him."

"Just shut up and listen," said Annie. "You cannot do this by yourself. We're talking about murder now. This isn't just some little adventure."

"It was never a little adventure," she growled.

"I only told him that you'd run into some trouble and he needed to find you," said Annie. "I didn't tell him about Nicola or the treasure. I just told him that he needed to find you."

"I do not want my father involved. He doesn't even know what I look like."

"He'll know you," said Annie. "He's already on his way to Mumbles."

Carys started to speak, then stopped.

"How did I know you were in Mumbles?" Annie asked. "Is that what you're going to ask?"

Her knuckles went white on the steering wheel.

"It's the only place in Wales that you know other than that unpronounceable town where your father lives," said Annie. "I knew you'd never go there. Mumbles is where he grew up. And the only place in Wales you've ever been. It was pretty obvious."

"I never told you my dad grew up in Mumbles," she said.

"Yes, you did. Remember when Mayor Menino got his nickname, 'Mumbles'? And you told me that your dad grew up in a town of the same name."

Carys had to smile.

"I forgot I told you about that. You have a good memory."

"Where are you driving to?" asked Annie.

"For your information I'm not in Mumbles anymore," said Carys. "You just sent my father on a wild goose chase."

"Goddamn it, Carys! Where the hell are you?"

"I'll call you later," she said and hung up. She pulled back out onto the highway and sped north toward Bardsey and, she hoped, more than almost anything she'd ever wanted in her life, toward Riothamus Arcturus.

◆ ◆ ◆ ◆ ◆

FRANK WAITED IN HIS CAR in the parking lot across the street from the Mumbles police station, watching its main entrance in his rearview mirror. The car was beginning to warm up, and he could have easily drifted off. Fortunately, the buzz of his nerves kept him awake. He didn't like being so close to the police.

Carys Jones's father looked just like his teenage son. And he looked just like his daughter. Dark, shiny hair, big eyes, high cheekbones, strong chin, tall, fit. But under it all, afraid. Frank could see that quite clearly. Kids were such a liability, a big open sore that anyone could press and torture and use against you. He'd made a career of doing just that. Children make you do crazy things.

Anthony came out of the police station and began to walk down the main waterfront road. He watched him for a moment, then got out of the car and followed half a block behind.

Then, Anthony stopped and answered his phone. Frank could just barely hear him.

"What do you mean she left?" Anthony asked the person on the other end of the phone.

He strained to hear the rest but could not. Anthony hung up and stood still, rubbing his head, then turned around and walked straight toward him. Frank knelt down, pretending to tie his shoe. After Anthony passed, he stood up, straightened his coat, and resumed his tail.

The maid thing rattled him. He hadn't meant to kill her. He'd killed before, of course, and in his experience, his victims usually deserved it. The maid hadn't, though, not really.

Although, on the flight over from the U.S., he realized that he had recognized the look in her eyes just before the gun went off. She'd known someone might be coming for the manuscript. When it happened, she offered herself up to save it. Crazy thing, that. Sacrificing yourself for a book. Just thinking about it gave him a sick feeling in his stomach.

Anthony stepped into one of the small inns that lined the main street. The Victorian. Frank approached and peeked into the window. Anthony showed the receptionist a photo. The receptionist shook her head no. Anthony shook her hand and walked back out.

Slowly, over the next hour, he followed Anthony as he checked every single inn and pub in Mumbles. There must have been twenty of them. It gave him plenty of time to think.

Gyles thought he was stupid. Gyles thought he wasn't paying attention. Gyles thought he didn't know that he was a dead man as soon as the tomb was located. Fuck Gyles. He had been studying that psychopath for twenty years, the whole time they'd been working together. Even a psycho has an ego, and Gyles's ego was his biggest weakness—as it is for most men.

But in Gyles's case, this affliction meant he didn't feel doubt or threat. Gyles would go into business with anyone who could help him make money—no matter who they were—because he was completely confident that he could out-terrorize the person if need be. He usually could. But the men he was working with now were on a completely different level of insanity. Gyles didn't seem to notice what he'd opened himself up to.

He, on the other hand, had a sixth sense. He knew within seconds of meeting someone if the person would rat, or if he'd stay loyal to the end. He knew if a person was completely unhinged, a danger to anyone who got too close, someone for whom contracts were never final. He knew who could be intimidated and who would lash out. It was his specialty. He wasn't too book smart, but when it came to reading people, he was a genius. Still, he had misread the maid until it was far too late.

Anthony stepped into another pub, and Frank stopped in front of an antiques store next to it. He looked through its big display window and examined the delicate Portmeirion tea set on a table at the front of the store.

Mum had collected Portmeirion, back when his father was around and they still had some money. The last time he'd seen her, before she went into the hospital that last time, she'd been so frail that it made him feel like a scared kid. Parents, mothers especially, are another vulnerability, but one you don't get to choose. She'd turned into a hornet that day when he offered her money for rent. She still took it. She had to. Her pension barely covered her food. As she crumpled the cash in her bony hand, her rage turned into loathing—he didn't know which of them it was aimed at. Mum had the sixth sense, too. He never should have made contact with the Jones woman. He shouldn't have tried to bribe her. He should have just taken what he wanted from the beginning. But he didn't have the stomach for the violence anymore. His mother's death had started a slow bleed of his aggression, replacing it with exhaustion. But the Jones woman—that was a mistake that he was going to own. A mistake that Gyles was going to try to make him pay for.

The good news was that the police had no idea he was involved with the murder. They couldn't know. He had traveled on a fake passport. No one, not even Gyles, knew where he lived—at least he didn't think he knew. The Jones woman had seen him, but to her he was just a nameless brute with a gun. There might be video, but Jones was the only one who could identify him, and she was here in Wales. Gyles wouldn't ever out him, because then he'd be tied to all the other murders, not to mention a thousand lesser crimes. And Gyles needed him to find this treasure.

The problem was that although Gyles would never rat on him, he wouldn't hesitate to kill him. Their long and fruitful relationship meant nothing the minute that gun went off in the mansion. As soon as he found the treasure, Gyles would hire someone to do the job. All those other people he had killed for Gyles had been in the business. They'd been a collection of liars, cheats, and scum. The maid was a civilian, a bystander caught up in something violent, and the employee of a famous billionaire to boot. The police would be far more diligent solving this one than they'd been with the junkies, or the thieving antiquities dealer, or the dozens of other players in this dark world who had crossed Gyles. And that meant Frank was marked.

He turned away from the store window when he saw Anthony leave the pub. Anthony walked a block and went into the next pub in line, the Farmer's Arms. Frank was beginning to get thirsty. It was time for a beer. He took a deep breath, waited a beat, and pulled open the door to the Farmer's Arms.

Anthony was at the bar, and he clearly knew the bartender, a gray-haired man smiling broadly to reveal a row of yellowing teeth. He took a position at the other end of the bar but within earshot. The bartender looked over.

"What can I get you?" he asked.

"Pint of the bitter, thanks," Frank said. He was actually looking forward to it. The man drew the beer and never stopped talking to Anthony. He slid the pint down the bar. He left a ten on the bar and took a gulp of the smooth beer.

"Dear god, man, it's been ages," the bartender said to Anthony. "How are you and the missus? What are you doing down here?"

"We're fine, we're fine," said Anthony. "Unfortunately, I can't stay, much as I'd love to catch up. I'm here looking for my daughter, Carys. She came to Mumbles, but she left and I'm trying to find out where she went."

"What's wrong?" asked the bartender.

"She's in trouble," said Anthony. "We haven't really seen each other…in a long time." He reached into his pocket and showed the man the photo.

The bartender looked at the photo, and his eyes grew wide.

"She was here. She stayed here, upstairs. Said her name was Jane. She's American. But she would be, wouldn't she? She checked out just a few hours ago. You just missed her."

Frank nearly choked on his beer.

"Did she say where she was going?" asked Anthony.

"No. Why are you looking for her?" asked the bartender.

"Her friend, the girl whose mother took Carys in when…who she grew up with, called me and said Carys needed my help, that she was in Wales," said Anthony. "She didn't give me any specifics. She just said I had to find her and that she was pretty sure she came to Mumbles."

"She didn't say a word to me about where she was headed," said the bartender. "Let me see that photo again." Anthony placed it on the bar. The bartender picked it up and studied it closely. "She really is the spitting image of you, isn't she? I can't believe I didn't see it."

The bartender put the photo down.

"Priscilla, the woman who took Carys in after Patricia, uh, died," said Anthony, "she'd send me photos every year on Carys's birthday and holidays and such." Anthony held up the photo. "This one was taken at her birthday dinner a couple of years ago. She's beautiful, isn't she?"

The bartender said nothing.

"She never forgave me for leaving, then I made it worse, didn't I?" said Anthony, almost to himself.

The old man silently examined Anthony's face.

"She seemed like a lovely woman," the bartender said. He turned his attention to cleaning the bar. Frank could feel the questions the bartender wanted to ask, but that friends wouldn't. He wanted to ask them, too. And he wouldn't be nice about it.

"How many years has it been since you've been back to Mumbles?" asked the bartender.

"At least ten. Haven't been here since I started at the university," said Anthony.

"Oh, that's right. Professor Jones. PhD. Too good to come visit the old stomping grounds now that you're educating the next generation of…what was it again?"

"Geopolitical historians," said Anthony.

"Whatever the hell that is…"

"Researching and analyzing shifting geographic and political boundaries, to you simple folk," said Anthony.

"Suppose you'd have to go into academia with something like that. Not much call for it out here in the real world, where people do actual work," said the bartender, a sparkle lighting up his eyes.

"Sod off," Anthony said, smiling. Then his smile faded. "Peter, did Carys say or do anything that might help me find her?"

"Not really. Did you talk to the cops?"

"Yeah. They said they'd ask around. They didn't seem much bothered about it. I guess missing girls are as common as cats."

"You know," said the bartender, "after she checked out this morning, I overheard her call a local guy, Dafydd Reynolds. Something about her wanting to hire him for something."

"He wouldn't hurt her, would he? You know him?" asked Anthony.

"He's a solid guy. Owns a salvage boat and a dive tour company for the visitors."

"Where can I find him?" asked Anthony.

"He's usually in here after work. You could come back at around six. You'll probably find him right where you're standing."

"I'm in a bit of a hurry," said Anthony. "Can you give me his cell phone?"

The man looked over Anthony's shoulder and squinted.

"I'll do you one better," he said, and pointed out the window. "See that guy right there climbing into his truck with a cup of coffee? That's him."

Frank did his best not to smile as Anthony turned and headed out the door. He stood glued to his spot, slowly drinking, just a normal guy enjoying an afternoon by the seaside. Once Anthony was gone, he and the bartender had the bar to themselves.

"Can I get you another?"

"Why not," said Frank.

The man slid another bitter his way. He drank long and deep again, and turned to look out the window just as Anthony was extending his hand to Dafydd. He watched the two men shake, watched Anthony retrieve the photo and hand it to Dafydd. Frank turned his attention back to his beer.

"That sounded like a pretty bleak tale," he said to the bar in general. "Daughter gone missing. Tough day for 'im."

"You don't know the half of it," said the bartender. "Anthony left the girl and her mother and came back here when his daughter was just a tyke. Then the girl's mother died when she was fifteen."

"What of?" he asked.

"Killed herself. They say she had the depression pretty bad. And he didn't go back to the States and get the girl after the mother died. He'd already remarried, started a new brood. Bloody selfish thing to do to a child, if you ask me."

He took another sip of his beer. "Which thing—killing yourself or ditching your family?" he asked.

"I guess they're about the same thing," said the bartender. "That girl's been through the ringer. Not sure how much help she's likely to take from him. But he's her only family. I'm not gonna get in the way of that."

The door swung open and Dafydd and Anthony came in, the tension palpable between them.

"Peter," said Dafydd before they'd even closed the door. "You know this guy?"

"I do," said Peter. "Known him my whole life. He's good people. Looking for his daughter."

"She said her name was Jane, but he says her name is Carys. He says she's in trouble," said Dafydd. "What kind of trouble?"

"That I would not know," said Peter, "but I don't think it much matters. If Anthony Jones says his daughter is in trouble, I'll be believing him. And I'd suggest you do whatever he needs."

Frank watched as Dafydd took another look at the photo. "She hired me for a job," Dafydd said.

"Where?" asked Anthony. Dafydd paused.

Peter looked hard at him. "Tell him," he said. "She's his child."

"Aberdaron," said Dafydd.

"When?" asked Anthony.

"I'm supposed to meet her tonight," Dafydd said. "She wants to dive on Bardsey Island tomorrow."

"Well, we'd better get moving then," said Anthony. "You can drive."

"I'm going to call her," said Dafydd. "I think I should tell her that you're looking for her."

"No," said Anthony, as the two walked back through the pub's door. "We'll never see her again if you do that."

◆ ◆ ◆ ◆ ◆

IF CARYS'S HEART HAD NOT BEEN BREAKING for Nicola, she would have been transfixed by the tiny seaside village of Aberdaron. It was everything beautiful and calming that she remembered about Wales from her childhood. Its narrow main road wound up and down the dune-like, grassy hillsides that clung to the gray ocean edge. The whitewashed, thickly thatched hotels, pubs, and houses of the village were, as in Mumbles, built right up against the road—but in this town there wasn't even room for a tiny sidewalk.

The walls of the buildings alternated from bright white to muted beige as the clouds rolled across the face of the sun, rolled away, then rolled across again, like a slow strobe light. Couples strolled in the streets, and she had to pull over and stop twice to allow an oncoming vehicle to pass. She was starting to crave this dreary, lovely country, to crave it like a nest, or a cave—an enclosed, safe place in which to hide for the rest of her life. She wished for a moment that she was in the cave and not Arcturus.

She called ahead for reservations at a hotel with an unpronounceable Welsh name that was near the town dock. The first, and it seemed only, language here was Welsh. She pulled into what she assumed was the parking area for her hotel—the sign next to the lot was composed entirely of consonants. She pulled her bag out of the back seat and entered the inn. It was all dark wood—on the floors, the walls, and even the coffered ceilings. As her eyes adjusted to the dimly lit space, she saw an older man sitting behind a simple desk.

"Hello," she said. "I'm Jane Roberts. I have a reservation."

The man moved his head slowly up to her, blinked, and without speaking pulled himself to his feet and went into the back room. He returned with a girl of maybe sixteen or seventeen.

"Can I help you?" she asked in a thick Welsh accent.

"Roberts. I have a reservation for two rooms for tonight and tomorrow night."

The young woman flipped through the book on the desk, made a check mark next to a name.

"I'll be paying for both rooms, but you can keep the key to the second room back there until my friend arrives. His name is Dafydd Reynolds."

"The diver," said the girl, smiling slightly. "We know him. I'll see he gets it. Room is upstairs on the third floor. I gave you one facing the sea. It's got a nice queen bed up there. Breakfast is down here in the conservatory"—she pointed out to the bright, glass-enclosed porch facing the ocean—"from seven to nine. We can make you takeaway lunches if you want. Just let us know at breakfast. Best to come down early if you want lunch though. We've got a houseful this week—only reason you got these rooms is we had a few cancellations this morning."

"Why so busy?"

"The pagans," said the girl.

"The what?"

"The pagans. They swarm Bardsey during the solstice. Like a sort of Stonehenge thing, but here. It's creepy, if you ask me."

"People without day jobs, I suppose," she said, winking at the girl and walking to the stairs.

Then, from the corner of her eye, she thought she saw Lestinus.

When she turned toward him, she saw instead a young, bald man wearing a full-length wool cassock with a rope belt almost identical to the one her hallucination favored. She stood and stared for a moment. When the girl at the desk handed the man a room key, then eye-rolled up at Carys, she realized that the man was real.

She smiled to herself and started up the stairs.

At the top, she stopped to catch her breath. Her legs were weak, and her lungs weren't working right. She was sick from the mold— but she'd think about that later.

Her room was bigger than her room had been at the Farmer's Arms. Two large windows gave her a breathtaking view of the sea. She could not see Bardsey Island, which was far off to the west and obscured by the highlands surrounding the little town. The room's cornflower-blue wallpaper was peeling in the corners and lent the chamber an archaic but not entirely unwelcome feminine touch. The queen bed's pure white duvet, edged in silk of the same blue, beckoned her exhausted, enervated body. She dropped her bags and flopped down on it.

She woke with a start an hour later. She rubbed her eyes and sat up. She almost felt good for a moment, then remembered that she had to call Harper. Nicola was dead. And by now, he knew. Her stomach flipped, and she thought she'd be sick. She could not postpone the inevitable. She dialed the number for Waggoner.

"John," she said when he answered, "I'm so sorry."

"Thank you," he said in an oddly flat tone. She recognized it as shock. "I can't believe she's gone. She was...she was a wonderful woman. She gave me something to be happy about after my wife died. She was my partner in this search. I don't know what I'll do without her."

"I know," she said.

"Don't ask me what you can do to help, because you're already doing it," he said. "I want revenge, Carys. Whoever it is that is responsible, I want them to go to jail for the rest of their lives. I want to take this prize away from them. They can't win. We can't let them win."

"They won't," she said. "We're so close. I'm in Aberdaron right now. I'm going over to the island tomorrow to work out where we want to focus our search efforts."

"I was working on the eclipse data on my computer before I… before JJ came by to tell me about Nicola," said Harper. "It's not helpful. There were no total eclipses visible from Bardsey during the sixth century, according to NASA data. There were a couple of partials, but nothing that lasted very long or would have created the sort of fat or large sun that was described in the poem."

Now she was meeting the cold-hearted, all-business Harper who had built his business singlehandedly, the man she had expected to meet before his illness got in the way. And without some more concrete directions to the cave, they were practically back at square one.

"What are we missing?" she asked.

"I don't know," said Harper. "Nicola translated this herself. If I could find her notes, I might be able to make more sense of the original words in the poem."

She thought for a fleeting moment about telling Harper Nicola's secret, about how she'd conscripted an army of linguists to help her translate the poem. She thought better of it. Although one of those linguists would come in mighty handy right about now.

"If you had to have this poem translated again, who would you go to? Who would you ask?"

"I wouldn't even know where to begin," he said. "I feel so powerless here. I could do some more research on my computer, but it won't be as thorough as Nicola would have done."

"Just see what you can come up with. I'll give you a call tomorrow when I find out what we're dealing with over on the island. There's supposed to be some sort of big pagan gathering there tomorrow, just to make things interesting."

"Why?" he asked.

"To celebrate the summer solstice," she said.

Lestinus appeared to her right and turned to her.

"The fat sun," he said softly.

"What?" she asked him.

"Who are you talking to?" asked Harper.

"Lestinus," she said.

She turned back to the monk.

"What did you just say?" she asked him.

"The fat sun," said Lestinus. "It is what the pagans are here to celebrate."

She stared at him for a minute.

The summer solstice.

"John," said Carys. "Lestinus just said the fat sun is the summer solstice."

There was silence on the line, and when Harper spoke again, it was barely audible. "Between the mother tree and the last light of the fat sun."

Her mind whirled, the poem and these new facts colliding with each other, then snapping into place to form a complete picture.

The spotted rock rose's blooming season was around the solstice. The meltwater in mid-June from the high mountains of Snowdonia would have made the Gamlan run high enough that it could have carried Arthur's casket barge all the way to the sea. The western shore of Bardsey, Dafydd had said, was riddled with caves. If she could get an unobstructed view of the sunset on the summer solstice while standing next to the mother tree on Bardsey Island, she could draw a virtual plumb line that would cross a point on the western shore— marking where the cave was located. Most important, the summer solstice would be the one thing guaranteed to happen every single year in exactly the same place in the sky. Unlike an eclipse.

"It makes perfect sense," she said to Harper. "It's the solstice."

Lestinus smiled slightly at her.

"But apparently I already knew that," she said.

"It fits everything in the poem," said Harper. "My god, you're right. I can't..."

Then Harper was quiet a long time. Finally, he said, "Arthur must really want us to find him."

"What do you mean?" she asked.

"How is it possible that you just happened to arrive in Aberdaron and figured all this out one day before the solstice? You end up in exactly the right place in exactly the right time? It's...it's inconceivable. How could this be luck?"

Harper was right. It was entirely impossible that all this had fallen into place at the perfect moment. She turned to Lestinus. He smiled broadly at her—his face open and genuinely happy, his eyes sparkling like the ocean.

"Carys," he said, "you have been judged worthy."

◆ ◆ ◆ ◆ ◆

IT WAS EARLY EVENING, but the sun rode high in the sky. This time of year, sunset didn't happen until close to ten. Frank liked it so much more than the short winter days, when the sun came up at eight-thirty and dropped purposefully and quickly down again before three. It was why the Brits drank so much—that and the rain.

His mood had cratered. Between the death of the maid and now finding out what the Jones woman had been through—there was no way she deserved the hell that Gyles likely had in mind for her. No one did, really. This was why it was always better not to know anything about targets except their location. Details just clouded things, made him less focused, more likely to hesitate when push came to shove, as it inevitably did when Gyles was involved. He just hoped things went smoothly. He didn't want to have to kill anyone else.

But Carys Jones was standing between him and his payday.

He stayed a few cars back from Dafydd's pickup. The two men, from what he could see, had been talking nonstop since they left Mumbles. He picked up his phone and dialed Gyles.

"They're on the move," he said. "Aberdaron. They're going out to do a dive on Bardsey Island tomorrow."

"They? How many are there?" growled Gyles.

"Three. The woman, her father, and the guy she's hiring to bring her on the dive," said Frank.

"A dive," said Gyles. "That's interesting. You know what, Frank, my man? She's not running. She's hunting. She's found the damn tomb." Gyles laughed out loud.

"What do you mean?" he asked.

"The burial site that the manuscript describes," said Gyles. "The one that's supposedly full of treasure. Why else would she be diving in the godforsaken North Atlantic unless she was looking for something? Or already found it."

"How do you want me to play this?" he asked.

"She'll lead us right to the damn treasure if we let her," said Gyles. "This is brilliant. Follow them. Get a boat. Get out there. When they're done, find out what they found, where it is. Specifics. Take hostages if need be. You know how to dive, right?"

"Yeah," he said. "Haven't done it in a long time, though."

"I'll send you some help," said Gyles.

He had not been expecting that. Not at all. And he knew just what he meant. Gyles was going to kill four birds with one stone, and he was one of the birds.

"I don't think I'll need help," he said. "I seriously doubt any of them brought a gun to their little diving party. The woman doesn't strike me as the violent type, the diver is just doing a job, and the father thinks he's on his way to a tearful family reunion."

"So be it," said Gyles. "I'll have someone on standby in case you change your mind. I've got a couple of blokes on contract who could get there pretty quickly."

"I'll let you know what I find," he said.

"Also, don't forget to grab the manuscript and translation," said Gyles. "We still need those. Can't imagine she'd take that on a dive. It'll probably be stowed wherever she's staying. Frank, this is terrific stuff. I think this deal might just be the solution to a little client-relations problem I've got."

"Well, I'm glad to hear it," he said. He hung up.

His stomach began to turn sour. He didn't like the plan. He needed a new one.

◆ ◆ ◆ ◆ ◆

THE WIND BEGAN TO KICK UP as Carys stood on the dock looking out over the ocean. It was around sixty-five degrees, partly sunny, and the wind wasn't very strong, but she couldn't get warm, even though she was wearing a sweater and a scarf she'd bought that afternoon. On the beach next to the dock, a very young man and woman, both pale-skinned and dark-haired, played with their tiny daughter, who was as improbably blonde as Carys had been at that age, before her hair had turned jet black.

The toddler screamed each time a thin wave surged up toward her feet. She ran back up the beach, looking behind her at the wave, right into her mother's arms. Her mother swung her around, put her down, and the child toddled back down to the water to do it all over again.

The voices around her were all Nicola's and her father's. She couldn't remember what her mother's voice sounded like. It made her heart ache. She could remember her mother's sayings, some of which she'd picked up from being married to a Welshman, like "tit for tat." Even as a child, Carys thought that sounded naughty. She remembered the way her mother would hold her face with both hands when she kissed her on the forehead, as if Carys might slip away. But mostly she remembered how her mother's eyes always seemed to be red and surrounded by dark shadows, and how some-times she just couldn't get her mother to smile, no matter how many cartwheels she did on their Cambridge lawn.

If there was some way that Lestinus could help her remember her mother's voice, she'd inhale those mold spores until her kidneys exploded. She was getting sick and was likely to get sicker as long as she kept smelling the book. But the tradeoff might be worth it. As much as she hated to admit it, Lestinus—or whatever part of her brain he was helping her access—was making this search easier.

She turned to walk back to the inn to inquire about dinner options when she spotted Dafydd's solid form striding down the dock toward her. She smiled and quickened her step toward him. He smiled back, but it was an odd, half-hearted sort of thing. She felt a pang of disappointment at this.

Then, from around Dafydd, strode on older man. He pushed past Dafydd and cantered toward her. She froze, unsure how to react. She backed away a step, and the man stopped short.

"Carys," he said. "It's me. It's Dah."

She squinted at him. Her brain seized up, refusing to process the words or their message. The last time she'd seen her father, he'd been young and handsome. This man had gray on his head and gray in his skin. He had a paunch. He was shorter than her father. Of course, she had been so young the last time she laid eyes on him.

Then the man smiled tentatively. The set of his mouth, the way his cheeks inverted slightly into dimples, and his voice…it was the same voice she could still hear in her head these decades later. The world began to pull away and push in toward her at the same time.

"What are you doing here?" she whispered. Anthony took another step toward her.

"You know him, right?" asked Dafydd. "Everyone in town knew him. Said he was your father, and your name was really Carys."

She glanced at Dafydd. He looked so worried.

"I'm sorry," she said. "I was trying to keep everyone out of this."

"Annie said you were in trouble," said Anthony, taking another step toward her. She put up her hand to stop him. Dafydd flinched. Anthony raised his hands and backed up. "She said she thought you'd gone to Mumbles. Peter—you met Peter at the inn where you stayed. He saw you and Dafydd together. Peter's known me since we were babies. It's not his fault I'm here." He jerked his thumb toward Dafydd.

"You shouldn't have come," she said. Her anger began to burn red. "I told Annie not to tell anyone I was here. You need to leave right now."

She began to walk back down the dock toward the inn. Anthony stepped in front of her and raised his hands to her shoulders. Dafydd stepped in and grabbed Anthony by the shoulder.

"She said she doesn't want to see you," said Dafydd.

She looked at them both, then sidestepped them and continued walking. Anthony shook free of Dafydd's hold and pursued her down the dock.

"Carys," Anthony said weakly behind her. "Please. Please let me help you. Just tell me what is happening so I can help you."

She heard his footsteps stop. She stopped and turned.

"Why would you want to help me?" she demanded, the words falling from her tongue like ice cubes.

Anthony began to speak, then stopped. He looked down at the dock, then over at Dafydd and then back at her. "Because I…I…you are still my daughter. If you're in danger, I want to help."

Carys smiled a thin, bitter smile.

"Now," she said. "You want to help now?"

"Yes," said Anthony. "I want to help now."

"I don't want it," she said. Her fingernails bit into the palms of her hands.

Dafydd took a tentative step closer. "Carys, are you alright?" he asked.

"I'll be fine as soon as this…person leaves," she said.

"I'm sorry," said Anthony. "I'm so sorry."

She glared at him, every bit of hate and anger she'd accumulated for the past thirty years shooting at him through her eyes. He looked down at his feet, unable or unwilling to say anything else. She turned back around and walked to the hotel.

◆ ◆ ◆ ◆ ◆

CARYS AND DAFYDD HAD THE DINING ROOM in the glass conservatory at the back of the inn to themselves. The setting sun illuminated the slate sea and the undersides of the clouds with a reddish gold. They'd ordered glasses of wine and a light dinner, but neither was eating.

"His bus doesn't leave for another hour," said Dafydd.

"As long as he's on it," Carys said as she flicked at the limp salad on her plate. She drained the last of her wine and motioned for the waitress to bring another.

"You shouldn't drink any more wine," said Dafydd. "You won't process oxygen as well tomorrow when we're diving."

"Take all the fun out of life, why don't you?"

"What's going on?" he asked.

"Which part—diving on Bardsey or my father appearing out of nowhere after three decades?" she asked.

"Both, actually, but let's start with Bardsey," he said. "What's the rush?"

She took a deep breath. Just the basics.

The waitress placed her wine in front of her. She lifted it and glanced at Dafydd, who scowled at her. She put it down without drinking.

"I'm trying to find a cave," she said. "Its location is written in a very old Roman parchment that I'm analyzing. The cave can only be located based on the position of the sun on the solstice. That's why I had to move so quickly, since the solstice is tomorrow."

Dafydd smiled.

"Intriguing," he said, his eyes twinkling. "I thought you were just trying to find modern locations for Roman place names?"

"Good memory," she said.

"What's in the cave?"

She smiled back. "I'm not sure. Right now, I'm just trying to establish that it exists and its location."

"And your father," said Dafydd. "Why does he think you are in danger?"

This would be much more difficult to explain.

"There are other people looking for the cave as well," she said. "I'm fairly confident that they have no idea where I am, or where I'm looking, but they would like to find it before I do. And they're not exactly…uh…subtle."

"It's treasure then," said Dafydd. "A treasure hunt."

"No," she said. "No treasure. It's just an important historical find—a previously undiscovered cave described by an old Roman manuscript."

"I don't believe you," said Dafydd, his blue eyes boring holes into her. She couldn't look away. "If this were just a historical search, you wouldn't be in danger, would you?"

"Historians can be very territorial," she said. "I will ask that you keep this expedition to yourself until it's completed, of course." She looked up at him and tried to grin. "I assume there's a client-dive-master privilege or something like that, right?"

"Of course," he said glumly. "Discretion is our motto." He finally relented and smiled back at her. "And how are you planning to find this cave? You have to at least tell me the truth about that."

"We'll have the exact location tomorrow," she said, "at dusk."

"Why dusk?" asked Dafydd.

"It's a long story," she said. "You're just going to have to trust me on this. I need to be on the west side of Bardsey tomorrow precisely at sunset."

"You and about five thousand of those freaks in robes," said Dafydd. "Why the west side? It'll be completely mental over there tomorrow night."

"There is an ancient apple tree on the west side of the island," she said. "According to the manuscript, the cave lies at the point on the coast that is on the line between the sun just as it sets on the night of the solstice and that tree."

"Where's the tree?" asked Dafydd.

"About a quarter mile up the hill from the water," she said.

Dafydd sat silently for a moment and she could feel him thinking.

"Then you have a problem," said Dafydd.

"What problem?"

He grabbed the salt and pepper shakers off the table.

"You'll only have a minute to determine the line," said Dafydd. "Right at the solstice. And there's only one solstice. You need to be as precise as possible."

He placed the pepper in the center of the table.

"Here's you at the tree," he said.

He tapped the edge of the table.

"Here's the coastline."

He folded his napkin and put it in his lap, six inches lower than the edge of the table.

"And here's me in a boat. From here in the boat, I can see the sun as it sets," he said, pointing to a button on his shirt, "and I can see the point on the coast where the caves are located." He pointed to the space between the table and his knees. "But I can't see you by the tree. The coast is a series of big cliffs. Obviously, you can't see the boat from the tree. How are we going to find the line from the tree to the setting sun, with only two people, neither of whom can see the other? And I'll need to drop two buoys that are right on that line if we're going to find the cave. We need three people to do this properly. We only have two."

"Can't I just stand on the edge of the cliff where I can see the tree and the sunset and then put a stake into the ground on the cliff edge marking the plumb line?" she asked. "Then we just dive directly below the marker?"

"You could do that, but we won't be able to see the marker once we are in the water up against the cliff face," he said. "We need a marker we can see from the water when we dive. That's why I said we need to set two buoys. We could set them with two people but the plumb line will be a lot more accurate with three. Accuracy is the most important thing if we're going to locate that cave, right?"

Her eyes drifted out to the ocean. She hadn't really thought any of this through.

"When do you want to dive?" Dafydd asked.

"Tomorrow. Right after sunset," she said.

He frowned.

"Bad idea. Why don't we wait until morning? It'll be a lot safer in the daylight."

"I want to locate and get into that cave as soon as possible. It'll be dark in the cave anyway, so what difference does time of day make?"

Dafydd took the salt shaker and wiggled it at her.

"Then we definitely need a salt," said Dafydd, placing the salt shaker on the edge of the table. "Not just to make the plumb line more accurate. We'll be diving at night, so we'll need someone in the boat to indicate the line on the cliff wall with a flashlight."

She looked at him silently.

"Do you know anyone here who you think would be willing to help out?" he asked.

She hated where this was leading.

"No. Do you?" she asked.

"Just one," he said. "But he's about to get on a bus."

They finished not eating their meal and sat in silence. The waitress brought the check and Carys signed it to her room.

"I'll let you go talk to him," said Dafydd, rising from the booth. "I'll be in my room, sorting out our gear and getting us a boat. I'll come by your room later and we can make sure your wetsuit is going to fit."

◆ ◆ ◆ ◆ ◆

IT WAS ALMOST DARK when Carys finally made her way out of the hotel and to the bus stop. It was only a short walk, but she took her sweet time. Her father was sitting under the bus stop awning. His legs were crossed, and he was shaking the dangling foot back and forth rapidly, as if it were on fire.

He used to do that all the time. Her mother said it made the whole house shimmy. Carys had never felt the house shimmy, but she knew that there was something bothering him when his foot started doing that. *Good*, she thought as she slowly made her way to the bus stop. *You should be bothered.*

She stopped about ten feet away from where he was sitting. He felt her presence and turned toward her, smiled broadly, and stood up. Her heart broke a little.

"I'm glad you came to say goodbye," he said. "I'm so sor—"

"Don't," she said, raising her hand.

He looked down at the ground. "I don't know what else to say," he said. "It's the only thing I can think of."

She walked to the bus stop bench and sat down. Her father sat down next to her. He smelled exactly the same as he always had—and the scent of him flooded her with memories that began to overwhelm her. Her mother's smell was in there somewhere, too. She looked at him. He had an expectant look on his face. The encroaching gray within his familiar black hair, the way his shoulders slumped forward. Her memories abated. This wasn't her father. This was just some guy who showed up.

"Dafydd and I need you to help us with something tomorrow night," she said. "It will only take a couple of hours, and then you can go home the day after tomorrow, when we're done."

"Of course, Carys," he said. "Whatever you need."

She cringed at his eagerness.

"We're going over to Bardsey tomorrow evening," she said. "I'll explain everything when we get into the boat. Until then, I need you to stay at the hotel. Don't go out. Just lie low. Can you do that?"

He turned his body to face her fully.

"You are in danger, then?" he asked. "Annie said you were. She sounded terrified. What's—"

"Please," she said. "Annie is exaggerating. She should not have called you. And as long as you're here, all I ask is that you make yourself useful and keep out of sight."

"What is going on?" he asked. "If you are asking for my help, then things must be pretty goddamn bad."

She opened her mouth to speak, then started to laugh.

"You are right about that," she said. He started to laugh, too.

"I can't tell you much," she said. "The less you know, the better off we all are."

Anthony placed a hand on her knee. She looked up at him angrily, then saw the softness in his face. The tension inside her loosened a little.

"I won't help you unless you tell me what's happening," said Anthony.

She felt like she'd been smacked. When she started to breathe again, she leaned into him, her face just a foot from his. His breath was a yeasty, warm perfume that brought on the memory of sitting in his lap in the big red leather chair as he read her *Le Petite Prince* before bed. She removed his hand from her knee.

"You are not even supposed to be here," she hissed. "And now you're making demands on me? Well, Dah"—she let the word slide out of her mouth as she stood up—"go fuck yourself."

She stood up and started to stalk away in long strides. She looked up to the hotel. Standing in a pool of light cast by the fixture over the hotel's front door was Dafydd, arms crossed. He cocked his head, raised one hand, pointed his finger at her, raised it to the sky, and spun it around in a circle and pointed it at Anthony. *Go back and get him.*

She stopped. Goddammit, he was right. They needed Anthony. They could probably have paid someone to help, but at the end of the day, her father was the only one other than Dafydd she could even begin to trust to keep his mouth shut about what was going to happen tomorrow. And she wasn't all that sure about Dafydd.

She slowly turned. Her father was standing, watching her. She stomped back toward him. Anthony looked like he was bracing himself for a blow. She threw herself back down on the bus stop seat like a petulant teenager.

"I'm looking for a cave," she said. "It's listed in an ancient manuscript. There is a man who is also looking for this cave. If I don't find it first, bad things will happen to whatever is in that cave and me and the man who owns the manuscript. I haven't told Dafydd any of this, because I need his help even more than I need yours and if he bolts, I'm screwed. Do you understand?"

"Not really," said Anthony. "But go on."

"Tomorrow we need you to help us find the cave on Bardsey Island," she said. "I have no reason to believe that this man can find us here. But it would be stupid to assume he can't. So we're going to stay put tomorrow and only leave the hotel when we're ready to head to the island. Do you understand?"

"Yes," said Anthony. "How did you get the manuscript?"

"Through work," she said. "The owner was a client."

"Oh, of course," said Anthony. "Sothington's. I started sending letters to you there when you kept returning the ones I sent to your house. I knew at least your work would accept delivery."

"I threw them away," she said.

She looked over to make sure the blow had landed. It had. Anthony sat silently, then looked at her as if the previous exchange had not happened.

"Why would your work send you on such a dangerous assignment?" he asked.

"They didn't," she said. "I sent myself."

"Why?"

"Because," she said. She opened her mouth to finish the sentence, then paused. There were so many reasons. Which one would he understand?

None of them. She stood up and went back to the hotel.

An hour later, after she'd managed to get her father a room and said a grudging goodnight, she sat on her bed. She retrieved the manuscript from her bag and held it in her naked hands, its nubbled surface like dupioni silk beneath her fingers.

Everything had spiraled out of control. Now her father was making things even more confusing. But this was real, this book. And despite what she now knew of the monk, the truth was that three times in the past two days, Lestinus had proved that he was invaluable to this search, that she did need him, and that she could not do this without him. She possessed all the knowledge she would need to survive this, but without Lestinus, it was hopelessly locked in her head.

She needed Lestinus. Not just to survive this, but to win—to avenge Nicola, to preserve the King's legacy, and, in the end, to secure her own future, though that was now tangential. She also needed Dafydd, and if she was honest, her father, too, if only for logistical purposes.

She'd never needed men before. She hated it. Since her mother died, she'd trusted only women and they had never, ever let her down. Now there were four men—one in an insane asylum, one she hated, one she barely knew, and one who was a figment of her imagination—who held her fate in their hands. And that wasn't counting the ones who were pursuing her.

She turned the manuscript around slowly, considering it again. How much exposure to this mold could she handle? At what point would she lose sanity and become like Harper had been? Institutionalized, incoherent, unstable, unable to think clearly or defend herself? How much time did she have left before that was her fate? How much damage had she already done? She opened the book and ran her hand over the writing.

It didn't matter how much time she had left, as long as it was enough to find the tomb. As long as she could hang on to her sanity and her health for another twenty-four hours, thirty-six at the most, it would be worth it. This was something worth being sick for, maybe worth dying for, as Nicola had known all along. It made all the uncomfortable neediness okay, at least until the job was done.

Carys slowly lifted the manuscript to her face and inhaled as deeply as she could. Her nose tickled as the mold spores entered, then her lungs began to burn slightly. Her head started spinning as she leaned back onto the thick white duvet and waited for Lestinus to tell her what to do next.

He appeared slowly in the corner, clear and crisp.

"Tell me why my mother killed herself," she asked in Latin.

"She was sad," Lestinus said. "A kind of sadness that made her feel like she was already dead. When even you could not bring her the faintest glimmer of joy, she knew it was time. And it wasn't all your father's fault. She was this way long before he left. Though he bears all the blame for what came afterward."

"But she botched it," she said. "She lived for another three weeks, all hooked up to machines. Everyone said it was a cry for attention."

"It was not. She was interrupted," he said. "She meant to die."

"How could she leave me?"

"How could she stay?" he asked. His eyes were filled with the tears she had never been able to cry for her mother.

"Carys, there was one letter from your father that you didn't throw away," he said.

She stared at the monk, trying to understand what one had to do with the other.

There was a soft knock on the door that jolted her out of her head.

"It's Dafydd," came the voice. He entered carrying two wetsuits.

"I figured we should make sure we have the right size for you, or else it's going to be a very uncomfortable dive," he said, smiling. "Let's see which one of these works."

He handed one over.

"I didn't bring a bathing suit," she said. "I wasn't planning on diving this trip."

"Just go naked," he said. "That's what I do. The bathing suit doesn't give you much protection anyway. It's more for modesty's sake."

She took the suit into the bathroom and pulled it on with great effort. It felt like the right size—she'd never worn one this thick before. She was already getting scared, and fear could be deadly underwater.

"How's it going in there?" Dafydd called through the door.

"Good. It fits fine," she yelled out.

"Come out and let me make sure," he said. She hadn't been able to reach the zipper on the back of the suit, and the top of her buttocks was visible. She opened the door.

"Turn around then," he said. She did.

"Nice butt," he said as he zipped her up and spun her around to face him. He smiled, then it dropped away. "Can I ask you something?"

"You've seen my butt, so I guess I have nothing left to hide, do I?"

"Quite right," he said, and sat on the bed, nearly on top of Lestinus, who looked straight at Dafydd, then turned to Carys and pursed his lips with disapproval.

"You shouldn't have strange men in your chambers," Lestinus whispered. Carys rolled her eyes and sat down on the stuffed chair in the corner of the room.

"Fire away," she said.

"Who were you talking to?" he asked.

"What?"

"Who were you talking to just now? I heard you very clearly."

Her words stuck for a second in the back of her throat, then she inhaled and spoke as calmly as she could. "I was just talking to myself."

"No, you weren't," he said. "You were having a conversation with someone in a foreign language. If there were phones in these rooms, I would have sworn you were on it."

"I know," she said, putting on what she hoped was a smile. "It's a crazy habit. Only child. I spent a lot of time alone."

"Uh-huh. If you say so," said Dafydd. "The wetsuit looks pretty good on you."

"Thanks," she said. "Neoprene complements my skin tone, don't you think?"

"Absolutely," said Dafydd. "Let's talk about tomorrow."

"Yes," she said. The fog of her last inhalation of the manuscript was starting to creep back at her. "Sunset is at nine forty-eight tomorrow night. So we should try to get everyone into position by no later than nine. What time do you figure we should push off for the island?"

"It's at least thirty minutes to get over there," said Dafydd. "We'll need to drop you at the boat ramp, which is on the east side of the island. One of you needs to walk over to the west side, the other to the apple tree. I'll show you on a map in the morning. I'll take the boat around to the west side as close as possible to where I think the line of the setting sun will be. The cell service is dodgy at best on the island. I'll get some radios. The pagans will be out in force. They'll be right down by the water—that's where they tend to congregate every year, bloody freaks. The land slopes down pretty sharply to the cliffs on that side, so whichever of you two is at the cliff edge needs to get in front of the crowd. They need to make sure they can see both me and the person next to the apple tree."

"You've thought a lot about this," she said.

"It's an interesting challenge isn't it? Navigation from an ancient book. Literally the only things that we can be sure didn't move on that island since Roman times are the tree and the setting solstice sun, so we're lucky those are the points of reference…"

"And hopefully the cave hasn't moved," said Carys.

"Yes, hopefully," said Dafydd He looked at her for a moment, then another. She started to squirm.

"These caves have been explored for hundreds of years. If you're looking to find something hidden in one of them, it's probably not there anymore."

"I know," she said, her voice wavering slightly. Dafydd pounced.

"What are you looking for?"

"A cave," she said. "Isn't that what I've been telling you?"

"You're lying."

"It occurs to me that I might as well pay you now, before we go," she said. She got up and walked over to the bureau underneath the picture window overlooking the sea. All she could see outside was the white foam on the waves crashing on the shore below, lit up by the lights from the hotel. Her purse was on the bureau, and she reached in. When she turned around, Dafydd was holding the monk's manuscript, which she'd left on the bed.

"Don't…" she said. He moved it out of her reach.

"If you're in danger, then so are your father and I," he said, slowly opening the book.

"That's a very delicate artifact…don't open—"

"I for one would like to know what I am risking my arse for," he said, and began leafing through the book.

She froze, eyes on the manuscript. She could see Lestinus rise up from the bed, a look of fear on his face, his eyes glued to the book as well.

"It's Arthur, isn't it?" Dafydd asked after a long minute. Carys did not answer and willed her face not to betray her. "You're an Arthur hunter."

She kept her eyes on the manuscript.

"That river you were asking me about," said Dafydd. "Afon Gamlan. Come on. We're weaned on that legend here. Bardsey? People have been looking for him there forever. It's like looking for the Loch Ness Monster or El Dorado. What I don't understand is why you'd be in danger from chasing some silly old legend."

Lestinus's nostrils flared, and her anger unexpectedly spiked. The words flew out of her mouth before she even had time to think about what she was saying.

"What if it's not a legend?" she barked as she lunged forward and grabbed the manuscript out of his hands and shook it at him. "This book was written in the sixth century. It's about a leader who lived and fought in Roman Britain during the Anglo-Saxon invasions. And if you know the legend so well, then you tell me who this sounds like—victorious at Badon, routed the invaders time and time again, slain by the Usurper in a battle on the Camlann. It's all in here. And it says that he's buried in that cave."

Lestinus lifted his hand to her.

"Stop," whispered the ghost.

Dafydd's eyes went wide at her outburst, and he stepped back slightly.

"He's in the cave?" asked Dafydd.

"But you know, you're right," she said through gritted teeth. "It's probably all just a silly myth. This ancient book could be just a story about any old Romano-British leader—maybe it's the Arthur of legend, and maybe it's not. It doesn't matter. If he's still down there,

I'm going to find him before someone else does. It's the only way to stop him from coming after me and my family."

"Who?" asked Dafydd. "Who is after you?"

He should know, Carys thought. He had as much right to the truth as her father. They both were now in as deep as she was, and Dafydd was the only one who didn't yet know what he'd signed up for.

"I don't know his name, but he's already killed a woman who helped translate and guard this book. I'm pretty sure he'll kill again if he has the chance."

"Someone's already been killed?" asked Dafydd, his eyes wide. "Why?"

"Because she wouldn't tell him where the manuscript was," she said. "And the manuscript leads to the tomb. And he and his employer really, really want to find the tomb."

"This isn't about finding a tomb," said Dafydd. "People don't kill for skeletons."

"If you don't want to help me, tell me now and I'll find someone else," she said.

"It's treasure, isn't it? There's treasure in that tomb. That's why people kill."

She put the manuscript in its bag, grabbed her wallet, pulled out five hundred pounds, and shoved it at him. "This is all I have right now. I can get you more tomorrow before we head out. I'll give you two thousand pounds total."

Carys swallowed hard. This is what happened when she let her anger bubble up.

Her head started spinning. She grabbed the edge of the bureau to steady herself.

"If you don't die tomorrow, you mean," he said. He looked at her for a long moment. Finally he said, "I'll need one hundred pounds for the boat rental tomorrow." He plucked the cash from her hands, counted out two of the fifties and put the rest on the bureau.

"Thank you," she said, the relief nearly washing her legs out from under her. She honestly had no idea what she would have done if he'd bailed.

"And I'll take a portion of whatever we find in the tomb. Ten percent of the value."

Her anger began to rear up, and she opened her mouth to say… well, she had no idea what. Dafydd smiled. "Or you could try to find someone else to bring you out there tomorrow, on the solstice."

She had no choice. She couldn't do this dive without him.

"Fine," she said. "Ten percent. Do you want me to put it in writing?"

"No. I trust you," he said. "I'm off to bed. Breakfast tomorrow morning?"

"I'll get room service," she sneered, not meeting his eyes.

"Good night, love. Sleep well," he said as he walked out and closed the door quietly behind him.

Carys stood still in the bedroom, seething. And she had no idea how she was going to get the wetsuit off.

◆ ◆ ◆ ◆ ◆

FRANK HAD PARKED JUST UP THE ROAD from the hotel where Carys Jones and her entourage were staying. For the past three hours, he'd stared at the hotel's warm, brightly lit windows beckoning him to come inside. As the night wore on, they flicked out, one by one. Now, the rain hammered the roof of the car and cascaded in sheets down his windshield. He could have yelled at the top of his lungs and it wouldn't have been as loud as the rain.

During the drive up from Mumbles, he had made some decisions. He knew Gyles was going to kill him as soon as this was done. He would be very surprised if there wasn't one of Gyles's contract men—maybe even Tommy—waiting at the dock tomorrow when he returned from this assignment.

So, tomorrow, he was going to follow this group out to the dive site and retrieve whatever they found, and then he'd bring them back to the hotel and convince them to hand over the manuscript and translation. If they didn't find anything, then at least he'd have the books. But no one was going to die. Then he would drive to Cardiff and hop on the first flight to anywhere but London, taking his bargaining chips with him. He'd need them when Gyles, or his hired assassin, came looking for him.

He was never going to kill anyone else ever again—well, except for Gyles if it came down to it, which it probably would. But then that was it. He was done with it. Carys Jones he would just scare. He would leave his gun's safety catch on. He'd let the sight of the weapon do the talking. She didn't deserve the same fate as the maid, not that the maid had deserved it either. *I'm sorry about that, old woman,* he thought.

Jones deserved to just go about her life, look back at this all as a big adventure, go get married and have babies or whatever it was she was going to do before she set off on this ridiculous chase. She was brave, he'd hand her that. But also incredibly stupid if she thought she'd outsmart them. Maybe she and her father would reconcile, although it sure didn't look likely based on their conversation at the bus stop. But it would be good if she did. A daughter needs a father, same as a son does, but for different reasons.

As soon as he had the books and whatever they brought up from the tomb—if they found it—he would head directly for his island in the sun. No need to wait for the big payday. He'd socked away enough. The chasing, the rain, the violence—he was done. Although he might make a call to Scotland Yard—tell them some stories about his friend Martin Gyles.

Frank leaned back in the car, closed his eyes, and dozed for the first time in over twenty-four hours. He dreamt, as he so often did these days, of his mother.

5

⋄⋄⋄⋄⋄⋄⋄

Thursday, the Solstice

Carys lay on the bed, letting the sun stream in. The day had dawned bright and clear. The wetsuit lay in a heap at the foot of her bed. She'd wrestled with it for ten minutes before she'd been able to grab the zipper strap dangling down her back.

Her first waking thought was of Dafydd. She should never have brought him into this. How was she going to explain this to Harper? *Yes, sorry, John, but not only does he know all about our top-secret search for King Arthur, but he's also an equity partner. That work for you?* Who knew what other demands Dafydd would make once they found the tomb? She smiled bitterly. As if that would actually happen. She never pegged him as a mercenary, but that was just foolishness on her part. He salvaged wrecks for a living. He made his money retrieving what other people couldn't. He'd told her that from the beginning. No surprise that he saw this dive the same way. It wasn't a sacred cause to anyone but her, Harper, and Nicola.

And her father…god, this whole thing was just going to shit. But what choice did she have?

If she was honest with herself, she'd had plenty of choices. She could have used a computer and solstice charts and a map to figure out where on the island's coast the line would fall. But that would have involved research and time and, frankly, knowledge that she did not possess, even with Lestinus's help. Doing it manually, on the scene, just seemed like the fastest way, and time was entirely of the essence.

She rolled out of bed naked; she'd been too exhausted to put on her pajamas after doing battle with the wetsuit. She threw on some clothes, went to the hotel restaurant and ordered coffee and some scrambled eggs, and brought them back to her room to eat. And then she had to figure out what she was going to do all day.

As the morning trod on, she watched groups of people, some in long tunics like monks, others in various stages of undress or re-creations of what they imagined ancient pagans dressed like, milling around down near the water. The ferry to Bardsey left packed with them, rounded the headland to the right, and came back empty. It was going to be an absolute carnival over there. Which was probably good. Easier to stay hidden if the bad guy was following them.

At around noon, her father rapped on her door and asked if she wanted to go out for lunch. She declined and strongly recommended that he not venture out. There was no telling who was waiting for them outside. They were going to go out once today, and it was going to be to get into the boat Dafydd had rented and get the hell to Bardsey as fast as they could manage. He said he'd bring a couple of box lunches up to her room and they could just talk. She said no. He said he was doing it anyway.

Anthony came back at one o'clock with two lunches and coffees. He fumbled in, hands filled with an array of sweeteners, milk, and cream.

"I didn't know how you take it," he said, smiling wanly.

No shit, she thought. They sat at the small table by the window.

"How do you like your job?" he asked as they nibbled on their sandwiches.

"Fine," she said. "I like the books."

"Your mother loved to read," he said.

She shot him a hateful glance. His back stiffened.

"Is there anyone special back home?" he asked. She chewed slowly on her sandwich.

"How's your new family?" she asked, staring out to sea.

"All healthy," said Anthony.

"You're still at the university?" she asked.

"Yes," he said. "I love it."

"I'm so glad for you," she said.

Anthony stopped chewing and put down his sandwich. Slowly, he took the napkin and brought it to his lips, wiped, and put the napkin down. He took a sip of his coffee and put the cup down.

"I know you'll never forgive me for leaving," he said. "I'm not asking for your forgiveness. I'm asking you to consider maybe, one day, trying to understand."

She glared at him.

"Fathers leave all the time," she said. "Happens a million times a day. That's easy to understand. You weren't happy. You bolted."

He started to speak. She raised her hand.

"What I'll never understand or forgive is you leaving me behind when my mother died," she said. "But I'm sure you already know that."

Anthony lowered his head.

"I know," he said. "It was wrong. But things were so confusing. I had a new wife and a baby and a new job at the university. We just couldn't bring a grown teenager into the house. We thought you'd be better off if you just stayed where you were, finished school. You're American—the citizenship issues alone would have…. You belonged there. Priscilla agreed it was the best thing for you."

"She got a say and I didn't?" she asked.

"You were a kid," he said.

"Your kid."

"I wrote you every week, and I called. Remember that? For a year. And remember how awful my two visits were. You barely communicated with me. Then you just stopped responding or coming to the phone when I called. It was pretty obvious you didn't want anything to do with me. It's not like we'd had much contact before your mother died."

"I was the child," she said. "You were the parent."

He shook his head, as if he were shaking her words from his mind.

"I supported you and your mother financially," he said. "I worked two jobs while I was going for tenure so you could go to all the best schools. You never wanted for anything."

"No. Just everything," she said. She pushed her sandwich away. "We're done."

She stood up and went into the bathroom, seething yet more exhausted than she could ever remember being. The ache in her abdomen was back, and a raging pain beat between her eyes. She would kick him out and never see him again if she didn't need his help. She was just going to have to deal with it for the next twenty-four hours. She splashed water on her face and opened the door. He was still sitting there, staring out the window. She stood in the doorway, looking at this man whom she didn't know and knew completely.

"Let's talk about tonight," he said. The remnant of a tear smeared his cheek.

"You should go," she said. "I'll come by your room before we leave. I can tell you the details on the boat." She walked over to the door and held it open for him. "Dress warm."

He didn't bother collecting the food off the table. He stood and left.

Carys closed the door and returned to bed. She wanted to sleep for a year. The smell of the sandwiches on the table was cloying. Their beige, half-picked-over triangles reminded her of lunches with her mother. They made her want to cry—she looked out to the bright sunshine to stop the tears. She needed to talk to Annie.

"Did your father find you?" Annie asked without saying hello.

"Yes," she said. "You shouldn't have contacted him."

Annie didn't respond.

"Have you had any luck with that business card I left you?" she asked.

"Yes," said Annie. "We got a hit on the bloody fingerprint on the card. Hottiecakes ran it through the fingerprint database internationally—on the sly, not an official inquiry yet. He also pulled the surveillance footage from the Mass Pike's toll plaza camera. I found the car the thug was driving the night he followed you to your house. Rented, of course. The name came back as a deceased English guy, so he used a fake ID and credit card to rent it. But we got a pretty good photo of him on the Pike cameras. Between that and the bloody fingerprint, we should be able to find out who he is, provided that print belongs to him. I also did some checking about the man whose name was on that business card—Roger Plimpton. He's a pretty well-known antiquities dealer in Birmingham, England—his photo doesn't match the thug's shot from the Pike camera. I have no idea how he's tied up in all this, but I'm going to call him today, see if he'll take a look at the photo of the goon. Hopefully he can tell us something about the guy. I'm getting more info on the fingerprint hit tomorrow. I'm pulling a lot of strings to get info without throwing up an official red flag, Carys, but at some point, people are going to start asking questions. I can't keep this secret much longer."

"I know," she said. "I just need one more day."

◆ ◆ ◆ ◆ ◆

"It's going to be crazy over there," the young receptionist warned. "Are you sure you and your friends want to go?"

Carys smiled and thanked her, and the three of them headed out of the hotel.

"Probably get heckled by pagans for blocking the view," Dafydd said as they walked down the narrow sidewalk. The big Boston Whaler that Dafydd had rented was docked at the marina down the street. It was filled with scuba gear, a few large waterproof flashlights, and a pile of what looked like blankets. Once they were inside, Dafydd released the lines holding the boat to the dock, pushed off, and gunned the twin engines. They roared into life and pushed the boat forward through the blue-gray water. The nose rose up, as if it were straining for the sky. As soon as they entered open water, the boat began to buck on the waves, which seemed to tower above their heads. She grabbed the sides of the boat and held on as tightly as she could.

"Takes a while to get used to the motion," said Dafydd. "Good thing it's a calm day."

About thirty minutes later, they arrived at the Bardsey marina dock. It was occupied by one of the ferries, so they waited just off-shore. Dafydd went to the back of the boat and grabbed two of the blankets.

"I got you a little present," he said, and tossed one of the blankets to her. She unfolded it. It was a hooded wool cassock, just like the ones the pagans were wearing. And very much like the one Lestinus wore.

"It'll be a lot easier to blend in, and if someone is following you, they'll never be able to pick you out of the crowd," Dafydd said. She nodded. It was a good idea. A great one, really.

Anthony pulled a cassock over his head and grinned from beneath the oversized hood.

"*In nomine Patris et Filii et Spiritus Sancti,*" he intoned while crossing himself. Then he pretended to bonk himself on the forehead with an invisible board. Dafydd laughed out loud. She grinned—Monty Python. She hated that her father loved it, too.

"You each get one of these," said Dafydd, holding up two walk-ie-talkies. "I'll hang just off the coast until I see you—who is going down to the cliff edge?"

"I will," she said.

She pulled on her cassock and they tested the radios, which worked fine when they were two feet away from each other. She was struck by just how tenuous and ill-conceived this plan was.

"Anthony, I'll walk with you up to the tree. You stand there," she said. "Then I'll go down to the edge of the cliff until I find a spot where I can see both you and Dafydd. Keep your eyes out for a large, no-necked man who looks out of place among all these hippies."

Dafydd gunned the boat up to the dock once it was clear and Anthony jumped out. Dafydd reached for her arm just as she was about to step onto the dock.

"Be careful," he said earnestly. "I mean it."

She glanced at him.

"I really do want you to find this tomb. I know that didn't come across very well last night," he said.

"That's putting it mildly," she said, and stepped out of the boat. Their eyes connected briefly, then he backed the boat away from the dock, spun it around, drove it between the two buoys that marked the short channel, and sped away south toward the headland and around to the west side of the island.

She felt ridiculous in her cassock until she looked around and realized she and Anthony were the least strange people on the shore. Some of the other revelers were dressed in togas. Some, including several women, were naked. One man had covered himself with mud and was wearing a very small and not entirely effective loin-cloth. She would have stared but she was just glad that she was surrounded by people who were not, in all likelihood, after her or King Arthur's tomb.

They took a narrow dirt road north from the dock across the barren island landscape. They walked in silence, along with about thirty giddy, unsilent pagans, for several minutes. Then the pagans peeled off to head west to the coast. Carys and Anthony continued north toward the treeless green hill that dominated the center of the island. Along its western slope, they'd find the old farmhouse where an apple tree, the oldest apple tree in Wales—perhaps in the world—stood silently tucked up against the wall of a barn, where it was shielded from the worst the Irish Sea could throw at it.

Bardsey wasn't a big island—about a mile across, a few miles long—but what it lacked in width, it made up for in height. The road climbed steadily, and after a few minutes, she noticed that Anthony was breathing heavily. She stopped.

"I'm just not in very good shape," Anthony said between gasps. "I mostly sit on my butt all…day at the college."

"You're doing fine," she said. The air hung still between them. She turned and continued, and a few minutes later, he fell into step behind her. They didn't speak again until they got to the farm, a small single-story whitewashed building with a thatched roof and dark green shutters. A half-hearted fence surrounded it. The place had become a B&B, and there was no activity anywhere. The occupants were likely down by the shore.

"We should probably not invade their property," she said. "The last thing we need is to have you chased away by an angry islander. Just keep the tree to your back and guide me into line when the sun sets. Check the radios."

As they looked toward the west, they saw clusters of people gathered on a slight rise by the shore about a quarter mile from where they were standing. She couldn't see the immediate shoreline, as Dafydd had predicted, but she assumed Dafydd had made it around to that point by then. She grabbed her radio.

"Dafydd, this is Carys. Are you there?"

She heard her voice come out of Anthony's radio, but there was no answer from Dafydd. She set off down the slope of the hill toward the crowds. Lestinus appeared and fell into step next to her.

"It has not changed since we were here," he said.

"Let's hope the coastline hasn't scrambled things too badly since then," she said. "The ocean levels have changed a lot in this part of the world."

Down below on the hillside, a slow drumbeat pounded. She could see some of the revelers dancing in slow, indeterminate movements. It looked like a seaside Woodstock. After a few minutes, she got near the top of the cliffs that dropped down to the sea and found herself engulfed by throngs of pagans and assorted solstice tourists. The drum was percussive now, and she could feel it in her chest. From where she stood, she could see Dafydd and the Boston Whaler tossing mightily on the rough waves below. He was hanging back, about a hundred yards offshore.

"The caves were in the side of the cliff," said Lestinus. "We had to climb down and then lower him. It took us a day to get him into his tomb. We had to do it all over again when we brought our people's belongings back here to bury with him for safekeeping. It was excruciating. The water is so high now. The mouth of the cave will be underwater. We never could have gotten him and the people's treasures into the cave the way it is now."

"If his tomb has been underwater, it's probably disintegrated, you know," she said.

"It's stone, and we sealed it well," he said.

"How can I open it?" she asked.

"You shouldn't. Let him sleep. Just knowing he is there is enough."

She stared at him for a moment.

"Dafydd," she said into the radio. "I'm in position. Can you hear me?"

A moment of static ripped over the radio, then a click.

"Loud and clear," came Dafydd's voice. "Wave to me so I know which of those freaks is you."

She slowly waved her hand above her head.

"Got ya," he said.

"Carys, you're still coming in on this end, too," said Anthony's voice, "although I can't hear Dafydd."

"Sounds good, Anthony," she said, looking back. She could see him standing by the house, directly between the tree and her.

"Now, we wait," she said. A man in a feathered hat standing next to her smiled.

"Yes, we wait," said the man. "Isn't it exciting?"

"Very," she said with a half smile.

Lestinus turned slowly, surveying the crowds.

"The godless pagans," he said. "Unwashed. No morals. They worship trees and rocks."

"That much hasn't changed in a millennium, has it?" she asked in Latin quietly.

It was 9:43 p.m. The sky was miraculously still clear, a rarity at this time of year, or at any time of year in this part of the world. For a moment, she let the heat of the fading light penetrate her. It was so beautiful here. She willed the beating of the drum, which matched that of her heart, to draw away some of the tension.

Suddenly, a pain stabbed like a knife into her abdomen and doubled her over. The man in the feathered hat reached for her. With difficulty, she stood back upright.

"Just indigestion," she said to the man, a cold sweat breaking out on her forehead.

"Too much partying last night, huh?" he said. She smiled faintly while trying not to collapse. The pain was now spreading out and dulling. Diving was probably the very worst thing for it. She took three deep breaths and stood up straight.

The sun kissed the horizon. The walkie-talkie chirped.

"About fifty feet to your right, Carys," said Anthony. She side-stepped people as she made her way through the crowd. "That's good. Hold right there."

She stopped and saw that Dafydd was now slightly to the left of where he needed to be. She directed him over until the boat was silhouetted in the sun as half of it sank below the waves.

"How we looking?" she asked, looking back toward Anthony.

"Perfectly lined up," he said. She could barely hear him above the crescendo of the maddening drumbeat and chants of the crowd. Lestinus stood silently next to her, taking it all in. She radioed down to Dafydd.

"You're right on," she said. "Drop the first buoy now."

Dafydd scrambled to the back of the boat and dropped an anchor attached by a rope to an orange, triangular float.

"Move forward now," she called. "We've only got a minute of sun left."

The boat motored forward. She directed him slightly to the right, then left, then, just as the sun slipped down below the horizon, she saw him drop the second buoy. Together, they pointed to the exact spot on the shore that was between the apple tree and "the last light of the fat sun," as Taliesin had called it. She felt a shiver up her arms.

"I'll see you both back at the dock," she said into her radio. She pushed her way through the crowd and looked up to see the purple glow upon the farmhouse and the tree. The mother tree, shaking lightly in the ocean breeze. It had seen Arthur buried. Tonight, it might see him again.

Around her, hundreds of people swayed and sang. Some cried, some prayed on their knees. A man in a cassock walked toward her. She thought it was Lestinus until he veered sideways, embraced a naked woman, and swung her around.

◆ ◆ ◆ ◆ ◆

BY THE TIME CARYS AND ANTHONY GOT BACK to the main dock on the other side of the island, Dafydd was waiting for them. They hopped into the boat and sped back through the pounding waves to where he had placed the buoys. The lingering twilight had turned the ocean purple, and the temperature was falling fast. She wondered if she'd get to see the sun again.

Getting into the wetsuit was even more difficult in the back of the rocking boat than it had been in her hotel room, but by swallowing every ounce of modesty and with some help from both Dafydd and Anthony, she got the thing on. Dafydd watched her carefully as she put on her tank vest, weights, and regulator, to ensure that she at least appeared to know a little bit about what she was doing. It was a task made more difficult in the fading light. She put her mask on upside down at first, then quickly corrected it.

Dafydd went through a short overview of the usage of the equipment. She absorbed it all, pretending that it was all just an unnecessary review.

"I'll swim next to you until we get to the cave, then I'll be behind you," said Dafydd. "Never out of view of each other, got it? At the first sign of trouble, thumbs-up means we're surfacing, no matter what. I mean it. This"—he made a circle of his thumb and forefinger, the A-okay sign—"means we're good to go."

"Got it," she said.

"We have about one hour of air," he said. "If you hyperventilate, you'll go through it even faster, so breathe steady and slow." He switched on a flashlight and slipped its strap around her wrist. He clipped another one to her belt.

Dafydd sat on the edge of the boat and dropped over backward with a quiet splash into the darkness. Her heart pounded furiously.

"Deep breaths," said Lestinus and Anthony, in unison. She gave them both a thumbs-up, then corrected herself and flashed the A-okay sign. She sat on the edge, grabbed her facemask, and dropped over.

She fell into a tight, black, bitter cold nothingness. The sound of bubbles consumed her, and she lost all sense of the surface. She'd forgotten this part, the confusion. The freezing water dug into her skin like a thousand tiny knives. For a moment, she panicked and began to struggle against the water. She gasped for air, and the mouthpiece dug into her gums. She wanted up and she wanted up now.

Then a voice, this time her own, told her clearly that the panic would ruin everything. She had to get herself under control or this dive would be over before it had even begun. She willed herself into stillness and she forced herself to slow her breathing, to let go of the panic, to let the water take her wherever it wanted. Her vest began to float her up. She surfaced slowly in the roiling water, next to Dafydd.

Anthony pointed his high-powered flashlight toward the coast to the spot where the buoys were aiming. Somewhere below that spot of light would be a hole in the wall of rock, an entrance to a cave, inside of which would lie the tomb of the King—if the manuscript was true, if the coastline hadn't shifted or changed or eroded too much, if they'd interpreted the ancient Welsh words correctly, if no one had found it already and cleaned it out…if, if, if.

Dafydd flashed her the A-okay sign. She flashed it back— although it was another of her lies. He submerged slowly, letting the air out of his vest. She did the same. They sank silently into the blackness. She began to warm, but pressure built in her ears. She pinched her nose and blew through it gently, and her ears cleared. She swam along, trying to focus on keeping her breathing steady, but she was not in shape.

This was all an incredibly bad idea.

She and Dafydd surfaced periodically to find the spot of light on the shore and make sure they were on the right track. Then down they went again. Swimming was a lot easier under the waves.

After fifteen minutes of kicking into an endless impenetrable blackness about six feet down, Carys began to feel the water pushing and pulling her strongly back and forth in a rhythmic pattern— waves. They were near the rocks. Then the light from both of their flashlights fell on a sheer wall of rock that loomed up in the darkness. She shined her flashlight down, through the clear, frigid water, and the wall seemed to have no bottom. Dafydd shined the light on himself and turned his thumb down, to indicate they should descend. They slowly dropped down along the wall of rock that had once been an exposed cliff.

After they dropped about twenty feet, Dafydd flashed his light at her. They hadn't encountered anything that looked like a cave opening yet. They slowly kicked across the face of the cliff to the right, sweeping the flashlights up and down the cliff face in opposite directions, looking for something like an opening. She felt her limbs and abdomen relaxing into a comfortable, slightly warmer state. The fear was beginning to dissipate. She began to kick her legs more slowly and deeply and she thought she heard…

Something like a giant hand grabbed her, shoved her, rapidly and with a force she had never experienced, directly into the cliff face. She hit with a force that dislodged her mask and filled it partially with water, and smashed her arm. She worked to contain her panic. She tried to reach up and adjust the mask, but she was being dragged, like a doll, down the face of the craggy cliff, down, down, faster and faster, as if she were falling through air.

Water washed into her mask and blinded her completely. She grabbed for her mouthpiece as she smashed again and again into the cliff wall. Pain shot into her arm, her hip, her leg as each hit the cliff face. She could hear the tank's metallic clunk as it too bounced along the wall. Then her arm was yanked back, as if by a forceful, angry hand, and with it went the regulator. She swallowed a small amount of water but it was enough to make her gag. She couldn't see anything and she was falling and flailing, trying to put the mouthpiece back in her mouth.

With a clank, she landed on her back on something hard. The powerful hand was holding her down on top of rocks. Her eyes were closed tightly against the stinging salt water. Her lungs began to burn, her mouth full of saltwater. Panic slowly filled her, but she held it partially at bay. She began to windmill her arms behind her, searching for either her primary or backup regulator. She couldn't find them.

She let the panic take over. She began to scratch at the rocks to right herself and get to the surface. But the powerful force of the water, or whatever it was, held her firmly in place. She was drowning. This was how it ended.

An instant later, a mouthpiece was being guided into her mouth, the air flowing strongly through it. She clamped down and inhaled the fresh, beautiful oxygen. There were hands on her shoulders, human hands this time, pulling her horizontally along the tops of the rocks, and then she felt the pressure ease on her body and she began to float again. Her mask was adjusted against her face. She let herself go limp for a moment and tried to get her breathing under control. The hands on her shoulders helped.

She held the top rim of her mask with her hand and began to blow water out of her nose. As the water drained away, she opened her eyes. Through the window of the mask was Dafydd's face. His eyes were wide but not panicked. He had his regulator in his mouth, and she had his secondary in hers. He had her primary in his hand and was pushing her regulator's purge button. Air bubbled out in spurts. It was working fine. It was dangling off her tank right near her right shoulder, exactly where it was supposed to be. How had she missed it?

She took a few more breaths until she felt her heart slow down. She removed his secondary regulator and put hers into her mouth. He waited, breathing in the air slowly and calmly, as if nothing out of the ordinary had just happened. They sat there on the bottom of the ocean together for a few moments, lit by the flashlights, looking at each other. She was alive. She was not going to die. Not at the moment anyway.

Dafydd reached over and touched her shoulder. With his other hand, he made the A-okay sign. She flashed it back to him, then again, so he knew she meant it. He swung around and pointed the flashlight above them at something on the cliff wall.

There was an opening in the cliff, about four feet wide, ten feet above the ocean floor. In front of the opening was an enormous flat boulder that ran like a second wall parallel to the cliff about four feet away from it. There was just enough room for a person to get between the boulder and the cliff. It was just like the bookshelf that obscured the opening to the vault at Adeona. If they hadn't been exactly where they were, looking over at the wall from this precise angle, they would not have been able to see the cave.

They kicked gently over to the tall, flat boulder and pointed their flashlights around its base. It was smoother than anything surrounding it, almost as if it had been hand-hewn. It was about seven feet wide, and the sides were almost completely vertical. It had an unusually uniform thickness, about two feet for its entire height, which she estimated to be about fifteen feet. Its top was slightly rounded. It reminded her of something.

The longer she moved the flashlight across it, the more convinced she was that it was man-made. Dafydd swam at its base, examining something there. He wiggled his flashlight at her to get her attention and then laid his flashlight on the ground, pointed right at the base where the rock met the sand. The light hit a deep, straight vertical scratch in the rock. With both hands, he very gently and slowly began to brush the soil away from the base where the scratch dropped down below the dirt.

As Dafydd moved the dirt and rocks aside, the water filled with silt, and before long they were surrounded and temporarily blinded by the reflected light. When he finished digging, he swam backward with the flashlight and waited for the silt to dissipate. As it did, on the side of the rock, there emerged a carving, about eight inches in diameter.

It was a circle quartered by a cross—an ancient Christian cross.

Dafydd looked up at her. She looked at him. Then he raised two fists high above his head in a victory stance. She couldn't help but laugh through her regulator.

Now for the hard part.

Dafydd swam slowly around the boulder and into the small space between it and the cliff wall. She came in from the other side. He motioned for her to go into the cave. Protocol was for the less experienced person to go first. That way, if she got stuck, he could still get out. Go for help. Only one person had to die. If this was the cave they were seeking, it had to be big enough for a group of men to be able to bring a makeshift casket through it—or whatever they had used to carry the King. If it got too narrow, they would know it wasn't the right one and they'd back out. Unless it had collapsed in the fifteen hundred years since.

All that was left to do, finally, was to go in and see.

Carys pointed her flashlight farther into the opening. The cave became wider once they entered its mouth. She swam in, focusing all her mental energy on keeping her breathing steady. Silvery fish flashed like shots of light past them.

It must have been excruciating to bring Arthur down through here. One of the men must have scouted it beforehand. Where the tunnel walls pushed inward, the rock walls sported long scratches. They looked like the doorjamb at her apartment after she'd tried to push a too-wide table through it. She and Dafydd swam on, and the tunnel leveled out flat and opened up wider, then began to climb upward again.

In about twenty yards, the tunnel split into two distinct paths. They both knew better than to split up. Dafydd motioned to the one on the right. Carys glanced at the walls inside both tunnels, and only one—the one on the left—had scratch marks.

She pointed at the scratches and motioned for them to go left. They swam on, the bubbles clinging like liquid mercury to the cave's ceiling before dancing off farther into the cave. Her heart began to pound a little faster, but from anticipation this time, not fear.

After about seventy-five feet, the tunnel narrowed and stopped—a dead end.

She stopped swimming. This was the right way, she knew it, but a rockfall blocked their way. She swam up to it and shined her flashlight along the walls on either side of the blockage. The white scratches dug into the wall right up to the fallen rocks and disappeared into them. She spun around slowly, wiggled her light at Dafydd, and pointed straight ahead. He shook his head no. She knew she was asking for something that was not only dangerous but violated one of the basic principles of diving—disturb nothing. But this was different.

She nodded her head emphatically yes and stabbed her finger toward the rocks and the scratch marks on the wall. She swam back away from the wall, and Dafydd swam toward it and reached for the rock at the top of the stack. He gave it a push. It didn't move. He pushed again. Again nothing.

She swiped her flashlight beam back and forth along every inch of the rockfall. On the third pass, she saw something she'd missed before: a rock, almost perfectly spherical, of pure white marble—it matched no other rocks she'd seen on the dive. It was at the very bottom of the rockfall, nearly obscured beneath a larger rock. She swam in closer to it, got right down at the level of the floor, and shined her light on it, brushing away the sand that had accumulated around its base.

As the full stone was revealed, Carys noticed a series of indentations on it. She leaned in closer. There, in tiny Latin script, were etched the letters "*SUSCITATEVIVEQUE.*"

Wake and live.

She turned to Dafydd, her heart pounding. She pointed at the rock. He swam in close and looked at it. He turned back to her, his eyes wide underneath his mask. She pointed at the rock again and made a rolling motion with her hands. He motioned for her to get back. She obeyed.

When she turned back around, she saw Dafydd reach down and shove the white stone to the left, then swim toward her as fast as he could in an explosion of effort. There was a thud, then a crack that pierced the silence of the tunnel, like wooden twigs snapping. The lowest row of stones seem to drop down, underneath the rockfall. Then the wall of stones collapsed methodically downward into itself—not backward or forward but inward, the way a building implodes, as if the whole thing were dropping into a chamber below the tunnel.

Dafydd, who had pressed himself against the side of the tunnel, turned in shock to look at Carys. She flashed him an A-okay. When the silt cleared, they could see open water on the other side.

They swam on and the tunnel veered sharply upward again. She led the way. They were so close. She could feel it. For one short moment, she let herself hope that maybe this was really going to happen.

Then the pain hit her. It started in her center and radiated like a shockwave through the rest of her body and her limbs, convulsing her completely.

She doubled into a fetal position. She could not breathe or think or process what was happening—her mind was filled only with the pain. She felt Dafydd grab her shoulders and turn her toward him. He motioned with his thumb. *Up.*

She could not let that happen. She pulled away and kicked her legs hard, every stroke torture, sending herself deeper into the cave as it climbed upward. It had to be here. Somewhere. She had to know, even if it was the last thing she ever knew.

The narrow cave widened before her into an enormous black void. With knife strikes of pain in her midsection, she kicked up, up.

And then her head popped out of the water. She instinctively ripped out her mouthpiece and inhaled what she prayed would be air.

It was.

Dafydd surfaced behind her. The light from their flashlights shined on their faces, and his was filled with the beginnings of panic. Seeing this made her more scared.

"What's wrong?" he asked.

"I'm okay," she said. "I'll be okay." She was sure of it. Oh hell, she wasn't sure. That was another of her lies. But they were almost there. That was something that she did know, as certainly as she knew her own name.

"We have to get you back out," he said. "What's happening?"

"I don't know," she said. "Whatever it was, it's done."

Dafydd's face turned resigned as he realized he was going to lose the fight. He shined his flashlight past Carys's head, upward, to illuminate the space they were in. It seemed, for a moment, to have no limits. But as their eyes adjusted, they could see that they were in an enormous underwater cavern, a huge natural cathedral filled with stalactites, like statues of the twenty thousand saints, dangling from the ceiling. Some nearly touched the water.

And there, in front of them, was a flat platform carved like a stage into the wall of the cavern. Upon it rested a rectangular object, huge, of dirty white stone. On the side facing them, etched into the side, was the same symbol that had adorned the enormous rock slab that marked the entrance to the cave: an ancient Christian cross.

Tears sprang from Carys's eyes, from pain or joy, she couldn't tell.

"Oh my god," said Dafydd softly. "It's here."

Dafydd's light illuminated a series of stone steps that extended from the stage down into the water and continued down far beneath where they were swimming. He grabbed her vest and swam her up to the stairs, and they rested there, half in and half out of the water. Dafydd sat staring at the sarcophagus. Then he turned to her.

"What's going on? Tell me what you're feeling," he said.

"It's just an abdominal thing," she said. "It happened a few days ago, but I thought it was nothing."

"It's obviously not nothing," he said. "We've got to get you back out of here." He grabbed her air gauge. "We're low."

She smiled wanly. The pain was beginning to abate.

"We have to look inside it," she said. "We have to see if he's there."

"No," said Dafydd. "We have to get you out of here. We can come back now that we know where it is."

"No. We may not get another shot at this," she said. "I am going nowhere until we open that tomb."

She knew he wanted to look, too. If she could stand, he'd see she was alright. She hoisted herself with her arms up another stair so she was completely out of the water. She unclipped her tank vest.

"Help me with this," she said.

Dafydd looked at her for a moment, unmoving, then reached over and held up the tank and she pulled her arms out of the vest. She pulled off her fins and stood up. The pain in her stomach was still there but not as knife-like.

The stage was in a large alcove with a rounded back wall. The floor was about ten feet deep and twelve or fifteen feet wide. The alcove extended up about ten feet before merging again with the cave's natural contours. It looked like an enormous version of the tiny nooks carved in church walls that hold statues of the Virgin and saints. There was nothing else on the floor of the alcove but the sarcophagus. It had been carved directly out of the cave's stone. It could never be moved. It was enormous—about four feet high, eight feet long and four feet wide. Dafydd stripped off his gear and came to stand beside her.

It was a remarkable work of art. A treasure unto itself. As permanent a thing as the people of that time could create. One of the last human beings to stand in this spot was likely Lestinus, offering his benediction over his master's casket. She wished he was with her so he could see the tomb again—and then wondered briefly why he wasn't. Perhaps her mind was so focused on the task at hand that there was no bandwidth for hallucinations.

"Where do we start?" asked Dafydd.

She bent over to examine the stone more closely. The lid, about three inches thick, fit cleanly with no gaps between it and the sides of the sarcophagus. She marveled at the workmanship. There was no way Arthur's men could have built this, and certainly not the alcove. It must have already been built, reserved for the burial of someone very important.

She put her hands on the edge, Dafydd joined her, and slowly they pushed. The lid slid away a few inches without much resistance. They looked at each other. It shouldn't have been that easy.

"Let's keep going. Very gently. Twist it away to the side so we don't have to lift it off."

Dafydd walked to the far end, and pushing the lid clockwise, they angled the lid so it was resting across the top of the sarcophagus.

She stepped back. So did Dafydd. They looked at each other, and the same fire burned for a moment in their eyes. Moving slowly, her awareness of the pain in her gut all but gone, she stepped to the side of the sarcophagus and pointed her flashlight inside.

There was nothing in it.

The pain rushed back, but this time it was from the clench of her heart. Her face must have fallen, because Dafydd moved next to her and looked in.

"Empty," he said. "It's bloody empty."

"It can't be empty," she said. "It's not possible. No one has been here."

She bent her body over the top of the tomb and stuck her head as far inside as it would go, to the point where it looked like she might climb in. She swept her flashlight back and forth deep inside.

There, in the very end of the tomb underneath where the lid obscured their view from above, were three lumpen objects.

She grabbed Dafydd's dry bag off his vest and took out a package of sterile gloves. With a grunt, she reached as far back as she could into the tomb and grabbed the objects. They were two leather sacks and a manuscript, bound in red leather and grander than the

Lestinus manuscript. She placed the two sacks on the floor of the alcove. Dafydd reached down for them.

"Don't touch," she said. "Please."

He backed away, a frown on his face. He had expected treasure—books were not treasure to him.

Carys carefully peeled back the cover to reveal the first page of the manuscript. It was handwritten, the penmanship good, the ink still surprisingly strong given its obvious age. The first page opened with the words "*Peregrinatio mea—Madoc Morfran.*" My journey—Madoc Morfran. She turned the page and translated it out loud for Dafydd. "I am Madoc Morfran, the son of Riothamus Arcturus, and herein I tell of my voyage to the place across the sea. It is there that Arcturus lies with the gentle people of the sand."

"Arthur," said Dafydd. "You were right. That manuscript was..."

Her mind was spinning, and she placed the manuscript on the top of the tomb.

Arthur's son had taken him away and buried him somewhere else.

She dropped to the floor. When was this going to end? She sat there and let it sink in, trying not to cry.

How would she ever tell Lestinus? He would be devastated. Then she remembered and felt like a fool.

She reached over and picked up the first sack, and pulled open the top. It, too, was in remarkably good condition. The air temperature, unchangeable humidity, and lack of sunlight inside the tomb must have conspired to create perfect preservation conditions. She reached into the sack and drew out a small object—a gold brooch, about two inches across, with a small red stone at its center. The design was clearly mid-sixth-century Romano-British. Dafydd stepped forward to look more closely.

"Bloody hell," he whispered.

She slowly pulled out seven more golden objects—combs, pins, belt hardware—each adorned with rough-cut, colored precious gems. She lined them up on the floor.

"These belonged to the people Arthur defended from the Anglo-Saxon hordes," she said. "They left their wealth with Arcturus and his men with the hopes of retrieving it when the hordes were defeated."

"That didn't work out quite as planned, did it?" he asked, leaning over to examine the objects closely with his flashlight.

"Nope," she said, and slowly returned each item to the sack, which she then placed in the dry bag. She grabbed the second sack. It was much lighter. She slid open the pouch and reached in. She couldn't quite get her cold fingers around the tiny objects in this sack, so she gently dumped them out into her hand.

It took her a minute to realize what she was looking at. There was a seashell. A carved, flattened stone—like an arrowhead—made of some sort of white rock. And seeds. A few that were very tiny, and several larger, almost like kernels of corn.

"What on earth…?" she asked.

"Is that what I think it is?" asked Dafydd, pointing at a shell. "Why would someone put this stuff in a coffin?"

She shook her head. Dafydd placed his hand on her shoulder.

"We need to go," he said. "And we'll need to surface as soon as we get out of the cave. We're too low on air to swim underwater all the way back to the boat."

They closed the sarcophagus, put their scuba gear back on, stowed the dry bag with the manuscript and the two leather pouches in Dafydd's satchel, and lowered themselves back into the icy water. They kicked steadily back the way they'd come without interruption. Her stomach pains stayed relatively in check, and she felt calmer than she had on the way in, although a twinge in her side let her know that things weren't entirely right.

They slid silently back out of the cave opening, navigated around the tall stone pillar and into the pushing and pulling of the dark, surging waves. Dafydd pointed the flashlight at himself and signaled for them to swim out a little farther, away from the shore, the rocks, and the downdraft. About thirty yards out, the wave action seemed to lessen and they slowly surfaced.

Once their heads broke into the cool, fresh breeze, they removed their masks and let their eyes adjust to the relative brightness of the moonlit night. Dafydd began to raise his flashlight out of the water to signal at Anthony. Then, he paused.

"Carys," he said. "Turn off your light. Now."

She obeyed.

"How many boats do you see?" he asked.

In the fading light of the solstice, aided by the glow of a newborn full moon, Carys could see their Whaler bobbing up and down on the waves. Just one boat, she thought. Then, for just a split second, she saw the bow of another boat poke out from behind the front of theirs. She peered more closely. There was someone on the Whaler with Anthony.

"Police maybe?" she asked, gasping out the words between waves. "Marine patrol?"

"Nothing like that out here. How many people do you see? I see one with Anthony."

She willed her eyes to focus despite the wind blowing into her face.

"I see one," she said. *It's the thug*, she thought. *Who else would it be? But how?*

"Can we swim to shore? Call for help?" she asked.

"Nowhere to get out of the water," said Dafydd. "All cliff this side."

"Back to the cave? Wait him out?"

"Not enough air," he said.

They let the inevitable sink in for a moment.

"We have to go to the boat," she said.

"I know," he said. "All I have is a knife."

"We don't have a choice. We can't take the manuscript on the boat. Got enough air to hide the dry bag in the cave opening? We can get it later."

"Another diver could find it," he said. "Or it could be swept away."

"We can't risk bringing it on that boat," she said.

"Right. Hang tight." Dafydd began to swim back to the shore, and at the last minute, just before he was about to get pulled into the rocks, he went under and was gone.

Carys bobbed in the water, kicking slowly, and watched the figures move around on the boat about a hundred feet away. There was definitely just the one guy with Anthony. He was big. That big head. The lack of a neck. The slope of the shoulders. It was him. The goon.

All she and Dafydd had were the element of surprise and the darkness.

When he surfaced next to her, she had a plan. It wasn't a great plan, but it was the only one they had.

A few minutes later, Dafydd dropped his tank, vest, fins, and weight belt to the ocean floor and they split up. Carys, still in full gear, swam straight for the back of their boat. Dafydd set off on a silent swim to the left of where they'd surfaced, in a wide arc that would bring him around to the far side of the boats.

As she got closer, Anthony spotted her splashing through the waves. He began to raise his hands to warn her off, but the goon, directly behind him, jammed something in his neck and he stopped.

She pretended she hadn't seen anything. She swam up to the stern of their boat, gripped the platform next to the engine, and readied her best performance. Anthony leaned over the stern, looking down at her.

"Anthony," she said, gasping dramatically. "The cave. It collapsed. Dafydd is trapped down there. We have to send for help." Anthony said nothing and made no move to her. "Did you hear me? Radio for help right away."

"Carys, I think…" Anthony began, but then the thug's head came around Anthony's shoulder and looked down at her.

"Hello, Carys."

"Who are you?" asked Carys, feigning great shock.

"Ah, you don't remember me? We met at your house. I came to see how your dive went," said the goon. "Find anything good?"

"The cave collapsed," she said. "My dive guide is trapped down there and he's running out of air. We have to get help. Anthony, radio for help."

"I'd be pleased to help, but first I need to know what you found," said the man. Anthony stood frozen.

"We found nothing," she said, still clinging to the boat. "The rocks came down before we were able to get very far. Help me out— we need to get help right away."

Anthony made a move to grab her, and the man jammed the object, which she could now see was a gun, into the back of his neck.

◆ ◆ ◆ ◆ ◆

FRANK COULD FEEL THE MAN SHAKING against him, and it wasn't because he was cold. No matter how often he held a gun on a man, watching him beg for his life, it gave him a sense of control that he felt at no other time in his life.

"Please, call for help on the radio," said the woman. It sounded genuine. She looked scared. Of course, now that she'd seen the gun, he expected her to be scared.

"Pull her out," he said to the father. The man stepped over the transom of the boat and onto the small ledge next to the engine. He started to bend from the waist, toward the water, and reached out his hand toward the woman. She reached up to grab it.

He moved the gun away from the father's neck and opened his mouth to tell them that all he wanted was the treasure and the books and he'd be on his way.

"I..." he began.

Out of the corner of his eye, he caught a glint of moonlight off a large swell rearing up to his left. It was moving fast and it rose up underneath them. Before he knew it, the world shifted underneath the rolling giant.

Everyone and everything in the boat was shoved hard to the right. He grabbed the gunwale to steady himself, and he heard the father fall down into the water, right on top of the woman. The two immediately disappeared under the waves.

He righted himself, still holding on to the gunwale. He spun around to reach into the water to pull the two out. He felt a little panicked, worried that maybe they were drowning. That wasn't what he wanted. Not at all.

As he started to bend over, something heavy and swift crashed down on the back of his skull. The world instantly went black. He dropped hard to the floor of the boat.

The last thing he saw as his brain closed down was a slow parade of the faces of every person he'd ever killed, with the face of the maid lingering longest. He panicked very briefly as he realized what was happening, the utter finality of it, there in the solitude and blackness of his mind. Then he was washed by a great relief and a final brief image of his mother, smiling, improbably; she never smiled...*she barely even looks at me anymore when we talk I love you Mum I'm sorry I'm so sorry I never wanted*...then there was total release.

◆ ◆ ◆ ◆ ◆

CARYS SURFACED, HER HEAD POUNDING. She grabbed the back of the boat, yelling before her eyes were even clear.

"Anthony!" she yelled. Dafydd stood on the back of the boat with the boat's small fire extinguisher in his hands. Just then Anthony surfaced, coughing hard, right next to her. She grabbed him around the waist.

"Anthony!" she yelled. "Dafydd, help us."

She felt a hand on her scuba vest, hauling her up. She sat down hard on the platform next to the engine. She opened her eyes to see Dafydd.

"Are you hurt?" he asked, his eyes wild.

"No," she said. "Anthony?"

"I'm alright," she heard Anthony yell from the water.

"Where's the gun?" she asked. "The man…"

Dafydd said nothing as he pulled Anthony up onto the back of the boat.

She spun to look behind her and saw the man splayed out, his head resting in an enormous pool of dark fluid. She cried out.

"I had no choice," said Dafydd, reaching for her, holding her by her arms. She looked into his eyes as best she could in the shifting light.

"Is he dead?"

"I think so," said Dafydd. "I haven't checked."

She took off her fins and vest, then moved to the body. She pressed two fingers against the side of the thick, muscular neck, the warmth already draining away. There was no pulse.

"Oh my god," she said.

Dafydd and Anthony exchanged glances, and there was a short silence but for the slapping of the waves.

"We've got to put him in the other boat," said Dafydd. "Take it out to sea. Drop him over. Let the boat drift. I'm not going to jail."

"It was self-defense," she said.

"So we say," said Dafydd.

They stood silently for a moment. She looked at Dafydd, waiting for him to speak again. He didn't.

"Let's get going," said Anthony.

"He's right. We need to move," said Dafydd. "We need to get out of here."

With a businesslike manner she found disturbing, Anthony and Dafydd hauled the bulky body over the side into the other vessel and dropped it on the floor with a great thud. The sound nause-ated her. Dafydd took the helm of the thug's boat, and Anthony, wiping his hands down again and again, came back aboard their boat and approached her. He stood in front of her for a moment, then reached out and embraced her—and for the first time in decades, she returned the embrace.

"I thought he was going to kill you," she said.

"I'm fine," he said, holding onto her. "We're going to be fine."

They drove both boats at full throttle for about an hour directly west. When they finally stopped, there were no lights visible from land, from buoys or from any other boats. The only light was the moon and the reflection off the gathering waves, which tossed their two vessels around like bathtub toys. She sat at the bow of their Whaler as the two men readied the thug's body for his voyage to the bottom. There was a splash. She lowered her head. They were murderers. No matter why it had happened, no matter if it was self-defense, it was done. And it was entirely on her.

Dafydd started the other boat's engine, steered it around to face west, locked the steering column, and jumped back onto their boat. They watched as the empty vessel plowed slowly and deliberately through the waves and swells, on its solitary journey far out in the Irish Sea.

Dafydd came up to the bow a moment later. She was shivering. He sat next to her on the bow seat, wrapped a blanket and then his arm around her, and pulled her close.

"I'm so sorry," she said. "I didn't mean for any of this to happen. We will never report this. We'll never talk about it. To anyone, ever. It never happened."

"I'd do it again," he said. "I didn't think it was real, Carys. I thought you were just another crackpot. Now…I…I'm in. Whatever you need. This isn't business anymore."

"You should get as far away from me as you can," she said.

"I've spent my entire, boring life on this stretch of Welsh coast-line. So have my parents, and their parents before them. You're the most interesting thing that has ever happened to me, Carys Jones," he said. She looked up at him, and he was slightly smiling. "I'm in. All the way."

She grabbed his hand resting on her shoulder and squeezed it tightly.

"Whether you like it or not," she said.

An hour later, they were back at the buoys marking the dive site and Dafydd was in the water. He emerged a short time later with his pack containing the dry bag. He got in, took the helm of the boat, turned it toward the mainland, and pushed the throttle forward as far as it would go.

6

Friday, June 22

The trio crept back through Aberdaron to their hotel. It was just before three in the morning. The last of the pagans were drifting through town, nodding drunkenly to them as they passed. Carys was still shaking, frozen to the core and sure she would never be warm again. The three of them plodded, exhausted, up the stairs. Her numb fingers fumbled with the keys. Dafydd took them gently and opened her door. They all entered her room and arranged themselves on the chairs and bed and stared off in different directions, immersed in their own version of the night.

Finally, Dafydd broke the silence.

"Let's show your father what we got."

Dafydd pulled the dry bag out of his pack and laid it out on the bed next to her. She looked over at it, and a flash of anger passed through her. *That's it*, she thought. *That's what this was all about. We paid two lives for these sacks and another manuscript? We've become murderers for this?* She felt an indifference to the contents of the bag that she couldn't have imagined just twelve hours earlier. She resented it and what it had put her through. And she couldn't stop that resentment from slowly bleeding over to Harper. The old man. Safe in an asylum. Giving orders that he knew he'd never have to carry out. What had he thought he was doing getting her involved in this? And what had she been thinking getting Dafydd and Anthony involved in it?

"Carys, open the bag," said Anthony. He shivered slightly, and semicircles of gray formed hard under his eyes. His lips were tinged with blue, his graying hair swept up and matted into odd shapes by the salt wind. He was slumped in the lounge chair in the corner and looked like he was too exhausted to ever rise again. But his eyes were burning.

The dry bag lay next to her. Inside was possibly the answer to one of the biggest unanswered questions in history, and all she wanted to do was heave it out an open window back into the ocean. But things had a momentum now—the time for stopping was long past.

She took a deep breath and reached for the bag, then stopped herself and retrieved a pair of clean gloves from her luggage. She unzipped the watertight enclosure carefully and slowly drew the manuscript from the bag. Then she pulled out the two pouches. She laid them both on the bedspread. Anthony lifted himself with effort out of the chair and walked to the side of the bed. Dafydd leaned in.

Carys smoothed her hand across the leather-bound manuscript. It was of finer quality than Lestinus's manuscript. It had remnants of gilt detailing on the cover. A mark of wealth. She slowly and carefully opened the front cover. "My Journey—Madoc Morfran," she said out loud.

"Who?" asked Anthony.

"Madoc Morfran."

"Jesus Christ," said Anthony, and he sat down heavily on the bed next to her.

"Who is it?" she asked.

"A Welsh explorer," he said. "Legend says he sailed to North America."

"Well, how the hell did his travel journal get into King Arthur's tomb?" Dafydd asked. Carys shot him a glance.

"King Arthur's what?" asked Anthony, his eyes wide.

Dammit, she thought. She turned to her father. *Here we go. Another moving part added.*

"The manuscript I told you about was written by the personal priest of the man that we believe was the inspiration for the legend of King Arthur, Riothamus Arcturus. The manuscript led us to Bardsey, and tonight we discovered the tomb where, according to the manuscript, Arthur and, eventually, the wealth of his people were buried after he fell at the Battle of Camlann."

Her father sat there, mouth dropped open.

"Except neither he nor the treasure is there anymore," she said. "All we found was this journal, some jewelry, and some seeds and seashells. Everything else was gone."

Her father's mouth continued to hang open. He finally closed it.

"And that's why that guy was following you," said Anthony. "He thought you'd lead him right to the tomb."

"Yup," said Dafydd. "And we dutifully complied."

"I don't know how he found me," she said. "But I guess it doesn't matter now. What matters is we figure out where this Morfran guy buried Arcturus."

"That's not really all that matters. There's also the jewelry," said Dafydd.

"All the property of the Welsh government," she said, placing her hand on the leather pouch. "So don't get any ideas."

Dafydd scowled a bit.

"Don't worry," she said. "You'll get your ten percent."

Dafydd was about to speak, but Carys turned and opened the other pouch. She pulled out the arrowhead, shell, and some of the seeds. She looked up at the men.

"We've got to figure out what these are. They're obviously intended to be some sort of clues," she said. She closed her eyes. "More clues," she mumbled to herself.

"We can bring the shell and seeds to the university," said Anthony. "We have a lab that can analyze these and tell us what types they are, where their habitats are, all that. We'll leave first thing in the morning."

They sat silently for a few minutes more.

"King bloody Arthur," said Anthony. He let out a long, low whistle.

"I wouldn't have believed it if I hadn't seen that tomb with my own eyes," said Dafydd. "It was the most ancient thing I've ever seen in one piece."

"Carys," said Anthony, smiling, "my girl. You're going to be famous."

She looked up at him.

"Only if we find him," she said.

"Isn't that tomb, the jewelry, the manuscript, aren't they considered incredibly important historical finds in their own right?" asked Anthony.

"I suppose," she said.

"I should think so," he said. "Either way, king or no king, you're going to be famous. And wealthy. The government has to pay you the value of those things before they can take them, you know. It's the law."

Despite the enormity of what she had in her hands and the events of the evening, she was so tired she could barely keep her eyes open.

"You look knackered," Anthony said. He touched her on the cheek. She didn't push him away.

"'Night, love," he said. He turned and walked away, leaving Dafydd and Carys alone. When Anthony had closed the door behind him, Dafydd turned to her.

"You're a very brave woman," he said. "Very brave. You did good tonight."

He bent over and kissed her on the cheek and stroked his hand softly against her hair. She smelled the salt and sea on his skin.

"Goodnight," he said. "Make sure to double-bolt the door behind me."

She watched as he left the room. Something warm stirred in her, erasing a bit of the cold that had been there for hours. She turned back to the manuscript. Despite her exhaustion, she knew she wouldn't sleep. She had reading to do.

◆ ◆ ◆ ◆ ◆

Two hours later, the journal had managed to crush Carys's heart like another death.

According to his record of the journey, Madoc Morfran, who claimed in the journal to be Arthur's natural-born son, had whisked Arthur's body away and buried it somewhere far across the sea. Location unknown. Location very likely forever unknowable.

Morfran had painted himself as a brave explorer in his journal, sailing an uncharted route. Yet even between the small, carefully drawn lettering, written along the tiny rows of pinpoints in the pages that helped the literate of his era write in straight, tight lines to conserve the precious parchment, it was clear he had acted out of fear.

He wrote that the British Isles had grown cold and dim, a sign from God that man had overstayed his welcome. The skies had filled with ash and brought a drought that had already killed most of the livestock in the western part of Britain. The people, who had survived decades of threat from the northern hordes, were now facing death by starvation and disease—and the hordes were on the move again. Morfran wrote that he desired to carry on the work of his father. He wanted to save his people and find a safer place for them where food was plentiful and they could rebuild without interference or threat. He wanted to help create a new society based on the governmental and societal structures that the Romans had brought with them, and that they had instilled in the Britons through centuries of intermingling and education—a level of sophistication that was again in danger of being swept away.

Carys couldn't tell yet in what year he had written the manuscript, or in what year he had left the British Isles, but a little bit of research would solve that matter. One thing was clear, though. His voyage had come around the time that the Anglo-Saxons had renewed their resolve to crush the rest of the British people and had begun to descend once more. Arthur's legend had grown so large by then that, Morfran wrote, he feared it was just a matter of time before someone would be tortured into revealing the location of Arthur's body—it had become more or less common knowledge that he had been taken to Bardsey. There was a reason that particular legend had flourished for fifteen hundred years. It was the only one that was true.

For the illiterate northern hordes to find and defile Arthur's body would have cemented their psychological victory over the survivors in western Britain, and all would be lost, Morfran wrote. It was up to him to save this legacy.

So Morfran decided to leave. Arthur's body and his treasure were removed from the crypt on Bardsey. Morfran took him and the people's wealth and sailed with a small fleet of specially built sailboats into the setting sun for a month, by way of the frigid north islands "that steamed and boiled"—probably Iceland with its natural springs and geysers—then south again, hopping from island to island for sixty days and nights until they made land somewhere with lush, dense forests of mighty towering pine trees, where birds, animals, and fresh water were plentiful. There lived friendly "sand people," as he called them, natives who welcomed Morfran and his crew.

It was with these people that Arthur had finally been laid to eternal rest.

There was very little in the way of clues or directions, just vague language about his final grave, in the sand people's traditional burial grounds among tall dunes by the sea, the source of the people's life. He wrote that the dunes formed a long spit of sand, behind which was a marshy land.

Ambrosius's ring and the riches of the people, given to Arcturus over the years for safekeeping or to help fund his battle against the hordes, were buried with him in his new tomb in the sand. To do anything else would have been blasphemy—the wealth was rightly, and for all time, Arcturus's, wrote Morfran. But Morfran did give Arcturus's great sword Caledfwlch to the sand people as a gift for their kindness and as future payment for guarding the tomb at all costs—and he warned that other, bad men might be coming to seek the grave.

Then he sailed the fleet back to Britain. Half his crews remained behind, smitten by the beauty of the people and the land. Morfran wrote that when he returned to Wales, he desired to memorialize his father's legacy. If pagans ever did find the burial tomb on Bardsey, they would know they had been thwarted. He wanted the people who came after to know that Arthur was safe, his legacy protected for all time and out of reach of the illiterate northern hordes. "You have lost," he wrote. "He shall live on forever."

He placed the shell, arrowhead, and seeds in Arcturus's Bardsey tomb as proof that he had been to a land far away, the land of the King's final rest. The few pieces of jewelry he left as proof that Arthur had truly been there—for only a warrior fighting the hordes would have possessed the riches of his people.

Her head hurt at the thought of spending the rest of her life trying to find Arthur. It was five in the morning, and the sun was beginning to kiss the ocean with sparks of yellow and red.

Lestinus formed next to her.

"Why didn't you tell me he wasn't going to be there?" she asked.

"I didn't know. This all happened long after I left. You've done everything you can now. You can stop looking."

"We're right back where we started."

"You must call the old man later and tell him what is happening," said Lestinus. "They fear for your life."

"That makes two of us."

"You have completed the task," he said. "You found the tomb. Tell the people so they can preserve it."

That was what she should do, but she already knew she wouldn't. She had done exactly as Harper had asked. She'd found the tomb. Technically, she was done with her mission. She could go home to claim her prize from Harper. Tell the historical authorities in Wales. Have the site preserved. She pondered that for a moment. Just for a moment.

"The task was to follow the clues wherever they led," she answered. "And now they're leading us somewhere else."

She closed the journal and put it back into the dry bag, then pulled out the sack. She removed a shell. It was broad and pure white on the inside, with a light gray exterior. She'd seen ashtrays made of these shells. It was some sort of clam. Could be from anywhere in the North Atlantic. And the seeds. Maybe they'd have luck with those. She put it all back into the bag.

"You'll find him," said Lestinus, beginning to fade. "But you'll need my help. Don't let me go."

He was right. He was invaluable. She still thought of him as a separate being, which she knew was the entirely wrong way to look at it. But it made it easier. She went to her luggage again, unzipped the front flap, retrieved the Ziploc bag with Lestinus's manuscript, opened it with bare hands, stuck her nose between the pages, and inhaled as hard as she could.

The twinge came into her nose, then the head rush, and then she lay down on the bed and drifted off into a fitful sleep, filled with dreams of the ocean, and people in loincloths, and miles of sand.

She slept later than she'd intended to, and the men didn't wake her. When she emerged from her room, it was noon and the pagans had more or less cleared out.

"You need to go back to Mumbles," she told Dafydd over lunch in the hotel's conservatory.

"I told you. I'm in this. What if there are more thugs coming after you? You'll need help."

Dafydd refused to leave them, so they drove to Aberystwyth in a convoy—Anthony with Carys, Dafydd in his truck. She and her father barely spoke during the drive to the university. He tried to initiate conversation a couple of times, but she just couldn't muster the energy.

The only conversation was in her mind, the same phrase, repeating—*I can't believe this isn't over yet.*

She dialed Harper to give him an update. Again, he sounded stronger than he had even just the day before, and his enthusiasm poured through the phone into her ears. It would have been infectious if she weren't so disheartened.

"John, we found the cave," she said.

Harper gasped but said nothing.

"It was right where the directions said it would be," she said. "We dove on it last night after the sunset. We found a stone crypt."

"Was he there? Was the sword there?"

"No," she said.

"How is that possible?" Harper burst out. "How do you know it was his tomb if he wasn't there?"

"It was right where the manuscript said it would be, and when we opened it, we found some jewelry—Dark Age workmanship. But we also found another manuscript."

"A what?"

"Another manuscript," she said. "Same era. Written by a man named Madoc Morfran. In Latin. I read it last night. It's about his journey across the Atlantic Ocean with Arcturus's body, not sure how

many years exactly after he was interred in the cave. Morfran rebur-
ied him somewhere on the other side of the Atlantic Ocean, near the
sea, with a community of natives."

"Oh my god. Native Americans. You mean he's been here the
whole time?"

"It said natives, not native Americans. He's somewhere on the
eastern seaboard of either North, Central, or South America. I wouldn't
really classify that as 'here.' There was a sack of shells and seeds and an
arrowhead in the crypt as well. The manuscript says they're from the
burial location. We're trying to figure out where they're indigenous so
we can try to narrow down the general section of coastline. He left the
sword with the people he found, to ensure that they would protect the
burial site. We'll probably never find that."

"I don't care," he said. "The most important thing is that we track
it to the end and find the burial location. Have you run into any
trouble?"

She opened her mouth to speak, then closed it again. She took a
deep breath.

"No," she said.

"You can finish the research here then," he said. "Come back
right away. We can work on it together."

"I will. John, what do you know about Madoc Morfran?" she
asked.

"Historically identifiable person," he said. "He sailed across the
ocean to escape a drought in mid-sixth century. Came back to Britain
a few years later."

She paused to think. Then she remembered what was happening
back home.

"When is Nicola's funeral?"

There was silence on the other end of the phone, then she heard
Harper cough slightly.

"Monday," he said. "I hope you'll be back for it."

"Are they going to let you go?"

"Yes. Yes, of course," he said. "They are considering discharging me."

"But you've been so sick for so long."

"I had the doctor check me for a kidney infection," he said.

"And?"

"There's damage," said Harper. "They called it moderately serious and possibly permanent. They put me on medication that cleared the hallucinations immediately. You need to stop exposing your lungs to that manuscript. It's serious. Please promise me you'll use a mask when you read it."

"But I still need…" She halted. Anthony did not need to know about Lestinus.

"I know," said Harper. "But we can take it from here without his help. You're in enough danger as it is. You don't need to make yourself sick, too."

She looked in the rear-view mirror, and Lestinus's vague shape was there, looking back at her.

"I've gotta call Annie. I'll give you a call once we know more about the shells and seeds."

"Come back to the States right after that. Don't linger there," said Harper.

Annie picked up after just one ring.

"How did it go?"

"Fine," she said. "I'll fill you in when I see you."

"You're coming home?"

"Yeah, but not sure exactly when. Next couple of days."

"Did you find the tomb?"

"I…. You know what? I just called to find out if you've made any progress on the thug."

"Yeah," said Annie. "Interesting thing there. The guy whose bloody business card you gave me—Plimpton—he ID'd the guy. His name is Frank Marshfield. We found some of his old military and criminal records. His military photo matches the picture from the Pike's toll booth cameras."

"Who is he?" she asked.

"I asked that question of Plimpton. He would only say that he had had dealings with Marshfield, and I suspect they were unpleasant."

"So he's a known commodity," she said. *Or was*, she thought.

"Yup," Annie said. "I'm betting, based on the looks of him, and the few police reports in the U.K. I was able to access, that he was hired muscle. Which means someone else is pulling the strings."

"Annie," she said. "No police yet. We still have work to do."

"A woman has been murdered," said Annie. "And Frank Marshfield is probably the one who killed her, for chrissake. Don't you and Harper want to see him in prison?"

"Of course I do," she said, swallowing hard. "Don't worry. I absolutely promise you. He'll get what he deserves."

◆ ◆ ◆ ◆ ◆

THEY ARRIVED AT THE UNIVERSITY OF ABERYSTWYTH at five that afternoon. Students were gone for summer break, but Anthony said there were a few postdoc students doing research projects in the Life Sciences department. One of them led a team of scientists who could help identify the habitat of the shell and seeds. They wound their way through the sprawling campus, which hugged the hillside above the ocean, and parked at a large building that looked like Hogwarts.

"I'm going to find out if they have any vacant professor housing that we can stay in for a little while," said Anthony as he hopped out of Carys's car. "We should stay away from my house—if someone is still following us."

"What did you tell your wife?" asked Carys.

"Nothing, except I suggested she and my youngest son go visit some friends out of town for a few days." He trotted up the wide stone steps and into the building. A few minutes later, Anthony walked briskly back out.

"They have a vacant three-bedroom apartment on the other side of campus," said Anthony, wiggling the keys. "I'll bring you two over there, we can drop off our stuff, and then we should head to the lab and see what needs to be done."

The apartment was bright and cheerful and well-appointed, the top floor of an old, blocky brick house reserved for visiting professors and their families. Carys suggested that Dafydd find a store and get some provisions for the evening while she and Anthony went to the lab, but he refused to leave them.

The Life Sciences building was a modern, angular, concrete and steel structure that looked like an awkward spaceship that had accidentally landed in this barren, windswept place. They walked down a deserted hallway to the only occupied lab. Inside were three young men in jeans and white lab coats, two of whom were studying something through an enormous, complex microscope while the other one sat at a computer. Anthony rapped on the window. They looked up and then broke into smiles when they saw Anthony. The one at the computer motioned them in.

"Doctor Rogers," Anthony said. "I'm in need of some of your brain power."

Rogers stood up and reached to shake Anthony's hand.

"Well, well," said Rogers. "Doctor Jones. What brings you here to the land of the living?"

Carys winced slightly at the honorific—she'd forgotten how accomplished Anthony was.

"Danny, this is my daughter, Carys," he said. She noted the brief puzzled look that flashed across Rogers's face. She nodded. "And her friend, Dafydd. We've got some objects that we need identified, and I knew you were here for the summer. I thought maybe you could help."

"What type of objects?" Rogers asked.

"Some very old seashells and seeds," she said. "We need to know what type they are and their primary habitat."

"James here is your man, then," said Rogers, pointing at one of the younger men at the microscope. He looked up and made eye contact with Carys. She reached into her bag and pulled out the sack.

"As you can see, we're in the middle of something here right now," said Rogers, "but we can probably get to this tomorrow."

"It's very important. If there's any way you could get to it first thing in the morning, we'd be really grateful," said Anthony.

"Shells and seeds are important? I'm glad you've finally seen the relevance of our work here, my friend," said Rogers with a laugh. "You spend too much time with maps."

"You're right about that," said Anthony.

Carys stepped up to the lab table and placed the sack there.

"Thank you very much for helping us with this, James," she said. "I'm going to leave you this shell and two each of the seeds."

James watched as she put on her gloves, retrieved the objects from the sack, and placed them in a plastic tray on the table. James nudged the shell with a pair of long tweezers.

"Hard-shell clam of some sort, probably North Atlantic," he said. He picked up one of the tiny pitlike seeds, then one of the round ones. "These are interesting. I'll check my identifiers and get back to you. Will these likely be North Atlantic region as well?"

"Unsure," she said.

"That clam will definitely be North America," he said. "Maybe New England or Canada. How old are the seeds? They look almost petrified."

She balked briefly. "Extremely old. About fifteen hundred years."

All three of the men looked up at her.

"Where…" Rogers began.

"We're staying in campus housing for a couple of days," Anthony said as he grabbed a pen and paper from a desk. "Can you please give us a call as soon as you know anything?"

"Sure," said Rogers, the shock lingering in his eyes. "We'll let you know tomorrow if we find anything."

"Can't tell you how much we appreciate this," said Anthony as he shook Rogers's hand. As the three left the lab, Anthony turned to Carys.

"Well, you sure got their attention," he said with a smile.

◆ ◆ ◆ ◆ ◆

THE APARTMENT WOULD HAVE BEEN a lovely, relaxing place to read or cook a meal or take a nap. But Carys was keen to stay in motion. Without any idea where to go next, however, it was all just energy, turned inward and spiking her anxiety. Dafydd had finally agreed to part with her to go for groceries. Anthony was in one of the bedrooms talking to his wife. She sat on the living room couch reading the Morfran manuscript, looking for alternative translations of the Latin that might give her a hint of his final destination, all the while plagued by the thought that someone bad—she didn't know who—was going to come crashing through the door at any moment.

When she heard Dafydd's truck arrive outside, she stood, went to the window, and watched him coming up the sidewalk. He was on his cell phone. He was ridiculously handsome. She smiled. She liked the way his legs moved when he walked. They were long and lean, strong, bowed out slightly, but he walked smoothly, without the bobbing that most people have when they stride. He almost looked like he was prowling. The sun was setting across the green yard, and his dark hair shone.

He stopped halfway up the sidewalk. He turned away from the house, and when he turned back, it looked like he was upset at whoever was on the other end of the phone. His face—angry, upset, she didn't know him well enough to know what he was feeling— took her by surprise, and her reverie crashed to a halt.

He hung up on the call, took a deep breath, shrugged his shoulders a couple of times, and disappeared from her sight as he came into the main foyer. She heard the door slam behind him, his footsteps on the stairs, the apartment door open and close, and the bag of groceries land on the kitchen counter.

"Honey, I'm home," Dafydd hollered in a fake baritone down the central hallway. She smiled. Her father used to do that.

She went into the kitchen. Dafydd was unpacking the grocery bag. "Thought we'd have shepherd's pie for dinner. They had nice ground lamb at the store." An unbagged potato rolled lazily off the counter and thumped to the floor.

"Everything alright?" she asked as she bent over to pick it up.

"Aside from killing a guy?"

"Yes. Other than that. I just...I saw you coming in. It looked like you were angry with someone on your phone," she said. There was a slight stiffening in his shoulders. He kept unpacking. After a moment, he turned to face her.

"I wasn't going to tell you," he said. "It seems counterproductive."

"What?" she asked. "Tell me what?"

"Remember the young receptionist at the hotel in Aberdaron?" Dafydd asked. His eyebrows were furrowed.

"Of course," she said.

"She's a friend. I dive up there a lot. She just called me," said Dafydd. "Someone was just looking for you, for us, at the hotel."

The blood drained from her face.

"I know," said Dafydd.

"What did she tell them?" she asked.

"Nothing," he said. "She said she didn't like the looks of them..."

"There was more than one? Jesus."

"She said she didn't know who they were talking about," said Dafydd. "Said it was so busy with the pagans that it was impossible to keep track of who was who."

"So that goon knew that we were staying at the hotel. And he told his boss before the dive, and now his boss is back on the hunt because the goon didn't check in today. How did that thug know we were staying at the hotel?"

"I have no idea," said Dafydd. "But again, I think it's an oddly hopeful sign that they're trying to pick up our trail there. That means they've lost us."

"What have I gotten you two into?" She turned and rested her hands on the counter.

Dafydd stopped unpacking, turned toward her, and grabbed her shoulders with both hands. He looked hard into her eyes. *Why do men get lashes that long?* she thought.

"Hear me clearly," he said. "I'm in this. I'm not going anywhere. Got it?"

"Why? We have no idea how long it will take to find what we're looking for. I assume you have bills to pay, family, friends, a girl-friend…. I don't under—"

"We are not talking about this anymore," he said, and turned to stow the milk and coffee in the refrigerator. "I bought wine and cheese so we could have a little snack before dinner. I'll pour us some wine now if you'd like."

She nodded.

Anthony emerged from his bedroom just as Dafydd uncorked the bottle of sauvignon blanc.

"Party?" he asked.

"Taking the edge off," she said as she sipped, not bothering to wait for a toast. She couldn't imagine what they'd toast to anyway. "How is your wife?"

"Mad and scared, but safe," he said. "She's demanding to know where I am and what I'm doing, but I just asked her to trust me that it was important and not to go back to the house until I tell her it's safe. She wants me to come be with her right away. She's really afraid."

"Did you ask her if anyone strange had been hanging around your neighborhood?" she asked. Dafydd handed Anthony a glass of wine. "Did you tell her to keep an eye out for someone tailing her?"

"No. I didn't want to make her any more concerned than she already was," he said, then raised the glass to them both and took a swig. "Should I have?"

Dafydd and Carys exchanged a glance.

"Someone was asking about us at the hotel where we stayed," she said. Now it was her father's turn to go sheet white.

"Oh my god," he said. "I have to warn her."

"No," she said. "That'll just upset her even more. They don't know where we are. That's why they were asking at the hotel. I just wish I knew how they figured out we were staying there."

"Do you think they know that guy is…?" asked Anthony.

"I can't imagine how unless someone found his boat," said Dafydd. "And it's in the middle of the Irish Sea right now."

The three of them stood silently for a few moments.

"I'm going to start cooking," said Dafydd. "Get my mind off this. You go sit down. I'll put some cheese and crackers together for a snack."

Anthony and Carys sat on the couch next to each other.

"He's sweet on you," Anthony said.

"You think?"

"He's making a cheese plate," said Anthony.

She smiled.

"He seems a good bloke," said Anthony. "He got any competition back home?"

"No," she said. "Just Harley."

"Your cat," he said.

She turned to him.

"Priscilla Brennan keeps me informed of your comings and goings," he said, "in place of firsthand contact."

"I was so angry," she said. "I still am."

"I know," he said. "You probably will be for the rest of your life. If you decide that's what you want."

"I didn't decide to be angry," she said. "You—"

"Yes, you did. You do. You decide every day," he said. "So do I."

"What have you got to be angry about?"

"I made some bad choices a long time ago," he said, looking directly up into the ray of sunshine streaming into the room as water welled up in the corners of his eyes. *So, that's where I learned that trick*, she thought. "I believed I had no alternative, but I did. I never forgave myself. I don't expect I will, and I don't expect you to either."

"You don't?" she asked.

"No," he said. "What I did was unforgivable. I know. But you're my daughter. Whether you like it or not. I just want to make sure that you're safe and happy."

"That's a tall order," she said.

"How did this all happen?" he asked.

"One thing has led to another and another, and now I'm here," she said, resting her elbows on her knees and leaning forward. "I have absolutely no idea how to do anything other than keep going forward until we get to the end, wherever it is."

Just then Dafydd walked in with a plate of cheese and crackers.

"I could use some help in the kitchen," he said. "Carys, can you chop?"

"Love to," she said, and hopped up off the couch.

♦ ♦ ♦ ♦ ♦

DINNER WAS DELICIOUS. It had miraculously taken Carys's mind off their predicament for two hours. They shared stories and drank wine. Anthony told of his first few years in America and meeting Carys's mother, Patricia, at the Green Dragon on Saint Patrick's Day—she was right; her mother had thought he was Irish. At first she wanted to lash out, tell him he had no right to speak of Patricia, to even think of her. But she couldn't find the words, and so she just sat quietly and then at some point, without meaning to, she was listening.

Then, for the first time in her life, she could hear how much Anthony had loved her mother. He talked about the day Carys was born. His eyes shone at the memory. She wondered how anyone could leave a child—and how both her parents had made that choice.

Dafydd shared his stories of growing up on and in the waters of Wales with his siblings. They had all believed that the South Wales coastline was the entire world when they were young. He admitted that he had really never been anywhere outside of the British Isles, to this day. What he knew of foreign places came from listening to the stories his customers told him on their long boat rides out to dive on wrecks, and by piecing together the travels of the ships that he had dived upon or salvaged as part of his work. He said he longed to travel and experience something outside of Mumbles, a town that four generations of his family had called home. His parents were still both alive and kicking, and in love, and had never shown an ounce of interest in living anywhere but Wales, which they loved as much as their own children, he said.

"That's why they charge a toll on the Severn Bridge to get into Wales," said Dafydd with a grin, "but not out."

Around ten o'clock, Anthony excused himself to go to bed. She and Dafydd found themselves staring across an unfamiliar table.

"How are you feeling?" he asked. "Any more of those pains?"

"I haven't had any since the dive."

"You need to get that checked when you get home. Is there anyone special there who…" He paused.

"A boyfriend, you mean?"

"Yeah."

"No," she said. "No boyfriend. Not much of anyone back in the States. But I've got my sister, Annie."

"You have a sister?"

"She's sort of my sister. Her mom took me in when my mother killed herself."

She glanced up at Dafydd's face. It didn't budge.

"Anthony bolted when I was seven. My mother had depression, and he couldn't handle it. He took off—abandoned both of us. You can imagine the effect that had on my mother's depression. When she died, he never came back to get me."

"No wonder you're so angry at him," said Dafydd. "But that has to be exhausting."

"It is," she said, realizing for the first time how true this was. "What about you? Girlfriend? Ex-wife? Wife?"

"Not that I'm aware of," said Dafydd. "But there are a few nights that are fuzzy. Anything could have happened." He smiled.

"I can't believe you're not married," she said.

"Me either," said Dafydd. "I'm quite a catch."

"Humble, too," she said. "But seriously, why? Why aren't you married?"

"I just didn't want to settle for what was available within arm's reach in Mumbles," he said. "I don't mean that to sound snobby. There are lovely women there. Absolutely beautiful. Smart. Funny. Strong. Good mothers. Good people. Most of my friends married local girls. I just always thought I'd…I don't know. I felt like my life needed to be bigger than that."

She waited for him to continue, but he looked up at her and smiled.

"Tell me about your sister," said Dafydd.

"She's a very successful defense attorney," she said. "Smart, loud, funny, takes no shit from anyone. She's a force of nature. She's actually been doing some investigating on the goon who—"

"Really," he said. "Did she find out anything?"

"Yes. His name was Frank Marshfield," she said. "Annie thinks he was some kind of an enforcer. Definitely not the mastermind type. She's trying to figure out who was behind it all."

She took another sip of her wine.

"Dinner was amazing," she said.

"Thank you," said Dafydd with a grin. She smiled back but was overtaken by a yawn.

"I should go to bed," she said.

"You didn't get much sleep last night, huh?"

"Couple of hours," she said. "I was up reading the manuscript."

"What's it like?" he asked.

"This Morfran guy thought quite highly of himself," she said. "He talked a lot about how his quick thinking saved the fleet. He spends a lot of time listing his daily grooming and eating habits. Unfortunately, he's not very specific when it comes to where the hell he buried the actual body. You know, little details like what continent it's on."

"That's not what I meant," said Dafydd. "I meant, what's it like reading a book that old? Being able to read it."

His eyes were glued to hers, and she could feel him waiting for her answer. She couldn't remember the last time a man had been so eager to hear what she actually thought about something. She considered for a moment how to answer his question. She'd never tried to put it into words before. She'd never been asked to.

"It's like…it's like watching a movie. This world sort of drops away, and all you can see is this other world playing in your head." She looked up at him. His eyes were riveted on her. "Latin isn't like English. It's very formal. People generally didn't use it to express their emotions. There were so few people who could write back then that they normally saved it only for recording official things. But to find a personal journal—to find two of them—it's like a magic window. Like climbing into the heads of people thousands of years ago. But mostly what you see when you read words that old is that humans haven't changed a bit over all the centuries. I'm not sure if that's comforting or disturbing. It's all the same—pain, anger, fear, joy, passion…"

Suddenly, Dafydd stood up and moved around the edge of the table. He put her head in his hands and brought his lips against hers, inhaling her as if he could draw her in. She threw her arms around his neck and stood up, pressing her body against his. Their mouths opened, their tongues entwined, and a hot flush ran up her body. Her breath caught in her throat. She held onto him as if she were clinging to a life raft.

7

◇◇◇◇◇◇◇

Saturday, June 23

Dafydd went to his room just before the sun came up, leaving Carys exhausted in a warm bed. It was another night without much sleep. He'd been insatiable, demanding, tender, passionate, and he knew his way around her body like they'd been together forever. They would make love for an hour, then she'd fall asleep, but she'd awaken half an hour later with his hardness pressing against her hip. Again and again they replayed the scene throughout the night. She hadn't pushed him away once or hesitated to take advantage of his enthusiasm for her. They connected again and again in a way that she had never experienced before.

She knew before the sun came up how badly she'd miss him when she went back home.

When she finally rolled out of bed and got into the shower, her entire body was aching and her most intimate parts were raw. It made her smile.

The two men were at the dining room table with tea when she got up. Dafydd smiled at her, and she lowered her head. Anthony glanced at them both.

"Sleep well?" Anthony asked. She grinned and walked into the kitchen. There was a pot of coffee already made, and a container of cream was on the counter. She poured herself a big mug and went back out to join the two. It was close to nine.

"I just got a call from the boys in the lab a few minutes ago," said Anthony. "Apparently they didn't get much sleep either." He winked at her. "They ran tests on the seeds all night. Rogers said they were the oldest ones they'd ever seen. They want to know where you got them."

"I'm sure they do," she said.

They arrived at the lab a half hour later. The scientists were haggard, and the room had the funk of takeout Chinese and unwashed men.

"What do we have, then?" Anthony asked Rogers.

"The seeds are remarkable samples for their age," said Rogers. "They'd probably sprout again if we planted them."

"What are they?" she asked.

"These"—he held up two tiny seeds, pressed into the flesh of his index finger—"are *Prunus maritima*, beach plum, native in ocean sand dune habitats from Maine to Delaware, and *Oxycoccus macrocarpus*, large cranberry, native to marshy areas of northern North America. The Native Americans of New England introduced cranberries to the Pilgrims in the 1600s as a food, and it helped save their butts. And this," Rogers said, holding up the shell, "is the North American hard clam, also known as quahog. *Mercenaria mercenaria*. Indigenous to the eastern coast of North America from Canada to Florida. The Native Americans of New England used them for money. Called them wampum. So if all these items were scooped up in the same place, it was most likely somewhere along the North American coastline from Maine to Delaware."

Her mind was yanked three thousand miles away.

The legendary King Arthur, a man whom historians had been seeking for fifteen hundred years all over Europe, was buried in a simple Native American burial mound on a barrier island beach somewhere just a few hours from her apartment. She started to laugh. The three scientists' brows all furrowed.

"Why is that funny?" asked Rogers.

"It's just strange," she said. "We really appreciate your help."

"Yes, we really do," said Anthony.

"Can we keep these?" Rogers asked.

"You can keep those two seeds," she said.

"Where did these come from? We've never seen samples this old," said Rogers.

"We can't share that info, Doc, sorry," said Anthony. Rogers frowned. She collected the shell and remaining seeds and put them back into their sack, which she then stowed in her purse.

"Let us know if you change your mind about that," Rogers said. "You've got a bit of a scientific treasure here. We would like to know where we can find more of these."

Carys just smiled and nodded.

◆ ◆ ◆ ◆ ◆

"LOOKS LIKE I'LL FINALLY GET TO SEE AMERICA," said Dafydd as the three of them walked back to their car.

"What are you talking about?" Carys asked.

"We should probably try to catch the night flight out of Heathrow," Dafydd said. "We can make it if we leave right away."

"You're going nowhere," she said. She looked at Anthony, who hadn't said much. He knew he would not be invited, and he didn't look like he was going to volunteer.

"He should go," said Anthony. "You'll need help."

"I have plenty of help back home," she said. "I managed to survive this long without you both." Anthony winced.

"I'm going," said Dafydd.

"You can do what you want, but I think it would be a mistake for you to come back with me. You'll just be in the way," she said to Dafydd.

It killed her to speak the words. As much as she craved his body again, even at that very moment, she knew he would be excess baggage back in America. Frank Marshfield's boss was likely still looking for her—and would be as long as she had the manuscript and the tomb and the treasure remained unfound. She didn't want to drag either man any further into the mess.

When they got back to the apartment, she retreated to her room. The bed sheets were still a tangled mess, and she wanted nothing more than to climb back in and beckon Dafydd to join her. She pulled off the sheets and pillowcases, bundled them on the floor, and put the blanket back on. She laid out her belongings on top of the blanket, taking an inventory to make sure that nothing had been left behind.

She refolded her clothes and shoved them into the overnight bag, followed by the manuscripts and the bag of Dark Age golden jewelry. Then she reconsidered. If she was caught by customs with these, she'd be detained indefinitely.

She carried the bag of jewelry out to the living room. Anthony was reading on the couch, and Dafydd was sitting at the dining room table typing on his cell phone.

"Anthony," she said. "I need you to do something for me." He looked up from the couch where he was reading.

"Of course," he said, hopeful.

She walked over and placed the sack in his hands. It clanked. Dafydd's head jerked up when he heard the sound.

"Morfran took almost all the treasure out of Arthur's tomb when he retrieved his corpse," she said. "So this might be the only remnant of the great treasure of King Arthur."

Anthony's jaw went slack.

"I need you to hold onto this until I call you and tell you we've found the King's burial site," she said. "Once I know we can secure it, I need you to call the British Antiquities Ministry and tell them where we found this."

Anthony looked like he might cry with happiness. The jewelry and this request were a bond between them, the first in thirty years.

"The buoys will still be there," she said. "The cave is slightly to the right of where the buoys pointed. Huge flat rock right in front of the entrance. It looks like…" She racked her brain trying to remember what that rock formation had reminded her of.

Lestinus formed faintly next to her father on the couch.

"Stonehenge," he said quietly. She looked at Lestinus directly.

"Exactly," she said out loud in Latin, and smiled at Lestinus before she could check herself.

Anthony raised an eyebrow at her. "Who are you talk—"

"Stonehenge," she said. "It looks exactly like one of the monoliths at Stonehenge. You literally can't miss it."

She turned to head back into her bedroom, leaving the two men speechless.

Despite the ungodly hour back in Boston, Annie picked up on the first ring. She sounded like she might cry when Carys told her she was on her way home.

"I'll hopefully be back tonight if I can make it to the airport by this afternoon," she said.

"How is your father?" asked Annie.

"He's fine," she said. "He was actually…uh…he was helpful."

"Who could have predicted that? Someone very wise no doubt," Annie said with an audible grin.

"Shut up."

"Absolutely," Annie said.

"I'll call you in half an hour with my flight info."

"I'll pick you up at the airport," said Annie.

"You don't have to—"

"I know, but I'll do it anyway," said Annie. "Love you."

"Love you back," said Carys, and hung up.

She put the last of her belongings and the remaining shells and seeds into the bag next to the manuscripts. Those she could get through customs without a problem. At some point, once this was all sorted, she'd need to give the Morfran manuscript back to the British authorities as well. She was, she realized, more concerned with breaking antiquities law than being an accomplice after the fact to murder.

Lestinus watched her silently.

"You must never feel guilty about what happened on the boat, Carys," said her hallucination. "There are worse things than killing."

She nodded silently to him and left the bedroom. The two men were sitting at the dining room table now. They'd obviously been talking.

"I have to go," she said.

"Please tell me when you've gotten home safely," said Anthony, rising from his seat. "I need to know you're okay."

"I will. I promise," she said. She put down her bag and took a step toward him. "I will be in touch. Please keep your eyes open and your family away from your house until we're in the clear. Both of you. Someone is still out there, looking for us. And for those." She nodded down at the sack of artifacts on the table.

"I will," said Anthony.

"Maybe, when this is all over, I'll come back for a proper visit," she said. Neither one of them made a move toward the other. "One where no one is trying to kill us or anything."

She smiled at him. His eyes were red and beginning to fill with tears.

"Carys," Anthony said, taking that last, final step into the space between them. He grabbed her with both hands and held her so tightly against his chest that she couldn't breathe.

"My beautiful girl," he said softly. He released her and turned away. She turned to Dafydd, who sat watching them both.

"I'll walk you to your car," Dafydd said, and got up. She kissed Anthony on the cheek again.

"Thank you for all your help. If we find him, it'll be your find, too. Put that jewelry somewhere very, very safe," she said.

Anthony nodded and looked away, embarrassed by the tears now streaming down his face.

Dafydd walked behind her as she left the apartment. They walked in silence down to her rental car, and she tossed her bag onto the passenger's seat and turned to find Dafydd moving her into an embrace.

"Dafydd," she said, "last night was amazing."

"Yes, it was," he said, grinning down at her. "You can't expect me to just let you go."

"You're going to have to," she said. "I have work to do. You know that. When this is over, maybe we can try to figure out some way—"

"Way to what? See each other? How romantic. No, you're heading home. You'll forget all about me," he said.

"There's no way I could do that," she said. "And the three of us are bound. If any of us talks about what happened this week, mentions it to anyone, we're all at risk. None of us can ever walk away from that."

"You can," he said. "You live thousands of miles away. I don't know where you live or where you work. I didn't even know your real name at first. You could just disappear."

"Finding me would be the easiest thing in the world," she said with a smile.

As the words came out of her mouth, she got a cold feeling in her stomach. This was a true thing. Anyone could find her in a minute. For the first time, it occurred to her that it might make sense not to go home. Maybe she'd hole up for a while at Annie's until the search was over. Or she gave up on it.

Dafydd was still holding her, the heat from his arms and belly making her sweat.

"I have to go," she said.

He bent down and kissed her, softly and deeply, and her knees literally went weak. She grabbed onto him more tightly to steady herself, and they kissed for a long minute. It took all her strength to pull away from him.

"I will see you again," she said.

He simply smiled and backed away as she got in the car. As Carys drove away, she looked in the rear-view and saw him raise his hand goodbye.

Trading the living for the dead.

◆ ◆ ◆ ◆ ◆

As she approached Cardiff, Carys finally called Harper. She told him about the lab results on the shell and the seeds, and she could hear him smiling across the phone connection.

"Remarkable," he said. "All this time. Right under our own noses."

"There's still a hell of a lot of terrain to cover," she said. "At least Morfran's journal didn't use a damn poem. I'll need to do a more thorough reading of the manuscript to see if we can tease out any more clues as to specifically where Morfran made landfall."

"I'll start research on the tribes of that era," said Harper. "It's funny. I know everything about what was going on in the British Isles at that time, and I know absolutely nothing about what was going on in the land under my own feet."

◆ ◆ ◆ ◆ ◆

Getting through passport control at Boston Logan International Airport was a long but relatively painless process. There was no extra scrutiny of Carys's fake passport—they obviously didn't run it through the international database of stolen IDs. As a white woman with a Christian name, Carys had racial and religious profiling as her ally. She pocketed the passport, patted the bag of shells and seeds in her pocket, and strode through the waiting throngs at the exit into the main terminal. She scanned the faces.

"Carys!"

She jerked her head to the right. Standing directly behind the barrier was Annie, waving. She walked straight to her and grabbed her in a bear hug across the waist-high metal barrier.

"Keep moving along, miss," said the security guard behind her. "Please exit the area."

She pulled away from Annie, who was grinning wildly and looked like she hadn't slept in a few days. Carys jogged around the barrier and over to Annie again, and they embraced a second time.

"You look good!" said Annie. "How is that even possible?"

"I managed to sleep on the plane," she said. "You look tired."

"I've been worried sick, bitch."

They walked, arm in arm, out of the terminal toward the parking garage. They climbed into Annie's car. She chose her words carefully as they drove through the twisting, logic-free streets around the airport.

"We found it, Annie," she said. "We found his tomb. It was right where the manuscript described."

Annie did her best to keep her eyes on the road, but Carys could see she was jolted.

"Oh my god," Annie whispered. "Was the body there?"

"No. Someone moved it. Fortunately, he left us directions. That's why I'm back. We think he moved it here."

"Wait, Boston?"

Carys couldn't help but laugh out loud.

"No, but pretty close. We think somewhere along the coast."

"Where?" asked Annie.

"That's the million-dollar question, right? According to the manuscript that we found, he's in a Native American burial ground on a barrier island or peninsula somewhere along the northeast coastline. That's all we've been able to make out so far. There are sand dunes. That's it. We just have to figure the rest of it out."

"So it's really just a process of elimination then?" asked Annie.

"There's a lot of coastline," she said.

"Did you see any sign of Frank Marshfield? Any chance he followed you to Wales, or followed you back here?"

Carys stared through the windshield into the shifting landscape of the highway. She could feel the cold waters off the coast of Bardsey. She could taste the metallic, salty panic as she struggled to breathe. Could hear the splash of Marshfield's body as it was tossed into the ocean.

"Carys? What happened?" Annie asked, staring at the side of Carys's face.

"I don't think I can—"

"Jesus," said Annie. She inhaled sharply. "Tell me when you're ready."

Carys needed to change the subject.

"I met a man."

"Did he try to kill you?"

"No. I had sex with him."

Annie's face broke into an enormous smile, a smile that always made Carys feel fifteen years old again.

"When did you have time to get laid?" Annie asked.

Carys started to laugh.

"Well, it was in the middle of the night. I didn't really have anything else planned at that hour."

"Oh, that's good. I'm glad to hear that you weren't being distracted from your mission. What's his name?"

"Dafydd. I probably will never see him again. But he sure has left a fine memory," she said.

"I'm glad to hear it. How were things with your father?"

"He was fine," she said.

Annie flashed her a smile. "I'm so glad I called him," she said. "By the way, they let Harper out of the asylum."

"Already? I just talked to him this morning. He said they were just considering it."

"When he found out that you were coming back, he somehow managed to convince his doctor to discharge him immediately," Annie said. "And I think there might have been some mention of a lawsuit. He hired a police detail at the house for protection."

Carys frowned. At least Harper would be safe. But what about her—and Dafydd, her father, Annie? She let the Boston landscape drift by, wondering when the man who sent Marshfield would dispatch the next goon to come after the King.

◆ ◆ ◆ ◆ ◆

MARTIN GYLES SAT IN HIS LEATHER RECLINER in his mahogany-paneled library overlooking the lights of Piccadilly Circus. When he couldn't sleep, this view usually relaxed him, but it wasn't working tonight. He spun his silver Montblanc pen between his fingers and flexed his feet up and down nervously several inches above the ancient Oriental rug that nearly filled the large room. The Lagavulin 30 neat sat untouched on the desk in front of him. He stared down at the drunken tourists milling around the statue below.

Where the fuck was Frank?

He reached over and flipped on his desk lamp. His reflection appeared, bald and wide-eyed, like a giant bug, in the room's picture window. It gave him a start.

He'd been calling Frank's burner phone for the past two days. He wasn't even getting a ring tone on the other end. His texts were no longer registering as delivered. It was like the guy had fallen off the face of the planet. As had Jones, her father, and the diver. The men he'd sent to Aberdaron the day before had found no trace of any of them—it was like they'd never been there. The man he'd sent to Jones's father's home yesterday had found no sign of the father or his family. Something had gone very wrong.

This left him with a significant problem.

The client who had hired him to retrieve the manuscript from Jones was threatening to pull the deal entirely and find someone else to do it. This person—man, woman, group; he didn't know who it was—was growing increasingly agitated. This person had been exceptionally skilled at keeping him-, her-, or itself hidden. Which was bad. It reduced his options for recovery if things went south. He could always convince people to do what he wanted as long as he knew who they were. He could identify their weak spots, their vulnerabilities. But he had no such leverage with a nameless, faceless client. He made a mental note to never make this mistake again.

Although he could be forgiven for biting at the deal, even with an anonymous client: five hundred thousand dollars, plus expenses, for the provable confiscation of the manuscript and translation. Odd thing, that. The client didn't even want it. Just wanted to make sure that it had been taken away from the woman. Once it became obvious to Gyles that she was actually searching for the tomb herself, the client insisted that the manuscript be grabbed *before* she found the tomb. That was an ironclad term of the deal.

Gyles—or rather, his black-market alter ego, JB—had already arranged the sale of the manuscript, translation, and contents of the tomb, whatever they turned out to be, to a senior member of the Saudi royal family. The idea of possessing a Dark Age body linked to a historical manuscript seemed even more intriguing to the prince than any treasure that might be found. He didn't really need more treasure. But an ancient human skeleton? He didn't have any of those yet.

All Gyles needed to do was find the woman, have Frank follow her until she found the tomb, off her and her search party, grab the books, and scoop up the contents of the tomb. Quick, easy, lucrative: the prince would pay five million dollars, less Frank's fee.

Normally, Frank's disappearance and the plan's failure would not be of such great concern. He'd just call all the parties involved in the transaction with his usual lie: the item was far too hot to handle. Deposits returned. No harm, no foul. Deal unwound. Everybody still friends. They'd all live to do business another day.

Except the successful completion of this deal was becoming increasingly urgent. He was probably going to need the proceeds to pay off a certain ISIS commander in Syria, Mr. Yasser Alahwi al-Iraqi, who was talking about beheadings, specifically of JB's head.

Although JB's real identity was a well-kept secret, this terrorist, medieval and uneducated, still gave him a very bad feeling.

A month ago, Alahwi had agreed to sell an ancient, perfectly preserved, extremely rare and well-provenanced Assyrian deity sculpture from Palmyra to Gyles for five million bucks. He had in turn agreed to sell it for eight million to a billionaire black-market antiquities collector in Hamburg. He would pocket the nice little spread of three mill. Between that, the manuscript deal, and the deal with the prince, it would be a very, very profitable month.

The sculpture deal was routine. He'd done dozens of them with Alahwi. The commander's pillaging had turned into a nice revenue stream—as had the back-end "repatriation" business when one or two had ended up in museums and highly visible private collections.

As was standard practice, the commander relinquished the sculpture to Gyles's couriers, and in return, the terrorist received electronic confirmation that five million dollars had been placed into an escrow account in Grand Cayman. Upon completion of the transaction—when the sculpture arrived in a special free-trade warehouse zone in Geneva—the escrowed amount would be released to any account Alahwi desired.

But Gyles didn't like escrow. There was no escrow account. There was no money waiting to be transferred. It was all smoke and mirrors, electronic sleight of hand. Not a penny of actual money would be transferred anywhere until the sculpture was safely tucked away in

Geneva and Gyles had gotten the buyer's money. He never used his own money for deals. Never.

Unfortunately, a few days after the first courier picked up the sculpture from the commander, it disappeared, somewhere between delivery checkpoints in Serbia. Some aggressive interrogations of the couriers involved in various parts of the delivery chain had yielded nothing. He had learned through painful experience that once something went missing in Serbia, it stayed that way. Expending valuable resources to search further would be a waste.

JB had been lying to Alahwi about the progress of the sculpture for two weeks, waiting for a solution to present itself. When Alahwi texted several days ago, the real threats began. JB again assured him things were proceeding apace, except for some small border issues. He knew the man didn't buy a word of it. Alahwi texted that he'd give him another week and if the money didn't arrive, then JB should expect "retribution" for his "dishonor." Words like "dirty dog" and "infidel" and "head" were being thrown around. It occurred to Gyles then that maybe he was relying a bit too heavily on his own anonymity to protect himself. He had no idea how, but he couldn't shake the feeling that Alahwi knew who he was.

Still, he had worked too damn hard and killed too many people to start bowing to the demands of every client who threatened his life. He had been threatened before. Many times. The only time it had terrified him was when he was twelve, in the shared bunk room at his boarding school, in the dark, surrounded by bigger boys, some bent on buggery, some just on mindless violence against someone smaller than themselves.

Back then, he'd begged. He'd made deals and promises. But in the end, he'd been their toy. The next day, he vowed his revenge, and although the assaults went on for several more nights, three of the boys involved in his humiliation, one by one, had to be rushed to hospital by ambulance because of a mysterious ailment that the school nurses couldn't diagnose.

They all died.

The school's laundry room lye proved very reliable. The buggering and mindless violence stopped after the third one got sick. No one bothered him after that.

He had learned in that hellhole of a boarding school that you can always reason with a man as long as he thinks you are crazier and more dangerous than he is. Of course, he had never had to reason with a man who bought his C-4 by the ton and beheaded children on TV.

To make matters worse, a source of JB's in Scotland Yard had texted that somebody was snooping around Frank Marshfield's criminal record. Somebody from the U.S. How they had gotten Frank's name, he had no idea. As if this search weren't complicated enough already. The inquiry had sealed Frank's fate. Frank was one of only two people who could link him to the maid's death. As much as he hated to eliminate such a valued asset—his best; the man was as close to a partner as Gyles had ever had—business was business. But he had to bloody find the man before he could have him killed.

He was just fine with the killing. Always had been. It was the waiting, the not knowing, that would drive him even madder than he already was.

He scowled at his ugly bug of a reflection again, reached over, and turned out the light.

PART 3

Boston

1

Sunday, June 24

The next morning, Carys woke at four, jet-lagged and jangled. She made coffee in the built-in Miele machine in the kitchen of Annie's spacious Back Bay brownstone overlooking a darkened Storrow Drive and Charles River.

Thoughts of Frank Marshfield crashed the gates of her momentary peace. She went to take a shower. Annie was up, bleary and hunched over a cup of coffee, when Carys padded back into the kitchen. She placed a quarter in front of Annie.

"I'm retaining you as my lawyer," she said.

"My rate is a little higher than that," said Annie. "But I'll give you the friends and family discount."

"You can't reveal anything I tell you?"

Annie's eyes opened wider.

"Correct," Annie said.

She made herself another cup of coffee, tightened the bathrobe she'd borrowed from Annie, finger-combed her wet hair, and sat down.

"Something bad happened in Wales. The short version is that it was self-defense."

"Did you...?"

"No, it was the man I met there," she said. "He did it. He killed the thug. Frank Marshfield. But I helped him get rid of the body."

She studied Annie's reaction. There was a slight loosening of Annie's jaw, but that was it.

"How did you do that?" Annie asked.

"We dumped him into the ocean."

"Who else knows?"

"My father."

"Your father?" asked Annie, leaning back in her seat. "Jeeezus."

Carys spent the next half hour telling Annie every detail of the dive: figuring out the location of the cave, her near drowning, finding the tomb and the artifacts, surfacing to find Anthony being held hostage, and Dafydd saving them all with the blunt end of a fire extinguisher. The long boat ride out past the lights, the splash, sending Frank's boat on its solitary journey. How she couldn't stop shaking. Their vow never to speak of it.

"I've already broken that promise," she said.

"I am not legally allowed to say anything without your permission," said Annie. "And given Frank Marshfield's history, I could make a case for self-defense. But we would still need to find out who sent him to prove you were in imminent danger and it wasn't just some boating-related altercation."

"How about we just never report it?" she asked. "He just disappeared? He's a bad man working for someone even worse. There's no way anyone would trace it back to us."

"Maybe," said Annie, "but you've got two co-conspirators. Most of the time, these solemn-silence pacts last about one month. In your case it lasted, what, two days? How do you know they're not talking also?"

She had no idea.

"And, more importantly," said Annie, "what if the one pulling the strings already knows Frank is dead and has sent someone else to finish the job?"

"I don't know. That's why we need to track down the leads we have on Marshfield. And make sure that no one knows I'm back. Except you and Harper."

"Your co-conspirators know, yes?" asked Annie.

"Yes. They know. But they don't know where I am."

"Well, since you're not at home, it probably wouldn't take your father long to figure out that you're with me," said Annie.

A cold shot of panic ran through Carys. Annie was right. She was so easy to track down. She needed to get out of here and away from Annie. She couldn't put anyone else in danger. She stood up.

"Sit down. Sit down," said Annie. "You're safe here."

She slumped back down in her chair and lowered her head. Her wet hair dropped down around her face.

"I have no idea what to do," she said. She could feel tears welling at the back of her throat. She choked them down.

"We'll figure it out," said Annie. She put her hand on Carys's shoulder and gave it a squeeze. "We'll figure it out, I promise."

✦ ✦ ✦ ✦ ✦

ADEONA GLOWED IN THE SUNSHINE as Carys and Annie drove up the stone driveway two hours later. The police detail checked their IDs halfway up the drive and waved them along. She had never been so glad to see any place in her life. She wanted to lock herself in the vault and never come out. It was the only place where she felt safe.

When they got to the door, she knocked, waited, knocked again, waited, then slowly opened it.

"Hello," she called out.

JJ's tall, muscular form strode into the foyer, his body tensed for confrontation.

"Oh hi," she said. "No one answered…"

Confusion flitted through his eyes, then went away. She could feel Annie next to her sizing him up.

"Carys," said JJ, his hard features softening slightly. "It's nice to see you."

Great, she thought. *One more person who knows I'm here.*

"Who is it, JJ?" bellowed a voice from behind the partially closed door of the library. Harper. His voice was stronger than she'd ever heard it. It sounded almost hard.

JJ laughed to himself and shook his head, then strode over to the library door and flung it open. "It's Ms. Jones and a friend."

Harper, seated at his desk, spun around. His face broke into a wide smile.

She grabbed Annie's hand and pulled her through the dark door that led to the library. The morning light filtered dimly through the tall windows into the library. As she approached him, he pushed back the Harvard chair and rose. He was dressed in dark khakis and a pink Polo shirt, and his hair was washed and combed back. His eyes shone like she had never seen before. She was struck for the first time by how handsome he was.

"You're back!" he said, and walked toward them.

"You're home," she said. "And you're looking so well."

"Thanks to you," said Harper as he hugged her tightly and spun her around. Over Harper's shoulder, she could see JJ standing at the library door, watching with a bemused expression. He was clearly glad to have his father home. She smiled at him. JJ smiled back, turned, and walked toward the kitchen.

"And who is this?" asked Harper.

"This is Annie Brennan, my best friend and closest thing I have to family. I thought it was time you met her," she said.

Harper looked her up and down.

"Thank you for your help these past few days," he said. Then he looked at Carys, the unspoken question in his eyes.

"She knows everything," she said. Harper's face hardened. "I trust this woman with my life. She's helping identify Nicola's killer. Using back channels. No police."

Harper studied her a moment longer.

"We require absolute secrecy," he said to Annie.

"Carys retained me as her attorney," said Annie, looking Harper in the eye. "I legally can't say a word without her permission."

Harper nodded gruffly. "I don't like it," he said. "There are already too many people involved in this."

"I know," said Carys. "But we need her. I need her. She can help us figure out who is behind this."

There were still signs of the struggle that had taken Nicola's life. The glass in all the bookshelves was missing, and a section of the floor had been sanded down and needed to be revarnished. Most of the books were back in their perfectly aligned rows on the shelves, but several of the manuscripts were on Harper's desk, one with a cover torn off, one opened to the place where pages had been ripped out. Another was covered with a dark spatter of dried blood. The sight of it made her sick to her stomach, and she began to feel woozy. She sat down heavily in Harper's chair.

"Carys?" asked Annie.

"Just tired," she said. Harper's brow furrowed, then it softened. He had more important things on his mind than her kidneys.

"Let's see the new manuscript," he said.

She handed it over. He opened it slowly, reverently.

"Entirely in Latin," he said as he carefully paged through Madoc Morfran's journal. "Who could have imagined that we'd surface two journals, both with absolutely no provenance information, in our lifetimes? It's remarkable. And the ink on this one is so sharp and clear that it looks as if it was written yesterday. The parchment is nearly unblemished."

JJ walked into the library and approached the desk. Harper moved a notebook over the top of the Morfran manuscript as he approached.

"Dad, I'm meeting some friends in the city," said JJ. "You gonna be okay here?"

"I sure am," said Harper. "I'm feeling better than I have in a really long time. Thank you for checking in on me, son. I'll talk to you later."

"I'm glad you're back," said JJ. He lingered for a beat at the library door, studying his father, before closing it behind him.

Carys turned to Harper.

"John," she said. "There were some complications in Wales."

Harper looked at her. She looked at Annie. Annie's face was hard and set.

"I think we need to be careful about how we proceed," she said. "The man who tried to bribe me and who killed Nicola was…is just hired muscle. He was working for someone else. I'm sure of it."

Harper removed his eyeglasses and rubbed his eyes.

"Who?" he asked.

"I have no idea," she said. "Someone who's not on our radar."

"But likely someone in the antiquities business," said Harper. "Someone who sees this as a financial asset—instead of a histor-ical one."

"We have a name on the man who killed Nicola," said Annie. "Frank Marshfield. English citizen. Veteran of the British Navy. Rap sheet with a variety of charges—from petty theft to attempted murder."

"I've told Annie that we can't go to the police with this informa-tion yet," she said. "Not until after we find the tomb."

"Right," said Harper.

"But if the police can get more information on Marshfield, they might be able to figure out who he worked…works for, and we can stop this before anyone else gets hurt," said Annie.

"No. We'll deal with it later," said Harper. "Right now, we need to focus on the search. The police will just slow things down—and if they find Marshfield, then he'll tell the authorities about the manuscripts. We're not supposed to have either one of them, and they will be confiscated. You can be assured of that. We can't let anyone know about either of these manuscripts until we're done."

Annie's back straightened.

"I'm sorry, Mr. Harper, but don't you think it's reckless to continue this hunt when you know that there's someone—someone willing to kill—who is probably following your every move? I think you've dragged Carys far enough into this."

Annie's voice was strong, controlled, a half-octave lower than normal. Her lawyer voice. "I think she needs to hand this off to you and someone else at this point. She's in enough danger."

Harper glanced at Annie dismissively.

"Carys?" he asked.

She wanted to stop, to go back to Wales and find Dafydd and make love and drink beer and stare out at the sea and the green hills for a month straight and never think about any of this ever again. But the bad guy, Frank's employer, whoever he was, would be after them as long as they had the manuscript and the clues to the location of the tomb, and neither she nor Harper would ever willingly part with those.

"I'm not quitting," she said. "Annie, I'm sorry. You told me sometimes there are things worth fighting for, and this is one of them."

"A thousand-year-old dead guy?" asked Annie, her voice back to normal.

"Fifteen-hundred," she said. "And you know it's more than that. It's one of the most important historical discoveries in the world. And it's in danger."

She watched the fight drain out of Annie.

"How can I help?" Annie asked.

"You can't," said Harper. "Although we may be in need of your services once this is resolved." He smiled at Annie.

"I'm planning on it," Annie said.

"Let's figure out what this book is telling us about where Madoc Morfran landed," said Harper, beaming.

He stroked the cover of Morfran's manuscript as if it were a pet. He put the book on the long antique table in the middle of the room, then retrieved a large rolled document from one of the bookcases. He unspooled it on the table, placing other books on all four corners. It was a map of the northeast coast of North America.

"We know he landed here," he said, sweeping his hand across the map. "Which is strange. Did he mention why he came all the way to North America?"

"Yeah," said Carys. "He wrote that he needed a safe place to bury his father where the hordes could never find him. But he was also searching for a safe, green, and fertile land for his people to start over after the drought and plague that hit the British Isles. He wrote that the northern peoples had already sailed as far as what is now Greenland. He called it the great icy land past the smoking island, or Iceland."

"But that was a good five hundred years before any recorded Viking settlements in Greenland," said Harper.

"Not all explorers stick around long enough to build settlements," she said. "The fact is that Morfran specifically states that the hordes had already made it that far. But neither Iceland nor Greenland were green or fertile, so he decided to keep looking."

"Next stop would have been Newfoundland, then Nova Scotia, then New England," said Harper. "Remarkable. Read me the part where he describes the location of the tomb."

She picked up the manuscript with her bare hands and opened the heavy pages. Out of habit, she began to lift the book to her face for a sniff.

"Carys," said Harper. She looked up at him. He furrowed his eyebrows at her slightly and shook his head. She lowered the book and continued to flip through Morfran's dense Latin writing until she came to the section that described the beach where they had buried the King.

"Here it is," she said, placing the book on the table. "'We interred our lord in a grave constructed by the native ones. The people gathered around with their sacred objects—bones, shells, bowls of food, offerings to ensure my father's safe passage to his next adventure. As was the people's custom, we laid him in a pit dug in the sand above the waterfront, surrounded by short and bushy trees. In front of us was the ocean, behind us was a great green marsh, filled with every sort of bird, with the broad flat land of the natives farther on still. The dunes around us were on a long narrow spit of land, like a finger pointing toward our homeland.'"

"Clearly a barrier island or narrow peninsula," said Harper, his eyes closed in concentration. "'Pointing toward our homeland'—east?"

"Probably," she said. She continued reading. "'We laid him in line with the shore, which ran straight and true as far as the eye could see in both directions. We placed his head toward home, and his feet toward his final glory. I laid him on his back, his right arm outstretched and wearing the ring of Ambrosius. He shall point to the ocean and his star for eternity. I placed our people's treasures from the cave crypt into his grave, and the native people placed their sacred objects there as well. I conducted what I could remember of a Christian burial rite and made the sign of the cross. Then we stacked the gravel and rocks and sand upon his body. We then placed stones in the shape of a cross upon his grave. I wept.'"

"Toward whose star?" asked Harper.

"*Ad aeternitam stellam suam indicabit*," read Carys. "*Suam*—it's a possessive male pronoun. And it refers back to Arcturus."

"Okay, his star. And they laid him in line with the northern shore, so parallel to it," said Harper. "'His head toward home.' East."

"That makes sense," she said. "So, if his head is facing east, his feet are west, and if they laid him on his back, his right outstretched arm would point north."

"Is there a star named Arcturus?" asked Annie.

They both looked at her. Harper went to his desk and flipped open a small laptop computer, typed quickly and then stood, staring at the screen. A broad smile spread across his face.

"'Arcturus,'" he read, "'the left foot of the constellation Bootes. Visible in the northern celestial hemisphere. Next to Ursa Major and Ursa Minor. It is called the guardian of the bear.'" He looked up at them triumphantly. "Due north in the northern hemisphere."

Carys smiled, despite the exhaustion that now penetrated down to her very core. Her knees were beginning to weaken, and the pain in her gut had made a reappearance and was beginning to gnaw away. She placed her hands on the table to steady herself.

"If they placed him in line with the shore of the island, and the island was straight as far as the eye could see, the barrier island would have a due east-west orientation," she said.

"And his hand pointed north toward the ocean," said Harper. "So the barrier island would have a north-facing shore."

Harper bent over and began to scan the coastline on the map. Annie and Carys waited silently, stealing only a short glance at each other. Annie's eyes were wide.

Harper took a pencil and lightly drew a circle on the map on a section of the Maine coastline, then continued scanning down through Connecticut.

"Do we think he could have been talking about Long Island?" asked Carys. "That's almost due east-west in orientation."

"But no northern-facing barrier islands," said Annie. "They're all south-facing."

She and Harper looked at Annie, puzzled.

"What?" Annie asked, shrugging her shoulders. "I used to date a guy from Southampton. I know the beaches there by heart." Carys shook her head and smiled.

Harper stood up and rubbed his eyes.

"There's only one place that meets our criteria on the entire coast from Maine to Delaware," he said. "We'll need to confirm that it was inhabited by aboriginals fifteen hundred years ago, but it looks like this might be it."

He drew a circle on the map and stabbed his pencil into it. She and Annie looked down at it.

"You've got to be kidding me," said Annie. She burst out laughing.

◆ ◆ ◆ ◆ ◆

The office of Professor Lydia Grant was not much more than a closet, yet she'd managed to pack more Native American art and artifacts on the walls and shelves than Carys had ever seen in her life. Not that she'd seen that many. She tightly clutched a plastic bag containing the arrowhead, afraid that after one look, this guardian of Native American history would demand to take possession.

Harper, a major benefactor at Harvard University, had pulled strings and wrangled a meeting on short notice with Grant for that afternoon. Annie went into work for a few hours. She said she had things to do—and that she'd seen quite enough of Harvard, thank you very much, during her law school years. Carys drove Harper's Range Rover into Cambridge, pleased to be back on the right side of the road again.

Grant was one of the preeminent scholars of Native American anthropology, not just at Harvard but in the United States, which was impressive considering her young age. She was in denim shorts and a tank top, makeup-less, her short, cropped Afro covered in part by a bandana. She clearly had plans that, until a couple of hours earlier, had not included being in her office on a glorious summer weekend afternoon. She sat across from Carys and Harper at her small desk, all but glaring at them.

"What can I do for you, Mr. Harper, on this fine day?" she asked.

"Thanks for meeting us," said Harper. "I certainly owe you and President Davidson."

Mention of her boss's boss's boss seemed to temper her anger a bit.

"We are trying to determine the age and provenance of some artifacts," said Harper. He nodded at Carys. She placed the plastic bag containing the arrowhead on the desk. Grant reached across and picked it up.

"We'd be most appreciative if you could tell us anything at all about this," Harper said quietly.

"Where did you get it?" asked Grant. "You realize that if you disturbed a gravesite or native lands, you've committed a felony."

"I assure you that we did not," said Harper in a voice that made it clear they would not discuss its provenance further. "We're trying to confirm that it could have been crafted by a tribe in New England during the mid-sixth century."

Grant put on her eyeglasses and picked up the tiny arrowhead from the desk. She leaned over to take a closer look, and as she did, her eyes widened. The professor reached into her desk and pulled out a loupe, like the ones jewelers use to examine gems, and snapped it onto the front of her right lens. She flipped the arrowhead over, studied it for a moment longer, and then peered over the top of her glasses at Carys.

"Who are you again?" Grant asked her.

"She's my associate," answered Harper. "What can you tell us?"

Grant's gaze lingered on her for a moment longer, then her eyes returned to the arrowhead.

"It's a pristine example—the best I've ever seen—of an arrowhead from the Middle Woodland period. That's roughly mid-sixth century," said Grant. "There were aboriginal people in the northeast at the time, from Maine down through the mid-Atlantic. Their territory spread all the way west to the Mississippi River, so this could have come from any of those locations."

"We believe it came from a barrier island in New England," said Carys. "Were there Middle Woodland populations there at that time?"

"The aboriginal populations used barrier islands as seasonal villages," said Grant. "Burial mounds and graves from that era, some containing arrowheads just like this, have been found all over New England. There is one barrier island that has been particularly fertile for archaeologists over the years."

"Where is it?" she asked.

"Cape Cod," said Grant. "Sandy Neck. On the bay side, north of Hyannis."

Carys shot a glance over at Harper, who looked her way briefly then averted his eyes.

"We've recovered evidence from burial pits that it's been inhabited for several thousand years," said Grant, removing her glasses. "I actually did a dig there myself during my grad work. That's the only barrier island I've ever heard of with signs of long-term established communities on it. There have been other minor finds on some of the other barriers, but none as rich as Sandy Neck. There was a large, very developed population there. And they stayed there year after year, unlike other tribes that moved their base around. The fishing and hunting were particularly good in that area. Their homes would have been protected from the sea and wind by the big sand dunes there."

"What tribe would have been there?" asked Harper.

"They weren't really organized into tribes at that time," said Grant. "But the aboriginals who live in that region today are all part of the Algonquin peoples. That particular area would be…"

She turned to her computer and typed a few words.

"That barrier island would have been populated by ancestors of what today is the Mattakeese, a tribe of the Wampanoag nation," said Grant. "They had a great chief during the 1600s who was very helpful to the European invaders. As thanks, the invaders gave them all sorts of nasty viruses. Most of the natives died from it. But the surviving Mattakeese can be traced to that region since long before Columbus showed up. Sandy Neck is a state park now. There's some rare bird that breeds there, so there's no more digs allowed without jumping through all sorts of legal hoops. Bit of a nightmare actually."

Harper's hand shook.

"Do you have anything we could read about the Mattakeese—their legends, origin story, the gods they worshipped, anything at all?" he asked.

"I don't have anything specific to that tribe here in this office. There's a tribal office located not too far from Sandy Neck," said Grant. "Not sure if it's the Mattakeese or some other tribe of the Wampanoag, but I'm sure they'd be helpful in answering any of your questions. Let me get their address."

◆ ◆ ◆ ◆ ◆

GYLES STROLLED THROUGH THE RAIN to Boodles for a late Sunday roast dinner. The stately private club, made of granite, brick, warped ancient glass, wrought iron, and history, was just a few blocks from his flat. Although the rain was hammering down, the walk helped dissipate the stress that was gnawing at his stomach and threatened to suck the enjoyment out of the only meal to which he looked forward during the week.

Frank was still missing. But Jones wasn't. She was back in Boston. There'd been activity in her bank account—an ATM withdrawal. She was being very sloppy if she was trying not to be found. Of course, she couldn't possibly realize how easily he could track her.

Mounting the stairs to the lounge abutting the regal dining room, adorned with portraits of the royals and prime ministers who had been members for the past three hundred years, he felt, as he always did—like he was trespassing. *If they really knew me,* he thought with a grin, *they'd bar the door and set the place on fire before they'd agree to let me in.*

Despite his sterling reputation in the art and antiquities community, his international law and art history degrees from Trinity College, and his upper-class network of contacts, it was still his lower-class upbringing that had given the membership committee serious pause. Class structure still ruled here at Boodles. But there is nothing quite so influential as gobs of money to grease some wheels and change some minds. His membership had been unanimously approved after the delivery of a very large check for his initiation fee and the first year's membership, as well as a receipt for a donation of twice that size to a local orphans' charity in the club's name.

He sat in his usual spot, by a window in a black lounge chair. No one was sitting within earshot. He nodded to the barman, who arrived a minute later with his scotch, neat, and a side glass with four ice cubes. He placed one cube in the amber liquid, took a sip, felt its heat at the back of his throat, and pulled out his burner phone.

Plourde answered in two rings.

"Martin," said Plourde. "I'm not somewhere I can talk. Can I call you back?"

"No," he said. "You don't need to talk. Just listen."

"This really isn't a good time," said Plourde.

"I'll be brief. Then you can go back to whatever it is that you Yanks do on Sundays. Football, is it?"

On the other end of the phone, he could hear a television blaring and a woman's voice yelling at someone to pick up his damn shoes. Domestic bliss.

"Let me go somewhere more private," said Plourde. The background noises faded. A door shut, then all was quiet.

"What is it?" asked Plourde.

"I need you to watch Carys Jones for me," he said.

A long pause. He waited it out. Yanks hate silence.

"I'm afraid I'm going to have to decline," said Plourde.

"You're not in a position to decline."

"You're not in a position to ask," said Plourde. "Why don't you get Frank to do it? Or one of your other helpers? I can't go near her."

"Frank is indisposed. And I want you to do it. You've managed to keep your hands clean in our dealings so far, and it's time for you to put a little bit more of your own personal skin in the game."

Plourde took a deep breath. "I'm out," he said. "I provided a fucking murder weapon. How much more skin do you want?"

"Some more," said Gyles.

"Martin, I've been more than cooperative, and I've generated a great deal of value for you over the past years. But it's over. At least until this stuff with the maid blows over. It's just too hot for me right now," said Plourde.

"You don't decide when it's over," he said, his voice dropping an octave and to a near whisper. He could feel the chilling effect that his tone was having on Plourde, even from an ocean away.

"I am very grateful for our business relationship," said Plourde. "But I think it would be unwise to try to pressure me into doing something I do not want to do."

"Unwise?"

"I can connect you directly to the murder of that woman, and to a variety of other crimes, and you do not want to piss me off," said Plourde quickly, as though he were racing to get the words out. The man was scared.

Gyles smiled.

"Are you threatening me, Mr. Plourde?"

"No," said Plourde. "But you are not the only one with leverage here. I make one phone call and you won't see the sky for twenty to thirty years minimum."

"So, yes, then. You are threatening me. That's a very interesting play, Mr. Plourde. Bold. Thank you for your time and your years of service."

He hung up.

With Frank missing, presumed who knew where, he needed to know just how much of a risk Plourde represented in the matter of the maid. Now he had his answer. Soon, he would, at least, have this problem solved.

2

◇◇◇◇◇◇

Monday, June 25

Carys didn't want to go back to her apartment to get a suit, so Annie loaned her one that would look presentable for Nicola's funeral. Annie had argued with her against going, and the two fought harder than they had in years. In the end, she convinced Annie that she'd be fine. She would just go there and back. No one but JJ and Harper knew who she was. She wanted to do this one thing for Nicola—pay her respects, which seemed so small in comparison to what Nicola had done.

The funeral was in a small Protestant church in Wellesley, near the lush, perfectly manicured, colonial town green. She noticed, for the first time, how much the landscape resembled that of Wales.

Nicola had been cremated, and her urn sat on a table at the foot of the altar, the sun streaming down on it through the stained-glass windows, bathing it in reds and greens. JJ and Harper sat in the front row, next to five grieving people who looked to be Nicola's relatives or friends. She took a seat on a hard wooden pew in the back.

The eulogy, by Nicola's sister, was a revelation. Nicola hadn't just studied linguistics. She'd gotten her PhD. She'd taught at the university in Cardiff for many years before coming to the United States to do some postdoctoral work at Boston University.

That's where she and Harper had met. The parts that were left out of the eulogy—why she was at Harper's home, in his library, why she'd given up her life to protect an ancient manuscript—were the parts of Nicola's story that only she and Harper knew. Having shared this secret with Nicola made her feel closer to her in a sea of unfamiliar, grieving faces.

Afterward, Harper had a small brunch catered at Adeona for the mourners. From where she was sitting, she could see Harper's knee bouncing up and down under the table. He kept glancing over at the door to the hallway and his library. When brunch was finally over, Harper and Nicola's relatives took the urn to the flower garden far behind the house and scattered the ashes. She stood quietly watching from the living room window.

I got your revenge, Nicola, she thought as the cloud of powdery white ashes flew up on the wind, then fell back onto the earth. *We got him.*

A few minutes later, she and JJ stood together in the hallway, waiting for Harper to be done in the garden.

"I can't believe how well he's doing," said JJ. "He said you warned him it might be an infection, and you were right. The medicine worked immediately. How did you know that?"

"Just something I read about, thought it might be helpful," she said.

"But his doctors couldn't even figure it out," he said.

"Well, sometimes you just have to ask the right questions," she said. "May I go into the library?"

"Sure," said JJ. He walked her to the door, and she opened it with her set of keys. They entered. JJ stood just inside the library entrance, gazing up at the balcony above him. "I got so close to selling this all off."

"You did what you thought you had to do," she said.

"I haven't heard or read anything about my father's illness in the tabloids, so I'm hoping this chapter is closed. Except for finding Nicola's killer. The police say they don't have any leads. Wish I'd never called Sothington's in the first place."

"I know your father understands," she said.

JJ looked at her, his face intense, his eyes weary.

"You know, I'll never really understand him the way you do. I want to, but I never will. Nicola understood him, though. She loved him very much. And he her."

Carys flinched slightly.

"How long have you known about them?" she asked.

"Since they started up," he said. "It upset me at first. You never want to think your parents could ever love anyone but each other. But I was glad he had someone to look after him."

JJ smiled an odd little smile.

"And even if I hadn't known, today certainly would have made it pretty clear. I mean, look at the guy. He's absolutely crushed." He pointed out the long windows down to the garden, where Harper stood alone, his eyes lowered to the ground and Nicola's ashes. It looked like he was crying.

She turned to JJ. Her heart was aching for both of them.

"It's strange," she said, putting her hand lightly on his arm. "I didn't cry when my mother died. Sometimes pain is so deep and hard that you can't cry. All you can do is be numb. It's the only way through it."

JJ looked at her for a moment. Then he put his hand on top of hers and patted it lightly.

"I think I know what you mean," he said. "I'm not sure when I'll see you again, Ms. Jones. But thank you for helping my father." They shook hands, then he turned and walked out of the library, and out the front door of Adeona.

She glanced around the library again, and her eyes lingered on the sanded patch of library floor. She would never feel like this wasn't her fault.

Through the long, thin windows, she saw Harper down by the garden. She walked closer to the windows to get a better look. He had his hands to his eyes, and his back was heaving.

Grief washed over her. She put her hands against the window and her forehead against the cool glass. She let the tears stream down her face onto the wooden floor.

◆ ◆ ◆ ◆ ◆

WHEN CARYS GOT BACK to Annie's apartment, she found her sitting on the couch watching *The Real Housewives of Atlanta*, one of her very few mindless pleasures. She hadn't gone to work—she was serious about not wanting her to be alone for too long, although she wasn't entirely sure what Annie thought she would be able to do if someone really did come after her.

Annie scanned her face as she came into the living room.

"How'd it go?" Annie asked.

"Gut-wrenching," she said. "I am so jet-lagged I can hardly think right now. I'm going to go take a nap. Will you wake me in a couple of hours?"

"You know it," said Annie.

She sank into a deep sleep the moment her head hit the pillow. What felt like mere moments later, she woke to Annie shaking her by the shoulders.

"There's someone here to see you," said Annie.

She snapped fully awake. "What?"

"A man named Dafydd," said Annie, eyes wide. "Tall, handsome, Welsh. Ringing any bells? Do I welcome him in or get my gun out and call the cops?"

She bolted upright, her head still blurry from sleep. She rubbed her eyes.

"No, he's my friend," she said. "He's here? How the hell did he know I was here?"

"He said your father told him you'd probably stay here once you got home," said Annie. "He gave him the address. He's outside. He's the man who killed Frank, isn't he?"

"Quiet," she hissed. "Yes. Yes, it's him. Jesus Christ. Do not let on that you know. He can't know that I told you." She jumped out of bed and began to throw on the clothes she had worn the day before.

"No," said Annie, pulling a pair of jeans and a light sweater out of the bureau. "Please do not put those clothes back on. They stink." She shoved the fresh clothing at Carys, who dove into them without protest. She ran a comb through her matted hair and smacked herself on the face a couple of times to restart blood flow.

"I need coffee," she groaned to Annie.

"Pot's full," said Annie. "Now let's get out there, shall we?"

She left the bedroom and went to the front door of Annie's apartment and peeked out into the hallway. Dafydd was standing with his back to the door, a backpack over his broad shoulders. He turned when he heard the door open. Her heart skipped a beat, and she felt her knees wiggle, a physical memory from the night they'd spent together. He smiled broadly.

"Hi," he said. She opened the door wide and backed up to let him in, and then found herself wrapped in his arms. She stuck her face into the crook of his neck, then looked up and gave him a deep and long kiss.

"I'll just go melt into the woodwork over here," Annie said. She glanced back as Annie stepped into the kitchen.

"I asked you not to come," Carys said.

"Your father begged me to," he whispered. "And I wanted to. Neither of us could stomach the thought of you finishing this all by yourself. Not after everything that's happened."

"I'm not by myself. Harper and Annie are…" she said. Her protest was feeble. "I am glad to see you."

"I should hope so," he said. "Do we know where the old King is buried yet?"

"Believe it or not, we do. We located the only place on the northeastern coast that matches all the details," she said with a smile.

"Where is it?" said Dafydd.

"You're not going to believe it," she said.

"I don't really believe any of this," said Dafydd. "Let's have it."

"Cape Cod."

"Where?" asked Dafydd.

She shook her head and smiled.

"King Arthur is buried on a barrier island called Sandy Neck about one hour away from where we are standing right at this moment."

His jaw dropped open. Then his eyes began to twinkle and an enormous laugh, almost like a roar, bellowed out of him.

◆ ◆ ◆ ◆ ◆

ANNIE MADE SMALL TALK with them for a couple of hours, but when it became painfully obvious that she was in the way, she announced that she had some work to do down at the office. She hadn't been gone more than ten minutes before Carys and Dafydd were in bed in her room, making love with an intensity that seemed like it would make her head explode. Afterward, they lay there, both staring at the ceiling, sweating.

"I am so glad you came to help me," she said. "'Cause I definitely couldn't do that by myself."

He laughed.

"When are we leaving for Cape Cod?" he asked.

She rolled onto her stomach so she could look him in the eyes. "You aren't leaving for Cape Cod," she said.

"Why not?"

"It's not just me, Dafydd. This is my client's hunt."

"And now it's mine. You have to admit that you never would have found that cave without me. Or survived the rest of the night."

She stared at him. He was right. He had risked his life for her. He had saved her and her father. It was as much his search as hers now. She didn't have the right to include him, but she would fight for his right to be there.

3

Tuesday, June 26

Carys and Dafydd woke early the next morning and made love twice more before finally rolling out of bed and getting into the guest room shower. There they made love once more standing up. Wrapped in Dafydd's body, his thrusts making her come again, surrounded by the soothing drum of the hot water, she let her mind be completely empty of anything but the physical sensations of that moment. It was a level of blankness and physical awareness she'd never experienced in her life. She did not want to let the day's thoughts and plans intrude on her quiet, blessedly empty mind. But the search awaited.

After they were both dressed, she packed a bag and put the two bags containing the manuscripts and translation into her large purse. Annie drove them to Adeona. Carys was surprised when JJ opened the door. She hadn't expected him to move into the mansion with his father, but clearly some bond still held them.

"Good morning," said JJ, backing up to let them in.

"Good morning," she said. "This is my friend, Dafydd."

Dafydd shook JJ's hand, the two men sizing each other up.

"Nice to meet you," said JJ.

"You too," said Dafydd.

"Would you excuse me?" JJ nodded slightly and walked into the kitchen. Harper was in the library, hunched over his desk. She walked in and he turned around with a smile on his face, which disappeared when he saw Dafydd.

"Hello," Harper said tentatively. Dafydd strode forward.

"Hello, Mr. Harper," he said, extending a hand. "I'm Dafydd Reynolds. A friend of Carys's from Wales. I was with her on the—"

"Carys, what is he doing here?" asked Harper gruffly, ignoring Dafydd's outstretched hand.

"He's coming to the Cape with us," she said.

"No," said Harper, rising from his chair, his voice a barely controlled growl. A deep red splotch formed near the collar of his shirt. "No, he is absolutely not coming to the Cape with us. Jesus. Why don't we just issue a goddamned press release? Invite the whole town. How much did you tell him?"

"John," she said as calmly as she could, "I didn't know until yesterday that he would be here, but now that he is, he's in this with us. Dafydd is the only reason we found the original tomb. He is the only reason that we survived long enough to find out where Morfran's manuscript led. He is the reason I survived that dive. We owe him everything."

Harper stood, arms crossed, a foot jutted forward, his eyes narrowed and determined. He glared at Dafydd, who stood solidly, arms at his sides, meeting Harper's eyes fully and without a trace of intimidation or fear. She felt ridiculously proud of Dafydd, as if he were hers to claim.

"Mr. Harper," said Dafydd evenly. "I made a promise to Carys's father that I would look after her and make sure that she got through this search unharmed, and that is what I am going to do. If she goes, I go."

"Carys can take care of herself," Harper barked. "I don't think even she realizes how strong she is."

"I don't need Dafydd to go with us. We'll be fine. I'll be fine. My father will get over it. He doesn't really even know me," she said. Dafydd's shoulders stiffen. "But I want him to go."

"You trust him?" asked Harper.

"Completely," she said. Dafydd smiled at her.

Harper waited a beat longer.

"Fine," Harper said. "But there are far too many people involved in this now."

She put her large purse on the desk, and retrieved the two manuscripts, wrapped in silk and stored inside plastic sealable bags, and the translation.

"What should we do with these?" she asked. "They'd be safer here, in the vault."

"We may need them," said Harper. He pulled the monk's manuscript from its plastic bag, unwrapped it, and smiled at it like it was an old friend. He began to lift it to his face but stopped, glanced up at her, half smiled, and lowered it again. He rewrapped it and put it back in its bag, then put all the books back into Carys's purse.

"JJ," hollered Harper. "Can you come in here for a minute?"

"Be right there," he said from what sounded like the kitchen. He appeared at the door.

"My friends and I are going to be gone for a little while," said Harper.

"Your doctor said you're susceptible to infection," said JJ.

"I'll be fine," he said. "If I have any problems at all, I promise I'll come right home."

"Where are you going?" asked JJ.

"Cape Cod," said Harper.

"Strange time to take a vacation," said JJ. "Since you just got out of the hospital."

"It's work," said Harper. "Research for the library."

"Of course," JJ said. "When will you be back?"

"Not sure," said Harper. "Will you be staying at Adeona while I'm gone?"

"If you'd like," said JJ.

"Thanks, JJ," said Harper. "I'll call you when I know when we'll be back. It won't be long. I promise. Then maybe you and I can head up to New Hampshire to the cabin for a few days."

JJ examined his father closely for a minute.

"Sure, Dad," said JJ. "That would be nice."

Then he turned and strode out of the library.

"Don't let those books leave your side," Harper said to Carys. "They are incontrovertible proof of the identity of the man in that tomb—wherever it is."

They loaded their luggage into the back of his Range Rover. It had already been nearly filled with a collection of detection devices. The target of the search was not a skeleton or tomb per se but metal—specifically, the metal of Ambrosius's ring, and any other metal objects left behind. It was the only thing they could be certain had not deteriorated with age. To be careful, Harper also packed a crazy-looking ultrasound-like contraption that revealed whatever was below the surface of the earth in three dimensions. It looked like a very heavy, complicated vacuum cleaner.

Despite all of this advanced detection firepower, they had a problem, and it was the only one that mattered. Sandy Neck was seven miles long and thousands of feet wide. It had shifted, shrunk, grown, and evolved over the previous centuries. The grave might be submerged in wetlands or buried so far under a sand dune that even the complicated vacuum cleaner couldn't find it. It could take an entire summer to properly canvass even a square mile of the area. And if there was still someone after them, they most likely didn't have that kind of time.

They were counting on the Mattakeese having some kind of legend or song or history of where their ancestors had put the King. Mattakeese Sachem Mary Clark and her people's memories were their only hope of ending this search. And Harper had already made an appointment to meet her.

They drove silently. Carys felt like she was on some strange family vacation. She checked Dafydd in the rearview mirror every few minutes. He'd met her eye with a grin the first few times, but after twenty minutes his head was back against the headrest and he was dozing. Harper sat rigidly, his nerves tight.

"What do we do if the tribe doesn't know anything?" she asked quietly.

Harper sat still, staring straight ahead, and didn't answer.

About half an hour into the drive, Carys's regular cell phone buzzed from inside the cup holder in the armrest. She looked down. Plourde's name popped up on the caller ID.

She huffed and hit the "send to voice mail" button on the screen.

"Who's that?" asked Harper.

"My boss at Sothington's," said Carys. "The one who blackmailed JJ. Can't imagine what he's got to say to me."

"You don't have to worry about him or that job anymore," said Harper.

She smiled. She'd almost forgotten that the library was part of the original deal.

"Have you been to the doctor yet?" he asked her quietly.

"No. I haven't had time. This seemed more important."

"You need to do that," said Harper.

"The pain has mostly gone away. I don't think I was exposed long enough to do serious damage anyway."

Harper continued to watch the side of her face, and broke off his gaze only when she turned and faced him.

It took them an hour and a half to get from Wellesley to the Sagamore Bridge and onto Route 6A, which wound through sparse scrub and pine forests along the northern coast of Cape Cod, skirting around the lakes, rivers, inlets, and salt marshes that dominated the landscape. The road had been in use nearly continuously since the 1600s, when, according to conventional history, white men first arrived on the Cape, a peninsula of Massachusetts that resembles a flexed arm. But the Morfran manuscript had just shattered that piece of American lore.

Carys had loved coming to the Cape with her parents when she was little. Her favorite memory from those trips was of spending entire days with her father watching the horseshoe crabs in the marshes near the house they always rented in the town of Dennis. She thought they were little monsters. Her father said they were the oldest inhabitants of the Cape, dating back before there were men here. Had Madoc Morfran gazed at these little creatures, with their front-mounted spike, so like a sword, and their hard, shield-shaped carapace, and seen in them an omen?

The view, the sun, the memories lulled her, but behind it all lurked the knowledge that somewhere, someone was still after them.

The Colonial Inn was the definition of Cape Cod quaint. It was a one-hundred-and-fifty-year-old, rambling colonial-era farmhouse, sitting in a copse on the edge of a large pond. It was the only inn in Barnstable with Wi-Fi and three vacancies. Carys didn't feel comfortable sharing a room with Dafydd with Harper there. She didn't want to give him any more reasons to question her decision to bring him along.

They lugged their bags in and greeted the young innkeeper, who informed them that she and her husband had taken over the B&B the year before and were hoping to have a better summer than they'd had last year. There was talk of a broken furnace and mice in the attic, all rectified, and breakfast in the dining room from seven to ten. Harper, who was used to ignoring service people, interrupted her as she was about to describe their famous French toast.

"Can you show us to our rooms right away?" he asked. "We've got some work we've got to get done."

"On such a beautiful day?" protested the innkeeper. "That's such a shame. Sandy Neck is right around the corner. Five-minute drive. It's one of the most beautiful beaches in the area. You should—"

"We really need to get started," said Carys. The young woman looked crestfallen. She quietly retreated to the kitchen and returned with three sets of keys.

"Follow me," she said.

Once Carys dropped her luggage in her own room, she went to Harper's, which, like hers, resembled a page out of *Victorian Homes* magazine. Nearly every surface was covered with blue chintz, and there were so many pillows piled up on the bed that she wasn't sure which end was the head. Harper had settled into a wingback chair by long windows overlooking the back garden. She sat in the other wingback. The garden was in full, glorious bloom. The last of the peonies were wrestling with a tangle of new red tiger lilies and the green leaves of the hydrangea bushes were just beginning to sprout from the remnants of the previous year's plants.

They didn't speak a word for a long time. Harper was about to say something when there was a light knock and Dafydd pushed open the door. He instantly began grinning at the decor.

"It looks like my grandmother threw up in here," he said. He shoved some of the pillows over and sat at the end of the bed facing them. "What's the plan?"

"The meeting," she said to Harper. "How should we play it?"

"First of all, I don't think Dafydd should join us," said Harper. She began to speak but Harper raised his hand. "Hear me out. Three people against one will immediately put her back up against the wall. We need her to cooperate, and I think three will just be too intimidating."

He was right. She turned to Dafydd.

"You'll have to find something to do for an hour or two," she said.

Dafydd looked like he was going to put up a fight, then shook his head. She smiled and Dafydd winked at her. The briefest of scowls crossed Harper's face.

◆ ◆ ◆ ◆ ◆

THEY HAD AN HOUR before their meeting with the sachem, so Carys and Dafydd left Harper's room. They stood in the hallway.

"You'll tell me everything, right?" Dafydd asked.

"Of course," she said, and kissed him again before breaking free and going inside her room. When she was done unpacking, she went downstairs to meet Harper. He was sitting at a desk in the parlor just off the inn's main hallway, typing furiously on his laptop.

Harper's eyes popped up at her for a second as she entered.

"Come look at this," he said. She walked to his side and peered over his shoulder. He was examining a map of what looked like Sandy Neck. There were little X's drawn on it, clustered at various places along the Neck, each one accompanied by a handwritten date range.

"Those X's are the aboriginal burial sites that Grant was talking about," said Harper. "Sandy Neck has been an archaeological dig site for centuries. They've been finding aboriginal artifacts there almost since the Europeans arrived. The sites get younger and younger as you go east along the Neck." He pointed at the dates next to the X clusters. The first site seemed to be two thousand years old; the second, fifteen hundred; the third, around five hundred, and so on. "They carbon-dated these sites, and they also inventoried what they found. Guess what they found in this cluster of sites from fifteen hundred years ago?"

"Beach plum seeds, cranberry seeds, and wampum?"

"Bingo," he said. "The section with the oldest burial mounds is also the widest part of the Neck. Not much erosion or sand-shifting there. But lots as you go farther east." He clicked on a second window on his browser, and up popped a satellite image of Sandy Neck.

"The area of the dig site dating to the Dark Ages is virtually the same as the day those graves were dug," he said. "But who knows how many younger sites have been buried beyond discovery or washed away by storms farther down the Neck."

"That reduces the search area," she said. "Can we just go out there and start using that giant vacuum cleaner thingy or a metal detector?"

"No," said Harper. "We're still talking about dozens of acres that need to be searched, most of it sand dunes. It would take us months, if we could even get permission from the authorities to tramp around in those dunes. They're all considered sensitive environmental areas. But at least we know he's there. We know the place that he was buried could not have been eroded away—although he may be buried under half a mile of sand by now. We know that it's not a wild goose chase. He and whatever was buried with him are still there, waiting for us to find him."

"Unless someone already dug it up," she said.

"Carys," he said. "I told you before. If someone already found that burial site, I would have heard about it."

"Someone could have dug it up centuries ago. Looters have been around since…" Harper was actively ignoring this possibility, as he had been since the beginning of his search. The chance that someone had gotten to the King long, long ago was the only thing that would render his quest futile.

She sat down on the chintz-covered sofa. "What do we do now?"

Harper rubbed his eyes with the palms of his hands. When he removed them, his age was hard upon his face. He took a deep breath, leaned back in his chair, and stretched.

"I, for one, could use a nap," he said. "It's been a long few days."

She smiled.

"The service and the brunch for Nicola were really beautiful," she said. "She would have loved it."

He stared off into a far-away place.

"I can't believe she's gone," he finally said. "I keep wanting to pick up the phone and call her and tell her what's happening. She'd be so excited. All these years we worked on the translation. It is as much her find as mine and yours, you know. I could not have done it without her."

"I know," she said. "And she went to her grave to protect what you'd done together. You can never blame yourself for that."

Harper's eyes snapped onto Carys's and turned razor sharp.

"I want you to know that when this is over, I will make good on my promise to give you the manuscript and the library," he said. "I've already drawn up the documents and had them notarized. It's all legal. Every single thing in the library will be yours, to do whatever you want with. Remember our deal: I get credit for the find; you get everything else."

"Of course." She smiled. "And I can run my new business from your library, right?"

Harper's eyes continued to bore through her.

"I'll be selling the house when we're done," he said. "The books must go with you."

"Why on earth would you sell that place?"

"I won't need it where I'll be going," he said.

"Which is where, exactly?" she asked, leaning slightly forward.

"I'm going to find and kill the motherfucker who murdered Nicola," he said. "This Frank Marshfield asshole. Then I'll turn myself in. I'll spend the rest of my life in jail, happily. It's the only thing I have to offer her."

Her body stiffened. "You can't do that," she said.

You very literally cannot, she thought.

"I can and I will," he said. "I am looking forward to it almost as much as I am to finding Arcturus."

She had stolen his revenge. He'd hate her for that when he found out. The fire in her abdomen flared, and she winced slightly.

"What's happening?" Harper asked.

"Just a little pain in my gut," she said. "It's getting better."

"You need to start in on the meds they have me on," said Harper. "Are you still smelling the manuscript?"

Just then a racket arose as the front door opened and a morbidly obese, middle-aged couple wearing visors, loud Hawaiian print shirts, and knee-length khaki shorts clambered in. They glanced into the parlor, waved half-heartedly at her and Harper, and began their trudge up the stairs to their room, the stairs squeaking in protest. When the tourists had finally waddled their way up to the first landing, she figured they were out of earshot. She turned to Harper and whispered.

"I haven't seen Lestinus since I've been back in the U.S.," she said. "I don't know where he is."

"When is the last time you saw him?"

"The last morning in Aberystwyth," she said.

"Maybe he thinks his part is done," says Harper. "He led you to where he left the King." Then his expression shifted, and he looked at her long and hard. "What happened in Wales?"

She knew that he'd get around to asking, and she still didn't know how she was going to answer. So she didn't. Harper sat, staring at her, waiting for a response, and she continued to not give it. Finally, he took a long, slow breath, leaned his elbows on the desk, and put his head in his hands.

◆ ◆ ◆ ◆ ◆

THE TRIBAL OFFICE OF THE MATTAKEESE was located behind the Barnstable County Courthouse in the center of Barnstable Village. Main Street was dotted with clapboard-sided restaurants, a grocery store, real estate offices, a post office, a barber shop, a flower shop—and to the north of the road, immediately behind the stores, was the marsh that rimmed Barnstable Harbor. The deeper back into the harbor you went, the marshier it got, until you hit Great Marsh, which was a bird sanctuary and, according to historians, one of the most primitive marshes in all of the northeast. These were the marshlands referenced in Madoc Morfran's story.

The brick and marble courthouse stood at the top of a hill on the south side of Main Street. Behind it was a large parking lot ringed with low office buildings. Carys steered the Range Rover up the short, steep driveway into the parking lot and stopped in front of a nondescript, single-story brick building. Next to its front door was a small white sign with black lettering that read "Tribal Office." It looked like a dentist's office.

The door was already half open, so they walked inside. It looked like a dentist's office on the inside as well, with beige linoleum floors, a suspended ceiling, and fluorescent lights. There were four laminated wood desks and metal chairs with wheels. The space was sterile, giving no indication of what business was conducted within. There was no one in sight.

"Hello," Harper called out.

"I'm here," said a woman's voice. Carys and Harper walked toward it, down a short hallway to another door that was open. They entered what looked like a larger version of Grant's office. Every wall of the large, windowless room was lined with shelves filled with Native American artifacts. On the right-hand wall as they walked in was a filing cabinet with long, very shallow drawers, like architects use to store their flat drawings.

Running down the center of the room were three glass cases, like those in a jewelry shop, arranged end to end. At the very back was a small desk, where a middle-aged woman with short-cropped dark-blonde hair and green eyes was seated. She stood up as they entered. She was tall. Almost as tall as Harper.

"I'm Mary Clark," she said.

Carys was about to open her mouth, but Harper spoke first.

"Sachem Clark," said Harper as he shook her hand. "It's our honor to meet you, and thank you so much for meeting with us. We promise we won't take much of your time."

"I'm happy that someone of your reputation is interested in our tribe," she said. "Doctor Grant said you wanted to know about our origin legends. I've compiled some reading material for you."

"Thank you for that," said Harper, accepting the stack of documents and books. Then he placed them on the desk and sat down. Clark looked slightly taken aback. "Can we chat about this material for a few minutes?"

Carys walked to the first glass case, which was filled with dozens of small arrowheads of various shapes and sizes, some of which exactly resembled the one in the leather pouch from the cave. Her heart rate spiked.

"Sure," said Clark, and took her seat again. "Is there anything in particular you're looking for?"

In the second glass case, hundreds of smooth, highly polished stones were arranged in rows. Some were the size of a hand, others the size of a quarter. Each had a symbol or an image etched into its surface. Some were clearly of animals, birds and deer; some had human figures. Some carried symbols that were geometric, like squares, triangles, circles, and stars.

"Yes," said Harper. "We have uncovered some evidence that white Europeans visited this region far, far earlier than current historical records indicate. We were hoping there might be some legend, song, or folktale that memorializes such a visit."

"It's pretty common knowledge that there were visitors to this region who predated Columbus," said Clark. "They were mostly of Norwegian origin, but none of them stayed very long when they realized we didn't have gold or anything they considered valuable."

At the end of the second glass case was a series of very small stones, not as highly polished as the others. Carys bent over so her nose was almost touching the glass. The etching on these stones was extremely faint.

"I'm referring to a much earlier visit," said Harper.

"How much earlier?" asked Clark.

Harper paused. Carys glanced over at the back of his head.

"About fifteen hundred years ago," he finally said.

She looked at Clark's face to gauge her reaction. There wasn't one.

"No," Clark said. "There's no history of any visit that far back. The very first and oldest legends involving a visitor tell of our tribe's great god, Maushop, who was a giant. Our legends say he came to this area and helped the local people learn to farm the sea and cultivate the land for food. He created Martha's Vineyard and Nantucket by pouring sand from his moccasins. But then the Great Spirit Kitanitowit called him home and he walked into the sea, turned into a great white whale, and swam back across the ocean so that we could learn to fend for ourselves."

Harper sat silently for a moment.

Carys looked back down into the glass case. Her eye fell on a single stone, the smallest one. She took a magnifying glass that was lying on the top of the case and leaned over again. On the tiny stone's face was the very faint etching of a rudimentary human form. The form appeared to be shrouded in some kind of tunic or robe.

On the front of the robe was carved a circle, quartered by a cross with four arms of equal length.

Carys stood upright and stared at the wall.

An ancient Christian cross.

"What was his name again?" asked Harper. "This giant?"

"Maushop," said the sachem.

"Does he have other names in your legends?"

"Oh, many, but all are slight variations on that name. It's a legend we share with several other tribes as well. Ironically, before Maushop left, he warned our people that a new breed of man would visit us and that we should not trust them," she said. "Obviously, we didn't pay attention."

"Very interesting," said Harper. "Is there any legend involving Maushop in which he buries someone here? Like one of his family members?"

"Not that I'm aware of," said the sachem. "But legends live and die, as you know. There might have been a legend like that once upon a time. But I don't know of it."

Carys finally found the ability to speak.

"These stones," she said. "They're very interesting. This one in particular."

The sachem rose and approached her. Carys pointed to the tiny stone with the Christian cross.

"Yes," said the sachem, smiling for the first time since they arrived. "Many people ask if that's a Celtic or Christian cross. It's funny really. That symbol has been used by our tribe since its earliest beginnings. How typically ethnocentric of Caucasians to think that that symbol is not original to my people."

"It's such a simple design," said Carys. "It probably sprang up in many cultures independently of one another."

"Precisely," said the sachem.

"How old would you say that etching is? Have you had it dated?" she asked.

"Certainly," said the sachem. "It's…"

Just then a cloud passed across the woman's face. It was not a frown, exactly, but a hesitation. Carys recognized it as a flash of panic.

"Middle to Late Woodland period, we've been told," the sachem finally said.

"So sometime in the middle to late first millennium?" said Carys. "About one thousand five hundred years ago?"

"Yes," said the sachem. "But we haven't been able to narrow it down precisely."

"Do you have any more stones with this symbol on them?" she asked. "More specifically, do you have any stones with that symbol that predate this one?"

The sachem's face went entirely blank.

"No," she said. She turned and walked back to her desk. "Is there anything else I can help you with today? I'm afraid I don't have too much more time. My daughter and her children are visiting from Boston, and I promised we could go to the beach."

Harper stood and shook her hand. "No, and thank you," he said. "You've been very gracious with your time."

"I'm not sure I've been of much help, unless you were looking for a giant," she said, and smiled again, but this time only with her mouth.

◆ ◆ ◆ ◆ ◆

HARPER AND CARYS WALKED BACK to the Range Rover, the tension and excitement nearly arcing between them. They got in, slammed the doors shut, turned to each other, and began to talk simultaneously.

"Holy shit," Carys said. "That was an ancient Christian cross."

"Maushop," said Harper. "Madoc. Giants. Do you know how many giants there are in Welsh mythology? There's even a Welsh legend in the Mabinogion about a giant who walks into the sea. They're all the same metaphor. The Maushop legend is Madoc Morfran."

"It was a Christian cross," she said. "And she knows there was an earlier white visitor—earlier than any were supposed to have come here. I could feel it."

Harper stopped his own reverie and looked at her.

"Are you sure?" he asked. "I don't think she knows anything. Why would she tell me the Maushop legend if she already knew its significance?"

She reached into the back seat to the pile of documents Clark had handed Harper. On the top of the pile was an illustrated children's book called *Maushop and the Clambake*. She grabbed it and held it up to Harper.

"She wasn't exactly divulging state secrets in there," she said. She tossed the book back onto the seat. "She was humoring us. An ancient visitor to North America, earlier than any other previously recorded, is obviously the foundation of one of their most well-known legends. And as long as they treat it like an old myth, why would anyone read more into it? Hide it in plain sight."

"I didn't get the impression that she was hiding anything," said Harper. "I think she just honestly doesn't realize what that legend means. They don't know where he is."

"Listen. She just about jumped out of her skin when I asked her how old that stone with the Christian cross was. Until the minute we showed up today, they were perfectly safe showing that stone and claiming that that symbol was an ancient Mattakeese symbol. No one could ever dispute it. It dates to over five hundred years before any white men—or any men who would have used that symbol—were supposed to have set foot on this continent. But we knew better. And we told her so. And when she had to admit that that stone carving dates to the exact time period we were asking about…. I'm telling you, she knows."

Harper sat still and silent as she started the Range Rover and began to back up. Just then, Clark appeared at the window next to the tribal office door. She and Harper looked at the sachem, and Harper raised his hand and waved a slight goodbye. Clark raised her hand but did not wave. She did not smile. In her eyes was the unmistakable sharpness of anger, maybe even hatred. Harper lowered his hand and turned to Carys.

"Oh my god," he whispered. "She knows."

"Let's go to Sandy Neck and see what we're dealing with," she said.

Ten minutes later, they turned off Route 6A onto the winding, tree-lined side road that led to the entrance to Sandy Neck Beach. The road was the only way on and off the beach by land. They paid their entrance fee at the ranger station, took their parking pass, and drove up to the main parking lot that fronted the ocean.

The lot was on top of what had been a huge sand dune before it was paved over, and from it they could see the enormity of the Neck, which stretched for six miles to the east of where they were sitting. To the north and west, the shore bent around and became white cliffs just south of the entrance to Plymouth Harbor. And almost due north was a tiny spire sticking straight up out of the ocean. It was Pilgrim Memorial Monument in Provincetown, visible from this part of the Cape only on the clearest days, which this was.

Harper had printed out a map of the archaeological dig sites on the Neck. They got out of the car and set off down the beachfront, passing groups of sunbathers and their mountains of gear, their furiously smoking barbecues, their playing children and barking dogs. The sand was deep, and after only a few yards, they stopped to take off their shoes.

Half a mile down the beach, a trail appeared between two dunes that led south, away from the water, and they left the beachfront and followed it. Once they were over the great hill of sand and down again, she could not hear the ocean waves anymore. It was as silent as if she were in a great enclosed room, and the accumulated heat from the sun on the sand seemed to stagnate in the little valleys. The light southerly breeze wafted occasionally over the marshes in front of them and brought an organic, peaty smell. The sun beat down on her shoulders. It was so peaceful here. The perfect place to build your village and to fish and farm, or rest for eternity.

Harper had his phone out and was tracking their location on a GPS map of the Neck. He consulted the printout to see how close they were to the dig. After twenty minutes of trudging along the deep sand trail, Harper stopped.

"The oldest pit is due east about six hundred feet," said Harper. They were standing right next to a sign that had been stuck into the sand along the trail: "Ecologically Sensitive Area—Stay on Trail." The warning was backed up by a "fence" made of string stretched between low posts along both sides of the trail. She paused for a moment as Harper stepped over the string and marched into the forbidden area.

They'd gone not more than a hundred feet when the distinct sound of a bullhorn snapping on interrupted the peaceful surroundings.

"Please turn around and return to the trail," bellowed a stern female voice. They stopped in their tracks and turned. A park ranger was on the trail where they'd been a few moments earlier.

"How the hell did she know we were out here?" Harper asked quietly.

"She must have followed us," said Carys.

"But why?" asked Harper as they trudged back to the trail. "It's not illegal to walk on the trail."

"Hello," said the ranger, a woman not much taller than Carys but much thicker, with long brown hair pulled into a severe ponytail underneath her brimmed fabric hat. "You two realize it's a violation to enter these dunes, as clearly stated by this sign you just walked past?"

"Yes, ma'am," said Carys. "We're sorry. We were trying to be careful, but there's an archaeological site over there that we are trying to find."

"And did you not think that maybe we didn't want you to stomp all over that either?" asked the ranger, who was a little more agitated than she expected a park ranger to be.

"Ma'am," said Harper, looking more carefully at her name badge. "Ranger Collwood, I assure you we weren't intending to stomp all over anything. We're doing some research—which is why we're not in bathing suits."

"I'm going to have to ask you two to come with me," said the ranger, who slung the bullhorn onto her belt next to her gun.

They followed the ranger to the beachfront and got into the back of the ATV she had parked near the trail entrance. She drove them silently back to the ranger station. Harper and Carys looked at each other like errant schoolchildren waiting for their turn in the principal's office.

"Come inside please," said the ranger. They followed her into the ranger's building and back into a small office with a desk and a few bookshelves. Inside, standing next to a desk, was a tall man who had an angular face, closely cropped brown hair, and a look on him that let Carys and Harper know that he was already pissed off.

"Anna, these the two?" asked the man.

"Yup," she said. "They were off by the dig site when I caught up to them."

The man shot Collwood a look, and she backed up and stood behind Carys and Harper.

"You were following us?" asked Harper.

The man looked him up and down and did the same to Carys.

"Of course not," he said. "But we monitor those dunes very carefully. They're an extremely sensitive ecological area."

"And archaeological as well," said Carys. "Very sensitive."

The man glared at her. "Yes, it is."

"The dig sites back there," said Harper. "How would we go about securing official permission to access the area?"

"You can't," said the man, whose name tag identified him as Michael Heath. "That area specifically has been closed off for twenty years. No one is allowed to dig there or even walk there. Permission is not granted."

"Why?" she asked.

Heath didn't answer right away.

"They have been closed off indefinitely."

He turned in his seat behind him to retrieve a clipboard and a pen.

"I'm going to issue you both a citation," said Heath. "If you are caught out there again, I'll be authorized to arrest you both and charge you with criminal trespass. Do you understand?"

"Yes," said Carys and Harper in unison.

After they'd recited their names and home addresses, Heath put the clipboard back on his desk. "Are you staying locally?"

Harper brushed her arm lightly.

"No," he said. "We just came down for the day."

"I'll have Anna drive you back to your car."

"We can walk," said Carys. "It's not that far…"

"We'll drive you," said Heath. He stood up and extended his arm out to Harper to shake his hand.

"Have a safe trip back up to Wellesley," he said, pumping Harper's hand once, then holding on to it just a second too long.

She looked over at their clasped hands. Heath's long shirt sleeve had ridden slightly up his extended arm. Peeking out from underneath the edge of the cuff on Heath's wrist was a very old, slightly greening tattoo that was about the size of a dime.

The ancient Christian cross.

Once they were deposited back in the Range Rover, Carys turned to Harper once more.

"You see his tattoo?" she asked.

"You bet your ass I did," said Harper.

◆ ◆ ◆ ◆

When they returned to the inn, Dafydd was on the back porch in a lounge chair, reading a dog-eared paperback copy of *Carrie* and drinking a Budweiser. He smiled broadly, hopped out of the chair, and hugged Carys hard. It felt delicious.

"How did it go?" he asked with bright eyes.

"It was very, very interesting," she said.

"Tell me," said Dafydd. They moved to the sitting room. Harper laid the stack of books down on a small wicker table.

"You go to a library?" asked Dafydd.

"Sort of," said Harper, flipping through the books and documents. "This is insulting. We literally could have found this stuff in the public library."

"Doesn't matter," she said. "We found out what we needed to know."

"Which is what?" asked Dafydd.

"They know someone very ancient and non-native is buried on Sandy Neck," she said. "They probably have no idea it's King Arthur. They couldn't know that. He wasn't the Arthur of legend when he was buried here. The legend evolved long afterward. But they definitely know a visitor is buried here, and they are keeping it secret."

"The rangers at Sandy Neck are Mattakeese tribe members," said Harper.

"Is it possible they're just there protecting their heritage in general?" asked Dafydd. "Aren't there quite a few native burial sites out there?"

"Yes, it's possible. But remember that symbol on the huge rock, the one that looked like Stonehenge, when we dove on the cave?" she asked.

"Of course," said Dafydd. "Never been so happy to see a Celtic cross in my life."

"We've been seeing an awful lot of that symbol today. It was on one of the tribe's stones in their office archives. A stone that dates back to fifteen hundred years ago. And there are no others like it that date to before that time," said Carys.

"And then the ranger who almost arrested us for…" said Harper.

"What?" asked Dafydd. "Almost what?"

Carys smiled and grabbed his arm.

"They let us off with a warning," she said. "We went to Sandy Neck Beach after we met with the sachem. We took a walk along the beach, went into the dunes to find one of the old archaeological dig sites, and about two seconds after we veered off the trail, a ranger was on us. They were following us. Like they were warned we'd be coming."

Dafydd sat there, his mouth slightly agape. He hadn't taken a sip from his beer since they'd arrived. She reached over and grabbed it and took a long swig. The refreshing fizz cleared the layer of sand accumulated at the back of her throat. She burped. Dafydd laughed out loud.

"You look incredibly pleased with yourself," said Dafydd.

"I am," she said. "I am. They know there is an ancient visitor buried on their lands. Now we just need to figure out why they are keeping the burial site a secret. And we have to convince them to share that secret with us."

◆ ◆ ◆ ◆ ◆

THE SUN GLOWED LOW through the trees surrounding the Colonial Inn, there was a tinge of salt air and low tide on the breeze, and the beer was cold. There was no sign that they'd been followed since Carys had returned to Boston, and she was beginning to think that maybe Frank Marshfield's employer—whoever it was—had dropped the chase. But deep in her mind, she couldn't convince herself of it. The faint hum of anxiety still pestered her neck and shoulders.

Harper had gone upstairs several hours earlier. Despite his semi-miraculous recovery over the past couple of days, the after-effect of his infection reasserted itself after Harper had half a beer. He excused himself to take a nap and a shower.

She and Dafydd sat on the couch, sipping their beers, relaxing into each other. There was no one around and no sound from the rest of the house.

"It's really beautiful here," said Dafydd.

"Does it look like you thought it would?" she asked.

"I've never really given it much thought," he said. "I've never traveled. I guess I always thought that foreign countries would be strange and unfamiliar. But this could be my backyard back home."

"I guess that's why the sailors with Morfran decided to stick around," she said.

"Can I ask you something?"

"Sure," she said. "Not much point in having secrets now."

"Why aren't you..." He paused.

"Why aren't I what?" she asked, and smiled. "Married?"

"Well, yeah," he said. "Or with someone. I mean, it's inconceivable."

She laughed. She'd never been asked that before. She always figured it was obvious.

"You're quite a catch," said Dafydd. "Smart, beautiful, fearless, funny, great in the sack."

"Broken," she said, her happy mood fading slightly. "Deeply broken."

"What broke you?" asked Dafydd.

"My father leaving, my mother committing suicide, my father abandoning me, you know, the usual," she said. "Being raised like a stepchild in someone else's home just really did a number on me, I think. Annie and Priscilla, Annie's mom, loved me well. But no matter how wonderful they were, they couldn't make me believe that I hadn't done something wrong to lose both parents. Somewhere along the way, I just decided to keep people at arm's length. Less chance of getting hurt."

Dafydd raised his arm out in front of her, then moved it over her head and draped it around her shoulders.

"I'm closer than arm's length," he said. "You have failed in your mission."

She couldn't help but smile. "It appears so."

Dafydd looked into her eyes, and for the first time in her life, she enjoyed the sensation of truly being seen.

"Have you told Harper what happened that night?" asked Dafydd.

"No," she said. "And I don't intend to." She laid her head back on his arm and closed her eyes.

She draped her legs across Dafydd's, and it almost felt like this could be a real thing. She realized that it wasn't actually Wales that she wanted to run away and hide in—it was this.

Finally, Dafydd wiggled his arm.

"I'm famished," he said, kissing her on the cheek. "I'm going to go get ready for dinner."

They pulled themselves off the chair and walked, hand in hand, up the stairs. They each pulled out their keys to their adjoining rooms. She stood at one door, Dafydd at the other.

She slid the key into the lock. She turned it. Then she looked up at him. He grinned. She opened her door and he followed her in, and they were both naked before the door closed behind them.

"Woman," said Dafydd an hour later as they lay in each other's arms. "You are insatiable."

"You're very, very good at that," she said.

"Why thank you," he said. "You know, they say the Welsh have some special talents in that department."

"Oh really," she said, smiling at him. "Who is this 'they' of whom you speak?"

"Oh, everybody, worldwide," he said. "It's a well-known fact. I'll bet even the squaws of the Mattakeese were twittering on about the horizontal skills of my ancestors fifteen hundred years ago when those strapping Welsh sailors came to town with Morfran. Probably got so spoiled on Welsh cock that the homegrown boys couldn't get a piece."

"Those poor guys," she said. "They should never have let them onshore."

"Ah, but they did," said Dafydd. "And that was their first mistake." He leaned over and kissed her. She melted into him, and she could feel him getting hard again.

Then, like a bright flash of light, she realized why the Mattakeese band was keeping the burial site of their ancient visitor a secret.

✦ ✦ ✦ ✦ ✦

GYLES SWUNG OPEN THE BACK DOOR of his bulletproof chauffeured Mercedes SUV into another drizzly London night.

"Stay put, Kenny," he said.

He swung both his feet out of the car, hopped down onto the curb, closed the door behind him, and strolled across the sidewalk into the white stone, brightly lit facade of the Iraqi embassy in Kensington. A young Middle Eastern man greeted him at the door and took his name.

"Welcome, Mr. Gyles," said the man, slightly flustered once he realized to whom he was speaking. "It's our great pleasure to welcome you."

He nodded graciously and entered the building, already teeming with men in tuxedos and women in gowns and diamonds. Candlelight filled the main salon of the elegant drawing room, and champagne and sparkling water were being passed to the guests by waiters in white coats and gloves. The ambassador's attaché, a large, swarthy man with a long beard, his belly barely contained behind his cummerbund, strode over to Gyles, hand extended.

"Mr. Gyles," said the man. "Thank you for coming. I know you don't like these things."

"I wouldn't miss it, Fuad," he said, smiling and shaking the man's hand. "We have a lot to celebrate."

"We couldn't have done it without your help," said Fuad. "It's a great triumph against the thieves who are raping my country of its past."

"Indeed," he said. "A great triumph."

"I assume you'd prefer to avoid the photo session, as usual," said Fuad.

"I don't wish to be insulting."

"Not at all," said Fuad. "If only more people were less interested in getting their name and face in the paper and more interested in actually making a difference in the world."

Fuad took champagne and sparkling water from a passing tray, and the two toasted.

The ceremony, which acknowledged and thanked those who had been responsible for the successful completion of a three-year negotiation to repatriate nearly one billion dollars' worth of antiquities to Iraq, was blessedly short.

His mind wandered to more pressing matters as the ambassador read the names of the people who had been involved in the effort.

He'd had a very productive couple of days. He'd sent his second-most trusted associate, Tommy, to the U.S. to dispatch Plourde. That job would be done within twenty-four hours. It would, naturally, look like an accident. Then Tommy was to stay in the area and await further instructions.

Meanwhile, JB, through his trusted network, had hired a Boston-based guy named Patrick to tail Ms. Jones. Patrick already had eyes on her and had put a GPS tracker on the vehicle she was using to travel. The guy had been in charge of a gun-running operation between Boston and Belfast in the '80s, so he knew the area like the back of his hand, and he was an expert at being invisible. If Patrick ever talked to the authorities, he could still put half of the government of Northern Ireland into a maximum-security prison for the rest of their lives. He was, as they say, as silent as the grave. He was sending hourly status updates to JB via text.

Carys Jones had been joined by another man and John Harper, who, it turned out, was no longer being confined and was not quite so insane as Gyles had been told. Patrick reported that he looked just fine. It was clear—based on the gear they were toting around—that they were still hunting for the tomb.

So, the game was still afoot. Once Jones and Harper found the tomb, Tommy would take over operations from Patrick. Gyles didn't trust anyone else to manage those logistics, which would most likely involve some wet work and the removal of the tomb's contents. Patrick and Tommy would then transport the contents, along with the manuscript and translation, to a diplomatically registered private jet for a flight from Bedford, Massachusetts, to Saudi Arabia. He trusted Tommy to handle the details on the ground—which Gyles imagined would be formidable. Tommy had handled worse.

Most crucially, he had realized over the previous twenty-four hours, no one was to spook Jones and her hunting party. The anonymous client who'd started this whole treasure hunt—whom he had taken to calling Client A, for "annoying"—had just texted, again, to remind him that the manuscript needed to be retrieved immediately. Jones and Harper, Client A insisted, must not find the tomb. That was an ironclad condition of their deal.

That ship had sailed. Gyles had no intention of grabbing the manuscript until after they led him directly to the burial site. Let them find the damn thing and then kill them off. This would happen much more quickly if Jones and Harper didn't realize they were in mortal danger. Client A would never know they'd found the tomb if they were dead within an hour of doing so.

The room exploded into raucous applause, and everyone turned to Gyles, who was jolted from his thoughts. He nodded graciously to the crowd, putting his hand over his heart and bowing low toward the ambassador. A moment later, under cover of the continuing applause, he placed his half-empty glass of champagne on a passing tray and discreetly headed for the exit.

Once outside, he popped the collar of his cashmere overcoat against the cool, damp night air and hailed Kenny. A BMW sedan was parked directly in front of the embassy, and he took a few steps down the sidewalk to meet his vehicle. He heard the BMW's door open. A moment later, he felt a hand on his shoulder. He spun around.

"Mr. Gyles, may I have a word?" asked an impeccably dressed man. His accent was Middle Eastern—he couldn't quite nail the country—and his beard and hair were trimmed and shining in the embassy lights.

"Can you call my office in the morning? I'm afraid I have an appointment."

"I think you'll want to hear what I have to say, Mr. Gyles," said the man. "Or should I call you JB?"

His blood ran cold.

"Let's take a seat in my car, please," said the man.

"Do I look like a fool?"

"Fine," said the man. "We'll speak here. Quietly. I would not want to compromise your...what is the English word? Facade?"

He glared at the guy. Kenny was slowly moving the Mercedes toward him. He put out his hand to tell him to stop. He didn't want him to hear any of this conversation. The SUV halted.

"When will the sculpture be arriving in Geneva?" asked the man.

"Tomorrow," he said calmly, as if discussing the weather. He held the man's gaze intently. "As I mentioned several days ago, there were some hiccups at the border. I will alert your people as soon as it arrives at the warehouse."

"It's been two days longer than you promised Mr. Alahwi," said the man.

"These things aren't science," he said. "There are variables."

"We don't like variables," said the man. "The money will be transferred in forty-eight hours."

How did this man know who he was? His mind raced, but he kept his breathing steady. How had he tracked him? It didn't matter. There was only one way to handle this. He had to be crazier and more dangerous.

"Nice car," he said confidently. "Diplomatic plates. Based on the number, looks like...U.A.E., yes?"

The man flinched slightly.

"They know you do side work?" he asked. "Using the embassy car?" He laughed. "The ambassador would probably waive your immunity in a heartbeat if he knew he had a jihadi working for him."

"What makes you think he doesn't know?" said the man with a smile.

"He'd no doubt be displeased if that fact went public. And he probably wouldn't lift a finger to stop the Americans from doing one of their special midnight renditions on you, would he?"

The man's smile dropped away.

"You'd rot in a cell in Guantanamo undergoing enhanced interrogation for the rest of your life—if you were lucky," he said.

Gyles reached into his pocket and pulled out his cell phone. He held it in front of him as if to dial, then turned it toward the man and snapped his photo.

"These phone cameras are simply remarkable now. Mine is twelve megapixels," he said. "You wouldn't believe the resolution."

The man glared at him and then began to bare his teeth like an angry dog.

"Have you ever seen a man skinned alive?" asked the man.

Gyles swallowed but didn't miss a beat.

"No," he said, deepening his voice and dropping it to a confidential whisper. He leaned in toward the man. "But I have seen a man turned inside out. Reminds you that we're all just meat. You might want to take a vacation back home. As soon as you can."

The man stood his ground for half a second longer, but then he took a step back. He got into the driver's seat of the car and slowly pulled away.

This one was an amateur. The next one would not be.

For a split second, he felt that old fear, deep in the pit of his intestines. He could feel the bodies in the school's bunk room closing in on him, could hear the squeak of the bedsprings. Then he pushed the thoughts out of his mind, as he had learned to do so well over the ensuing decades. He was not going to let this become a problem.

◆ ◆ ◆ ◆ ◆

THE THREE OF THEM TOOK THEIR SEATS at a round table at a fish restaurant that overlooked the marina at Barnstable Harbor. Outside, fishing boats and sailboats buzzed back and forth in single file in the narrow, low-tide channel that led from the harbor to the marina's docks.

When their drinks arrived, Carys was ready to explain her theory.

"I think I figured out why they are keeping everything a secret," she said.

"What did you come up with?" asked Harper.

"They're pretending they don't know anything about ancient visitors," she said. "But that Christian cross is an embedded part of their most ancient history. And the cross was inscribed on the tunic of a human figure on the rock artifact in the tribal office."

"What's your point?" asked Harper.

"I did some research of my own," she said. "The aboriginals didn't wear decorated garments during the Woodlands period. They didn't know about weaving or fabric. They didn't have that technology—that was European technology. The tribe surely knows this. If they still have the sword that Morfran left behind, they know that that was European technology as well. My point is that they probably don't know *who* was buried in that tomb, but they have to know that he was European—in other words, white."

"That doesn't explain the secrecy," said Harper.

A light went on in Dafydd's eyes, and he smiled at her.

"The Morfran manuscript says that many of his men stayed behind after Morfran returned to the east, right?" asked Dafydd. "You best believe those Welshmen didn't stay behind so they could become celibate."

Harper sat motionless, processing. Slowly, realization crossed his face.

"Imagine what it would do to the tribe if it were ever revealed that they have been partially white since a thousand years before the official arrival of white men," she said.

"Probably nothing," said Harper. "Tribes get to determine the rules about who is a member and who isn't."

"But if the Mattakeese have had white blood in their veins for fifteen centuries, the surrounding tribes likely would have it as well," said Carys. "They all intermarried. Every tribe in the Wampanoag nation would have their sovereignty questioned. Everything they have would be at risk. Any federal money they receive, all the sovereign lands they hold, the right to build casinos, everything. Their entire identity, their entire history, would be questioned—very publicly. It could affect all the native people in this part of the U.S. I'd bet the Mattakeese would do anything to hide the truth."

"Every native tribe in America has been intermarrying with white people for centuries," said Harper. "Why would it matter?"

"Because this would rewrite their most ancient origins, their most sacred legends," she said. "Their very foundation. Their creation legend is Maushop. What do you think would happen if they found out their great creator was, provably, a white guy? And not just any white guy, but the son of King fucking Arthur?"

"I didn't get into this to destroy an aboriginal people's identity," said Harper. "But we're so close. There has to be some way to get them to give us the location of the tomb without damaging them."

"We can't claim credit for discovering Arthur's tomb unless we also reveal the two manuscripts to the archaeological community," she said. "Without them, our claims would be entirely invalid."

"I know," said Harper. "Jesus."

"Maybe we should blackmail them," she said. "Show them the Morfran manuscript and tell them what it says and threaten to reveal it if they don't cooperate."

Dafydd started to laugh. "Oh, that's a great idea. Blackmail Indians. You'll get yourself killed."

Just then, heaping plates of fried food appeared before them.

"Can I get you kids anything else right now?" asked the server.

"No, thank you very much," said Harper. "This is great."

As hungry as Carys and Dafydd had been before they got to the restaurant, neither touched a bite. The waitress nodded and moved briskly away.

"Dafydd's right. That's a bad idea," said Harper.

"But what other bargaining chip do we have?" she asked. "If we show them the manuscript and explain what it says, at least we'll have some leverage."

"They'll never believe us," said Harper. "They'll never believe it's authentic. We have nothing to negotiate with if they won't even acknowledge that Morfran's manuscript is real."

"They will," she said. "All I have to do is read them a few paragraphs. If those paragraphs even remotely match their tribal legends, they'll know we're not making it up. And if they continue to pretend they have no idea what we're talking about, we'll let them know we can have the book carbon-dated, made public, big announcement, most important historical find, blah blah."

"And then what?" asked Harper. "Their options are literally to tell us the location and rewrite their entire history, or don't tell us the location and rewrite their entire history when we reveal the manuscripts to try to strong-arm them. What incentive do they have to cooperate?"

The three of them sat silently. Dafydd finally dug into his plate of fried scallops.

"I suppose it depends on what they want," said Carys. "Besides us going away."

4

Wednesday, June 27

Carys rolled out of bed into the cool grayness of her room, leaving a snoring Dafydd wrapped in the duvet. She crept into the bathroom and looked out the window into a thick white mist that shrouded the view of the surrounding yard. She could barely see twenty feet. It was pure and silent.

She took a quick shower, and Dafydd was still asleep when she emerged. He looked like a young boy in the bed, surrounded by pillows and blankets. She felt a pang of something in the center of her chest, something warm and electric that seemed to expand when she looked at Dafydd. At its center was a desire to protect, to never be without, to entwine. She enjoyed it for a moment, then inhaled it away. There would be time for that later. She put on some jeans, a T-shirt, and a cardigan and went downstairs for coffee.

Harper was already up and working on his laptop in the parlor.

"Sleep well?" she asked. His head popped up, and he smiled at her.

"Nope," he said. "Not a wink. Couldn't stop thinking. We need to set up a meeting with the tribe today. Let them know we have proof. Then we can start negotiations to get to the tomb. I have an idea."

"What if they still insist they don't know what you're talking about?" she asked.

"Call their bluff, like you said last night," he said. "We could let it leak to the press that we uncovered some ancient artifacts found in a cave in Wales that have been traced to a Native American tribe. We can have your father deliver the jewelry to the Welsh antiquities authorities, reveal the location of the original tomb. We slowly ratchet up the heat until they agree to play ball."

"But what does 'playing ball' mean, exactly?" she asked. "How can we prove it's Arthur without ruining the tribe? Revealing who is in that burial site is a losing proposition for them on every level. They have no reason to cooperate."

"I'm working on something," said Harper. "I'll tell you about it when it's a little more fully formed. In the meantime, we should let them know what they're facing. We can't waste time trying to find a perfect solution before we get things moving here."

"It's going to be ugly," she said. "They'll be fighting for their identity."

"I know," said Harper. "I'll call Sachem Clark and tell her we need to meet with the Tribal Council. Today."

◆ ◆ ◆ ◆ ◆

HARPER'S PHONE CALL WITH CLARK did not go smoothly. Harper reminded her of their conversation the previous day, that he had some evidence that white men had come to the Mattakeese fifteen hundred years ago. This time, however, he also mentioned that he had evidence that many of them had stayed when their leader left. Physical evidence—scientifically verifiable and conclusive.

This new wrinkle was met with the same blank, emotionless denial that had greeted them at the office the day before. When

Harper pushed, insisting that he understood what this discovery would mean for the Mattakeese tribe of the Wampanoag nation of the great Algonquin peoples, and its future, the denial changed to anger, then rage, and then, like the final stage of grief, something that Harper thought sounded very close to acceptance, or at least defeat. Clark agreed to arrange a closed-door meeting that night with the five-member council.

"I told them I'd bring the manuscript," said Harper. "So they can see for themselves that we aren't making it up. Can you translate a few of the meaty parts—the burial scene, the part where he says half his men stayed behind, gifting the tribe the sword as payment for their promise to guard the tomb—things like that. Stuff they might recognize."

"Of course," she said.

"Oh, and translate the part about Morfran's warning about other strange men who may follow after him," said Harper. "The tribe will definitely recognize that part of the story. Sachem Clark especially."

She spent most of the day on her task, while Dafydd sat in the backyard, soaking up the sun. Harper busied himself with documents and phone calls. He was setting something in motion legally—some sort of offer for the Mattakeese, something to persuade them to go along with Harper's search. She couldn't wait to find out how he was going to do it.

She called Annie and told her about the meeting.

"Be careful," said Annie. "The Morfran manuscript is the closest thing that this tribe has to a Bible—and this one is actually true. There's no telling what they'd do to get their hands on it."

The thought sent a chill up her spine.

That bible might turn out to be the best bargaining chip they had.

She worked for the rest of the afternoon on the translations, barely touching her lunch. Dafydd came and went, checking in on her from time to time, lightly kissing her on the neck, but she barely acknowledged his presence.

When the translation was done and printed out, she spent several more hours photographing, in high-definition on her phone, every single page of the manuscript and taking careful notes on its construction and materials. She transferred the images to her cloud account and set them up on her computer so they would run in a slide show. She highlighted the pages that contained the text that she'd translated. It was like doing a book report.

Then she slid both manuscripts and the monk's translation into a plastic bag, sealed it, and went outside, where she hid it somewhere she was sure no one would find it—a hole she dug at the base of the wisteria plant growing up the secluded arbor in the forest behind the inn. She could have given them to Dafydd. But if the worst happened, if someone came after them, it would be better if she was the only one who knew where they were. She knew she would never tell.

At quarter to six, Harper came by her room.

"How did the translation go?" he asked.

"Very well," she said. "Pretty straightforward. I also photographed the entire manuscript so that we don't have to take it with us to the meeting."

Harper bristled.

"We have to take it," he said. "Why on earth would they agree to the deal if they weren't sure that we actually have the book?"

She spun her computer around to face Harper and hit the play button. A video started—Carys, stating her name and the date. Then the video zoomed in on the date on the front page of that day's *Barnstable Patriot* newspaper. In the same continuous shot, she placed the newspaper down next to Morfran's manuscript and carefully flipped through the first few pages to show that they matched the ones in the photos.

"Huh," said Harper. "You sure you weren't a spy in a previous life?"

"Pretty sure," she said, grinning. "If the tribe believes us—if they believe this manuscript is authentic—they're going to want to just take it and make us go away. They have guns. And they outnumber us."

Harper sat still as he processed this. It was obvious by the tightness in his jaw that he hadn't even considered this possibility. She waited while he thought it through.

"You're right," he said. "We can't risk bringing it with us. Tonight is just about making our case."

"John," she said.

"Yeah?"

"What are we going to offer them?"

"Their past...and their future," said Harper.

She couldn't imagine what he was talking about, but they didn't have time to chat about it. This was Harper's show, not hers. She had to keep remembering that.

"I'll go get Dafydd," she said. "I think we'll need safety in numbers."

"No," said Harper. "Just you and me. Too many people and they'll get scared. Best we leave Dafydd out of this."

Carys was going to fight, but he was right.

"I'll go tell him we're leaving," she said.

"Did you put the manuscripts somewhere safe?" asked Harper.

"Very safe," she said.

Harper left. She went to Dafydd's door and knocked.

"Hi, beautiful," he said, then pulled her in and began to kiss her. With great effort, she pulled away.

"I just came to tell you that we're heading to the Tribal Council meeting now," she said.

"Oh," said Dafydd. "I didn't know it had been set. Let's go."

She swallowed.

"You're not invited, I'm afraid," she said. He started to open his mouth, his shoulders thrown back, and she put her hand on his chest. "These are just the preliminary negotiations, and it will be best if it's just me and Harper. We don't want them thinking that their secret has gone international."

"I don't like it," he said. "Are you going to give them the manuscript tonight?"

"Absolutely not," she said. "It's in a safe place. We won't let them near it until we have some assurances that they'll cooperate." She smiled at him. "I'm sorry to leave you behind. I'll make it up to you when I get back."

He smiled and then kissed her softly.

"You better," he said. "Good luck."

♦ ♦ ♦ ♦ ♦

CARYS KEPT HER BAG containing the computer and the Morfran translation on her lap during the drive to the tribal office. She didn't like being so far from both of the manuscripts. She felt like she was missing a piece of herself.

They arrived a few minutes early, and a couple of cars were pulling up in front of the office. She and Harper got out of the Range Rover and met the eyes of the two other arrivals but exchanged no greetings. The drivers, a middle-aged man and an old, gray-haired woman with a slight stoop, shook hands with each other silently and proceeded inside the building, not bothering to hold the door open for she and Harper. Harper stood in front of the closed door and looked over at her.

"Well," he said. "This is getting off to a great start."

She shrugged.

"It's not like they are happy about this," she said.

Harper reached for the door handle, then paused.

"We can't tell them who is in that grave," he said. "If they knew, they would never let us near it. We have to keep that to ourselves until we've arrived at a deal."

"What if they already know?" she asked.

"I guarantee you they don't," said Harper. "Arcturus was just a brave warrior when he was buried here. Only time turned him into King Arthur, and they haven't been part of the story. We have the only link between the legend and the man in that tomb—the Lestinus manuscript."

They pulled open the door and entered. There were three men—one a very old white-haired man they were seeing for the first time—and two women, including the sachem. The council ranged in age from around forty to well past eighty. The youngest was Michael Heath. He glared at Carys with his deep-set eyes, then looked away. This was going to be bad.

Harper approached Clark.

"Good evening, Sachem," he said, extending his hand. "Thank you very much for agreeing to meet with us today."

She did not shake his hand. "It didn't seem like we had much choice in the matter," she said. "Let's get started."

The tribal council members took their places on one side of the conference table, and Carys and Harper sat on the other. She pulled her computer out of her bag, put it on the table, and fired it up. It sprang to life with an unexpectedly loud musical flourish that couldn't have been more out of place. She cringed.

"I call the Mattakeese tribal council to order," said Clark, "and seeing that we have a quorum, I ask you to state your name and tell us what business you have before us."

Harper took a deep breath. Tension radiated off of his body.

"Councilors," said Harper. "My name is John Harper, and this is Carys Jones. I thank you for seeing us this evening. It is an honor to—"

"Just get on with it," said Clark.

Harper closed his mouth and reset his shoulders.

"Ms. Jones and I have a manuscript written by a man named Madoc Morfran. It was retrieved by Ms. Jones last week from a cave on the coast of Wales. The manuscript she recovered was written in the sixth century. It is entirely in Latin, a version that is also traceable to the sixth century. It is the first-person record of a journey made by Morfran and a small fleet of sailing vessels from the British Isles, across the Atlantic Ocean, to a location on the eastern coast of North America that he describes in detail. The purpose of the journey was threefold. He wanted to find a place where the people of the British Isles could potentially escape invading Anglo-Saxon armies, which were on the move again after decades of peace. He wanted to find a land that was not experiencing the crippling drought that had plunged his country into famine and illness. But more important, he made the journey to find a safe place to bury his father."

Carys sat silent and still, watching the expressions on the faces of the councilors. Each maintained a look as stony and impenetrable as the next. It was almost as if they had rehearsed it.

"When Ms. Jones found this manuscript, she also found a sack of ancient artifacts that have been identified by scientists in Wales as originating from the northeastern coast of North America. These artifacts included several seeds of plants indigenous to this area as well as several quahog shells. There was also an arrowhead from the Middle Woodland period and several pieces of gold jewelry, British in origin, all dating to the mid-sixth century. This cave had not been entered or breached since its entrance was sealed up by the person who left the manuscript and those items there, Madoc Morfran, who returned to the British Isles several years after he had left on his journey."

Harper paused, took a sip of water from the glass that was in front of his seat. The stony-faced councilors had not flinched. Not one of them.

"The manuscript describes the location and conditions of the burial of his father," said Harper, turning to Carys. "Ms. Jones has taken the liberty of translating the sections of the manuscript that describe the location and the manner in which his father was buried, and the people he encountered while he was in North America."

She reached into her bag, pulled out the translations, and slid them across the table to Clark. Clark slid them to the old, white-haired man. He began to read them and his hands shook slightly.

"We believe, due to the various data points referenced in the book, the origin of the artifacts, and the specific details about the burial location and the native population that lived there, that Morfran landed here, and that the ancestors of the Mattakeese were the gentle people of the sand who showed Morfran and his crew kindness and allowed his father to be buried here," said Harper.

He paused dramatically and looked at each councilor in turn.

"This is complete nonsense," mumbled Heath to the other councilors. Clark shot him a hard glance. No one said a word. Carys felt a cold sweat begin to break out on her back. Harper took another sip of water and continued.

"I direct your attention to two sections of translation," said Harper. "The first is where Morfran is describing the bargain he struck with the native peoples. In exchange for guarding the burial site of his father, he gifted those people with a great sword, described in detail in the translation. It was made of iron, a material that would have been entirely unknown to the native people at that time period. It was topped with a single large ruby."

Despite the fact that the room was air-conditioned, a small bead of sweat broke out on the forehead of the ancient female councilor. Her thinning gray hair was beginning to get wet at the roots. She lifted one frail hand and wiped the drop of sweat away.

"There is also a section of the translation in which Morfran describes his departure from the area," said Harper. He looked at each councilor in turn again. "It states that before he left, he warned the native people to be on the lookout for other men, a strange breed of man, who might arrive. He warned them that these men would be very dangerous and that they should be avoided."

Clark lowered her eyes briefly, then raised them again to lock stoically on Harper.

"And lastly," said Harper, "I direct your attention to the portion of the translation in which Morfran states that when he left the native peoples and sailed back to the British Isles, half of the crew members—all males, all white European—stayed behind because, and I quote, 'so lovely were the native people, and so verdant and fertile were the land and seas.'"

At this, the middle-aged councilor, who had a head of dyed black hair and green eyes, his shirt straining at the buttons around his stomach, gripped the edge of the table with his hands. "I've heard enough," he said. "This is complete nonsense. I move that we adjourn. I'd like to get home for dinner." He began to stand. Clark looked at him.

"We remain in session, Cedric," said Clark. "Please sit."

"Thank you," said Harper. "Carys has prepared a video showing you the manuscript in great detail—"

"You didn't bring it with you?" asked Clark. "As we agreed?"

Carys interjected. "With respect, Sachem Clark, we thought about that and Mr. Harper and I decided that until we had come to trust and understand one another, it might not be…wise…to have this ancient manuscript physically present in this meeting. But this video shows we have it."

"That's not what we agreed," said Clark, her eyes burning into Harper.

Carys hit the play button on her computer for the video program and spun it around to face the councilors. All eyes were glued to the screen for the tape's three-minute length.

"That could be any old book," yelled Heath when the video was done. "You just made this all up to blackmail us into giving you something. I have no idea what, but I've had it." He stood up abruptly. The old, white-haired male councilor stood, too. Carys stood as well and stared into Heath's face.

"If we were making it all up," she barked, "then how do we know your tribe possesses an ancient sword? Made of iron? A sword that can be conclusively dated to fifteen hundred years ago—long before any aboriginal tribes were in possession of the technology to smelt iron. How would we know that for the past fifteen hundred years, your tribe has been protecting the tomb of a man, a white man, buried on Sandy Neck? How would we know that before you were even a tribe, your people were descended from white Europeans—information that you're sworn to keep secret?"

Heath and the white-haired councilor remained standing, mouths slightly agape, each waiting for the other to say something. Neither did.

"You know what we say is true," she continued. "It matches your legends exactly, except you called this great visitor Maushop, not Madoc. You have the sword, and this manuscript describes it exactly, so you know that's true. You know where the tomb is, and this manuscript describes that location perfectly. You're keeping its location a secret. And this manuscript provides a clear, verifiable explanation for why you feel you must do so."

The two men looked briefly at each other. The elderly female councilor had her head down and was fidgeting with her hands.

"I'm sorry," she said. "I really am. But you know we are not making this up. And pretending we are won't change the facts."

There was dead silence as Heath glared at her. She held his gaze. Harper slowly reached over and touched her hand. She flicked it away and continued to look at Heath.

"Is it possible," she continued, "that in this manuscript, there is information about your people that even you don't know? That this is the closest thing to the Book of Genesis that your tribe has?"

The silence continued until Clark rose slowly.

"Ralph and Mike," she said. "I realize tempers are high right now, but let's please show our guests some courtesy and respect." She looked at Carys. "Could we all please sit?"

The three of them stood for half a beat longer before breaking their gaze and slowly lowering themselves into their seats.

"Let's say that, for the sake of argument, this manuscript is authentic and the story it tells is true," said Clark. "I'm not saying it is, but let's explore the logic here a little further."

The other councilors turned sharply toward her, faces worried, teeth gritted. She raised her hand. "If such a burial site existed, and if everything that book says is true, there would be no worldly reason for a tribe to reveal its existence or any portion of the story you just told us. It would be cultural suicide."

Harper's shoulders stiffened.

"Such a tribe, when confronted by the fact that their secret was no longer secret, might choose to reevaluate its position," said Harper. "And, perhaps, working with the individuals who have discovered their secret, come to some mutually agreeable solution."

"What would such a solution look like?" asked Clark. The elderly woman had the beginning of a tear in her eye.

"Stop this," the old woman whispered. She looked like she had been broken in half. "Please."

Carys felt the enormity of what they had brought down on these people. Until their dying breath, they would be the ones who failed in their oath to protect the most important secret in their world.

"How many people know about this manuscript and what it says?" asked Heath.

"Aside from this tribal council, there are five people who know," she said, "including Mr. Harper and myself."

"How do we know those other people will not reveal the secret even if we make some sort of an arrangement with you two?" asked Clark, the worry etched into a crease between her brows.

"We speak as one," said Harper. "The three others were instrumental in finding the manuscript and, like Ms. Jones and I, are interested only in being shown the burial location. And being given permission to conduct a thorough archaeological dig to confirm the identity of the person buried there. That's all."

Clark laughed.

"Mr. Harper, that is everything," she said. "If that tomb is exca-vated, you have rewritten the history of our people."

The pretense of the hypothetical had dropped from Clark's words.

"We would be willing to work with you to ensure that our find does not impugn any of your tribal claims," said Harper.

"And how the hell would you do that?" growled Heath. Clark scowled at him, and Heath backed down.

"There have been archaeologists digging on our burial sites for a couple of hundred years, and we have always managed to keep them away from the Ancestor's burial ground. Working with the parks service, we finally were able to prohibit digs entirely," Clark said. "How will we explain why we have decided to give you permission?"

"I should think you are under no obligation to reveal your reasons to anyone," said Harper. He paused. "You are also under no obliga-tion to reveal that I will endow an irrevocable trust in the amount of thirty million dollars and will name the tribe as sole beneficiary."

The jaws of all five councilors dropped in unison.

"Now you are bribing us?" asked Ralph.

"Compensating," said Harper. "Not bribing. I propose to compensate you for your assistance in completing an important archaeological expedition. Perhaps one of the most important in North American history."

Carys could taste the bitterness of the offer in her mouth.

"The trust fund would provide the financial resources to pursue federal designation for the Mattakeese tribe, and to fight off any challenges to its status," said Harper, "as well as the status of any other tribes that might be affected by our findings."

That last point seemed to hit home particularly with Clark, who nodded lightly. Then the elderly woman slammed her hands on the conference table with a force that surprised even the other councilors.

"You think you can buy us out of our sacred obligation to guard that site?" she bellowed. "You think you can buy that?" She slowly stood up. "We have guarded that tomb for fifteen hundred years. I don't care about your archaeological expedition."

She walked, very slowly, around the end of the conference table and headed for the door. The other councilors eyed one another. She could feel them trying to decide whether to follow the old woman or stay where they were and tacitly accept the bribe. Clark watched the old woman leave, then turned to either side to look at her fellow councilors.

"The councilors and I have a great deal to discuss," she said. "We will call you when we've made our decision. Is there anything else we should know before we adjourn?"

Harper rose.

"I'm prepared to give you Madoc Morfran's manuscript," said Harper. "It contains the story of your oldest ancestors, and it rightfully belongs to the tribe."

This time, it was Carys's jaw that dropped. She spun around toward him. Heath laughed out loud.

"It looks like your colleague may not be in agreement with that plan, Mr. Harper," he said. Harper looked at Carys.

"It's the right thing to do," Harper said to her. Then he turned back to Clark. "Ms. Jones is right. It is your Book of Genesis. And it is right that you should have it. But I want the sword. We are assuming that such a meaningful historical artifact is still in the tribe's possession."

He looked at Clark. Her lack of response answered the question.

"Until we excavate the tomb, the sword is the only object that can definitively link your tribe to Dark Age visitors, and I need some assurances that once you get the Morfran manuscript, you'll allow me to access it for verification purposes. We will begin immediately on our archaeological dig, and we will document each of our findings thoroughly. But in order to preserve the tribe's heritage, we agree to wait until you've received your federal designation to reveal our findings. However, we must have access to Morfran's manuscript when we request it to substantiate our claims when we go public. That sword will be my insurance policy."

The councilors sat silently for a moment longer, waiting for Clark to speak.

"We'll contact you with our decision," said Clark.

"When?" asked Carys.

"Tomorrow," Clark said.

"If we don't hear from you by five o'clock tomorrow afternoon," she said, "we'll assume that you have declined. The following day, we'll fly back to Wales and present Morfran's manuscript, and the artifacts recovered from the cave, to the British antiquities authorities, which we are legally obligated to do. Those authorities will go over this stuff with a fine-tooth comb. It will be translated; the artifacts will be chemically and electronically analyzed. They will identify with pinpoint accuracy where those artifacts came from. And trust me, there aren't enough rangers to keep away the crowds who will descend on that beach when those findings are made public."

Heath stood up to his full, broad height and again stared down Carys.

"Are you threatening us?" asked Heath.

"No," she said. "I'm just telling you what we are legally obligated to do. We wouldn't want to break the law, would we?"

She rose, Harper rose next to her, she closed her computer, put it back into her bag, and the two of them left the silent councilors behind.

◆ ◆ ◆ ◆ ◆

CARYS AND HARPER CLIMBED UP the creaky stairs to the second floor of the inn. She slid the key into her door, and Dafydd poked his head out of his room.

"How did it go?"

"Tense," she said. "We'll know tomorrow if they are going to take us up on our offer."

"What offer?" he asked.

"Come inside and I'll tell you about it," she said. "I don't want to talk about it out here."

He entered her room and immediately wrapped her in his arms, then landed a long, wet kiss on her. She let herself relax for just a minute, then broke off and looked up at him.

"What have you been up to?" she asked.

"Went for a walk," he said. "Hitched a ride to this beach you're all worked up about. It's beautiful. We should take a walk there tomorrow."

"That's a great idea," she said. "We'll just have to stay out of the dunes so I don't get arrested."

"My favorite criminal," he said, and kissed her again. "So tell me about tonight."

"We made them an offer we hope they won't refuse," she said.

"Which was?"

"We'll give them Morfran's manuscript and a huge trust fund in exchange for the location of the burial site and permission to excavate. Once they've received federal tribal designation, we can go public with our findings. They agree to give us access to the manuscript to support our claims in the future, so Harper can finally get credit for the find."

She could feel his body tense up in her arms.

"You're going to give them Morfran's manuscript?" he asked, looking down at her with a look of surprise. "After everything we went through to get it? I can't believe Harper would agree to that."

"It was his idea," she said. "Believe it or not, this really always was about finding that tomb. Everything else was just a means to an end."

"But you're not giving them the monk's manuscript, right?" asked Dafydd.

"No," she said. "That one is going to stay stuck to me like glue until this is all over and we can reveal what we've found to the world."

Dafydd pulled away and sat down on her bed.

"When is this all going down?" asked Dafydd.

"We gave them until five tomorrow to accept our terms."

◆ ◆ ◆ ◆ ◆

TWILIGHT IN LONDON was pink and noisy. Black cabs swung around the traffic circle below Gyles's library window. A glass of Lagavulin, one cube, lay in his hand. Its weight was assuring; its cool surface calmed him. Things were slowly, oh so slowly, falling into place.

He'd heard from Patrick, who had bugged Jones's room in the resort community near Boston where she and her little posse were staying. He hadn't had time to put devices in the rooms of the two people she was traveling with, but Patrick had heard enough to piece together what Gyles needed to know. There had been some sort of meeting with a local council. There was talk of an offer being made to trade a manuscript for the location of the burial site. Deadline of 5:00 p.m. eastern.

He would have the manuscript and the location of the tomb, and would be one step away from the prince's money by the end of the day. Then, if he absolutely had to, he would have the means to pay off the terrorist and save his skin. Money, however, once earned and deposited into Gyles's offshore account, tended to stay put. That was never more crucial than now, since his very lucrative arrangement with Plourde was no more. He needed a plan to deal with Alahwi once this job was done.

Tommy, who had successfully finished his assignment in Boston, was sent to take over the stakeout of Jones, and Patrick was on his way back to Boston to await further instructions. They could no longer wait for Jones to find the tomb on her own sweet time. He instructed Tommy to do whatever he had to do to get the exact location of that burial site; collect the manuscript, translation, and whatever was in that tomb; exterminate any witnesses; and get to the airport to meet the Saudi's plane.

A text-message ping came from his personal phone. He glanced over at it.

"Where my money, Gyles?"

Alahwi. This madman could send both of Gyles's worlds crashing down around him if he didn't get what he wanted. How had Alahwi learned his identity?

"Please be patient," he texted. "I need a couple of days."

"You have twenty-four hours," came the response.

◆ ◆ ◆ ◆ ◆

CARYS, DAFYDD, AND HARPER were just finishing some takeout pizza in the lounge area of the inn when her phone rang. It was Annie.

"Hi," said Carys.

"Have you seen the news at all today?" asked Annie, her voice cold as ice.

"No," she said. "Why?"

"It's your boss," said Annie. "He's dead."

"What?" she exclaimed.

Dafydd's eyes popped up at her, and he mouthed, "What happened?"

She held up her hand. "What are you talking about?"

"He was killed in a car accident last night," said Annie. "Single vehicle. Drove off the road in Framingham right into a tree. The car burst into flames. He and his whole family. Wife, two kids. They were burned alive."

"Jesus Christ," she said. "Do they know what happened?"

"No," said Annie. "They don't. The cops are baffled. There weren't even any rubber skid marks on the road. It looks like he was going something like seventy miles per hour and just veered directly into a tree. He didn't even brake."

"Maybe he fell asleep at the wheel," she said.

"Maybe," said Annie. "I just thought you should know."

"I can't believe it. His whole family," she said.

She hated the guy, but the news was a gut punch. She shuddered at the momentary vision of the children in the back seat of the car, on fire, then shook it off before it grabbed hold of her. She was sure she'd dream about them tonight.

"How is everything going there?" Annie asked.

"Okay, we think," she said, standing and walking to the other side of the lounge. "We made an offer to the tribal council: Morfran's journal and a whole bunch of money for the tomb. They agree to let us make it public after they secure federal recognition, so there won't be any way for them to be stripped of their status, no matter what is revealed about their origins."

"When do you find out if they take it?"

"We gave them until tomorrow afternoon," she said. "Have you found out anything else about Marshfield?"

"No," said Annie. "I'm at a dead end unless I can escalate this to a formal investigation."

"Not yet, we—"

"I know, I know," said Annie. "I won't do anything until you have the deal locked up down there. Call me tomorrow as soon as you hear?"

"I will," she said. "Thanks for the call. I…this is awful. But I honestly can't say the world is worse off without that guy. But his wife. The kids. Jesus."

"I know," said Annie. "I've gotta go. Love ya."

She hung up and walked back to Dafydd and Harper. Their faces were expectant.

"My boss and his family got killed in a car accident last night," she said.

Dafydd gasped.

"His children, too?" he asked.

"Yeah," she said. "It's horrific. Burned alive. He hit a tree speeding."

"I'm so sorry, Carys," said Dafydd.

"Your boss at Sothington's?" asked Harper. "Who blackmailed JJ?"

"Yes," she said. "George Plourde."

"Didn't he call you yesterday?" asked Harper.

Carys stared at Harper. She had completely forgotten in all the excitement. She pulled her phone back out and called up voice mail, found his message, hit play, and sat down on the sofa to listen.

"Carys, this is George. Plourde. It's Tuesday, around ten. Listen, I know you and I don't, didn't.... I, uh, was very angry with you for threatening to reveal certain details about my past and I did something I'm not proud of and now, I'm, uh, afraid we're both in some trouble. There's a man, Martin Gyles. The repatriation expert. He's actually a black-market antiquities dealer in London. I've been doing some side deals with him for years. He's bad news, Carys. He's very, very bad news. He's involved in...uh, that woman who was killed at the Harper mansion. That was him. His guy did it. On his orders."

Her face drained of blood and her hands went cold.

"Couple of weeks ago, he asked me for information on you. He never told me why. But I gave it to him.... I'm sorry.... I...I was very angry. And they pay me very well. Anyway, he's coming... for...for you. He wanted me to track you. Said you were back in Boston. I told him no. But he'll find someone else. I can't be part of this anymore. It's getting...it's not what I signed up for. I wanted to warn you. I hope you get this message before...well, before anything happens to you..."

Carys raised her hand to her face and looked up at Dafydd and Harper. The two men were chatting, paying no attention to her. How did they know she was back? Her mind began to churn.

"There's one other thing. I'm...I found a letter on your desk when you were gone. I opened it and read it and I told Gyles that it was from your father and I gave him the return address on the envelope. He might be in...ah...some danger as well...so you should warn him."

Carys gasped. That's how Frank had found them in Wales. He'd tracked her father. She'd forgotten all about the letter. The goddamn letter. Her brain froze.

"Don't call me back. I'm going to get my family out of here, just find somewhere to hole up for a while. I think Gyles may try to...do something to me or my family...I'm sorry, Carys...I never meant for any of this to happen...it just got...out of...hand...it...it was bigger than me. I'm so sorry. Be careful. I hope one day you'll forgive me."

She hung up and looked up at the men. Plourde and his family were dead, and it wasn't an accident. Gyles had gotten to him. And now she couldn't ask him what other information he had given Gyles. Did he know about Annie and Priscilla? Did he know about Dafydd? Harper?

Dafydd glanced over and did a double take when he saw her expression. He stood up and came over to the sofa.

"What's wrong? What did he say?" asked Dafydd.

"John," she said. "The man who killed Nicola...he was under orders from Martin Gyles."

Harper's brow furrowed in confusion.

"*The* Martin Gyles? How is that even possible? He's one of the foremost experts on—"

"It's him," she said. "He's sent someone after us. He may already know we're here."

5

Thursday, June 28

Carys and Dafydd barely slept that night. They lay wrapped in each other's bodies, wide awake. Every few minutes, Dafydd fell into a soft, rhythmic breathing, then he woke and held her tightly. She'd stare for a few moments at the ceiling, then out the window at the stars above the treetops, and then she'd listen intently for the footsteps of the killer who was coming for them. She repeated the process all night.

The previous evening, Harper, Dafydd, and she had decided, jointly, that they were as safe at the inn as they would be anywhere. Neither she nor the men could recall seeing any signs that someone was following them. There had been no strange people lurking around the place, no cars following them. Then again, they hadn't been looking for such things until the threat became real just hours earlier. And it was likely that whomever Gyles had sent would be much better at staying hidden than they were at noticing a tail.

She suggested they leave and return to the Mattakeese when things had cooled off, but Harper refused. He wanted this done and he wanted it done immediately. She felt herself, in the darkness, growing bitter at the old man's single-mindedness, at his willingness to sacrifice them all for his dream. But she had to admit that she agreed, in her heart, with this course of action. She wanted this done, too.

Harper had promised that as soon as he knew the location of the tomb, he would steer every one of his resources and call in every one of his law-enforcement contacts to find and punish Marshfield and Gyles. Then they'd be safe, he said, even before they publicly disclosed the location. She still hadn't told him the truth about Frank, and didn't intend to unless it became unavoidable.

Meanwhile, Dafydd was concerned about his own family and her father. They were all, every one of them, in danger. It was too much for her to absorb. She'd called her father the previous evening, but his phone must have been off—it was after midnight in Wales. She left him a voicemail telling him what she'd learned. She said Anthony and his family would need to stay away from their house—not going back for any reason—until it was safe.

"They know where you live, Anthony," she said. "They followed you to me."

When the sun came up and she could hear the innkeepers in the kitchen below starting their day, she finally drifted off for a couple of hours. Around nine, her phone rang.

"Carys," said Anthony's voice through the phone. "What the hell is happening?"

"I'm so sorry," she said. And then, improbably, she began to cry. "You can't go home. You have to keep your family safe."

"You're my family," said Anthony, and she could hear that he was crying also. "Can you come back here?"

"No," she said, "not right now. But I will soon. I promise this will be over soon."

"There's no way you can know that," said Anthony.

"Please don't go to the police yet," she said. "We're so close."

Then she went downstairs to the lounge, where she could be alone to call Annie—if Gyles knew about her father, he probably knew about her best friend, and she had to warn her.

"We know who Marshfield was working for," she said. "Plourde left me a message before he was killed in the accident. His name is Martin Gyles. He's a famous art-world consultant. He's behind it all. He hired Marshfield to tail us. Marshfield killed Nicola."

"Where does Gyles live?" asked Annie, her voice hard and all business.

"London, I believe," she said.

"I'm notifying the Wellesley police and Scotland Yard right now," said Annie.

"No! Annie, please, we have to wait until this deal is done."

"No, we do not have to fucking wait!" said Annie. "We've waited long enough, and there are six people dead."

"I promised Harper we wouldn't—"

"Well, I didn't promise Harper anything," said Annie. "It's done. It's happening. You can tell him or not, but it's happening."

"I just called you to warn you that there might be someone following you," she said. "Plourde said Gyles probably sent someone to the U.S. to follow us."

"If you're trying to talk me out of calling Scotland Yard, that is a really terrible way to do it," said Annie. "Carys, this is insanity."

"Do what you have to," she said finally. "I'm not going to tell Harper anything. But I know I can't stop you."

She hung up and, despite her protests, she felt relief wash over her that Annie had finally taken that decision out of her hands.

She and Dafydd showered, dressed, and went to breakfast, surrounded by a gaggle of tourists eagerly discussing their plans for the sunny day. Carys just stared at her eggs, sipped her coffee, and watched the front door, flinching every time it opened.

Harper didn't come down.

After breakfast, Dafydd and Carys went back upstairs to her room. A few minutes later, a knock came on the door. Carys's heart jumped. Dafydd got up and stood next to it.

"Who is it?"

"It's John."

Dafydd let him in.

"I just heard from Clark," he said. "They want to meet us in two hours at the tribal council office."

"Did they take the deal?" she asked. Dafydd gripped her hand tightly.

"Yes," said Harper with a wide grin. "The Morfran manuscript in exchange for the sword and the burial site. We agree to hold off announcing the find until the recognition is approved. They get the manuscript and the trust, and they allow us access to Morfran's journal to verify the chronology of the body's travels."

He put his hand on his forehead.

"I can't believe it," said Harper. "After all these years, today I'm finally going to see the final resting place of Riothamus Arcturus."

Dafydd turned to her.

"There's a sword?" he asked, his jaw slackened. "Is it…?"

"Excalibur," she said. "You'll be able to touch it with your own hands today."

◆ ◆ ◆ ◆ ◆

THE MEETING WAS SET to begin at 1 p.m., Dafydd insisted that he be allowed to join them. Harper refused. He didn't want to do anything that might make the tribe members more skittish or change their minds about the deal, and meeting a brand-new face at the last minute might be a deal-breaker. Dafydd was insistent. They compromised. Dafydd would stay outside with the car and keep watch in case someone showed up unannounced during the meeting.

They pulled up to the tribal offices at 12:55 p.m., and there was only one car in the driveway, a pickup truck. They all hopped out of the car, and she kissed Dafydd on the cheek.

"See you soon," Dafydd said. "Good luck."

She and Harper entered the tribal office. No one was in the front room.

"Hello?" yelled Harper.

"We're back here," said Clark.

They walked down the short hall toward the archive room. In her bag was the plastic bag containing the Morfran manuscript, as well as the monk's manuscript and the translation. She wanted to show the tribe all the hard evidence and they deserved to see the originals. She'd left her computer back in her room. It made her smile to think that in her two-hundred-dollar tote bag, she had airtight, verifiable proof of the location of the tomb of King Arthur.

Clark was standing behind the desk at the far end of the archive room. Heath was the only other councilor present. He was in his ranger uniform standing stiffly, almost at attention next to the desk. She noticed his gun holster was empty.

"Sachem Clark, Mr. Heath," said Harper. "We're so pleased we could come to an agreement."

Neither of them said anything. They just stood where they were.

On the right-hand wall, one of the flat, shallow filing cabinet drawers was pulled out. Carys peeked inside the drawer. There was a long, thin object about six feet long, draped in a leather cloth.

"May I?" she asked Clark. The woman barely nodded. Harper came and stood next to Carys. She reached into the drawer and, with the reverence of a priest, slowly pulled the leather aside.

She and Harper inhaled at the same instant. The blade of the sword was around four feet long and about three inches wide. Though rusted, it looked as strong and lethal as the day it was forged. Its handle was about ten inches long. It was solid and healthy, with what looked like the wear of human hands on it. At the top of the handle

388 ♦ KRIS FRIESWICK

was a single large red stone, an enormous ruby, shining brightly as it caught the light of the room.

"Caledfwlch," said Harper softly.

Excalibur. She hadn't believed it was real until that very instant. She reached out her hand to touch it.

"Ah, now we're all here," came a voice from behind them, with a thick English accent. She and Harper pivoted around to face it. The man was tall, forties, thickly muscled, and he was standing with his back to the wall next to where they'd entered the archive room. They had walked right past him on their way in and hadn't even seen him. Now, he was blocking the hallway back to the front office.

He was pointing a handgun with a long silencer directly at her.

She reached for Harper's arm. He pushed her behind him, blocking her from the gun.

"Step away from that drawer," barked the man. He looked like he'd done this a few times. He held the gun low, comfortable with its weight.

"What do you want?" asked Harper. He took a step toward the stranger.

"I'm here for what we're all here for," said the man. "The tomb. I just need one of you fine Indian chiefs to lead me there right now, and then we'll be done. Simple. So which one wants to do it?"

"Go fuck yourself," said Clark. The man's face hardened.

He raised the pistol, aimed it at Clark, and pulled the trigger. Its bark was muffled and percussive. Blood exploded from Clark's abdomen and a guttural exhale burst from her mouth. Clark was thrown backward against the wall, then slid down into a heap on the floor.

Carys yelped and Heath jumped back.

"I guess it's you," said the man to Heath, as he trained his gun on Heath's head. Heath was bent over Clark, who was conscious and moaning. Blood flowed heavily from her gut.

"Did Gyles send you?" Carys yelled out, trying to distract him.

The man turned toward her.

"You've been expecting me," he said.

"Yes," she said. "We have."

"You certainly made it easy for me to find you," he said.

"What do you want?" asked Harper. "I have money."

"Oh, I know," said the man.

"How…" Carys said meekly.

"How did we know about the tomb?" asked the man with a grin. "We know everything. I also know you're Carys. I have specific instructions on how to deal with you."

The blood drained out of her arms and legs.

"All of you," barked the man. "Move to the back of the room now."

"Why?" she yelled. "Why would he care about me?"

The man turned toward her. Out of the corner of her eye, she saw Heath reaching behind his back.

"You've been a real pain in the ass," said the man, locking eyes with her fully. "You killed Gyles's partner."

Harper's shoulders flinched.

"He tried to kill us," she said.

"Tragic," said the man. "Now move!"

Just then, Heath pulled back his arm, raised it, and heaved a long, bright knife at the intruder. It sailed directly at the man, and his left arm jerked. He staggered backward, the knife lodged in his chest just below his left armpit, but then he reeled around.

As if in slow motion, Harper heaved himself at the man and body-slammed him. The collision sent the two men backward with an enormous crash into one of the wood and glass display cases. It tipped over and shards of glass and artifacts scattered across the floor.

The two men wrestled, grunting and bellowing, punching, arms and legs flailing, kicking. It seemed to go on and on. Heath jumped in on top of the man and tried to grab the gun, but the man pushed him off and Heath fell backward.

Carys ran a few steps toward the melee, unsure what to do or how to help.

There was a shot.

The arms and legs continued struggling for a moment more, then stopped. The two bodies lay on the floor, and she could not tell where the bullet had landed.

She took another step forward.

The man sat up, pinning Harper underneath him. A plume of blood was expanding slowly across the front of Harper's shirt. His mouth was agape with shock. His eyes found hers.

She opened her mouth to scream, but no sound came out.

In one movement, the man hopped off Harper and began moving toward Heath, blood streaming from the knife that was still lodged in him. He raised his gun, pointing it straight at Heath.

"If you kill me, you'll never find the tomb," said Heath.

This gave the man pause, and he took a few steps toward Heath, so that his back was mostly toward Carys. He looked down at his chest and grabbed the handle of Heath's knife and pulled it out, hollering mightily as he did so.

Harper was on the floor, still moving, gasping for air, but bleeding so heavily that she couldn't imagine he'd survive. A rage came over her like a wave. Her heart rate shot up, and her arms and legs grew hot.

With a speed and power she did not know she possessed, Carys grabbed the handle of the sword in the drawer. She lifted it up and ran at the man's back, hoisting the massive piece of metal with both hands high above her head.

It was heavy, but her muscles welcomed the weight. It gave the sword momentum. Her rage powered her forward silently and she arced the sword down toward the man. Heath's eyes glanced up at her just as the sword fell and the man began to turn.

The sword caught him full in the side of the neck and became wedged there. He spun around, but she gripped the end tightly and moved with the sword, keeping it between herself and him, knowing full well that all their lives depended on her grip.

She stared at the back of the man's head. Blood flowed from the wound over his shoulders. He dropped his gun and reached for the blade of the sword with his hands and tried to push it off his neck. The ancient deadly edge instantly drew blood from the insides of his hands. She heard the beginnings of a scream. It quickly turned to a gurgle.

He sank to his knees, and as he did, she realized that the sword had sunk nearly halfway through his neck.

The ruby seemed to glow and throb in her hands, as if fueled by the first blood it had seen in over fifteen centuries. This mighty sword had done, once more, what it had been created to do. What it had done over and over again in the hands of the King.

Protect the innocent.

Carys marveled briefly at this weapon in her hands. At the strength it had given her. At Caledfwlch.

The man's body crumpled into a pile, and the blood coursed from his neck onto the linoleum. She sank to the floor with him, still holding the sword in both hands, watching the red pool spread.

Soon, the pool was all she could see. Red and smooth, like a quiet, dark sea.

Somewhere, far away, she could hear screaming. A woman's. Maybe her own. The lights in the room grew dim.

Then it all went dark.

♦ ♦ ♦ ♦ ♦

CARYS HEARD MOVEMENT AROUND HER, and light slowly filled her eyes. She was lying on the ground. She was wet and sticky. When she could see again, her eyes settled on the glowing red stone. She was lying in a pool of blood. Her entire left side was drenched in it. The cold reality of what she had done sent adrenaline coursing through her. She dropped the sword handle and sat upright on the floor. She scanned the room quickly and saw Heath carrying Clark's limp form. Dafydd had Harper on his feet, but Harper wasn't moving them and Dafydd was using all his strength to drag him toward the door. Heath's eyes flashed at her.

"I'm bringing them to Cape Cod Hospital," Heath said. "There's no time to wait for the ambulance."

She got to her feet unsteadily.

"Take the sword out and put my knife in the wound," Heath barked. He tilted his chin down to the floor next to Carys. Heath's knife was on the floor next to her. "Clean the sword off and take it and get out of here. We can't let the police find it."

Clark looked pale, and her lips were already blue. Harper grunted next to Dafydd.

"I'll be right back, Carys," Dafydd said. "I'll come with you. Just hang on."

She heard the front door slam shut behind them.

Then it was silent. She was alone in the room with the body of the Englishman. She looked at her hands. They'd managed to remain clean, even though her left sleeve was bloody. A story began to take shape in her mind.

Heath had stabbed the intruder, who had shot Harper and Clark. It had been a robbery gone wrong, and Heath had saved them all. Heath was a ranger. Harper was a billionaire philanthropist. The cops would believe their story. The police wouldn't investigate the specifics of the Englishman's death—or the weapon used—with such respectable witnesses testifying to their version of the truth. It was a small town.

The Englishman was in a fetal position on his side. The blood had stopped flowing out of his neck, and his skin was the color of pure white paper. She'd never seen so much blood. She pulled off her bloody sweater and put her right hand into the clean right sleeve. Gingerly, she gripped the handle of the sword.

She pulled the sword handle straight up, away from the man's body. The blade remained lodged, and his body shuddered from her effort. She jumped back away from him and almost lost her footing in the pool of blood. Bile rose in her throat. She swallowed hard and took a deep breath.

She approached the body again, bent over, gripped the handle, placed her left foot on his back, making sure that it was on an area of his shirt already completely saturated with his blood, and pulled with all her might. The sword broke free all at once, and she nearly fell over backward.

A small trickle of blood flowed from the open wound at his neck. She turned her eyes away from it before she saw too much of what lay beneath his skin. She reached for Heath's knife, positioned it over the cut in his neck, closed her eyes, and slid it back down into the wound.

She stood back up, battling mightily not to throw up, and wiped the sword's edge with the clean right sleeve of her sweater. Once, twice, three times. The sword's metal seemed to glow from within. She turned back to the filing cabinet and wrapped Excalibur in its ancient leather covering.

The front door swung open and Dafydd rushed in. He was covered with blood as well.

"Come on," he said. "Heath said to store the sword somewhere safe and meet them at the hospital."

They turned to leave. Standing in the hallway was a man, silhouetted by the bright sunlight.

"Carys?" asked the figure.

She froze. He looked familiar, but it took her a moment for her brain to untangle exactly who she was looking at. He was tall, with a wide figure and thick blond hair. She blinked.

It was JJ.

"JJ, what are you...?" she began to ask.

"Are you two hurt?" JJ asked as he moved swiftly toward them. He grabbed her arm. His grip was strong.

"What are you doing here?" Dafydd asked.

JJ surveyed the room slowly, ignoring the question, seemingly immune to the blood splattered everywhere, the dead body in the middle of it. She studied his face, confusion roiling her mind.

"What happened?" he asked, seemingly in shock.

"Your father," she said. "He was shot. We were meeting with the tribe for some research and—"

"He was shot? Why?"

She checked herself. She was still guarding the secret, a compulsion stronger than the shock of the carnage that surrounded her.

"Why are you here?" she asked.

"My father called me," said JJ, spinning slowly to survey the room. "He said he had something he wanted to show me."

Carys pondered this with the one remaining logical section of her mind. The bond. Father and son. Stronger than anything. He wanted to share his victory with his son. Finally. After all this time.

"We should go to the hospital," said Dafydd.

"Yes," said JJ, with a blank look. "I don't know where it is."

"Carys can go with you," said Dafydd. "I'll follow you in Harper's car."

"What is that?" JJ pointed to the sword, wrapped in leather in her arms.

"It's an artifact," she said. "Your father will explain it all when we see him. Let's go."

"Carys," said Dafydd. "The manuscripts." He pointed to her tote bag, lying in the blood on the floor. She reached down and picked it up.

As they left the tribal office, police sirens wailed in the distance. Dafydd put the sword in the back of the Range Rover and hopped in. "Don't lose me," he said. "I don't know where we're going."

JJ remotely unlocked the doors of his car. Carys got in on the passenger side, putting her bloody sweater and tote bag by her feet. "I'm so sorry, JJ. Your car is—"

"Don't worry," he said. "It's the least of my concerns right now."

She pulled her cell phone out and mapped the address of the hospital.

They pulled onto 6A, and JJ eased into the slow traffic, Dafydd following closely behind.

"I'm so glad he called you," she said.

JJ just nodded slightly and smiled. "Yes," he said.

"How much did he tell you about what we were doing?"

JJ drove on quietly, staring straight ahead, then turned to her.

"I know everything," he said.

This was new. She thought JJ knew nothing.

"When did he tell you?"

"He didn't tell me," he said. "He told my mother a long, long time ago. She told me."

"I'm…I'm surprised. I thought Nicola and I were the only ones who knew."

JJ nodded.

"My father told my mother because he was trying to explain why he couldn't spend more time with her when she was sick," said JJ.

They approached a junction, and she looked at the map.

"We make a right here," she said.

JJ did not put on his blinker. As the turn approached, he continued straight.

"You missed the turn," she said.

He stared ahead.

"JJ," she said. "That was our turn back there."

He didn't answer.

"I'll reroute it," she said. "Do you want me to drive? Are you okay?"

"My father has been shot. So I suppose no, I'm not okay."

"I'm so sorry," she said. "Pull over at the next driveway and I'll drive."

"But on the other hand," he said, "I actually feel better than I have in a long time."

She examined his face and began to see something she hadn't noticed before. He didn't look upset. He looked completely relaxed.

"You want to know the last thing my mother said to me before she died?" he asked.

"Your father isn't going to die," she said. "He's strong. He'll pull through."

JJ smiled at this and looked over at her.

"That's not what I was getting at," he said. "Do you want to know what she said?"

"If you want to talk about it."

"I do," he said. His eyes were steel. "She said, 'Promise me he will never find what he's looking for.'"

Carys looked at the side of his face, trying to make sense of the words. Slowly, like ice melting, she began to understand.

JJ turned to her again, his eyes burning brightly.

"She hated him," he said. "So did I. He abandoned us. From before my earliest memory. He was there. But he wasn't. Know what I mean?"

She knew.

"For a long time," he said, "I had no idea how I would keep my promise to her. Then he lost his mind. And finally there was a way."

Her hands were cold. He was driving faster now, ten miles over the speed limit. Four police cars roared past them headed toward the tribal office, their lights flashing and sirens wailing. She turned to watch them pass. Heath must have made it to the hospital and reported the shooting.

"But he'd hidden the monk's manuscript," said JJ. "It was the one thing that would have allowed him, if he ever did get better, to pick up where he left off and find that tomb. So I had to get rid of it. But

I didn't know where it was. He didn't even tell my mother where it was. I knew it was in a vault in the house somewhere, but I could never find it. So, once I got power of attorney, I decided to do two things. First, get rid of all the source material that proves what's in the monk's manuscript. Without the library, the monk's tale was just a wild, unprovable story about a warrior. But I also had to find the monk's manuscript and the translation and get rid of them too.

"That's why I called Sothington's in the first place. I knew they'd send you to do the appraisal for the library sale. I knew my father and Nicola would eventually show you the manuscript, and I also knew my father would ask you to take up his hunt. He talked about you all the time, you know."

He glared at her.

"He said you could practically read his mind when it came to manuscripts. You weren't supposed to accept his offer. Once you found out about the monk's manuscript, you were supposed to put it into the estate, make it part of the collection like a good, law-abiding rare-books authenticator. Then I was going to sell it all off—manuscript included—and my father would never be able to find the tomb.

"But you didn't play by the rules, did you?" said JJ, his face seething with hatred. "You stopped the sale, you accepted my father's offer—you stopped everything in its tracks. This thing would have been so smooth; no one would have gotten hurt. No one would have gotten killed, if you'd just played by the rules."

JJ looked at her with an expression of the purest contempt.

"I don't understand," she said.

"I know," he said. "It's not important that you understand. All that matters is that now I've got the monk's manuscript."

Carys, through the fear gathering slowly in her gut, noticed that JJ didn't seem to know about the Morfran manuscript. Which, with the monk's journal, was lying at her feet.

"Even if my father recovers and somehow manages to find the tomb, he'll never be able to prove who's in it."

He smiled to himself, basking in his victory.

"I kept my promise," he said. "So, as I said, I'm feeling better than I have in a long time."

Another piece clicked silently into place in her mind.

"You hired Gyles?" she asked.

"Yeah," said JJ. "Once your idiot boss called off the sale, I did some research of my own on Gyles, who was so obviously in on the scam to blackmail me. I'm surprised you didn't see it. It took quite a bit of digging—Martin Gyles is very good at keeping himself hidden away, but I'd have no right to my doctorate in computer science if I couldn't figure out how to hack him."

He smiled to himself.

"Found out Gyles, or I should say JB—that's the name he uses to do all his dirty business—was just the kind of person I needed for the job."

"What job?" she asked.

"I offered him five hundred thousand dollars to find and steal the monk's manuscript and the translation," said JJ. "I told him it led to an ancient treasure and that he was free to launch his own search once he could prove he had grabbed the books. Part of the deal was he had to snatch the books before you found the tomb. But he didn't play by the rules, either. He decided he was just going to let you find that tomb and then he'd sweep in and steal everything in it. He thought all I wanted was the manuscript. But the point was for my father to never find the tomb. Gyles didn't understand that."

If she could toss the tote bag out the window, she could at least warn Dafydd. He'd stop. At the very least, the books would be out of JJ's reach. Carys slowly lifted her bag and placed her hand on her window button. JJ glanced at her and hit the driver's side master lock button. The locks thunked down like the lid of a coffin.

"Then, I got lucky," said JJ, smiling as if he were telling a funny story. "Remember the day you came to the house and you and my father were marking up the map where he thought the King was buried? Well, he put a big X right where you were going."

He turned to her and looked hard at her face. She had gone entirely numb.

"JB texted me yesterday to say he'd have the manuscripts today," said JJ. "Said there was a meeting at a tribal office and the books would be in hand by end of day. I came down to make sure things went the way I instructed. Good thing I did. Looks like his man really screwed up. I'm beginning to think that Gyles is as big of an idiot as your boss. Now I've got everything and all Gyles has is… well, nothing. No treasure, no money, no manuscript. Teach him to fuck with me. And he doesn't know that I know his real identity. He still thinks I only know him as JB."

"JJ," said Carys. Her hands were shaking uncontrollably. "Please pull over."

"No," said JJ.

"I'll scream," she said. "I'll break the window."

He reached into his pocket and pulled out a gun.

"Go ahead," he said. "It'll be the last thing you ever do."

JJ took a right down a narrow lane off Route 6A, somewhere in Dennis. Dafydd turned in after them, then slowed down and beeped the horn. It was clear to him now that they were not going to a hospital. He beeped again, the sound getting more urgent. The car bounced down the rocky narrow lane.

She started to text Dafydd, but JJ saw and pressed the gun into her side.

"Put it down," he sneered. She obeyed. She wanted to turn around, warn Dafydd off. All she could do was sit and watch this nightmare unfold.

"You don't know what you've done," she said softly. "Gyles is not an idiot. Not at all. He has people everywhere. He'll hunt you down."

"Oh, I know exactly what I've done," said JJ. "I leaked Gyles's little nom de guerre to some very bad people he's doing business with in Syria. I'm not at all concerned about Gyles. Gyles is finished. Payback for trying to rip me off."

Bushes scraped the car's sides, setting the metal yowling like a distant scream. In a few hundred yards, they emerged into a clearing along the shore of a small, swampy lake. A long boat dock stuck out about one hundred and fifty feet. Carys quickly scanned the shore, looking for houses, people, anything. There were none.

"Get out of the car," said JJ.

She had to think. She had to stall.

"Get out of the car!" JJ yelled. It was the first time he'd raised his voice. She opened the door and got out. JJ got out, keeping the gun trained on her. Dafydd pulled up next to them and jumped out.

"JJ," said Dafydd, "what the hell are we—"

JJ raised the gun into view, and Dafydd raised his hands.

"What are you doing?" asked Dafydd.

"Take that thing out of the back of the Rover and put it in my trunk," said JJ. "Do it now or I'll shoot her." He pointed the gun at Carys.

Dafydd hit the button on the key ring, retrieved the sword, and put it into the opened trunk of JJ's car.

"Now walk around to the front of my car," he said. "You too, Carys."

He wiggled the muzzle of the gun at her. Slowly, she walked to the front of the car. Her legs nearly buckled out from underneath her.

"Kneel down," said JJ. "Both of you."

Dafydd searched her face.

"Dafydd," she said. "I'm sorry."

"We'll be okay," said Dafydd. "Just do what he says."

"Please, JJ," she said. Her hands were shaking. "Don't do this. You're not a murderer."

"Yes, I am," he said. He walked around behind Dafydd and struck him once in the back of his head with the butt of the gun.

Dafydd dropped forward, unconscious. Before she could react, she felt a sudden searing pain on the back of her head and the world went black.

✦ ✦ ✦ ✦ ✦

THE HILLSIDE FILLED the entire landscape. It was soft and wet and strewn with oddly shaped rocks. Carys moved slowly across it, as if her feet were being pulled back down by hands. Each step she took was leaden. Her vision was blurry and darkened. She looked down. Her feet were nearly black with mud, but it was thinner than mud. A strange odor, tinged with something like metal, or meat, penetrated her nostrils.

And her lungs.

She could not breathe. The air itself was choking her. She raised her hands to her face to wave it away, but the gray sky and the space around her were composed of something denser than air. Every move she made was constrained, as if the air were struggling to push her down.

She screamed, but no sound came out of her mouth.

Up ahead, standing on top of a small rise in the middle of the hillside, was Lestinus. His cloak flowed around him in great billows. She tried to call for help but was mute. If she could only reach that hill, if she could reach Lestinus, she knew she could get away from whatever it was that was holding her. But no matter how hard she tried, the heavy air would not let her go.

Lestinus turned and saw her. His face brightened into a smile. She wanted to raise her arm to wave to him so he would come help her, but it was too heavy and she was so tired. Lestinus took a step toward her, then another, and soon he was running toward her, hard and fast, his cloak flowing out behind him. He moved more swiftly than she could imagine ever moving again. She watched him, her heart glad and peaceful. It had been so long.

Lestinus stopped a few feet short of her. He raised both his arms and held them out to her. Then he opened his mouth. The words that emerged from him did not sound human. They were instead like a clean, high note, with a visceral sharpness—a clear, perfect sound, a crystal glass being struck.

"*Suscitate viveque!*"

The words penetrated right to Carys's bones and filled her muscles with a freezing bolt of energy. She was pulled rapidly up, as if a great hand had reached down out of the leaden gray sky to yank her heavenward. As she ascended, the world went black again.

When the light returned, she was surrounded by green murk and impossible cold. Water. She was in water.

Her lungs were screaming. She tried to swim up. But she was going nowhere. Her head was hitting something.

Slowly her eyes cleared and she saw that she was in a car. The Rover. It was in the water. And next to her in the back seat was Dafydd. He was completely still. She reached for him. Shook him. Nothing. A small bubble of air escaped from his lips. Carys reached for the door handle and pulled it hard. It would not open. She looked around her for something to smash the window with and saw the silvery wobble of a pocket of air in the back, near the rear window, as the Rover descended into the murky, brackish water. She struggled to pull Dafydd over the back of the passenger seat to get him to the air, but her lungs were screaming for a breath. She let go of his arm and swam over the back seat to the air bubble, popping up into it, gasping in the oxygen, once, twice.

The bubble slowly disappeared around her. She took one last breath and pulled Dafydd to the trunk area near the rear window. She yanked open the rear hatch handle, and it slowly opened outward. She grabbed the collar of Dafydd's shirt and pulled him behind her out through it, then up, up to the blue, clear air above.

They popped up and she gasped.

"Dafydd. Dafydd. Breathe. Please breathe."

He was dead weight in her arms. Silent. He was not breathing. His face and lips were blue. She was at the end of the long pier. There were no ladders. She swam to one of the pilings and held on with her leg as she tried to give him mouth-to-mouth resuscitation in the water. He kept sinking down, away from her, so she grabbed his collar again and swam as hard as she could back to the shore. She pulled him up on the sand far enough so his torso was out of the water and began CPR and mouth-to-mouth again.

A minute. A trickle of water escaped his mouth. A good sign. She alternated chest pumps with breaths. Thirty compressions. Two breaths. As she'd been taught.

Five minutes. His skin was colder. A deeper blue. His eyelashes were so long. So beautiful.

"Please, Dafydd," she begged. "Please wake up."

She bent over him and tried, again and again, to breathe life into him.

Ten minutes. She was exhausted. Breathing into him as hard as she could made the world spin. Her hands were numb from pressing on his broad chest. She ripped open his shirt, bent forward, put her ear on his soft, cold skin and listened one last time for a heartbeat.

Nothing.

She sat back on the sand, her own heart wrenched from her body. A long wail, like that of an animal, began to emerge from deep inside her. With no beginning and no end, the sound moved through her, around her, composed of every bit of pain, loneliness, sadness, regret, and betrayal she had ever felt, and would ever feel again. When the sound finally ended, she was empty. Dead. There was no Carys left. Just a shell where her soul had once been. She fell backward, flat on the warm sand. She could feel the blood coming from the back of her head. The darkness closed in again.

6

⬥⬥⬥⬥⬥

Friday, June 29

Carys slowly opened her eyes, and her vision was blurry. She felt drugged. She was in a bed, underneath a thin sheet. She wiggled her feet and looked down at herself. She wore a white nightgown. As her eyes slowly cleared, she saw that she was in a hospital room. Annie was asleep in the chair next to her. The light coming through the window shade was dim. Dawn or dusk? Her right arm felt stiff. She looked down at it. She was hooked up to an IV. She touched the back of her head. Covered in bandages. There was no pain. Annie stirred and then woke up with a jolt.

"Hey," Annie said, trying to smile. "How are you feeling?"

"Dafydd," she said, still not fully conscious.

"I know," said Annie. "Honey, I'm so sorry."

"JJ," she said.

"The police are trying to find him," said Annie. "He still doesn't know his father's...been shot."

"No," she said, struggling to sit up. Her head nearly exploded, and she lay back down. "He tried to kill me. He hired Gyles. He killed Dafydd…" She tried to get out of the bed, but Annie pushed her gently back down.

"Hold on," said Annie. "Lie down. Tell me what happened."

"JJ showed up at the tribal office," she said. "He said his father called him. I got in his car to come to the hospital after Harper and Clark were shot by that Englishman, and Dafydd followed in the Range Rover. He pulled off to a pond. He had a gun. He knocked us out and put us in the Rover and drove it off the pier. Dafydd…"

She tried to sit up again. Annie pressed her back.

"Dafydd's gone, honey," said Annie.

Her vision began to close in, and she leaned her head back on the pillow.

"Carys, stay with me," said Annie. "Stay with me. Did JJ say where he was going?"

She struggled against the heavy weight of consciousness.

"No," she said. "Oh my god. Annie, he killed him. He was next to me in the water. I couldn't save him. JJ tried to kill me, too. He thought we'd both drown in that car. But Dafydd…"

"Carys," said Annie. "Did JJ say anything that might tell us where he went?"

"He has everything. The manuscripts. The sword. The translation. And…" she said, "Dafydd. He killed Dafydd. He's dead. He's dead. How can…?"

Annie leaned over and embraced her. Carys began to weep.

"Try to calm down," said Annie. "You're in rough shape. The doctors say you have a concussion. You shouldn't get your heart rate up."

"JJ hated Harper," she said through her tears. "He hated him. For abandoning him and his mother when she was so sick."

"We'll catch him," said Annie.

"How long have I been out?"

"Since yesterday afternoon, when they brought you in," said Annie. "Some guys found you next to that lake. You lost a lot of blood. They stitched you up. They want to keep you for another day."

Just then, the door opened and a nurse came in. She greeted Carys half-heartedly, checked her vitals, and was about to leave when she turned back to them.

"Ms. Jones, did Mr. Harper have any other next of kin? Other than his son?" the nurse asked.

"No. None that I know of," she said. "How is he?"

The nurse's expression went blank. She looked at Annie.

"Thank you," said Annie to the nurse. "We'll get that information to you in a few minutes."

She turned to Annie as the door closed. Annie put her hand on her arm.

"I'm so sorry," said Annie. "I was going to tell you when you felt a little stronger."

"No," she said. "He can't be."

She wept deeply and inconsolably. Annie was quiet, and handed her tissue after tissue.

They were gone. Nicola. Harper. Dafydd. They had been snuffed out. By Frank. By Gyles. Ultimately, by JJ.

"This can't be happening," she said. "How can he be dead? How can they all be dead? It's not possible."

"Harper bled out during surgery," said Annie. "The bullet severed an artery, and they just couldn't stop the bleeding."

She tried to breathe her way back to composure. There wasn't time for tears. She had to do something.

"JJ won," she said. "He got what he wanted. His father never found what he was looking for."

"That's not important right now," said Annie. "The only thing that matters is that you get better."

"It is important," she said through the last of her tears. Then fear replaced her sorrow.

"Annie, Gyles will be back," she said. "I have to tell the tribe. He knows the tomb is here. Gyles knows about the tribe. He'll come for the burial site. Can you get Mike Heath? I need to talk to him. How is Sachem Clark?"

"She's going to survive, but it was touch and go for a while," said Annie. "You are going to need to talk to the police at some point."

"I have to call Dafydd's family." She closed her eyes, and the sobs threatened to come up again.

"I'll take care of it, I promise. Please sleep a little longer," said Annie. "I'll track down Heath. I'll have him come by in a couple of hours."

Carys couldn't fight off the sleep that descended on her like a heavy blanket.

She woke to a soft knock on the door. Heath was peering at her through the window. She motioned him in.

"I'm not supposed to be talking to you," said Heath. "Police said they want to talk to you first."

"Thank you for coming," she said. She tried to smile but it hurt too much. "Did Annie tell you what happened?"

"I heard Mr. Harper didn't make it," said Heath.

She nodded. She wanted to tell him about Dafydd, but he wouldn't care.

"It was his son."

"His son?" asked Heath.

"His son, JJ, was the one who attacked me," she said. "He was behind all of this. He paid a man named Martin Gyles to stop his father's search for that grave. Gyles sent the man to the council office. And now JJ has the Morfran manuscript and the sword. And Gyles knows that the burial site is here."

"What do you mean he knows?" demanded Heath. "I thought you said that you were the only people who knew about it. The whole deal we made was based on that."

"We…I was wrong," she said. "I had no idea, no way to know that JJ and Gyles knew the burial site was here. I just found out yesterday."

She closed her eyes against the throbbing pain in her head.

"I brought hell down on your people. But you can scream at me later. I need you to know something. Gyles will come for the grave."

"Why? Is he an obsessed archaeologist, too? Does he want to ruin my tribe as well?" snarled Heath.

"He wants what's in the grave," she said. "He doesn't care about the tribe."

"What are you talking about?" asked Heath. "It's an old skeleton. It's not like it's worth killing over now that the sword and manuscript have been stolen. Those were the only things worth any money."

She paused, confused. Was it possible they still didn't know about the treasure buried with that skeleton? Then she remembered that they hadn't read Morfran's journal. They'd seen only the translations she'd provided. And none of them mentioned the true identity of the man in the grave or what his son had buried with him. For a split second, she considered withholding the rest of the story. But Mattakeese lives were in danger, and they deserved to know why.

"This is going to sound crazier than anything you've ever heard in your life," she said. "But I assure you that it is the historical, verifiable truth."

"What now?" asked Heath sternly.

"The man buried in that grave you're hiding, that you've been hiding for fifteen hundred years. He wasn't just any man."

"Who was he?" asked Heath.

She tried to pull herself up into more of a sitting position, but the pain of movement made her lie back down.

"He was a general in the wars against the Anglo-Saxons in the sixth century," she said. "He became famous, and then he became a legend. Stories were told over the years, almost none of them true. But there's one story that is true. It's in another ancient manuscript that we have—or had. The one that started this whole search. It was written by the warrior's personal priest, a man named Lestinus, who traveled with him."

"So we have the skeleton of a general from the Dark Ages. Again, who but an archaeologist or a historian would care?"

"This general's sword, the one you had in your vault," she said. "That sword had a name. In Welsh, it was called Caledfwlch."

She paused and took a deep breath.

"In English, it's Excalibur," she said.

Heath stood absolutely motionless. For a long minute, there was no sound except the hiss of the IV pump next to her bed.

Then Heath snorted—a half laugh. He rolled his eyes to the ceiling.

"I hope you feel better soon, Carys," said Heath. "I'm sorry about Mr. Harper."

He started moving toward the door.

"Wait," she said. "Everything else we've told you so far is true. I've verified Lestinus's manuscript myself. The man in the grave is King Arthur."

She was now Harper. Trapped in a hospital room, trying to convince someone she wasn't crazy. She had to convince them. They needed to know and prepare before Gyles came back.

Heath pulled open the door to her room.

"Wait," she said.

He stopped and turned toward her.

"You have to believe me," she said. "Your tribe is in danger. How can I convince you?"

"Well, unless he's got Guinevere buried next to him, you probably can't," said Heath.

Her mind spun, trying to think of something she could say to make him at least consider her story. She couldn't prove anything she was claiming without the monk's manuscript. Without that, the Mattakeese would have no reason to believe they had King Arthur on their land.

Then it came to her. They didn't need to believe it was King Arthur. They just needed to believe they and their families were in danger. That, when all was said and done, was what had gotten her to go to Wales and take up the hunt in the first place.

"He's buried with a considerable treasure," she said. "Probably worth millions of dollars—triply valuable because it's buried with King Arthur. And the monk's manuscript, the Morfran manuscript, the ring he's buried with, and the sword form airtight proof that he is who I say he is."

Heath stood silently.

"It's not the King but his treasure that Gyles will be coming for," she said.

"Gyles wouldn't be able to find the gravesite even if he does come back," said Heath. "It'd take him years."

She didn't want to have to spell it out for him, but he didn't understand what they were up against.

"If I had to guess exactly how he'll do it, I'd say he or one of his thugs will come here, take a councilor or a councilor's family member hostage, and threaten to kill them unless the tribe reveals the location. It won't be a bluff. You already saw how willing he is to kill people. He's already killed many."

Heath's face lost some color, but he stood rigid, unswayed.

"Look, even if you don't believe it's King Arthur, the things buried there are as real today as they were then," she said. "A metal detector will prove the treasure is there—your tribe didn't have the technology to make any type of metal when the King was buried."

Heath's expression turned curious.

"You can prove me right or wrong in two hours," she said. "Please just go look for yourself."

Heath's eyes bored into hers. Then he pulled open the door.

"I'll let you know what we find," said Heath. Then he left, and Carys was alone with her dread and sadness and a crushing headache.

7

Saturday, June 30

The texts Gyles received the previous evening had been vague yet, each in its own way, quite specific.

From Alahwi: "We are coming."

From Client A: "Have the manuscript. Thanks for nothing."

And then there was the call. A detective at Scotland Yard had phoned Gyles on his official business line, asking him to come to their offices for a conversation.

"We've received some information about an artifact that we need your help with," said the detective. It was bullshit. He had checked, and the investigator worked in the homicide division, not art and antiquities.

That had sealed the deal. JB was done.

Gyles cleaned out the numbered bank accounts, transferred the cash to an offshore account. Took his small black paper notebook—hackproof—with his client names and cell phone numbers, and shredded everything else. Both of his careers were over—just as soon as he finished this one last job.

The bag he kept packed for just this sort of thing, but which he had never had occasion to use, was on the seat next to him. Fake passport. Fake credit cards. Ten thousand euros and ten thousand U.S. dollars. Several burner phones. An entirely new life in a small leather carry-on bag.

The ferry rolled mightily in the English Channel. He hated being on the water. Seasickness. He sat up on deck, in the fresh air, keeping the horizon in sight. It was the only thing that helped. He'd be in Calais in a few hours. Then, well, he hadn't quite decided. Probably Switzerland. It was remarkably easy to disappear there.

When he hadn't heard from Tommy, he'd texted Patrick to find out what happened. It was worse than he could have imagined. Tommy dead. Manuscript and translation gone. Harper dead. Burial site location still unknown. But those natives knew where it was. And he was sure as hell going to get them to tell him.

The manuscript, the tomb, the treasure, the deal with the Saudi prince, they were all still out there, waiting for him. But so were Alahwi and his men, and they were on the move. He was going to have to pay them off. That was increasingly obvious. But he couldn't do that without the manuscript and treasure. Keeping his cash reserves intact had never been more crucial now that both of his revenue streams had been shut down. He was going to need that cash to live. To survive.

He would figure it all out. He just needed more time. But first he had to find a place to hide. Just for a little while.

◆ ◆ ◆ ◆ ◆

CARYS HAD SPENT THE PREVIOUS AFTERNOON and most of the morning telling half-truths to the police about Dafydd's death and her near drowning. She did not like the way the cops were looking at her as they questioned her. Annie did her best to deflect any questions she knew would lead them to the real motives for their trip to

Cape Cod, and whenever they pressed too hard, she feigned amnesia about the details. JJ was nowhere to be found, of course, and there was no way for her to prove that what she was saying was true. The Mattakeese were being as opaque as she was. The cops advised her not to leave the area when she was released. Annie assured them that she'd stay put.

About noon, Heath returned to her hospital room. He was slightly pale, with a nervousness hiding just below his subdued surface.

"There was metal there," said Heath. "Lots of it."

"Did you dig it up?" she asked.

"No," he snapped.

"Do you believe me now?" she asked. Her head was still throbbing a bit, but at least she could think now.

Heath just stared out the window, then he turned to her.

"What do we do?"

"I don't know," she said.

"Why wouldn't that Gyles guy just come at us right now?" asked Heath. "Now that he knows the burial site is here."

"He might."

"Obviously, we can't tell the police," he said. "It'll just mean more people who know about the Ancestor. We need to get those manuscripts back. They're like a goddamn time bomb out there."

"We?"

"You and me," he said. "You, because you owe us. Me, because I don't trust you. None of us trusts you."

"You have no idea what you'll be getting yourself into."

"I'm already in." He paused, took a deep breath, and stood silently for a moment. She watched him staring out the window, thinking hard.

Suddenly, he shivered slightly, turned, and moved toward her.

"I may have an idea," he said. "The tribe isn't going to like it. I don't like it. But I think it may be the only way."

"What is it?" she asked.

"We have to move him," said Heath. "Him and everything in that burial site. Leave no trace he was ever there, and put him somewhere far away. Even without the manuscripts, treasure is treasure. That guy will come. And as long as those manuscripts are out there, my tribe is in danger—physically and historically."

Heath was right. This was the answer, at least to the Mattakeese's problems. It was the only way to keep Gyles away from them and protect their secret.

"The big question is where to take him," said Heath.

She thought for a few moments. Then the answer formed in her scrambled mind and she smiled, in spite of her pain.

"I know where," said Carys.

8

_{◇◇◇◇◇◇}

Sunday, July 1

Carys walked several paces behind Heath through the deep sand, her head still aching but not enough to keep her from this moment. It should have been Harper here. Not her. But she insisted that she be allowed to attend, in exchange for everything she was about to do, every risk she was about to take, the sole purpose of which was to protect the lives and the secret of the Mattakeese Tribe of the Wampanoag Nation of the Algonquin people. Forever.

After he'd left her hospital room, with Clark's permission, Heath had called an emergency meeting with the other councilors at Clark's home—the tribal office was still a crime scene—to tell them what they intended to do. They needed to take the Ancestor, and everything in his grave, and leave.

One day, when they had the sword and manuscripts back, they would lead authorities to the King's body and treasure. Harper and Nicola would be credited with the find. That was Carys's promise to them both. For the Mattakeese, no link would ever remain of the Ancestor's place in their history. Their secret would remain safe for all time. But they had to make sure Gyles knew that there was no longer a treasure buried on Mattakeese land. Draw his attention toward her and Heath, make him follow them, and keep him away from the tribe.

At first, the councilors refused. There would be no further discussion, they said. They insisted that there was nothing that anyone could say to change their minds. But Heath explained that the threat now facing them was far graver than the revelation of their true history. This threat could end them, literally.

The councilors, especially the two oldest, said they would willingly sacrifice their lives to protect the Ancestor's burial site from being pillaged. But when Heath asked them if they would be willing to sacrifice the lives of their children or grandchildren, they finally agreed to the plan. They knew that they were not prepared to stand in defiance of an evil that would happily do whatever it needed to do to achieve its ends.

Climbing through the dunes, the elderly, gray-haired female councilor carried a long wooden staff topped with an iron object that looked like a spear point. It was probably something off one of Morfran's boats, left as a gift when half the crew sailed away those centuries ago.

Five of them trudged through the sand—four members of the tribal council and Carys. Clark, recuperating in the hospital, had given them her blessing. They had been walking for forty-five minutes. The surf pounded the beach on the other side of the dunes. Ancient scrub brush surrounded them. A breeze was kicking up, and wind-driven sand pelted their faces from time to time. No one spoke.

The five walkers crested a large dune and half stumbled down its steep back side until they stood on a section of ground that was oddly flat. In the center of the plateau were four ancient, gnarled cedar trees, weathered and broken down, with trunks the width of a man's torso, each about three feet high, arranged in a square. Two of the councilors had brought old wooden brooms, and they began to sweep the sand between the trees.

Slowly, the sand parted to reveal flat, perfectly round, sea-smoothed black stones. After more sweeping, it was clear the stones formed the shape of an ancient cross with its four equal-length arms and a circle. With the stones revealed, the burial site was as obvious as it would have been if it had been marked by a formal headstone.

The elderly woman moved to the top of the cross and drove the staff deep into the sand so it stood on its own, like a sentinel. Each of the three other councilors stood next to a tree. They waited until the moment when the sun was at its highest point.

When the appointed time came, the old woman raised both of her hands to the sky and began to chant, and the councilors followed each chant with a response. It was an ancient language, as old as the Latin that Carys immersed herself in each day, and it cut back through the hundreds and hundreds of generations that had conducted this ritual for fifteen centuries.

The wind nearly drove away the sound of the councilors' chant. When they were finished, they bowed their heads and spoke quiet incantations, each in turn. Heath had explained that they were going to offer thanks to the Visitor, the great Maushop, father of them all. They also spoke to the Ancestor, the great father in the ground, telling him that they were honoring their promise and would continue to do so. No one had disturbed this site since the day the final stone was placed in the cross.

But they would disturb it today.

The four councilors began to remove the stones, one by one, and place them in a clay jar, a jar that was nearly as old as the tribe itself. When they were all removed, the middle-aged male councilor, Cedric, and Heath continued to sweep away the sand. It took about an hour, but eventually, a new pile of rocks, smaller and very tightly packed, revealed themselves. Again, the four councilors removed the rocks, slowly and reverently, placing them around the clearing in a perfect circle where the cross had been.

Finally, after a few more minutes, the elderly woman picked up a rock, and beneath it was the skeleton of a hand. It pointed north, toward the star Arcturus. Carys gasped. On the middle-finger bone was a ring, dulled by time, set with an emerald flanked by two sapphires. The old woman began to weep silently.

In two days' time, at 8:00 a.m., Heath and Carys were scheduled to board a merchant vessel departing Bourne with two very large suitcases and a rollaway steamer trunk. Neither they, nor their luggage, would be searched, thanks to some of Heath's connections at the dock.

The trip would be long. By the time they got where they were going, which no one but she and Heath knew, JJ could be anywhere with the manuscripts and sword—he could have sold them a hundred times over. But it was more important to get the King and his treasure away from the Mattakeese. She'd find JJ and the manuscripts after she had protected these people.

She made another vow as well. When they landed on the other side of the ocean, she would finish what she'd started. She'd make things right with the people who had died on this search: Nicola, Harper, and her beloved Dafydd. Whom she would never forget.

And she would bring the King home.

ACKNOWLEDGMENTS

Although this book is a work of fiction, it includes many facts gleaned from years of research. I drew inspiration, plot twists, background, foreground, and information about rare-book collecting, Native American history, and the potential identity and history of the legendary King Arthur from many sources. They include: *A Gentle Madness*, by Nicholas A. Basbanes; *The Story of Britain*, by Rebecca Fraser; *Journey to Avalon*, by Chris Barber and David Pykitt; *The Discovery of King Arthur*, by Geoffrey Ashe; *Arthur's Britain*, by Leslie Alcock; *1491*, by Charles C. Mann; and interviews with the rare-book curators at the British Library, the Widener Library at Harvard University, and the Boston Public Library.

I owe an enduring debt of gratitude to the readers who gave so generously of their time, energy, ideas, and insight: Barry Schuler, Jenna Blum, Richard Fifield, Janice Lombardo, and Benjamin, Natalie, and Stephanie Rotstein. A special thanks to Christopher Castellani, Eve Bridburg and the team at Grub Street Writers in Boston, and the team at The Writers Room in New York City, two crucial resources that helped me bring this book into being.

To my manuscript editor, Claire Wachtel; my agent, Richard Abate, and his assistant, Rachel Kim, at 3Arts; and my editor at Post Hill Press, Debra Englander, all of whom believed in this project—I thank you from the bottom of my heart. To my cover artist and brilliant author in her own right, Whitney Scharer—a million thanks for your creativity and patience. To all the people who, over the many years it took to write this book, have been on Team Ghost Manuscript—each page is for you.

Lastly, I couldn't have done any of it without the support and love of my husband, Andrew Robinson, the best man I have ever known.

ABOUT THE AUTHOR

Kris Frieswick is a journalist, editor, humorist, teacher, and author whose work has appeared in national magazines, newspapers and books for over twenty years. She is an avid cyclist, cook, and traveler. She lives on Cape Cod, Massachusetts, and St. Croix, USVI, with her handsome Welsh husband.